A GAME of HEARTS

A GAME of HEARTS

a regency romance

JOANNA BARKER

Joanna Barker
www.authorjoannabarker.com

First Printing: October 2022

❀ Created with Vellum

To Grandma Jean,
for telling me stories until I was ready to tell my own.

Chapter One

MARIGOLD

I WAS GOING TO WIN.

It would never do to acknowledge such a thing, of course. No one liked a braggart. But I'd played this game long enough to recognize the coursing energy inside me—the unrelenting certainty that I could not be beat.

I nocked my arrow, and the crowd milling about the makeshift archery range quieted. I paused, forcing an expression of extreme concentration to my face. I did not want to make it look too easy; stodgy Lord Beauford already disliked me enough. I would win, but I would do my best not to embarrass my opponent.

I glanced to where the audience had gathered, standing outside the staked strings that marked the field of competition. Mama stood arm in arm with Papa, who chatted amiably with his neighbor. She caught my wandering eye and tapped the side of her head with a stern glance. *Focus*, she was saying. I sent her a wink. She sighed and hid a smile.

I spared one more second to search the rest of the crowd. *He* still wasn't here.

I pushed away the disappointment that pricked inside my chest and faced the target. In one fluid motion, I raised my bow and drew back the arrow. The feathers tickled my ear as I steadied my aim, adjusting the tip of the arrow to account for the slight afternoon breeze from the east. I held my breath, knowing even that small motion could affect the path of my arrow—then I released.

"A center hit!" Cora cried delightedly. "Well done, Marigold." My friend had been given the task of keeping score, darting to the target between shots to judge the arrow's placement and award points. She grinned at me now as she poked a hole through her card to mark the score, my fifth center hit of the day.

I lowered my bow, unable to keep my own smile from bursting forth. I'd never done so well at a prize shoot.

"Are you certain?" Lord Beauford's haughty voice came from behind me. I turned to see him glowering at Cora, his drooping jowls more pronounced than ever. "It looks to be in the red."

"You are more than welcome to examine the arrow yourself, my lord," she called out. Even from across the field, I could hear the false sweetness of her voice. "But seeing as the tip is nearly at the center, I see no room for error."

Lord Beauford grumbled something under his breath, likely a word not meant for any proper lady's ears. That only made my grin broaden. Not a gloating grin, of course. Just a pleased one.

Well, perhaps it was a bit gloating.

"You've each three more shots," Mr. Rogers said as he checked his own scorecard. He was Sandcliffe's vicar, but today he also served as our archery marshal. He stood between Lord Beauford and me, ensuring we did everything properly. "The score stands at fifty-three to sixty, in favor of Miss Cartwell."

I wanted nothing more than to send a pointed look at the baron. Here it was before him, proof that I was talented, able, equal. But I stopped myself. It would help nothing, and Lord Beauford's features were already dark as he cleaned the tip of an arrow with the archer's tassel hanging from his belt. I did not know if he realized I was holding back, but he had to know he was in dire straits. I'd outshot him last year, and the year before, though it still hadn't been enough to prove myself. Nothing was enough.

I chewed the inside of my cheek. At least I *could* defeat the baron. That was more than I could say for a different, equally provoking gentleman. I surreptitiously glanced around as Lord Beauford prepared to shoot again. The crowd was thick, but I wasn't searching for a bystander. I was searching for calculating brown eyes and a maddening smirk.

I was searching for my *real* competition.

How was it possible that he hadn't come? A victory today meant little if Tristan Gates was not here to stand defeated.

As I faced the field again, I caught Lord Beauford nodding at someone in the crowd. Then he turned to smile at me, showing his crooked upper teeth. Why was he smiling? I couldn't imagine he enjoyed losing to a woman, based on his refusal to allow me to join the Sandcliffe Bowmen, the society he'd founded. But this prize shoot, held during the annual town fair, was open to all, and it was my only chance to show my quality. If I won this year, if I beat every member of his society, he would *have* to let me join. Wouldn't he?

Lord Beauford focused on the target, raising his bow and drawing back the string. After a few moments, he released his arrow. It hit the inner red circle, just outside the gold center. A good score, but it only earned him three points compared to the nine that my center hit had given me. I applauded politely along with the audience.

"Curse it." Lord Beauford shook out his right hand, his face scrunched up in an expression of exaggerated pain.

"Is something the matter?" I asked, all careful concern.

"My hand." He cradled it in his left hand, glancing to ensure Mr. Rogers was paying attention. "It has seized up. I do not think I can continue."

My heart dropped. I should have seen this coming. A withdrawal would save the esteemed Lord Beauford the shame of being defeated by a nineteen-year-old girl. I tried to breathe evenly. He was taking my victory from me. If I won by default, it would mean nothing.

"Perhaps you might allow it a moment," I said, a desperate edge in my voice. "I am sure it's just a spasm."

"No, no," he said, holding up his hand as if it were evidence. "I have these every so often. It takes hours to recover."

Mr. Rogers raised an eyebrow. "Would you like to withdraw, my lord?"

I bit back the protests that rose to my tongue. It would do no good. Instead, I exhaled and reached to unstring my bow.

"Perhaps we could consider a different option." Lord Beauford planted the bottom of his bow in the grass. "Might I substitute another archer to finish in my place?"

I brightened. It was an unexpected suggestion, but Lord Beauford was the best of those I'd shot against today. I would have little trouble with anyone else *and* I would get to finish the meeting.

"If Miss Cartwell is not opposed." Mr. Rogers turned to me.

"That is acceptable," I said, trying not to show my eagerness.

"Excellent." Lord Beauford handed his bow to his manservant standing nearby, then motioned to someone from the crowd behind me. "Here he is now."

I turned, expecting to see another of Sandcliffe's curmudgeonly bowmen.

But no. It was *him*.

Tristan Gates strode toward me, towering and self-assured, bow grasped in one hand, his quiver of arrows in the other. I'd been searching for that dark chestnut head for the last hour, short hair so perfectly neat one might think he carried a mirror about with him for the purpose of arranging his tresses. He walked with such confidence, as if he could have been blindfolded and still not missed a step. My stomach lurched. His eyes met mine, a biting brown that sprung countless childhood memories to my mind—and not any of them good.

"Miss Cartwell," he said, offering a slight nod, face expressionless. I hadn't seen him in six months, not since I'd left for London for the Season, but his clipped baritone still sent a skitter up my spine. Tristan had always been like that, cold and immovable as a boulder. A handsome, irritating boulder.

"Mr. Gates." I wasn't sure how I managed his name. Everyone

was watching. I forced my knees to bend into a curtsy. A short curtsy.

I managed a sweeping inspection as I rose. His clothes were as unremarkable as ever. Finely made, of course—he was a gentleman —but would it hurt the man to wear a touch of color among his blacks and greys and whites?

The onlookers craned their necks, whispers sweeping through them. This was what they'd come hoping to see, after all. A number of archers competed at the fair each year, mostly members of the Sandcliffe Bowmen, but the last two summers it had come down to Tristan and me in the end. I'd won the first time, but Tristan had won last year. I did not like to lose, and I had only ever lost to Tristan.

He never let me forget it either, somehow finding cause to mention it every week when he and his uncle came to dinner. I did not begrudge my father his long friendship with Tristan's uncle, but heavens, did the man have to have such a vexing, arrogant nephew?

I'd been determined to beat him this year, but when the shoot had begun two hours ago, Tristan hadn't shown. I'd swallowed my disappointment. He was the only opponent worth shooting against. What, then, was the point of competing?

Now he was here, setting his tin quiver in the grass, studying the target. I should have been elated—now I had my chance. Except this was not at all what I'd wanted. I'd allowed the match to grow too close, to leave Lord Beauford some dignity in hopes he might soften towards me. Now Tristan was swooping in, which my strategy had *not* planned for.

I was in terrible, terrible trouble, and I could not allow Tristan to know.

"I was surprised to see you missing this morning," I said, my voice unaffected. "Your uncle said you were meant to arrive last night."

Tristan slipped on his shooting glove and buttoned it around his wrist, his fingers deft and practiced. "My travel was delayed by bad roads."

"How unfortunate." My dry tone told him precisely what I thought of his excuse.

He narrowed his eyes but said nothing. He strung his bow by bracing the lower tip against his Hessian boot and bending the upper limb to slip the loop over the string nock. He made it look easy, his shoulders taut beneath his jacket. When I strung my bow, it strained every muscle in my body.

My mind raced, attempting to find an escape from this debacle. Perhaps I could intimidate him. Archery was a physical sport, but there was mental strategy to it as well.

"Lord Beauford has shot well," I said. "But I'm afraid you'll find the deficit too difficult to overcome."

Tristan flexed his hand within his shooting glove. "A lead of seven points is hardly an assured victory."

Stay calm, I told myself. I had to keep my head, especially with every eye upon us.

"Miss Cartwell," Mr. Rogers interrupted. "It is your turn."

Tristan took an arrow from his quiver and inspected it, not looking at me as he spoke. "Best of luck, Miss Cartwell."

I stopped myself from saying what I thought of his *luck*, and turned to face the target. Cora watched me from down the field, eyes wide. She knew my situation as well as I did. Now that Tristan was shooting, I needed every point I could claim.

I gave Cora a confident nod. I had three shots and I would make them count.

I took an arrow from my pouch, nocking it carefully against the string and ensuring the cock feathers were pointing up. I'd done this a thousand times—ten thousand—and I'd never practiced so much as I had in the last year. My defeat at Tristan's hand last summer had tormented me, his derisive smile taunting me in my mind's eye with every arrow I drew. I'd vowed that I would never lose to him again.

I took a deep breath and raised my bow as I drew back the string. I aimed, taking more time than usual. The crowd quieted. It was too quiet. I could hear Tristan breathing. I could hear his smug smile.

I released the arrow. It hit white. Not the gold of the center, not the red of the innermost ring, but white, the *third* ring.

"Two points," Cora called, sounding as if she would rather muck out a stable stall than call my score for the whole town to hear.

I lowered my bow, heat building in my face.

"Hmm," Tristan said behind me. "Perhaps you would like to move closer?"

I sent him a glare. Ladies generally shot from a distance of fifty yards, but I'd trained at a hundred yards for years, as he well knew.

"I've already had five center hits today," I said coolly as I moved to the left and allowed him to take my spot.

"Only five?"

He was trying to irk me. Lucky for him, Tristan Gates irked me just by existing.

"I thought you might appreciate the opportunity to catch up," I retorted.

"How kind," he said, stepping forward and raising his bow.

I eyed him closely. If he was indeed telling the truth about his travel delays, and he *had* just arrived, then his arms would be tight, especially without any practice to warm his muscles and bow. But this was Tristan. He always fought to the end, always wanted the last word in our arguments. I could never rule him out.

He aimed, the line of his arms strong and sure. I tried to find any flaw in his stance, but his left arm was straight, wrist bent in a perfect angle, his feet the exact right distance apart.

His arrow went flying, a blur too quick to follow, and hit the target with a thud.

"Three points," Cora called, carefully avoiding my eyes as she marked her scorecard. I swallowed. He'd hit the red ring on his first shot.

I couldn't let this happen. Not here in front of everyone.

Tristan lowered his bow and gestured me forward. "Please do not hold back on my account, Miss Cartwell."

I did not dignify that with a response. I stepped forward and aimed again, determined not to let him affect me. I'd known Tristan over a decade, and in my opinion, it was a decade too long. I could beat him. I *could*.

I aimed and released my arrow.

"One point," came the call. The outer white ring. I gritted my teeth. What was wrong with me?

"Fifty-nine points to sixty-three," Mr. Rogers said, announcing the new total. "In Miss Cartwell's favor."

Too close. Much too close.

Tristan stepped forward to take his final shot. I closed my eyes, unable to watch. His bowstring creaked as he drew, my heart pounding into the still silence. A pause, then the flitting whir of his arrow as he released, the distant thump of it hitting the target. My hands fisted around my bow, every limb tense.

"A center hit," Cora called, disbelief painting her every word. "Nine points."

My eyes flew open and I gaped. A center hit on his *second* shot of the day? The crowd clapped wildly as Tristan turned back to me. I immediately pressed my mouth into a line, pretending to be utterly unimpressed, but my pulse betrayed me, skipping like a rock over water.

Tristan's face also held no hint of his feelings—he simply slung his bow over his shoulder as he watched me. I knew better. Oh, he must be gloating to see me in such a position. He was now five points ahead, and I had only one shot left.

I needed a center hit to win.

I rallied myself. It was nothing I hadn't done before. Two summers ago, I'd beaten him by an even smaller margin. This game was far from over.

I raised my bow. I went over every aspect of my stance: head, chest, and hips drawing a straight line to the ground, the top of my bow angled a few degrees to the right, arrow settled in the groove between my left knuckles and the bow. The breeze had calmed, so I adjusted my aim.

I held my breath. It was now or never. I released. The arrow flew from me in a rustle of feathers. The world slowed around me, and I watched it dart away, nothing but a blurred spot on my vision. But I felt it, the surety that came from a solid shot. I'd done it.

The arrow struck the target and quivered, its point piercing the canvas, buried deep into the straw behind. From this distance, it seemed to be on the very edge of the gold center. *Nine points*, I willed Cora to say. I could not breathe.

Cora's voice shook, barely audible over the distance. "Three points."

The words echoed in my head. Three? No. She was wrong. She'd meant to say nine. Hadn't she?

"The final score is sixty-eight to sixty-six," Mr. Rogers announced. "Mr. Gates is the winner!"

The crowd burst into applause, shouts and whistles echoing. It all came from too far away, hazy and unreal. I lowered my bow to hang at my side, staring at the target. I wished I could act like Lord Beauford and insist Cora check again. But she would not have called my score if she hadn't been sure. My stomach was a hard pit.

I hadn't yet moved my feet. My eyes sought my parents. Papa clapped politely, his gaze apologetic. Mama clapped as well, but her eyes were closed, as if she did not want to see how badly this had hurt me.

I was only just recognizing the ripping in my chest, the dull pounding of my heart. All the hours of practice in the last year, my dreams of finally beating Tristan. They were gone. Vanished within a single moment. It had been my chance to prove to Lord Beauford, to *everyone*, that I was good enough for his dratted society. Now that chance was gone, snatched from me like a ribbon in the wind.

A hundred eyes watched me. I knew what to do—it was what I'd always done. Smile graciously, applaud, be the perfect young lady I was meant to be. Women of gentle breeding did not stalk angrily from archery ranges, after all.

But today I did not want to be a woman of gentle breeding.

"An admirable effort, Miss Cartwell." Mr. Rogers smiled at me kindly.

I mustered a smile in return. It wasn't his fault. "Thank you."

He moved away to present Tristan with the silver arrow that was the prize for this shoot. I watched as Tristan took it with a nod, not even smiling at his victory. The crowd began dispersing, eager to return to the food and music of the fair. I was left alone on the field with Tristan, who was already unstrapping his shooting brace. Not even a glance in my direction, or a "well done." Not that I'd want either.

I stared blankly at my bow. It was my favorite one, the one I'd used two years ago to defeat Tristan in this very contest. I had thought it would bring me luck, and it seemed inconceivable that I should be standing here, a failure. I could not have lost. Not a quarter of an hour ago, I'd had Lord Beauford on the run. He'd known it, too. He'd—

I stared at Tristan, pulling off his brace and shaking out his hand. My breathing grew shallow. How was it that he'd arrived just when I was about to defeat the baron? It seemed an enormous coincidence. An impossible coincidence.

My shock slid away, like morning mist under an unrelenting summer sun. Simmering anger took its place. It was no happy accident, Tristan's delay in travel and then his fortuitous arrival. It was precisely the sort of scheme Lord Beauford would instigate, cad that he was. He could not bear to lose to me, and so he'd made certain he would not—with the help of his society's most skilled archer.

And I would *not* let Tristan get away with it.

Chapter Two

TRISTAN

I UNSTRAPPED my shooting brace and shook out my hand, a pleased smile fighting to spread across my face. I could still feel the reverberation of my last shot in my hands. A center hit, *and* after traveling in a bumpy carriage for three days. It was as near to a miracle as I'd ever witnessed.

I would never admit that aloud, of course. Marigold stood not ten feet away, boiling mad. I could tell even though I was currently ignoring her. We'd done this before, and I knew how it went. She would glare daggers at me and I would pretend not to care. Indifference ignited her irritation more than anything—a fact of which I took full advantage.

I bent my bow against my boot, loosing the string. My lips twitched at the memory of Marigold's face when the score had been announced. Her wide, disbelieving eyes and that gaping mouth. If only I could have a portrait made of that moment. That was something I would enjoy reliving for years to come.

"Gates."

Marigold marched towards me, bow still in hand, blue eyes flashing. It seemed she was still determined to call me by my surname, though of course she only omitted the "Mr." when it was just the two of us. I wasn't sure why she did it. Perhaps it made her feel we were on more equal footing, as if she was just another gentleman.

"Miss Cartwell," I said without a hint of inflection. "Might I commend you on your—"

"I do not want your insincerity." She stopped an arm's length away. "I am far more interested in why you have decided to compromise your honor."

"Pardon?" I asked, my defenses already rising.

She raised her chin. "You knew you could not beat me on merit alone, and so you resorted to conspiracy. Will you truly do anything to win?"

I laughed, simply because it would irritate her. "I don't know what is more ridiculous, that you think I cannot beat you or that you think I would conspire with Lord Beauford." Of all the absurd things.

She ignored that. "I was holding back against him. And then you made me—"

She stopped, pressing her lips together, eyes wide as she caught herself.

"And then I made you what?" I raised an eyebrow. As if she would ever admit that I flustered her.

"Nothing," she said too quickly. "But I've been shooting all morning. I was tired. It wasn't fair."

It wasn't fair? What was she on about? "You agreed to the substitution," I said, my jaw tight.

"Before I knew you were scheming against me."

This was broaching on insanity. She thought Lord Beauford and I had hatched some plot to defeat her? I generally thought of myself as a level-headed man, but even I had limits. She was assaulting my honor, and I would not stand for it.

"I did no such thing," I said sharply. "My coach was delayed because a bridge washed out near Faversham. I had to stay the night in a drafty, dirty inn and I arrived only minutes before you saw me. Mr. Hutton asked if I would finish for Lord Beauford and I had no reason to refuse. I am sorry if that ruined whatever plan you had concocted, but I'll not allow you to accuse me of cheating when I can outshoot you any day of the year."

It wasn't a particularly witty insult, especially since Marigold *was* good. Very good. But if she was going to throw baseless accusations at me, I would defend myself.

Marigold glared at me. Normally, she was all collected propriety, but today, after hours of shooting, she seemed a touch unhinged. "How is it you grow more awful every year?"

I took up my quiver and bow, my pulse like a drum in my ears. "That is progress, at least. While you remain precisely the same."

I did not bother with a farewell as I left. The girl was deluded, truly. She thought far too much of herself, imagining such a story. I headed for my coach, still waiting along High Street where I'd left it after Mr. Hutton had stopped me. I hadn't hesitated when he'd asked me to shoot in the baron's stead. In fact, I'd been elated. I had thought I'd missed the competition entirely because of that bridge. As much as I disliked Marigold—spoiled, haughty Marigold— shooting against her was a singular thrill.

Especially when I came out on top.

As the crowd dispersed, I spotted Uncle. He came toward me with an open smile, raising a hand in greeting. Just the sight of him made the tightness in my chest loosen. There were few people I trusted and loved in this world. Uncle Matthew was one of them.

He embraced me, slapping my back with two concussive thuds. If only allowed one word to describe Uncle, *broad* would be most people's choice. Broad shoulders, wide face, and a smile that spread from ear to ear.

"You've finally arrived," he boomed as he pulled back. When I'd first come to live with him twelve years ago, his voice had frightened me. Too loud, too full, and so unlike anyone I'd known. Now his voice sounded like home.

"An unavoidable delay," I said, grasping his shoulder with my free hand. "I'm sorry I did not have a chance to send a note."

"Not as sorry as poor Miss Cartwell." He grinned, looking over my shoulder to where Marigold was no doubt pouting. "That was an impressive showing, Tristan. She'll not be speaking to you for the next month, you know."

And she would no doubt think it an awful punishment, depriving me of her wit and company. "Not the hardship you think it is."

He laughed. "Ah, I've missed you."

I'd missed him too, a fact that always surprised me.

"How was Staffordshire?" he asked. "Might I guess you are now running the entire operation?"

"Hardly," I said. "But I was impressed."

While most of Sandcliffe's high society had removed to London for the Season, I had better things to do than flirt and dance and play cards. I'd been watching the ceramic industry closely the last few years, and when I'd heard of a kiln in Stoke-on-Trent that was seeking new investors, I leapt at the opportunity.

"You stayed a long while," Uncle said. "Your vetting must have been quite thorough."

"It always is," I said. "I like to know who I am doing business with."

I'd been pleased with the kiln and its owners, though. It was a solid investment. After signing the papers, I'd journeyed home, looking in on a few of my other ventures along the way—a print shop in Oxford and a bakery in Tilbury. I wasn't one for large gambles or risky speculation; I liked to invest in businesses and people who knew their craft. People who simply needed someone to take a chance on them.

Like Uncle had taken a chance on me.

"Come," he said to me now, wrapping an arm around my shoulders and leading me away. "I've someone I want you to meet."

I went with him, my brow furrowed. I thought I knew all his friends in Sandcliffe. Who could he want to introduce me to?

A middle-aged woman stood near the edge of the field, the temporary wooden booths of the summer fair behind her. She held a hand over her eyes as she looked out over the crowd, the sun lighting up the graying brown hair beneath her towering bonnet.

"Mrs. Penrose," Uncle called, catching her attention with a wave. She spotted us and brightened.

"Good day," she chirped as we approached, her voice high and breathy. She fixed her eyes on me with alarming interest. "You must be the infamous Mr. Gates. I've heard so much about you from your uncle."

I opened my mouth to respond, but she went on without pausing.

"What a performance that was! I must say, I thought Miss Cartwell was beyond catching, but you certainly proved me wrong. I used to be something of an archer myself in my younger days, though of course I hadn't your talent. How thrilling, truly." She said it all in a rush without stopping for breath and now she inhaled deeply as a result, beaming at me.

"Tristan," Uncle said with amusement in his voice. "May I present Mrs. Penrose, a new . . . friend of mine."

Friend? Did he think me simple?

But I forced a smile and bowed. "A pleasure, Mrs. Penrose."

"Oh, it is all mine, I am sure." She bobbed a curtsy as she inspected every inch of me. I returned the favor, noting the expensive fabric of her dress, the gold and pearl earrings dangling from her ears.

Uncle had had several interested parties over the years, women who thought a lonely, rich widower an easy mark for the taking. But he'd never returned anyone's attention as far as I knew. Not since he'd lost his wife so long ago, when I was young enough not to remember my aunt.

"We'll not keep you any longer," Uncle said, winking at me. He knew very well how much I disliked both meeting people and filling empty conversations. "You'll want to settle in at home, no doubt."

"I hope we'll meet again soon, Mr. Gates," Mrs. Penrose said brightly. "I so look forward to knowing you better."

I gave a short bow. "Likewise, Mrs. Penrose."

I started away, glancing back a few seconds later. Mrs. Penrose had moved close to Uncle's elbow, gazing up at him with fluttering lashes. He had a silly look on his face as he regarded her, smiling and happy.

I pressed my lips into a line as I faced forward. There was something about this Mrs. Penrose that had my instincts on guard. She was different from the other ladies who had set their caps at Uncle, mostly because *he* seemed just as interested in her. I would have to keep a close eye on the situation. I needed to ensure she did not have any unsavory motives toward my uncle.

"Mr. Gates."

I stopped as Mrs. Cartwell approached with a kind smile. It always startled me how much she looked like her daughter, the same fair hair and blue eyes. Marigold, however, would never smile at me like her mother did.

When I'd first come to live with Uncle twelve years ago, I hadn't any idea what I was getting into. He and Mr. Cartwell were long-time friends, and that meant never-ending dinner invitations and forced friendships with the Cartwell children. I could not escape the family, though I'd certainly tried. They were exhausting—all so energetic and talkative and prying, Marigold in particular.

But I never seemed to mind Mrs. Cartwell as much as the others. She had a sense about me, finding moments to talk with me when I most needed it. She was as kind a human as I'd ever met and yet a force when provoked. Sweet and insightful, whip smart and strong. Unfortunately, her oldest daughter had only inherited the latter two of those qualities, along with a healthy dose of obstinance and superiority.

"I am glad you've arrived safely," she said. "How strange that we've not seen you since Christmas."

"It has been a long while," I agreed. "I assume the Season went well?"

"Well enough," she said. "Though I am always glad to return home."

I nodded, not entirely sure what to say in reply. It had been Marigold's first year on the Marriage Mart. A successful Season would have seen her married off, but I'd yet to hear of any such luck.

16

Mrs. Cartwell turned to look back the way she'd come. "You shot well today."

I frowned. Her tone, slightly reserved, hinted there was more she wished to say.

"So did Marigold," she said. "I wish we might have been able to see just the two of you compete."

Had Marigold been spreading rumors already? My mouth went dry. "Do you also think I planned a coup?"

Mrs. Cartwell shook her head. "Tristan, that is not what I meant. I haven't even spoken to her yet. She disappeared before I could."

I looked over my shoulder. The archery range was nearly emptied, Marigold nowhere to be seen. I spotted Mr. Cartwell striding off towards the trail that led down to the beach. He glanced my way, frowning at me before turning back. Marigold's father and I had never liked each other. We were perfectly polite, of course, but I knew he disapproved of me—probably because unlike everyone else, I did not treat Marigold as if she walked upon clouds.

"I only meant that I was sorry you were delayed," Mrs. Cartwell said, pulling my attention back to her. "I know how you both enjoy the contest. No one was at fault today." She paused. "Well, perhaps save for Lord Beauford. But do not tell him I said so."

I managed a smile. "I promise."

She sighed. "She is frustrated, that is all. This is her only chance to compete."

I knew that, I did. But it might have been forgotten in the rush of victory. Sandcliffe's archery society did not allow women, though Marigold had petitioned Lord Beauford a dozen times or more. I was a member myself and enjoyed the summer season all the more because of it, attending prize shoots and pitting myself against the best the society had to offer. Which, truthfully, wasn't much compared to Marigold.

I set my jaw, pushing away the guilt. It wasn't my fault Marigold could not join.

Mrs. Cartwell sighed. "I hope she'll be all right," she murmured as she stared thoughtfully into the distance.

That confounded guilt again. I had done nothing wrong.

Mrs. Cartwell shook off her stupor. "I'll leave you be. But you'll come to dinner in a few days?"

The last thing I wanted was an evening surrounded by Marigold and her far-too-protective family, but I'd given up fighting these weekly dinners. And I did not want to offend Mrs. Cartwell. "Of course."

She smiled again, her eyes crinkling at the corner more than when I'd last seen her, and left with a gentle touch to my shoulder.

I watched her go with a grimace. Had Mrs. Cartwell meant to make me doubt the integrity of my win? Or had she just been making conversation? The silver arrow in my pocket seemed to weigh more with every second, and the thrill of victory faded. I knew well how exhausting a prize shoot could be. Marigold *had* been tired, while I'd been—well, not exactly fresh, not after my night at that awful inn. But I'd been keen. Ready. Eager. Too eager. I hadn't stopped to think. I should have realized how it would look, taking Lord Beauford's spot with only two shots left.

I shook my head, adjusting my quiver over my shoulder as I started off again. Mrs. Cartwell was right. This wasn't the way I wanted to win. I wanted it to be perfectly clear who the better archer was, once and for all. But I'd allowed myself to be caught up in the excitement and now my win was hollow. I swallowed back the surge of dissatisfaction.

Blast.

Chapter Three

MARIGOLD

I DUG my toes into the rocky sand, closing my eyes and letting the rushing sound of the waves fill my head. I did not want to leave any room for thoughts of Tristan, or Lord Beauford, or the archery shoot. I had only space for the call of sea birds, the crash of water on the rocks. I inhaled. There was nothing I loved more than the tang of salt on the air as the breeze toyed with my hair.

Except for winning.

I snapped my eyes open, needing a distraction. I let my gaze run over the black pebbles that met the sea, the deep blue water speckled with reflected sunshine. Immense, white cliffs rose up behind me, hiding me from view. I'd come here often as a girl. The cliffs and the beach below were a child's dream, full of sea glass and shells and feathers. I hadn't visited for a long while. Too busy, I mused, with the life of a proper Society lady. But it was the first place I'd thought to run when I'd so desperately needed to be alone.

I wrapped my arms around my legs, blowing out a breath. Why was Tristan the way that he was? So cold and arrogant. Unfeeling, almost. I didn't know how anyone tolerated him.

"There you are."

Papa's voice came from behind. Of course he would find me. How many times had he discovered me here over the years? I didn't turn as he came and sat on the sand beside me, mirroring me as he linked his hands around his legs.

"I took your bow and things to the coach," he said, looking out over the sea. "I thought you might still want them after deciding you don't entirely hate the sport."

I blew out a puff of air. He was trying to tease me from my sour mood, but I wasn't ready yet.

He sighed, his expression sobering. "I'm sorry, Mari. It wasn't fair. I'm sure everyone realizes that."

I gave a dry laugh. "Except the people who matter."

"I assume you mean Tristan." He frowned. "I confess, I cannot comprehend how your mama has always had such a soft spot for him."

"Mama loves everyone." Besides that, Tristan was an orphan and she couldn't help but take him under her wing. But she didn't actually *like* him, did she?

"True enough," he said. "I, however, am not so generous."

My lips pulled upwards. I might look like Mama, but I'd always been more like Papa in terms of temperament. We loved without reservation, but we also held grudges. And heavens, did I feel a grudge now.

"Shall you challenge Tristan to a duel?" I said. "He is abysmal with a pistol."

"Indeed," he said. "His uncle will be very put out with me for shooting his heir. After all the work he put into finding one."

My smile faded, and I pressed both hands to my face. "Ugh. I cannot believe it. Tristan is awful, but this is low even for him."

Papa paused before speaking. "As much as I would like to place this fault entirely at his door, I do not think he is the one you are truly angry with."

"No?" I turned to face him. "Because I feel like I could hit him over the head with my bow and feel very little remorse. Is that not anger?"

He grinned. "That would certainly make any upcoming dinner

parties somewhat awkward." Then his grin faded. "I think you understand my meaning, though."

I did. But it was easier to hate Tristan, because he at least was at my level. Lord Beauford was *untouchable*. A baron with unparalleled influence and infuriating prejudice.

"I have done everything I can think of to sway Lord Beauford," I said, trying and failing to keep the pain from my voice. "*Everything*. I hold myself back in competitions. I've sat through hours of mindless chatter with his wife in hopes of her speaking a kind word about me. I've written letters to him explaining why, like the London leagues, women would only benefit his society. I've been logical and patient and long-suffering."

"You have," he said simply. "But, unfortunately, men like Lord Beauford do not change their minds. He has an old way of thinking, especially about women. Especially about bright, talented, *determined* young women." He gently bumped me with his shoulder.

I bit my cheek. Was he right? Would Lord Beauford never change his mind? So many other archery societies allowed women, but not his. It sometimes seemed that sheer stubbornness held him back. Men and their pride.

"But," he went on, "I know better than to tell you to give this up. You simply must find another way."

My hands tightened around my elbows. "I feel as if I have exhausted every option. Save for Lord Beauford's untimely death, I cannot see a solution."

Papa laughed. "Plotting a murder, are you?"

"You were the one who encouraged outside thinking."

"Perhaps something within the confines of the law."

I sighed dramatically. "You are no fun at all."

"If I had any influence with the man, you know I would have used it by now," he said. "But he holds no fondness for me either."

"Yes, thank you for that," I said. "Do try to lose to him more often at the gaming tables."

He laughed. "Never. Despicable man."

I grinned, slipping my arm through his. "Excellent answer."

We sat in silence for a few moments, the waves breaking a few feet away, the sun bright overhead. Finally, he patted my hand. "Come. Your mama is waiting."

I brushed the sand from my feet and replaced my stockings, shoes, and garters, then Papa helped me stand and we started back up the winding, rocky path.

The archery range was empty when we reached the top of the cliffs, save for Mama waiting near the targets. When she saw us approach, she hurried to meet us, her eyes sad.

"All your hard work," she said, embracing me. "I am sorry, Marigold."

I held her tightly, tears pricking like needles at my eyes. But I did not know if Lord Beauford—or Tristan—was still nearby and I would never allow either the pleasure of seeing me cry.

She pulled back and examined me. "Should you like to go home?"

"And miss the rest of the fair?" I cleared the lump in my throat. "No, indeed not. I shall stay and enjoy myself just to spite Lord Beauford."

Mama laughed softly, though she squeezed my shoulders. "You are your father's daughter, through and through."

"I will pretend that is a compliment," Papa said.

"Always," she said, stepping to his side and kissing his cheek.

"Mari!" came a shout from behind me, and I turned to see Iris running toward us. In usual form, her bonnet hung from its ribbons around her neck, her white-blonde curls sticking out every which way. Hawthorne—Harry to us—was right behind her, his shorter hair in matching disarray. Something about the mischief in their bright eyes made the twins look younger than fifteen.

"Oh, stop," Mama called in exasperation. "Your hair, Iris."

"Never mind my hair," she said, throwing her arms around me and nearly knocking me to the ground. "How terribly unfair that was! I am so upset with Tristan, I cannot breathe."

"You seem perfectly alive to me," Hawthorne teased, stopping nearby. He crossed his gangly arms, which seemed to grow an inch every day. Mama constantly bemoaned having to let out his jacket sleeves.

Iris ignored him as she stepped back. "But what a competition. You were brilliant, of course."

Iris's dramatics made it easy to pull away from the emptying pain of losing. I wanted to escape. "I am never anything less," I said with a wink.

Mama sighed as she and Papa moved past us toward the fair. "My daughters. Humble and unpretentious."

"You'll never guess what we did," Iris said to me in a low voice as we followed after our parents, a grin tugging at her lips.

"Iris," Hawthorne protested. "We said we would not tell."

"It's only Mari," Iris said. "She won't tell Mama."

I leveled a wary look at Hawthorne. "Harry, what's she done now?" Generally, Hawthorne was the more level-headed of the two but was prone to being swept up in Iris's schemes.

"No, no, we *both* did it," Iris said, her eyes sparkling with mischief. "We have been seeking revenge in your honor."

"Revenge?" I raised an eyebrow. "You'll need to explain a bit more than that."

Iris and Hawthorne exchanged a glance before leaning closer. "We hid a fish in Tristan's carriage," Hawthorne admitted.

"You haven't!" I exclaimed, causing Mama to glance back. Iris hushed me and Mama sent us a suspicious look before facing forward again.

"We have," Hawthorne said, quieter but with a gleam in his eye. "In a few days, his seat will take on the most awful smell and he'll be positively baffled."

"It serves him right," Iris said, her voice taking on a more serious tone. "Swooping in like that at the end. You had Lord Beauford on the run and everyone knew it."

I could not help but feel strangely touched, though, in truth, it seemed more likely that a servant would suffer from the ill effects of the fish rather than Tristan. But I slipped an arm around both their waists as we walked. "I cannot say it is the method of revenge I would have chosen, but I accept your offering. May that fish stink worse than Harry's feet."

Iris laughed and Hawthorne protested and Mama insisted we tell her what we were talking about, though of course we refused.

My mood lifted in spite of everything. Tristan Gates might think he'd beaten me. Lord Beauford might think he'd outsmarted me. But I was not defeated. Not in the least.

Once I set my mind to something, I always accomplished it. I *did* enjoy the fair. I found Sylvia and Cora, and my two friends were so fierce in their condemnation of Tristan that I was immediately cheered. We spent most of the afternoon laughing together, perusing the various booths filled with brightly colored ribbons and feathers, meat pies and roasted nuts. It was an excellent distraction from the unrelenting pit in my stomach.

There was no hiding from it that night, however. After dinner, I retreated to my room and dressed for bed, then sat before the fire with a book in my hands. I was no great reader, but I was desperate. Nothing put me to sleep faster than attempting more than two pages of a book, and I had no desire to lay awake staring at my ceiling, reliving the prize shoot over and over until I went mad.

A knock came at my door before I'd read even one sentence, and Mama poked her head inside. "Good, you're not in bed yet."

I closed my book. "Not for a long while, I imagine."

She offered a sympathetic smile as she stepped inside. "Still thinking of the shoot?"

"I cannot help it," I grumbled. "My mind refuses to let it be."

"Perhaps this will provide a welcome distraction," she said, holding up a folded paper. "Your father received a letter today."

She knew I could not resist an intrigue. "Go on, then," I said with a short laugh. "Distract me."

"It is from Mr. Eastbrook," she said, unfolding the letter. "He has accepted our invitation to visit Crossdale. He means to travel with Oliver and arrive next week."

I sat forward, a grin lighting my face. "Truly?"

"See for yourself." She handed me the letter.

I quickly read the short note, admiring the slant and strength of the writing. Mr. Eastbrook was a new acquaintance—and a handsome one at that. He was a friend of my brother Oliver's, who had introduced us a few weeks ago at a ball in London. I'd liked Mr. Eastbrook immediately. He was worldly and charismatic, and he dressed as well as any man I'd ever seen. We'd spent much of the last social events of the Season together, dancing and flirting. Mama and Papa approved of the match, of course. He was well situated in wealth and status, being the grandson of a viscount, though neither my parents nor I cared much for that. He had simply charmed us all.

Which was why I'd asked Papa to invite him to visit us. We hadn't had enough time in London for me to know if I loved him. But if I saw Mr. Eastbrook here at Crossdale, if I knew him better outside the glamour of the London Season, then surely I could decide if he was the right man to marry.

"I'll let you keep that," Mama said with a teasing wink. "You can show it to Cora and Sylvia and try to glean additional meanings from every word."

I folded the letter, giving her a superior look. "Oh, no. We are far too grown up for such silliness."

She laughed. "You'll go see them in the morning?"

I grinned. "First thing." I stood and kissed her on the cheek. "Thank you, Mama. I needed something to look forward to."

"Try to sleep," she said quietly. "Lord Beauford does not deserve another minute of your time." She kissed my forehead and left.

I watched her go, holding the letter tight. If only it were that easy. If only I could brush off what had happened, pretend I did not care. But I *did*. Archery was not just another pastime to me. It wasn't like arranging flowers or painting, something to fill the day. Archery drove me. It pushed me. It demanded perfection, and when I failed, it cut to the bone.

I'd asked myself *why* so many times. Why should I care this much for a game? Why did I feel the need to be the absolute best? I'd tried quitting. After last summer's defeat at Tristan's hands, I'd refused to touch my bow for a month. But it had lured me back. Even as heartbreaking as it could be facing rejection and humiliation, I never felt more right than when I had a bow in my hands, an arrow pulled to my ear, and a target in my sights.

That's all I needed, I decided, sitting before the fire once again and unfolding Mr. Eastbrook's letter. I needed a new target. And if Mr. Eastbrook proved himself worthy, perhaps I might have one.

Chapter Four

TRISTAN

I ROSE EARLY the next morning. It was more of an effort than it should have been—these past weeks of travel had disrupted my usual schedule. But I was determined to find my stride again. Besides, I knew Coultry would be up already.

I had my horse saddled and I rode to town, enjoying the cool air that would soon turn uncomfortably warm in the summer sun. I wound through the streets, beginning to come alive as windows opened and servants called to one another. When I reached Coultry's shop, I dismounted, tied my reins to the post, and knocked loudly on the small wooden door.

The shop was quiet, but there was no doubt Coultry was already awake. In the two years since I'd met him, I'd never known him to miss a day of work.

"Who's there?" came a disgruntled voice a moment later, proving me correct.

"Your long-lost business partner."

The door jerked open a moment later and John Coultry's dark, alert eyes filled the opening. If I thought he might be glad to see me, I saw no sign of it.

"About time," he grumbled, leaving the door open for me as he returned to his work counter. Older than my twenty-two years by a decade, Coultry had rough, worn features, his messy hair pulled beneath an old woolen cap.

I removed my hat and stepped inside, hiding a grin. The man had no social graces—it was one of the reasons I liked him so well. No pretense, just hard work and skill. That was precisely what I looked for in a business partner.

"I didn't see you at the prize shoot yesterday," I said, dropping my hat onto a table crowded with feathers, wood shavings, and paint. "Did you not attend?"

"What for?" he asked, already focused again on his task of sanding the bow on the counter.

I sat on a tall stool beside the table. "To see your work in action, of course."

Coultry was the finest bowyer outside of Canterbury, though not many knew it yet. I'd been lucky to discover his talents two years ago and commissioned several bows before eventually investing in his business. His reputation had begun to grow, though slowly. It would certainly grow faster if he made an effort to attend shoots and hawk his wares.

Coultry didn't spare me a glance. "Seems a vanity to me."

"A bit of pride in your work wouldn't hurt."

He shot me a look. "Perhaps you just wanted me there to watch you shoot against Miss Cartwell."

I narrowed my eyes. "Hardly. But I do think the business would benefit if you attended shoots and ensured everyone knew who had crafted the winning bow."

He snorted. "I'm no peddler, Gates. My quality will speak for itself."

That was true enough. I had yet to be disappointed in any of the bows or arrows he'd made me.

Footsteps came from the stairs at the back of the shop, and Mrs. Coultry appeared a moment later, carrying a plate with sausage and toast. She smiled when she saw me, her round face framed by dark curls.

"Why, Mr. Gates," she said, coming to set the plate beside Coultry, resting one hand on her husband's shoulder. "I hadn't realized you'd returned. Shall I bring another plate?"

"No, thank you," I said. "I've eaten already. I was simply trying to convince your husband to attend target meetings. It would be a boon to the business."

Mrs. Coultry sighed. "I have been trying to convince him of the same thing."

Coultry grunted. "Why would I need to seek out customers when they come so willingly to me?"

I furrowed my brow. "What do you mean?"

Mrs. Coultry sent her husband a searching glance. "Have you not told him yet?"

"Told me what?" I asked.

He finally looked up from the bow he held. "Lord Beauford came here yesterday."

I blinked. The baron, lowering himself to visit a craftsman's shop? "Go on," I said, curious.

"He commissioned a bow," Coultry said. "Wants it as soon as I can make it."

"And what did you say?"

"He agreed, of course." Mrs. Coultry leaned forward. "One cannot refuse a baron. Besides, this is the chance we've been waiting for."

"It very well could be," I said. "Lord Beauford has connections far beyond my reach. If he is pleased by your work, you'll have more orders than you know what to do with. But he can be . . ." I paused. "Temperamental."

Coultry took up the bow again. "That doesn't frighten me. My work is good enough."

I hesitated. This felt odd, Beauford's sudden interest. I'd been singing Coultry's praises for months now, but the baron and most of the other bowmen in Sandcliffe were stubborn—they preferred to use their own bowyers. Why was Lord Beauford making such a change now? Was he desperate to find some new advantage in the face of defeat?

"What do you think?" Coultry asked, a note of unease in his voice. My hesitation was worrying him.

I shook away my lingering doubts. "I agree with your wife. It is an unparalleled opportunity." I clapped him on the shoulder. "I cannot wait to see this bow."

He looked pleased, or as pleased as he could manage without truly changing his features. This was good, I reassured myself. A chance for him to prove himself, and to ensure his family's future.

I couldn't help thinking I would feel better if it had been anyone but Beauford.

"I'd best be off," I said, standing and taking my hat from the table. "My uncle needed a word before he left to see Mrs. Penrose."

Mrs. Coultry had been leaning against the doorframe, but straightened at my words. "Mrs. Penrose?"

I set my hat on my head. "Yes. She and my uncle are new . . . acquaintances."

"Mrs. Meredith Penrose?"

I turned at her unnerved tone. "Do you know her?"

She cleared her throat. "Only by reputation."

She was certainly going to have to explain *that* comment. "And what is her reputation?"

Mrs. Coultry sent her husband an uneasy look. He shrugged, so she faced me again with a sigh. "I believe you know I lived in Bath before I married John. Mrs. Penrose did as well, though she went by a different name then."

I tipped my head. "Her maiden name?"

"No," she said. "Her first husband's name. He and his mother were quite popular in Society there. When he died, I heard she married another wealthy, older gentleman." She paused. "Just like her first husband."

A dull weight slipped into my stomach. "You don't mean to say—"

Mrs. Coultry shook her head. "I only know the rumors, Mr. Gates, but they were not kind to her. Most painted her in a terrible light, claiming she marries rich old fools and then drives them into terrible debt with her extravagance and wastefulness."

"Then she is a fortune hunter." My voice was even, as if we were still discussing business. But this was not business. This was my family. Uncle.

"It is just a rumor," she said, holding up a hand.

But I knew well enough that there was usually a grain of truth in every rumor. My instincts were rarely wrong, and they had certainly been on alert after speaking with Mrs. Penrose yesterday. Now I knew why. She'd set her aim at my uncle's fortune. *My* inheritance.

Well, she would find that I was not so easily fooled.

Uncle Matthew was waiting for me when I arrived home with the worst possible news—the Halfords were hosting a ball tonight and apparently I would be attending.

I groaned. "Uncle, I only arrived yesterday. Surely I won't be expected at a ball *tonight*."

He would hear nothing of it. "You were supposed to arrive two days ago. Why should I have hesitated to send our acceptance?"

"Because there is nothing so tiresome as a ball?"

He grinned. "There is nothing so *delightful* as a ball."

While Uncle Matthew's enthusiasm for life was often catching, I did not find myself infected by the time evening came. I took as much time as possible to arrange my hair and tie my cravat, futilely hoping that Uncle would grow impatient and leave without me. He only laughed and pulled me from my room.

"You'll miss the first dance," he said as he climbed into the coach, "and earn the ire of all the matrons."

"A tragedy, to be sure," I said dryly, following him inside and sitting opposite.

"Mrs. Penrose, of course, would hardly notice." He unconsciously straightened his jacket. "She cares little for such social mores."

At her name, I straightened. Now was my chance to learn more about Mrs. Penrose—and how deeply she'd already dug her claws into my uncle.

I cleared my throat. "Where is it Mrs. Penrose comes from?"

"Derbyshire most recently, I believe," he said.

"And has she connections here in Sandcliffe?"

"Indeed," he said. "Our good vicar, Mr. Rogers, is her younger brother. After her husband died, she grew lonely and came to live here."

I pressed my lips together. Of course, there was no reason a lady could not live with her brother. But it did lend some support to the idea that Mrs. Penrose was not financially secure. No doubt she was looking for a way to ensure a comfortable future.

I tried for careful nonchalance. "How is it you were introduced?"

He furrowed his brow. "It must have been a month ago now. The Cartwells had a garden party when they returned from London."

Only a month. Obviously, matches had been made more quickly than that, but it was still not a substantial amount of time to know a person. Especially if one was considering marrying that person. And it seemed clearer and clearer that Uncle *was*.

I still could not comprehend it. Uncle was a favorite among Sandcliffe's society, and he had such a vast array of friends that when people greeted him in town, Uncle often admitted to me later that he could not quite remember their names. But despite his friendliness, he was only close to a chosen few. For him to develop such a connection with any woman, let alone in a *month*, was unheard of in all my time of knowing him.

I did not like it.

Admittedly, I was not the most trusting of fellows. I knew that. But my nature had served me well in the past. I could not allow

Uncle to marry someone who was only after his money. I simply did not know *how*.

We arrived at the Halford estate and I trailed behind Uncle as we entered. Perhaps we could avoid the worst of the socializing and I could escape to the card room without much effort.

"You see?" Uncle said, nudging me with his elbow. "This is not so terrible. There are some very pretty girls here, don't you think?"

My eyes skipped over the line of dancers. "I hardly care if a woman is pretty. I think character the far more important quality."

Uncle laughed. "You are only saying that so I won't play matchmaker. Fear not, I won't force you to dance with anyone."

"Then why, precisely, are we here?" I grumbled as we moved to join the crowd watching the dance. I wished I was back home with a brandy and the delightful new billiards table Uncle had purchased while I'd been away. I'd taken a liking to the game during my stay in Stoke-on-Trent and had gotten quite good at it.

"So *you* can choose who to dance with," he said with a grin. "I do not ask for much, but some great-nieces and nephews would not go amiss."

Uncle had always treated me as his son, from the moment I'd become his ward at the age of ten, surly and silent, to the day he'd named me as his heir. He'd never pushed me to marry, but he loved children. It was one of the reasons he'd spent so much time with the Cartwells over the years, with their young, active brood.

One of these days, I would have to choose a wife, if only to give something back to the man who had given me everything. But that did not mean I had to pretend to enjoy this particular ball.

"Why is it," I said, "that of all things *balls* are such a pillar of Society?"

He humored me, a twinkle in his eye. "Most seem to agree that it is the best method for those of marriageable age to interact and form attachments."

"What of those who dislike dancing?" I challenged. "There must be a better way to determine one's life partner than who looks prettiest dancing a cotillion."

"What would you suggest?" Uncle asked. "An archery competition, wherein everyone is matched according to their score?"

I barked a laugh. "Heavens, no. Then I would be matched with Marigold Cartwell."

"Do my ears deceive me?" came a singsong voice from behind me. "Or did the inimitable Tristan Gates admit to having an equal?"

I forced down my groan as I turned to face Marigold. She wore a dress of pale pink silk, with pearls at her neck and in her hair. She grinned wickedly as she curtsied, head tipped to one side. Of course she would overhear the one thing I would wish her not to.

"Miss Cartwell," Uncle greeted her cheerfully as we both bowed. "How lovely you look this evening. Doesn't she look lovely, Tristan?"

Marigold raised an eyebrow. Daring me.

"Yes, lovely." I wished I was lying. I wished Marigold was a hideous crone with wrinkled skin and missing teeth. But despite her freckled nose and her too-wide eyes, Marigold Cartwell was a perfectly acceptable sort of attractive. It was most unfortunate.

"How very kind," she said demurely, clasping her gloved hands before her. "Now, do go on with your conversation. It sounded most intriguing."

"I daresay you heard it all," I said. "You mustn't let us keep you from dancing. Though it seems you haven't a partner at the moment." I looked pointedly at the empty space beside her.

Her jaw tightened. "Mr. Howard is fetching me lemonade."

"I am certain he is." No doubt the man *was* fetching her lemonade, not avoiding her as I would have done, but I couldn't resist putting her on the defensive.

Uncle shot me a look of warning, and I bit my tongue. I never *planned* to spar with Marigold. The girl always managed to taunt me into it with that infuriating spark in her eyes.

"Are all your dances claimed for the evening?" Uncle asked Marigold, not nearly as slyly as he thought.

"Yes, they are," she said with a smile just for him. I could tell she was lying, but thankfully Uncle could not. He always wanted me to

34

dance with Marigold, as if that would finally make us friends. I'd given up telling him what a useless cause *that* was.

"I'm not surprised," he said. "You are always in demand, Miss Cartwell."

"More's the pity," she said with an exaggerated sigh and a quick glance at me. "Sometimes I wish *I* had the time to sulk about the edges of the ballroom."

Unfortunately, she said this at the exact moment Uncle spotted a friend across the room and waved, so he did not hear her slight. It was unfair considering how often he lectured me about my interactions with Marigold.

"Yes, a shame," he said distractedly. "Do excuse me, Miss Cartwell."

"A shame or a sham," I muttered under my breath as he left.

Marigold snapped open her fan. "Would you rather I told him my supper dance was still available and have him force us through that incomparable torture?"

I shuddered. "Do not even suggest such a thing. Dancing is horrible enough."

"How you remain unmarried, I'll never know," she said tartly.

"I cannot say the same of you."

She narrowed her eyes. "What is that supposed to mean?"

"Just that the men of the *ton* are clearly discerning."

She gave a cool, calculating laugh. "You haven't any idea what you are speaking of."

"Haven't I?"

"No," she snapped. "In fact, I expect a proposal of marriage quite soon."

I glanced around. "There does not seem to be a line. I hope you don't mean me."

Her eyes flashed. "If ever I heard an offer of marriage from you, I would laugh before the words finished leaving your mouth."

"And I'd hope Uncle would send for the doctor because surely I would be suffering from an episode of madness."

The corner of her mouth twitched. As much as I liked to win

our verbal tussles with deft wit, sometimes it was a greater victory when I made Marigold laugh. It went against her core belief that I had no sense of humor, and I enjoyed watching her fight that realization.

Marigold regained control of her expression and raised her chin. "Then it is fortunate that we will never find ourselves in such a situation."

"A man can only hope."

She flicked her fan closed impatiently. "As pleasant as this has been, I have other places to be." She began to push past me and then stopped, her gaze catching on something behind me. An impish gleam filled her eyes. "But before I go . . ." She raised a hand and called across the room. "Miss Kingsley!"

I froze. Not Miss Kingsley, all fawning compliments and insincere laughter. The young woman, despite my best efforts at polite indifference, had set her sights on me and Marigold knew I avoided her at all costs.

She wouldn't.

She *would*. Marigold continued waving, her smile false and bright. "Do join us, Miss Kingsley."

I glanced over my shoulder to see Miss Kingsley hurrying toward us, those sharp eyes already latched onto me.

"Don't do this," I said to Marigold through clenched teeth.

Marigold leaned close, our shoulders nearly brushing. Her warmth reached across the space and her perfume, a subtle floral, drifted to my nose.

"I did not hear a 'please,' Gates," she whispered, her lips curving up into a saucy grin.

My eyes locked onto her mouth. For a moment, I forgot that Miss Kingsley was coming at me like I had a target on my back. I forgot that we stood amidst a hundred or more guests, and somehow, inexplicably, I even forgot how much I disliked Marigold Cartwell.

Instead, I was distracted entirely by those smooth, pink lips.

Their tempting fullness. I stared, my head strangely clouded, my stomach lurching—

I tore my eyes away, cursing myself. I did not believe in witchcraft, but there was little else to explain what had just happened. Or perhaps she was a siren, luring me to my death. That seemed more likely.

I cleared my throat. "You won't hear a 'please,'" I finally managed, my pride the final nail in my own coffin.

Marigold sighed with a shake of her head. "And I *so* wished to help you."

Miss Kingsley was closing in. I knew Marigold well enough to guess her plan—she would foist the lady upon me and then we would have to dance together if I did not wish to cause enormous offense. My mouth soured. Miss Kingsley always peppered me with questions, no doubt wishing to appear interested and thoughtful. But talking about myself was the last thing I wished to do at a social event. Well, it tied with dancing, at least.

The music for the previous dance ended, applause filling the air, and another idea presented itself. Marigold was stepping around me to greet Miss Kingsley, but I grabbed her hand.

Marigold looked down at our joined hands then blinked up at me. "What are you—"

I tugged her toward the dance floor. I did not glance at Miss Kingsley, hoping it seemed as though I hadn't seen her coming from behind me.

"Tristan, stop," Marigold hissed, though she did not pull away. She was just as aware of all the eyes around us as I was. "I don't wish to dance with you."

"And I do not wish to dance with Miss Kingsley," I said evenly, enjoying her reaction a bit too much. "This seems the lesser of two evils."

"Wonderful," she snapped. "Now we both lose."

"Better than you winning."

Her eyes flashed to mine and her mouth opened to sound a retort.

Then she masked her expression and looked away. There was not much she could do or say, here in such a crowd with everyone watching. For a moment, that unfamiliar tug of guilt returned. I was not being very gentleman-like. But then, *she* had been the one to call Miss Kingsley over to torment me. This was simple retaliation. Battle tactics, as it were.

I led her to join the line of dancers. Uncle Matthew caught my eye as I took my place across from her, looking pointedly at Marigold. I only shook my head. Now he would have illusions of friendship—or more—all over again.

"You do recall the steps?" she asked crisply as we waited for the music to begin. "That is one downside of avoiding balls, I'm afraid."

"I know the steps," I said. "So you may give up the hope of me falling on my face."

"You know just how to disappoint a girl."

The hum of violins filled the air, and I bowed as she curtsied. We started into the movements of the quadrille. Her hand was featherlight in mine, as if she wanted to avoid touching me at all. The tension wound tightly between us, a bow string stretched to its breaking point. Why had I thought this was better than dancing with Miss Kingsley? No man wanted an unwilling partner. I'd been a lout to force her.

I watched Marigold from the corner of my eye as we danced. Her lips were set into a flat line, her smile nowhere to be seen. And for the first time in my life, I did not like knowing I'd been the cause of its disappearance.

Chapter Five

MARIGOLD

I DID NOT ENJOY my dance with Tristan.

He was an adequate dancer, of course. I knew that of him already. We both moved smoothly through the steps, our gloved hands barely touching.

No, it was everything else. It was his stiff hand beneath mine. It was the look of extreme dissatisfaction on his face. It was knowing that he would note every mistake I made, that he wished—like myself—to be anywhere else in the world.

Except, when I did make a mistake, stepping right when everyone went left, he did not say a thing. He only pulled me with him to the left, making my mistake almost unnoticeable.

I allowed him a few moments to form a mocking slight, but . . . nothing came.

"It is unlike you to let a mistake of mine go unmentioned," I said shortly.

"What mistake?"

We parted with the movements of the dance, and I watched him through narrowed eyes. What was he about?

But he said nothing more the rest of the dance, and neither did I. When the music ended, he saw me to the edge of the dance floor and bowed.

"An unparalleled pleasure, Miss Cartwell," he said in that caustic tone of his.

"A dance never to be matched, I am sure, Mr. Gates," I said with a dramatic curtsy.

I swept away, though not before I caught the barest sketch of a smile on his lips.

"Did I see wrong, or were you just dancing with Tristan Gates?" Sylvia appeared at my side and took my arm, green eyes mischievous and red lips spread in a grin. Her delicate features, almost faerie-like, seemed softer in the candlelight, though she hardly needed such favors. There was rarely a day Sylvia did not look stunning, and when she made an extra effort, with her elegant, embroidered gown and her raven hair swept up with tiny white rosebuds, she made every other girl in the room wilt.

I sighed. "He forced me into it, I assure you."

"Forced you?" She tipped her head towards me. "Why would he have any need to do that? Every girl here is eyeing him tonight."

I hated that she was right. Tristan's aloofness notwithstanding, the young female population of Sandcliffe had been entirely deceived into thinking he was something of a catch. "For reasons I shall never understand," I muttered.

"Oh yes, it is strange indeed," she said. "That a wealthy, handsome young gentleman should be seen as an excellent match."

I blew out a breath. "I know you are teasing me and I shan't rise to it."

Sylvia's eyes twinkled. She liked Tristan even less than I did, though it probably had more to do with his refusal to return her flirtations than any particular loyalty as my friend. Sylvia was unaccustomed to rejection.

"No matter," she said. "Your brother will return home soon and reclaim his place as the most eligible bachelor of Sandcliffe. All will be right."

"Only if you are at his side," I said, nudging her ribs. For as long as I could remember, Oliver and Sylvia had flirted and teased each other. Neither had ever spoken of marriage, but no one in Sandcliffe would pretend any shock when an engagement was eventually announced.

She laughed. "Well, naturally."

I glanced around. "Where has Cora gone off to?"

Sylvia waved a hand. "Her mother still has her in her clutches."

Gray-haired and stone-faced Mrs. Atherton stood beside the lemonade table with her group of matronly friends. Cora leaned against a nearby pillar and looked resignedly miserable. The poor girl rarely danced at balls, considering Mrs. Atherton turned up her nose at any man brave enough to ask her. Cora watched the dancing couples with obvious envy, but when she saw Sylvia and me approaching, she brightened immediately.

"There you two are," she said. "I thought you would desert me all night."

"Of course not," I said. "We are your friends first and foremost."

"Indeed." Sylvia patted her hand. "We should never abandon you for a mere dance."

A gentleman appeared beside Sylvia as if summoned, a Mr. Lawrence. "Miss Halford, might I have this dance?"

Quick as anything, Sylvia flashed a smile. "Oh, certainly, Mr. Lawrence."

He took her hand and led her away, Sylvia throwing a playful wink at us over her shoulder.

"Should we be offended?" I asked, laughing.

"Heavens, no," Cora said, blue eyes shining, her honey-colored hair almost gold in the candlelight. "Or we should spend our whole lives feeling slighted. No, I am only jealous."

I cast a quick glance at Mrs. Atherton, who still stood sentinel a few feet away, her perceptive eyes always watching. "No good candidates tonight?"

Cora shrugged indifferently. "I do not think a man exists who might please Mother."

I turned away so Cora would not see me frown. She pretended she did not care, but I knew better. I hated to see my friend so downtrodden. I understood a mother wanting the best for her child, but Mrs. Atherton's rigid expectations were nothing short of delusional. Herself the daughter of a baronet, Mrs. Atherton was determined to find only the best match for Cora.

"Enough about that." Cora leaned her head closer. "Should we discuss how you might convince Mr. Eastbrook to propose?"

I'd visited Cora this morning with Sylvia, and we'd gone over every word of Mr. Eastbrook's letter. We had been positively silly, and it had been just what I'd needed.

I grinned. "I am hoping he will not need too much convincing."

Cora squeezed my arm. "To think, you might be engaged soon."

Her words unexpectedly brought Tristan back into my mind, the look of disbelief on his face when I said I was expecting a proposal soon. Impossible man. Believing that no man could want me simply because he did not.

· "My hopes are high, I admit," I said, pushing Tristan from my mind and into the dark night where he belonged. "But Oliver is traveling with him and will undoubtedly fill his ears with all kinds of terrible stories about me."

Cora's expression froze. "Oh. I hadn't heard your brother was returning."

"To the detriment of all who live in Sandcliffe," I said, though we both knew I spoke mostly in jest. Oliver could be a pest, as older brothers were wont to be, but I had missed him in the month since we'd returned to Kent and he'd remained in London. "Save for perhaps Sylvia."

Cora cleared her throat. "Do you think he shall finally propose then?"

I shook my head. "I cannot guess what goes on in that head of his. They are both such flirts, it is difficult for me to imagine either of them actually marrying."

Cora nodded, and her gaze seemed distant. I eyed her curiously. What had caused this strange mood? But then Mr. Howard finally appeared before me, lemonade in hand.

"There you are, Miss Cartwell," he said, handing me the glass. "I do apologize, I was held up by an acquaintance. But I've your refreshment, and I should also like your hand for the next dance, if you are willing."

I opened my mouth to refuse—something was amiss with Cora, I could tell—but she spoke for me. "She would be delighted, of course."

She took my lemonade and nudged me forward. That was just like Cora. Teasing me about abandoning her, but then being the first to push me back to the dance floor. She would never wish me to miss anything on her account. I gave her arm a small squeeze before taking Mr. Howard's hand. She raised the glass and sipped the lemonade with a smile.

I danced without pause for the next two hours, until my feet ached and my cheeks were sore from smiling. When kind Mr. Etchins escorted me to the next room for supper, I was happily anticipating the delicious repast the Halfords were well known for: flaky mushroom tarts, glazed veal, duck in orange sauce, delicate choux pastry flowers, and sweet rose ice cream.

That is, I was happy until I spotted Lord Beauford sitting at the table beside the one Mr. Etchins led me to. My jaw clenched. I almost suggested that we choose a different table, but I stopped myself. Why should I not sit wherever I pleased? The baron did not frighten me.

He saw me—I knew he did. But he neither spared me a glance nor a greeting. I responded in kind, seating myself with my back to him so I would not have to see his smug smile.

The meal began, and I tried to focus on the food and the other guests at my table. But when voices came from behind me, one of which was Lord Beauford's smooth, cultured tone, I could not help but overhear.

"It was a pity," he was saying. "This hand of mine is a curse. Only a few more shots and victory would have been entirely mine."

I stiffened. He was speaking of the prize shoot, and without any attempt to keep his voice down. The other guests at my table quieted, listening, including Mr. Etchins.

"Oh, of course," said a different voice. I glanced over my shoulder to see Mr. Hutton, one of the baron's favorite lackeys, who lived only to please the man. "The girl has nothing of your raw talent."

I had to force myself not to snort. Raw talent? Lord Beauford? He wasn't the worst archer, but neither would I describe him as anything beyond competent.

"Indeed not," said another man. "You had her pinned. She wouldn't have stood a chance had your hand not been injured."

It was so absurd that I did not even stop to think. I spun on my chair and looked directly at Lord Beauford. "It is unfortunate we will never know, shall we, my lord?"

A woman gasped behind me. My heart hammered. What was I doing, speaking against a baron?

Lord Beauford's eyes gleamed, as if he'd been waiting for this exact moment to occur. "Ah, Miss Cartwell. I did not see you there."

"It was an excellent prize shoot, don't you agree?" I hardly knew from where my words came, only that I would not stand hearing about his assured victory a moment longer. "I daresay it is always more competitive when *all* parties are allowed to participate."

Lord Beauford remained unaffected, taking a sip of his Madeira. "Parties?"

He was playing the fool. He knew precisely what I meant but instead acted as if he wasn't the sole reason I hadn't been allowed to join the only archery society within thirty miles.

"I speak of ladies, of course." I would not let him escape. "Many women are accomplished archers."

Lord Beauford leaned forward, slowly setting down his glass. Everyone was watching, conversations dying out through the room. Mama and Papa sat a few tables away. She was wide eyed, though Papa seemed amused.

"My dear Miss Cartwell," Lord Beauford said, fixing his gaze on me. "I hope you know we mean no offense by restricting the membership of the Sandcliffe Bowmen. It is not meant as a personal

44

slight, I assure you. I've seen what comes from relaxing such necessary rules. Once the fairer sex is involved, societies become more focused on flirting and parties than on the sport."

"Because women are not serious competitors?" I did not entirely manage to hide my irritation. "Plenty of societies allow women, including the Royal Toxophilite Society. Archery has long been an approved sport for ladies."

Lord Beauford shook his head. "I cannot speak for other societies. But the Sandcliffe Bowmen was formed to be a club for men, to practice a beloved art. It is a tradition that I am determined to uphold."

"A tradition?" I forced my voice not to rise any higher, though it did not matter. Every ear in the room was turned toward us. "The Sandcliffe Bowmen have existed for less than a decade."

His eyes hardened. "I did not realize traditions were held to any constraints of time. I am sorry, Miss Cartwell, but our rules will remain unchanged."

Because *he* would not let them change. Plenty of men in the society would not mind opening their doors to women, but because the baron opposed it, no one dared to oppose *him*.

Everyone still watched, whispers breaking out. Generally, I did not mind attention, but generally I did not cast myself in such a light. I'd never acted like this in all my life. I was Marigold Cartwell, the ideal eldest daughter. I never caused gossip or scandal. And while I did enjoy fairly beating the baron on the archery range, I certainly did not argue with him during balls.

Except now I had. And even though my stomach was a lead ball and I found it difficult to swallow, there was also a strange power coursing through me. To finally speak for myself, and make the unfairness known, was freeing in a way I could not have anticipated.

My gaze caught on Tristan, seated just beyond Lord Beauford. He watched me, like everyone else, but while all the other eyes were filled with variations of embarrassment and pity, his were not. No, his dark eyes were narrowed slightly, focused and determined. I'd seen that look so many times over the years. It was a challenge.

He was daring me not to back down.

I straightened my back. Lord Beauford would not change his rules. But if rules could not be changed, then perhaps I should change the game. An idea sprouted into life, growing and blooming in seconds.

"I suppose it hardly matters," I said, drawing Lord Beauford's gaze back to me.

He had lost any amusement, his expression irritated. "And why is that?"

"Since I will be establishing my own archery society, solely for women."

The room was silent, not a scrape of fork or whisper to be heard. I did not look away from Lord Beauford, though I could only imagine my family's and friends' faces.

"A women's archery society?" he repeated, arching an eyebrow.

I raised my chin higher. "Yes."

He tipped his head, regarding me a long moment as if deciding how to react. Then Lord Beauford laughed. He *laughed*.

"Well, certainly you should," he said, still chuckling. "That sounds perfectly reasonable to me. Let the ladies shoot with ladies, as it should be."

"I do not think we shall be content with that," I said, my voice laced with sharp edges. "Not with the Lady Patroness's Meeting approaching."

For the first time since our conversation began, Lord Beauford seemed taken aback. I knew it would strike a nerve. The Lady Patroness's Meeting was held each summer by the Earl of Englefield at his family seat of Highstead Castle. The prize shoot was attended by every society in northeast Kent, and the Sandcliffe Bowmen had attended for years. They'd returned last year boasting of Tristan's victory over the other archers, and I'd nearly died from envy. Although the meeting was open to public viewing, I had never attended. I knew it would be unbearable to watch Tristan and the rest of the Sandcliffe Bowmen shoot while I stood in the audience.

The baron paused, regarding me with those hard, unflinching

eyes. "The Lady Patroness's Meeting is by invitation only. I daresay a hastily-formed ladies society will not be high on the earl's list. Though I wish you the best of luck, Miss Cartwell."

He made a snort of amusement then turned back to Mr. Hutton, speaking in a low voice. I'd been dismissed.

The hum of voices filled the room again as everyone turned to their neighbor to discuss the newest development. I sat stiffly at my table. None of my companions met my eyes, and even Mr. Etchins, who had been such an attentive dance partner, was red in the face and far too intent on spearing a potato on his plate.

My face was likely just as red, though not with embarrassment. Hot anger edged through my bones. How dare he laugh at me. He knew very well that I could beat him in a fair match. Yet he disparaged me—and all women—with his careless words and cruel laughter.

But anger was not enough. Could I do this?

I let myself look out across the sea of faces. Most turned away from me. But there were a few that gave me hope: my parents, pride in their eyes. Cora, nodding her support. Sylvia, winking at me over her glass. A few men offered sympathetic looks. Most thrilling, however, were a few women—married and unmarried alike—who did not flinch from my gaze but instead looked excited and invigorated.

Cool determination slipped into my veins. I sat up straighter. I was not alone. I'd always assumed that Lord Beauford would relent sooner or later and allow me membership, and so I'd never imagined starting my own society. But now . . . I knew the rules and expectations. I knew the structure and necessities of a successful society, probably far better than the baron did. I *could* do this.

Of course, securing an invitation to the Lady Patroness's Meeting was a different matter entirely. But that was far from my biggest concern at the moment.

Against my will, my eyes went again to Tristan. Why, I could not say. I did not care what he thought of me or my decision. It did not involve him.

He was not looking at me. Instead, he'd risen from his seat and was making for the door to the gaming tables. Of course. He'd had his fun, spurring me on to butt heads with the baron. He was likely gloating inside, thrilled that everyone could finally see the truth of Marigold Cartwell, stubborn and competitive and snappish. Not traits a woman of good breeding wished to be known for.

But when Tristan reached the doorway, he glanced back and found me watching him. I met his gaze, narrowing my own. He offered a smirk, that irritating twist of his lips that was as close as he ever seemed to get to a smile, then disappeared into the corridor.

What had he meant by that? I shook my head. I could not afford to spend any energy trying to understand Tristan Gates. I had far more exciting plans on my horizon.

Even with most people in the room eyeing me like I'd grown a second nose, I could not help my own smile. Finally, something I could *do*. Papa had told me to find another way.

I'd found it.

Chapter Six

TRISTAN

I woke thinking of Marigold Cartwell, which was an unpleasant way to start the day.

I rubbed a hand over my face, squinting in the faint, grey light of morning. It had been three days since the ball, but I hadn't been able to stop thinking of that scene at supper. Lord Beauford's pompous pride, Marigold's stubborn insistence. It had been deucedly entertaining—not many dared speak out against the baron, let alone a young, unmarried woman.

I frowned at the ceiling. That being said, her idea for a female society would not solve anything. If she was aiming for the Lady Patroness's Meeting in a month, she couldn't possibly build a society of that caliber in such a short time. It was a fruitless dream.

But I would sooner sprout wings than understand the workings of a woman's mind, so I threw off my covers and my thoughts in the same moment. I had work to do. I had mountains of correspondence to catch up on after my long absence, and I was hoping to catch Uncle at breakfast to ask his advice on a business matter—one of my tenants was behind on his rent.

I dressed quickly and went downstairs, hoping to find Uncle in the breakfast room. The room was empty when I arrived. I filled a plate and sat at the table, waiting to hear his familiar heavy steps approaching. When a quarter of an hour passed without his appearance, I stopped a passing maid.

"Pardon," I said. "Has my uncle eaten already?"

"Yes, sir," she said with a quick curtsy. "He left word that he went to call on Mrs. Penrose."

My stomach tightened. Again?

"Thank you," I said absently, slumping back into my chair. I'd barely seen him the last few days, and when I did, he spoke of nothing but Mrs. Penrose. We used to talk of business, my work and his—running the estate. I needed his advice, but he no longer seemed to have the time for me.

It didn't matter. I'd solved problems like this before. I'd always been immensely proud of my investments, my financial independence. Instead of spending my inheritance from my father on horses, gambling, and drink like most young men of the *ton*, I'd saved. And when I'd grown old enough, I'd invested. When that investment proved fruitful, I invested again and again. I would never wildly speculate grand sums of money, and neither would I be wildly rich. But I had done well for myself, well enough that I was no longer dependent upon anyone, not even Uncle Matthew.

"Keep your eyes on your own path," Father had often said when I was younger, to keep me from comparing what little I had to others and their plenty. However, after Mother died, and after Father followed, I took the phrase another way. I kept to myself. I provided for *myself*.

I took a sip of my long-cold tea and grimaced, setting the cup down. Unfortunately, it appeared as if I would need to look after Uncle as well. With him spending this much time with Mrs. Penrose, I could only assume a proposal was forthcoming. And if she *was* a fortune-hunter, then I had to investigate and learn the truth about her before it was too late.

But how? I could not accuse her outright. I needed proof. And if I was to guess, most fortune-hunters did not leave evidence of their misdoings lying about for just anyone to stumble upon.

An idea lit in my mind. Mrs. Cartwell. She knew everyone in

town, and made it a point to befriend any newcomers. Besides that, she had the uncanny ability to read people, to take a person's measure with careful conversation and watchful eyes. She would know something, surely, and if she didn't, she would help me. I would need an ally to convince Uncle of this folly.

And soon.

Ignoring the stack of unanswered letters on my desk, I set out across the broad lawn to the east of Stavely Hall, which eventually met the small wood and stream that separated our land from the Cartwells'. I hoped to find Mrs. Cartwell outside in her garden, where I knew she spent every morning of good weather. I'd never met a woman more attached to plants than she. Her thriving garden was proof of that, not to mention the names of her children—Oliver, Marigold, Hawthorne, Iris. It seemed overly sentimental to me, but then, most things did.

I hadn't walked this path in years, though I'd gone often as a youth. Back then, Uncle had been worried about how I held myself apart from children my age, and endlessly tried to force a friendship between myself and Oliver Cartwell, since we were the same age. We'd gotten along well enough, but eventually we'd grown old enough to go our own ways. Oliver was too . . . Oliver. And I was perfectly happy alone. Well, content, at least.

Then, of course, there was Marigold, always wanting to do everything we boys did. That had truly been the only thing to bond us, trying to escape from his indomitable younger sister.

I was lost in thought as I walked, my gaze downward, but a sudden bout of laughter made me jerk my head up. I hadn't yet reached Crossdale, though the back of the manor house had come into view ahead, sprawling and white and cheerful as ever. Where had the laughter come from?

I heard it again, and then noticed two dozen figures assembled at the rear of the house. Ladies in pale muslin gowns and flowered bonnets gathered in small groups on the terrace and grass. Had I stumbled upon a garden party?

I stopped right there on the lawn. Should I retreat and hope no one had seen me? But it was too late. Heads were already turning my way, a few ladies raising their hands to block the sun from their eyes.

"Good day, Mr. Gates," came a voice, high and grating. Marigold. She stepped from her friends, Miss Atherton and Miss Halford, and brandished a sharp smile at me.

"Miss Cartwell," I managed, trying to focus on her instead of the multitude of curious gazes.

Marigold moved to meet me with a mischievous expression. "As flattered as I am that you've come, I'm afraid there is nothing I can do."

I furrowed my brow. What was she on about?

Her eyes danced. "You *have* come to join our society, have you not? But we are quite determined to keep it ladies only."

It was then that I noticed the targets set up in the distance, the bows and quivers arrayed on nearby tables and chairs. "You are meeting? Already?"

I should not have been surprised. Marigold Cartwell was not one to sit around when there was revenge to be taken, after all. Still, I was impressed with her initiative, though I would rather be eaten by a lion than admit it.

"Oh, yes," she said as the ladies behind her talked and laughed amongst themselves, flicking occasional glances at me. "And you may beg all you please to join, but I shall be forced to refuse. We have rules, you see."

"Believe me," I said dryly, "I hadn't any idea you had organized a practice or I would have avoided the estate entirely."

I searched the crowd and could not find Mrs. Cartwell anywhere, although I did recognize many of the ladies from town. How had Marigold managed such a turn out in just three days?

"Then might I ask why have you come?" Marigold placed one hand on her hip, leaning closer. She had a shapely figure and she knew it. I tried *not* to know it. "Are you a spy for Lord Beauford?"

"A spy?" I fixed my eyes on her. "I think you have overestimated the strength of my connection with the baron."

"Have I?" she said. "You certainly played the part of his lackey at the fair. I only assumed espionage was also part of your duties."

I crossed my arms, keeping my expression carefully composed. I could not let her see that I regretted my role in that ridiculous affair. "I am fairly certain Lord Beauford does not consider your little club worthy of espionage."

She grinned. "I anticipate that will change."

In truth, I thought she might be right. Not that Lord Beauford would send spies, but that this ladies' society might catch his attention in the wrong sort of way. He could easily ignore the existence of a female society in his own town—he controlled the prize shoots his society hosted, after all. But if Marigold managed to procure an invitation to the Lady Patroness's Meeting, then that was an entirely different matter. It was the most exclusive and popular shoot in Kent, and if Lord Beauford had to shoot against Marigold there, he would not take it kindly.

Not that I personally cared one whit what the baron thought or felt. But his displeasure would not bode well for this collection of ladies.

"So if you are not a spy, and you refuse to admit how much you wish to join us," Marigold said, "then you can imagine my confusion at your unexpected arrival."

I shifted my weight. Mrs. Cartwell still had not made an appearance.

"Is your mother here?" I asked, avoiding her unspoken question. "I don't see her."

She quirked her head. "Some issue with the tea, I believe. She is speaking with the housekeeper. Why do you ask?"

I frowned. I couldn't very well wait out here for Mrs. Cartwell to return, for then she would surely be occupied helping with the practice.

"Gates?" Marigold crossed her arms, impatient for an answer.

I eyed Marigold, weighing how much I could safely tell her. "There was something I wished to speak to her about."

"What, precisely?"

The way she spoke, as if she had a right to know. There was nothing more irritating.

"Nothing you could help with." I stepped back, preparing to leave.

"Are you so certain?"

I hesitated. I did not want Uncle to know about my investigation into Mrs. Penrose until I had enough evidence, but I would gather none of that if I did not talk to *someone*. And surely if Mrs. Cartwell knew something, her daughter would too. I would just be careful not to tell her anything too revealing.

"Very well, then." I moved closer again, and her eyes widened a touch. I lowered my voice. "Are you very familiar with Mrs. Penrose?"

Marigold blinked, but recovered quickly. "Not terribly. I've only met her a few times. But I like her a great deal. She is friendly and quite a good hand at whist."

As if skill at whist were critical in deciding a person's quality.

"I liked her so well, in fact," Marigold went on, "that I was keen to introduce her to your uncle. I thought they might make a good match."

I stared. "*You* introduced them?"

"Indeed," she said, waving a hand. "You may thank me at your leisure."

My jaw tightened, struggling to keep back all the sharp words that fought to escape my tongue. Of course. *Of course* Marigold would have been the one to bring such trouble to my life.

She noticed my reaction and squinted at me. "What is it? Are you not glad to have your uncle marry?"

What could I say to that? I did not trust Marigold not to go about spreading rumors about Uncle and Mrs. Penrose.

"I know too little of her to be glad yet," I said carefully. "Which is why I posed my question. My concern is for my uncle's happiness."

Marigold inspected me, her eyes intent. "I did not know you cared so much."

54

"How could I not?" Did she think me completely unfeeling? "He is my only family."

"Still," she said, moving a step closer. "You ought to guard your hard-earned reputation. You can't have everyone knowing you've a heart inside that stone chest of yours."

She tapped at my chest with one finger, right above my heart. As if it sensed her there, my heart jumped and sped faster. I scowled. Ridiculous thing. I took her hand and moved it away from me.

"There is something to be said for being selective," I said pointedly. "I would rather have one true friend than a thousand false ones."

She smiled, unruffled. "You wound me. But at least I have my thousand false friends to help me recover."

I looked again at the ladies gathered. There was a new energy in the air, a tangible excitement. "I admit I had not expected such a response, not after your unseemly scene at the ball."

She cast me a sideways glance. "How flattering."

I shrugged. "You will always have the truth from me, even if you do not like it."

"Truth." She huffed. "Tell me, Gates. What is your truth about Lord Beauford and his society? About his ridiculous rules and pride?"

I opened my mouth to offer a pithy response. I stopped. Her question was flippant, and yet I saw the serious set of her eyes behind her smile, the tension in her shoulders beyond her careful nonchalance.

"I think it unfair," I said.

She drew back her chin. Her eyes darted over my face, as if waiting for me to break into a mocking smile. In truth, I was surprised by my own admission. Generally, Marigold and I stayed safely within the confines of mild insults and spirited arguments. *This* was uncharted territory.

"Lord Beauford knows your skill," I said. "He is afraid of you, and he hides behind his rules, his traditions."

She recovered. "And are *you* afraid of me?"

I spread my lips into a flat grin. "Not in the least."

"Yet you hide behind Lord Beauford."

"Opposing him would do nothing," I said, not rising to her bait, "except finally give him reason to remove me from the Bowmen. As of now, I pay my dues and win prize shoots, so he is forced to endure me."

She eyed me as if she did not quite believe me. I could hardly blame her. Had I ever been candid with her about my situation in the society?

"But it is my personal belief," I said, "that the best archers should be allowed to compete." I wanted to be perfectly clear that I was *not* like Lord Beauford. I did not fear a challenge, and Marigold was the very definition of the word.

Marigold considered that a long moment, staring over my shoulder. When she finally met my eyes again, something had shifted in her expression. As if I were a painting she'd seen a thousand times but only now had noticed something new.

"I . . ." She shook her head. "You did not need to say that."

"You asked for the truth."

"But I did not expect it."

We looked at each other, a strange, drawing energy between us. It was too much, and too different. I found I did not care for it and hurried to break the silence.

"Perhaps you ought to open your mind to new possibilities, Marigold," I said, retreating to our normal repartee. "You might find you don't know everything."

Her thoughtful expression vanished. "Remind me again why you are so *selective* with your friends, Gates. Or perhaps *you* are not the one being finicky."

She turned on her heel and strode away, her golden curls bouncing with each determined step. Usually after Marigold and I talked—or argued, as was more often the case—I could declare one of us the winner. This time, I was not so certain.

I hadn't meant to share any of what I'd said. No doubt she

would find a way to use it against me in the future, even if it *had* been the truth.

I tried not to think of another truth as I started back across the lawn, but it bullied its way to the forefront of my mind anyway. Marigold was stubborn and impossible—yet somehow, the tiniest root of begrudging admiration had taken hold inside me.

If this was what came of talking candidly with my greatest rival, I would have to avoid it in the future.

Chapter Seven

MARIGOLD

"What did *he* want?" Sylvia nodded behind me as I rejoined her and Cora.

I forced myself not to glance over my shoulder at Tristan, hopefully walking away feeling defeated by my final comment. That was wishful thinking. He never cared what anyone thought of him, least of all me.

"Was it not obvious?" I said airily. "He has decided he wants to leave the Sandcliffe Bowmen and join our society."

They both stared, then burst into laughter. I grinned.

"He begged and begged," I went on. "I rejected him as kindly as I could, but I'm afraid he is somewhat put out."

"Oh, do stop," Sylvia said, holding her stomach. "I thought for a moment you were in earnest."

"Can you imagine?" Cora shook her head, still laughing. "Tristan Gates, joining our ladies' society."

I pretended to shudder. "No, and do not speak of it lest we make it happen."

"But what did he want?" Cora asked curiously. "You seemed to be having a rather intent conversation."

I twisted my lips to one side. "He never told me why he came. I think he meant to speak with Mama." But then our conversation had veered into strange territory. First his questions about Mrs. Penrose, then his unexpected admission about Lord Beauford. And at the end, he'd had an odd look in his eyes, looking down at me as if he did not quite recognize me.

Though, that might be a better description of how I felt about him at the moment. To have had any amount of sympathy from Tristan was unheard of.

I clapped my hands together once. "Let us have no more talk of Mr. Gates. We wouldn't want to ruin a perfectly good morning."

They followed me to the edge of the terrace, and I surveyed the gathered group with a ridiculous amount of pride. I had spent every second of the last three days preparing for this meeting, beginning the moment I'd arrived home from the ball. I made a list of all possible members for the society, then personally wrote and delivered twenty-four invitations the next day. Most were eagerly accepted, which had somewhat surprised me. I'd assumed Lord Beauford's intimidation might have proven stronger than any desire these ladies had to join, but thankfully I'd been wrong. I'd then had to scramble to procure more targets, ensure that every lady had a bow for her use, and arrange for the table of drinks and delicacies that now stood behind me. After all, what was the point of being a ladies' society if the food was not infinitely better?

I mounted the terrace steps and every head turned toward me. A thread of excitement hung in the air, and conversations quieted. I was used to being before a crowd, whether at a ball or a prize shoot, but sudden nerves claimed my stomach like a hill of ants. I swallowed hard, trying to find my voice. Then Mama was there, nodding reassuringly from behind Mrs. Vale, and I managed a quick, deep breath.

"Good day, ladies," I said with a smile, and thankfully my voice rang strong and clear. "I am so pleased to see you all here. Welcome to the first meeting of the Lady Archers of Sandcliffe."

There was a burst of enthusiastic applause, and I found my confidence again.

"I admit, I was unsure if we could gather enough willing ladies to consider this a success," I said, "but I should never have doubted. This will be a wonderful enterprise, even if *some* people do not consider us ladies worthy opponents."

A nervous, tittering laughter darted through the women, as if speaking ill of Lord Beauford would cause him to appear in our midst and condemn them.

"Now, there are several matters of importance that we shall need to decide," I said.

"What sort of matters?" Mrs. Atherton called from near the garden, her eyes suspicious. Cora stood near her mother and sent me an apologetic look. I did not mind the question, though. I was simply pleased Mrs. Atherton had allowed Cora to come, let alone come herself.

"Oh, several things," I said. "Deciding upon a subscription charge, choosing a president and other officers, commissioning uniforms for our prize shoots—"

Many of the women had wide eyes and open mouths, while still more whispered to their friends. Mama raised one hand slightly, easing me. I flushed. I'd pushed too far. Many of these women had likely come just for the novelty. I could not overwhelm them with such details.

"But," I amended, "I think we are all excited to shoot, are we not? We can save business for the next meeting."

Another burst of applause. I gave a relieved sigh. I wanted this to be a proper society, with the organization other groups depended upon, but I would do whatever I must in order to make this succeed. At least they seemed eager to start shooting.

But their eagerness, and my determination, took a turn within the next hour. Even with the targets only set thirty yards away—where most ladies typically shot at fifty—just a handful of women managed to even hit the targets, let alone a ring. I watched with increasing anxiety as the ladies laughed and teased. Young Eliza Vale —one of Iris's friends—was unable to raise her bow properly without dissolving into giggles. Iris stood beside her and was just as silly, though I knew she could shoot fairly well. I certainly could have used someone of Iris's skill, but one of Mama's qualifications for allowing Iris to join the society was that she would not participate in prize shoots until after she had come out in society.

"Oh, dear," Mama said, coming to my side. "I suppose I've forgotten that most womens' daughters do not practice archery day in and day out like you do."

"It is not so bad," I said, trying to remain optimistic. "Look, Cora is shooting."

On her second hit, Cora managed to hit the green skirt of the target, which did not count for any points but was a vast improvement on many. By her tenth arrow, she'd hit the outer ring twice, and earned herself a round of applause.

"Are you not glad I forced you to practice with me all those times?" I teased as she passed me to collect her arrows.

She laughed. "Glad? No. But I will not complain quite so bitterly next time."

My levity faded quickly as the shooting continued. Sylvia was also a terrible shot, though she at least tried. Besides Cora and myself, none seemed to have any natural affinity for archery. I had assumed that many would have been somewhat proficient, with this being one of the few approved sports for ladies. But based on what I saw today, I would hazard a guess that most had never touched a bow before in their lives.

By the time our practice ended an hour later, my determination had waned to a dismal level. This was not at all what I had imagined. Still, I kept a smile on my face. Everyone seemed to have enjoyed themselves, at the least. They all left with happy faces and a wish to be invited to the next practice.

Even Mrs. Atherton seemed pleased as she and Cora left. At least, she did not scowl too terribly at me before her carriage pulled away.

After they left, there was nothing to stop my heart from sinking as I accepted the pitiful state of my archery society. What had I thought would happen? That the women of Sandcliffe would be overcome with passion for the sport? That they'd practice for hours on end so that their skill might rival the men's society? That we could challenge Lord Beauford and come away victorious?

Yes. That had been precisely what I'd hoped for. I was a fool. These ladies, kind and sweet as they were, simply did not care as I did. It was no fault of their own, of course. They were the normal ones here. I was the obsessive, envious girl who hadn't thought to manage her wildly unrealistic expectations.

Mama came to stand beside me and patted my arm as we watched the Athertons' carriage disappear down the lane. "Do not worry," she said. "It was only the first meeting. I'm certain next time will be an improvement."

I blew out a breath. "It is my own fault. I allowed my hopes to rise too high."

"There is nothing wrong with hope."

"No, of course not." I sighed. "I am just realizing all the challenges involved. Not only must I convince everyone that this is a society worth investing in, but it appears I must also teach them the very basics of the sport."

"If anyone can, then it is you."

I smiled at her compliment, though it quickly faded. "I am truly worried, Mama. Have I taken on the impossible?"

Why had I announced my society so publicly? Now if I failed, the embarrassment would be unbearable. Lord Beauford would send me smug, knowing smiles at every social event. Besides that, I'd also revealed my hopes for the Lady Patroness's Meeting. How could we ever imagine to claim an invitation? And even if I somehow did, we would be laughed from the field.

Mama shook her head without hesitation. "I am not worried in the slightest. If you need to teach them, you will become a teacher. If you need to solve disagreements, you will become a diplomat. If you put your mind to it, it will happen."

My eyes pricked with tears. It was what I needed. She always knew.

"Thank you," I said, my voice scratchy.

"Do not worry, Mari," Iris said from behind us, her voice full of teasing. "I think Eliza and I shall soon be fearsome archers. We will take the archery world by storm."

I cleared my throat and regarded her with an amused smile. "Fearsome indeed. Only the bravest of souls would stand nearby when the two of you are shooting."

She laughed, and the three of us went up the stairs and into the house. As I closed the front door behind me, I tried to hold on to Mama's encouragement. But for some reason, it was Tristan's words instead that held me fast. *The best archers should be allowed to compete*, he'd said in that blunt, forthright way of his. And I believed him.

If only everyone else could think as he did.

Chapter Eight

TRISTAN

IF ONE WISHED to feel intimidated and insignificant, one only needed to wander past Camberwell Court.

I stepped down from my coach, apprehensively eyeing the towering columns and blinding white stone above me. The sheer enormity of the Baron Beauford's family seat was enough to make anyone tug at their cravat. Add to that my relatively low social status and it was safe to say that I never felt entirely comfortable at these meetings of the Sandcliffe Bowmen.

Not that I would ever let anyone know that. But I took a moment to touch my hand to the outside of my jacket pocket where I could feel the outline of the silver shilling inside. Just that small reminder gave me the fortitude to grab my bow and quiver.

I followed the waiting footman up the two flights of marble stairs and inside the front doors. I'd been here many times, but I could never stop myself from stealing glances at the decadence around me. A soaring, gilded ceiling presided over the entry hall, which was filled with a strange assortment of Egyptian styled furniture—an ebonized and gilt divan in the center, behind which a three-legged stand supported a clock made to resemble a sphinx. Six enormous gaudy, red columns lined the hall as we passed through.

The footman led me through the corridors until we reached the garden door that opened to the back lawn. I stepped outside, taking quick stock of the attendants. White-haired Mr. Markham and weak-eyed Mr. Rochester sat at a table with drinks and sandwiches, as was their norm. Neither of them attended these meetings for the practice—to them, the society was purely a reason to leave their homes. If either of them ever managed to hit the target, let alone score a point, it was cause for celebration.

A few gentlemen littered the lawn, the bright sun winking off pocket watches and cravat pins. Mr. Goodall and Mr. Hanson stood before the targets, taking their shots in turn. Mr. Lawrence and his son, Thomas, watched, though they seemed more interested in their own lively discussion than in observing the archers. Lord Beauford himself stood near them as well, his expression dark. The baron never looked cheerful, so it was difficult to tell if there was a particular reason for his scowl. Perhaps he hated sunlight.

I nodded at the two older gentlemen, who raised their glasses in return, then I strode across the lawn to join those shooting.

"Ah, here's Gates now," the elder Mr. Lawrence said cheerfully. "We were just wondering if you'd decided you were too good for a little town society after your time away."

"This society is as good as any in the country," Lord Beauford said stiffly. "He is fortunate to be included."

Mr. Lawrence was never one to take Lord Beauford's barbs personally. "As are we all, my lord," he said, perfectly serious save for the twinkle in his eye.

"Indeed," I said. "I did observe a target meeting while traveling and thought our society would be evenly matched with any I saw there." It was the truth, thankfully. Even if most of our thirty-odd members only attended the three prize shoots in the summer and none of the weekly practices, we still had many who shot regularly and enjoyed the competitiveness of the sport.

Lord Beauford nodded, jaw tight. "Quite right."

The baron and the elder Mr. Lawrence began talking of the last practice, and Thomas Lawrence moved to my side. "Good to have you back, Gates," he whispered with a grin. "It's been me and the old men for far too long."

I managed a smile. "I'm glad to be back."

As Thomas and I were the only men in the society under forty years of age, one would've thought that we would be close. But amiable as he was, I'd yet to discover how to deepen such an acquaintance into friendship.

I tried not to think of Marigold's parting words from a few days before. *Remind me again why you are so selective with your friends, Gates. Or perhaps you are not the one being finicky.*

She was right, though I would never tell her that. Most people had no particular wish to know me better, and neither did I want them to. I preferred to keep to myself, because making conversation with anyone I did not know well was torture akin to having hot oil poured on me. And while I never strived for rudeness, I did not know how to be anything but abrupt and frank.

But now Marigold's slight roiled inside me. Now I wanted to prove her wrong.

"How . . ." I cleared my throat, scrambling for the right words. "How have meetings gone in my absence?"

If Thomas seemed surprised by my sad attempt at conversing, he did not show it. "Dreadfully," he said, glancing at the baron to ensure he was not listening. "Without you here, no one has been able to beat Lord Beauford, and he's become insufferable."

Already I was backed into a corner. I knew I was the best shot, as did everyone in the society, but how did I go about responding to such a comment without sounding like a vain peacock?

I decided to work around it, matching his caution and speaking in a low voice. "More insufferable than usual?"

"Yes," he said with a laugh. "I, for one, was hoping to see Miss Cartwell knock him down a peg at the fair. But your victory was just as entertaining."

"Glad to be of service," I said dryly.

"What's this business with her starting a ladies' society?"

Thomas asked, crossing his arms. "I wasn't at supper when she made her announcement the other night."

"Are you speaking of Miss Cartwell?" Mr. Lawrence moved closer to rejoin our conversation. Lord Beauford did as well, expression carefully guarded.

"Yes," Thomas said eagerly. "I am curious to see if she will follow through."

"Have you not heard?" I said. "She already has."

All eyes swung to me, an experience I could have avoided completely if I had not insisted on *making friends*.

"Forgive me," Lord Beauford said slowly. "She has already formed her society?"

"How do you know?" Thomas asked me. "Have you and Miss Cartwell mended your bridges?"

"There were no bridges to start with," I said. "I only happened upon the meeting when I visited Crossdale for another purpose entirely."

Mr. Lawrence shook his head in amusement. "One must admire her tenacity."

Lord Beauford laughed, a sharp bark. "One mustn't do anything of the sort. And forgive me if I doubt Miss Cartwell's chances of success."

"Why is that?" I asked, my voice holding an unfamiliar edge.

"Because ladies simply do not have this sport in their blood like men do," he said. "The art of shooting with a longbow is part of our history, our identity. Women have many skills and talents, of course, but the passion that drives us simply cannot be replicated in a woman. I am sure Miss Cartwell, stubborn as she is, will muster up a little party to shoot, but nothing will come of it."

"A little party?" I raised an eyebrow. "Would you call two dozen women a *little* party?"

The baron's eyes fixed on me. "Two dozen?"

"Indeed," I said. "I daresay it proved to be quite popular."

Lord Beauford's eyes narrowed, which gave me a strange pleasure. I also was fully aware of my own contradiction—defending

Marigold even in my dislike of her. But she was not here to speak for herself. It did not seem fair.

Thomas and his father looked between the baron and me, not daring to speak up. I did not blame them for their silence. It was not a pleasant experience to be in Lord Beauford's black books. I only managed to stay off his pages because of my ability to win at the targets, elevating his society as a whole. Otherwise, I had no doubt he would be glad to set me adrift.

"Well," Lord Beauford said, his voice perfectly even. "I suppose we shall see. But an archery society is only as good as its members, and I cannot see this becoming anything more than a social club."

I bit my tongue. He could be right, after all. Perhaps Marigold's society would dwindle and devolve, its members growing bored. Marigold could be frighteningly obsessive about archery. No doubt she'd scare a few of them off.

But I did not think that would be the case. My concerns from a few days before returned. What would happen if Marigold's success threatened Lord Beauford's peace? He had been the one to refuse her membership in the Sandcliffe Bowmen, after all, and if her society proved at all successful, especially in tournaments outside of Sandcliffe, he would feel humiliated—and angry. I knew him well enough to realize that. He was the sort of man who liked to control every situation, and he could not control Marigold.

"Let us be done with this," Lord Beauford said. "We must practice. I am determined we do well at the Lady Patroness's Meeting."

I exhaled and checked the pull of my string. I might not care for the baron's opinion, but he was right. The Lady Patroness's Meeting was less than a month away. We all needed the practice. I'd won last year, but just barely. It was indeed the best of the best.

If one only counted the men, that was.

Lord Beauford moved away, and I eyed him as he left. I would not want him for an enemy.

I hoped Marigold knew what she was getting herself into.

Chapter Nine

MARIGOLD

I PRACTICED ALMOST CONSTANTLY for the next few days after the society meeting. Normally, I practiced for one reason: to beat Tristan. He was naturally stronger, which meant he handled longer bows and distances with an ease I could only wish for. Since I did not have Tristan's physical advantages, I had to make up for them with talent and perseverance. Those I had in abundance.

Now, however, I practiced for another reason. I had to learn how to *teach* archery.

I thought the task impossible at first. It felt akin to teaching someone to breathe or walk or smile. Some things just came naturally. But I refused to admit defeat before I'd even begun. I forced Iris and Hawthorne to shoot with me, and they let me practice on them, instructing on their posture and aim. I lectured them on the finer points of the game, though they yawned and offered saucy responses to my questions.

But I learned and I improved.

I also wrote a plan for the details of our society, which I had Mama read over and approve. No one knew better than I how it should be done. I simply needed to present my plan and hope they accepted it. Otherwise we would be mired in useless debates about society fees and whether our uniforms ought to have ruffles.

After four days of constant work, however, I needed time for myself, and I escaped to the back lawn with my bow and arrows. Oliver and Mr. Eastbrook were due to arrive this evening, but I had hours to practice before I had to ready myself to receive them. My target was set up a hundred yards away, as always, and I shot arrow after arrow, making tiny adjustments each time.

Eventually I had to pause and stretch my shoulders, rolling them from front to back. They were nearly as sore as my arms. Perhaps I'd pushed too hard these last few days. There was no use overtaxing myself into uselessness. One more shot, I decided.

But as I was raising my bow, I heard a voice on the breeze.

"Mari!"

I turned to see Iris waving frantically at me from the garden. I squinted. What did she want?

She cupped her hands around her mouth. "They are here! The coach has just turned down the lane!"

Heavens. They were early. We hadn't expected Oliver and Mr. Eastbrook until closer to dinner, and now here I stood, sweaty and wilting in the July sun. I grabbed my quiver from the grass and ran to Iris.

"Here, let me," she said, taking my things with a teasing grin. "You'd better look in a mirror before you greet him."

"How kind you are," I said tartly as I hurried past.

Mama and Papa were already waiting in the entryway when I reached the house. I was out of breath, though I hadn't run terribly hard. Was I nervous? That seemed silly. What was there to be nervous about? I liked Mr. Eastbrook. We got on splendidly.

Papa took one look at my face and laughed, handing me his handkerchief. "At least you don't need any rouge."

I stepped to the mirror hanging in the entry. He was right—my cheeks were flushed, my skin covered in a slight sheen.

"Hush," I said as I dabbed my forehead with the handkerchief. "They are early."

Mama gave me a look of exasperation. "It's nearly five o'clock, Marigold."

I checked the long case clock across the entryway. "Is it truly?"

Papa patted me on the shoulder. "We can only hope Mr. East-brook sees your love of archery as a positive recommendation rather than an unhealthy obsession."

"Ha," I said, handing him back his handkerchief. "I am perfectly healthy, thank you."

The sound of wheels and horse hooves came from outside, stopping right before the front door.

"Are you ready?" Mama asked me, slipping her arm through mine.

I steadied my breath and pushed back that rush of nerves, then nodded. We went down the front stairs just as Oliver emerged from the coach, blond hair tousled from travel but his mischievous grin ever-present.

"Ah, you've all gathered to greet me," he said, stopping directly in front of the coach door and running a hand through his hair. "How touching."

I shook my head but fought a smile. Oliver was ridiculous. He knew very well it was not *his* arrival we were anticipating.

"Lovely to see you, dear," Mama said with no small amount of exasperation. "Now do make room for our guest."

Oliver laughed good-naturedly and stepped to the right with a flourish, allowing Mr. Eastbrook to descend the coach steps. I let my eyes run over him, not realizing how hungry I'd been for the sight. I'd thought him handsome on our first acquaintance, and now I only agreed more firmly with myself. Light brown hair, a few shades darker than my own, and a wide, strong jaw. His blue eyes always smiled even when his lips did not—though he was certainly smiling now as he took me in. He stepped down, straightening his brilliant green jacket, hat in one hand.

"Mr. Eastbrook," Papa said with a bow. "How glad we are that you could come."

"The pleasure is entirely mine, I assure you," Mr. Eastbrook said as he returned the bow, his voice deeply masculine. "Kent has by far the prettiest countryside in all England, I should think." His gaze moved to Mama and me. "Made prettier by its ladies, of course."

That made Mama beam, even if it was just a pleasantry. "You are shameless, Mr. Eastbrook," she said, extending her hand.

"I shall not be ashamed of the truth," he said, bowing over her hand briefly. Then he turned to me, his smile pulling to one side. "I am glad to see you again, Miss Cartwell."

"Mr. Eastbrook." I offered a curtsy, trying to ignore the sudden pounding in my chest. *Silly,* I reminded myself. "I've been most anxious for your arrival."

Was that too forward? But then, what was wrong with a little honesty in matters of the heart? I *had* been anxious. I wanted to see how Mr. Eastbrook might fit here at Crossdale. He hadn't yet met Iris or Hawthorne. Would they like him?

His eyes softened. "It could not come quickly enough."

I smiled up at him. The perfect response.

Papa showed Mr. Eastbrook into the house, saying something about how excellent the fishing was in the pond. They'd gotten along well in London, so I had no worries for their relationship.

Oliver moved after them, raising his eyebrows at me suggestively. "'Most anxious for his arrival'? Do control your emotions, Mari."

I made a face at him. "Why did you not remain in London longer?"

"Mama missed me," he said, starting up the stairs. "And so did you. No need to deny it."

I cast Mama a look of pure exasperation, but she only laughed. "I did miss him."

"He'll remind you soon enough why absence makes the heart grow fonder," I said, shaking my head.

We followed the men into the house, and I forced myself to take a deep breath, releasing any remaining apprehension. It was an excellent start, to be sure. Mr. Eastbrook knew precisely how to charm my family.

For one strange moment, Tristan flashed through my mind.

Unlike Mr. Eastbrook, Tristan did not get along well with most of my family—Papa and Oliver only tolerated him, while Hawthorne and Iris had long given up trying to win his indifferent favor. Mama was the obvious exception.

I shook off that thought. I need not think of Tristan tonight, not when I had so many hopes set on our newly-arrived guest. If I was a betting woman, I would wager last month's pin money that I would be engaged within a fortnight.

I simply had to ensure my heart was ready.

∽

As it turned out, Iris and Hawthorne liked Mr. Eastbrook perhaps even more than I did. He'd recently traveled to Italy, and they begged him for tales of his adventures abroad. He indulged them, telling them of the sparkling blue waters of the Mediterranean, the rolling, fertile hills of the Italian countryside, the winding streets of Rome that suddenly opened up to one grand cathedral after another. I could not help but smile as I watched them.

"You are kind to suffer their attentions," I said when Mr. Eastbrook finally came to sit beside me on the settee, Mama having drawn my younger siblings away to give us a moment together.

He forced an expression of mock pain. "Yes, I am suffering indeed. In fact, I think you owe me quite a favor for enduring such a horrendous evening with your terrible family."

I laughed. His humor was impossible to resist, so light and quick. That was how a gentleman ought to act. Not dark and irritable and impossible to please, like a certain one I could think of.

"I suppose that seems a fair bargain," I said. "What do you require of me?"

"Perhaps a ride tomorrow? I should like to see more of Crossdale." He leaned towards me, lips curved. "And spend more time with you, of course."

A tingle ran up my spine. "I think that could be arranged.

Perhaps in the morning? I do have an archery meeting in the afternoon."

"An archery meeting?" Oliver was serving himself a drink at the sideboard but turned to send me a questioning look. "Don't tell me Lord Beauford finally gave in."

"No, Mari has started her own society," Iris piped in. "A female society."

"Indeed?" Oliver looked amused. "Well, a lady has to fill the empty hours, I suppose."

"Archery is not empty," I said, straightening in my chair. "You simply don't like it because you were never good at it."

He waved his hand dismissively. "It was all well and good when we were children, but it is hardly the sport of a grown man."

"I think thousands of archers across England would beg to differ," I said, perhaps a bit too heatedly. I quickly sent a sideways glance at Mr. Eastbrook to gauge his reaction. I had told him in London that I enjoyed archery, but enjoying a pastime and being impossibly devoted to it were two very different things.

He smiled at me, his eyes bright. "I would enjoy watching you shoot, Miss Cartwell, if you and the other ladies do not mind a man's intrusion at your practice tomorrow."

My cheeks warmed. "Of course not. We would be glad to have you."

We spent the next morning entirely in each other's company, riding and walking the grounds. We had a chaperone at all times, of course, with Mama or Oliver following dutifully behind, but based on the way Mr. Eastbrook continually looked at me with warmth in his eyes, I did not think that was how he wished it to be. Perhaps I might arrange to be conveniently alone in a corridor when I knew he would be passing by. Scandal could hardly hurt a couple who were planning to wed anyways.

After a light luncheon, we prepared for the society practice. I had no small amount of apprehension, considering how the first meeting had gone, and this time we would have spectators. As the members arrived, I greeted them all and introduced them to Mr.

Eastbrook. He was wonderful—charming and polite. I was not oblivious to the many pointed looks the ladies gave me, most accompanied by knowing smiles. I knew precisely what they were all thinking, and could not help a surge of indulgent pride. This man had come to Crossdale for me and everyone was well aware.

"Well done," Sylvia whispered, eyeing Mr. Eastbrook as he spoke to Mama. "One mustn't attribute too much importance to physical appearance, of course, but heavens, you've netted yourself a beauty."

"I haven't netted anything, you goose," I said, though I grinned.

"She is right," Cora said, eyes twinkling. "Be on your guard, because Mama might set her sights on him for *me*."

Sylvia's attention, however, was quickly diverted when Oliver stepped out onto the terrace. He sent her a wink, clasping his hands behind his back.

"Speaking of eligible, handsome gentlemen," she said, full lips widening. "Do excuse me."

I wrinkled my nose as she left. "She must stop saying things like that. She seems to forget he's my *brother*."

Cora laughed, the sound mildly forced. "Never fear. It is not something I ever forget."

I sent her a strange look, but she quickly straightened. "Come on, then," she said. "You've work to do."

Practice began, the targets still only set thirty yards away. I watched from the terrace steps to get a better view. I winced as the ladies shot, arrows falling short of the mark, laughter and conversation taking precedence over effort. I took a deep breath. I had to be patient, or this undertaking would fail before it truly began.

Thankfully, Mr. Eastbrook seemed not to know much about archery. Instead, he appeared much more interested in watching Oliver flirt with Sylvia.

"I wasn't aware your brother had any particular attachments," Mr. Eastbrook said from beside me as I overlooked the targets. Oliver was "teaching" Sylvia how to hold her bow, carefully adjusting her fingers as she giggled. I frowned. He was doing it all wrong.

"They've always been like that," I said. "I do not know that I would call it an attachment. They are simply two sides of the same coin."

Sylvia loosed her arrow, which arced upwards and then buried itself in the grass not twenty feet away. I sighed. I wanted nothing more than to stay there with Mr. Eastbrook, but I had work to do.

"Forgive me," I said to him with a wry smile. "Oliver is instilling some terrible habits in my friend and I simply cannot stand by and watch."

He grinned. "By all means."

After I banned Oliver from helping—to Sylvia's laughing protests—I focused as best I could on the other members of my society. I offered what aid I could, critiquing posture and correcting finger placement. By the end of the practice, I saw the slightest bit of improvement. Or perhaps I was simply fooling myself into believing it. But I could not stop a tiny bloom of hope from taking root inside me.

When the meeting ended, we all separated to dress for dinner. Mama had planned a small party, wishing to welcome Mr. Eastbrook without overwhelming him. Besides our family, Tristan and his uncle would be attending, as well as Mr. Rogers the vicar and his sister, Mrs. Penrose. While I was somewhat irritated that Tristan would be attending the welcome party, I was mollified by the fact that he would see I was indeed nearly engaged. I was already anticipating that warm surge of smugness.

As my maid helped me dress, my thoughts returned to the conversation I'd had with Tristan the other day and his questions about Mrs. Penrose. He had seemed so guarded, careful, about the idea of his uncle marrying. Did Tristan simply wish to keep Mr. Raines to himself? I could not see why he should disapprove of Mrs. Penrose, save for the fact that she was pleasant and sweet when he was quite the opposite.

I put it from my mind. Tristan's troubles were of his own

creation. He could not see what a good thing this was for his uncle, and I would not worry myself over it.

Mr. Eastbrook lingered at the base of the stairs when I stopped at the top. I could see Mama, Papa, and Oliver already inside the drawing room, and I thought it sweet of him to wait for me. I knew I looked well in my new gown, an ivory silk with a beaded bodice, and Mr. Eastbrook reacted just how a man should upon seeing his soon-to-be intended glide down the stairs. His gaze swept over me, lips turning up in a pleased smile, and he immediately came to meet me at the last step.

"You look stunning, Miss Cartwell," he said, offering his arm. "I do not recall seeing that dress during the Season. Is it new?"

"Yes, it is. How observant you are." He certainly had an eye for fashion. He himself was bedecked in a burgundy jacket and striped waistcoat, cravat tied in an elaborate knot.

"I always notice you," he said. It was perhaps a bit of an exaggeration, seeing as we'd both gone most of the Season without noticing one another, but it was a flattering sentiment nonetheless. He raised my hand to his lips, pressing a kiss to the back of my gloved hand. My heart flipped.

A cough came from my left. I turned to see Tristan stepping inside the front door. His mouth held a badly concealed smirk as he handed his hat to the footman. My face heated. Of course he would be the one to interrupt such a moment.

"Mr. Gates," I said stiffly, dropping my hand from Mr. Eastbrook's. "Terrible timing, as usual."

"Some might say I have impeccable timing," he said, tugging at the sleeves of his jacket, a conservative black.

I glanced behind him. "Did you not arrive with your uncle?" I rather depended on Mr. Raines to keep Tristan in hand.

He frowned. "He volunteered the use of our carriage to Mrs. Penrose and the vicar. I preferred a walk." He glanced at Mr. Eastbrook, who was watching our exchange with curiosity. "Besides, I imagine you've been anxious to introduce me to your new acquaintance. I did not want to keep you waiting any longer."

"Oh yes, waiting with bated breath," I said dryly. "Mr. Eastbrook, allow me to introduce Mr. Gates. He is a . . . friend of the family."

"I assure you, that is not how she used to describe me," Tristan said. "But then, ladies are not generally supposed to use words of the sort she preferred."

I glared at him, but Mr. Eastbrook only laughed. "I am quite aware of Miss Cartwell's spirit. It is one of the things I admire most about her."

"Is it, now?" Tristan raised an eyebrow at me. "Well, praise the heavens. We thought we'd never find someone to take her off our hands."

"I have never been in your hands," I said, my smile forced and frustrated. "Quite thankfully."

I linked my arm through Mr. Eastbrook's and pulled him with me to the drawing room, Tristan following. I could feel his eyes upon me, but I did not look back. I would not let him see how much he affected me.

"Do not listen to a word he says," I warned Mr. Eastbrook, leading him to stand by the window.

Mr. Eastbrook's eyes danced. "I can certainly handle myself against the likes of him. But you two seem to have a colorful history."

"I suppose that is one way of describing it," I said wryly. "He has only ever been a nuisance. You'll see once you have the slightest disagreement with him. He must always be in the right."

He grinned. "I look forward to seeing it for myself."

Mr. Raines's carriage arrived soon after, depositing himself, Mrs. Penrose, and the vicar, Mr. Rogers. As we greeted the newcomers, I watched Tristan from the corner of my eye. He, in turn, was watching Mrs. Penrose, his face set in stone, a strange contrast to his almost teasing levity of earlier. What did he see that was so wrong about her?

Dinner was served, a happy, lighthearted affair. Mr. Raines was always a welcome presence at parties, since he never allowed conversations to dwindle and his laugh could fill a ballroom.

"Mr. Eastbrook," Mr. Raines boomed across the table almost before we'd all taken our seats. "Has Miss Cartwell here told you of her archery society? It is the talk of the town at the moment."

Mr. Eastbrook smiled. "She has. In fact, I was fortunate to attend one of their practices this afternoon."

"And you survived?" Tristan cut in, seated across the table from me. "I have it on good authority that they use gentlemen like us for target practice."

The table laughed and I narrowed my eyes at Tristan, accepting his challenge. He was determined to embarrass me in front of Mr. Eastbrook. He met my gaze, that sly almost-smile still toying with the corner of his mouth.

"Oh, no," I said sweetly. "We only do that with men who are too afraid to face us on the archery range."

Another round of laughs, including an approving chuckle from Mr. Raines. It always amused him when I kept pace with his nephew.

"Perhaps," Mama interrupted, looking at me pointedly, "before you both send for your bows, I might share a bit of exciting news."

That claimed my attention. "What is it, Mama?"

Her eyes sparkled with her secret. "Have I ever told you that the Countess of Englefield and I were schoolmates when we were girls?"

I drew my chin back. "You and Lady Englefield are friends?" No, she had certainly never told me that. I would have remembered Mama being connected with the Earl of Englefield's wife. Then again, I had very carefully avoided ever speaking of the Lady Patroness's Meeting and its hosts. Being unable to attend every year had always rendered the subject too painful.

"Well, we *were* friends," she said. "Thirty years ago. Since then, I've seen her all but twice in London. But I thought it time to call upon that old friendship."

"What do you mean?" I asked cautiously. Hope surged within me, but I tamped it down.

79

"I wrote to her of your society," Mama said, her face glowing. "After your first meeting. She was most intrigued. In fact," she paused for emphasis, "she was so thrilled at the thought of a women's society that she extended an invitation for you to participate in the Lady Patroness's Meeting."

"Participate?" I blinked. "Do you mean as an exhibition?"

"No," she said. "As part of the competition with the men."

I stared at her. I gaped. She could not have said what I thought she'd said. I was dreaming, because her words were a firm impossibility.

"Truly?" I breathed.

She smiled. "Truly."

I did not remember standing, but in the next moment I was at the end of the table, trapping Mama in an embrace. "Thank you, thank you."

She laughed, hugging me in return. "You must give all your thanks to Lady Englefield."

"Indeed not," I said, kissing her forehead. "You deserve a goodly portion."

Her cheeks reddened, but she looked happy. "Oh, sit down, dear. We've a party, if you recall."

I grinned as I hurried back to my chair. "I daresay our guests don't mind."

"Not in the least," Mrs. Penrose exclaimed. "I think we are all pleased at the news. Save for Mr. Gates, perhaps, who will now have to shoot against you."

Tristan's eyes darkened slightly. Was it because Mrs. Penrose addressed him or because she was right? "I am far from worried, I assure you."

I ignored him. "Of course, Lord Beauford won't be pleased," I said, seating myself. "I imagine he will protest allowing us to compete against the men."

"No doubt," Mr. Eastbrook said from beside me. "And after seeing you shoot, Miss Cartwell, I shall take pity on this Lord Beauford."

"As you should," I said with a wink.

The dinner passed in a lovely blur, me questioning Mama for more details, the table discussing how such a prize shoot might look by including our ladies' society. I could scarcely take it in. My veins raced with barely-contained energy, excitement, anticipation.

And a drop or two of dread.

I swallowed hard. Would we be ready? The Lady Patroness's Meeting was in only a few weeks. After two practices, I had seen a sliver of improvement in my society, but would there be enough time to make us at all competitive with the mens' societies?

I shook off those thoughts. I'd had a golden opportunity dropped into my lap. I could not and would not squander it.

Tristan lapsed into silence for the rest of dinner. It was not unusual—he liked dinner parties about as much as he liked losing to me at shoots. But I eyed him anyways. What was going through that mind of his?

When the ladies separated, I followed behind Mama and Mrs. Penrose, who were discussing gardening, Mama's favorite topic. I was about to step into the drawing room after them when a masculine voice called my name from behind.

"Marigold."

It must be Mr. Eastbrook, finally finding a moment with me alone. I turned with a smile, fluttering my lashes.

But it wasn't Mr. Eastbrook. It was Tristan. He stared at me, perplexed. "Why are you looking at me like that?"

Of course he would not recognize flirtation when he saw it.

My smile immediately vanished. "What are you doing here?"

"Well, there is something called a dinner party—"

"I mean *here*," I said pointedly. "I would think now would be a prime opportunity to convince Mr. Eastbrook that I'm a wild, wanton woman ill-suited to marriage."

Tristan crossed his arms. "Why would I do that? If you marry, I'd finally be rid of you."

I narrowed my eyes. "Ah, so that is your new plan. Marry me off before you have to shoot against me again."

He blew out a breath of exasperation. "Why does everyone think I am frightened of you? Does no one recall that *I* won our last bout?"

"*Won* is a generous term for it."

He shook his head. "I came to try and talk to you sensibly, but I can see it is impossible."

He turned, no doubt to march away in a self-righteous fit. But, as always, curiosity got the better of me. I grabbed his arm. "Talk to me about what?"

Tristan froze, staring down at my hand on his arm. Why was he acting so strangely? I released his arm. He shook it out, as if I'd left some indelible mark on him.

"I only wanted to warn you," he said finally. "About Lord Beauford."

"What about him?" I asked, amused. "I am quite accustomed to being in his line of fire, I assure you."

"But this is different, and you know it," he said. "The baron is not a man one wishes to provoke. I fear you will push him too far."

"I am not pushing him anywhere," I said. "Lady Englefield is doing that for me."

He shook his head. "You do not know Lord Beauford as I do. The Lady Patroness's Meeting is of the utmost importance to him. Must you force this? Is it not good enough to have your own society?"

I blinked in disbelief. "Good enough?" I echoed. Was he in earnest? "I beg your pardon, but when have *you* ever settled for good enough, Tristan?"

He opened his mouth to speak, but I did not stop. "I have tried for years to join the baron's society, and have only been met with scorn and contempt. Now, when I finally have a chance to prove my worth, you wish me to step back and be pleased with *good enough*." I crossed my arms. "I thought you sincere when you said I should be allowed to compete. But you will say whatever it takes, I suppose, to get what you want."

His eyes tightened. "If you think that, then nothing I say will make a difference. I was trying to help you, but I can see you have already decided what to believe."

He stalked away, leaving me alone in the corridor. My whole body trembled, anger and frustration vying for attention. Trying to help me? No, I knew the truth. He *was* afraid to shoot against me and used Lord Beauford as a means of intimidating me.

And quite frustratingly, it worked. My fears from earlier quickly crept in. Our society was untested. I knew I could shoot as well as the men, but would my ladies be able to hold their own? I pictured Lord Beauford's cold smile upon seeing that my society was just as he'd imagined, silly and unfocused and unequal to the task of shooting against men.

I would have to find a way. I would not let Lord Beauford destroy everything I'd worked for. And I would not let Tristan play games with my mind.

Chapter Ten

TRISTAN

I STALKED DOWN THE CORRIDOR, jaw clenched and hands fisted. What was wrong with that woman? I'd only sought to help her, to make her aware of what she faced, and she'd bitten me like a viper. Marigold had a way of taking my words and twisting them until I looked like a cad and she felt justified in her righteous indignation. It was utterly infuriating.

Well, I'd tried. If Lord Beauford now declared a personal vendetta against her, I could wash my hands of the whole affair. I'd done my gentlemanly duty.

A small part of me laughed. *Gentlemanly? Have you not goaded and teased her since the second you arrived this evening?*

Strange that my inner self sounded just like Uncle.

But the circumstances were entirely different, I assured myself. Seeing Marigold with that Mr. Eastbrook when I'd first arrived had knocked me off balance. She'd said at the ball that she had a suitor, and yet I hadn't entirely believed her. Surely anyone who spent more than a few minutes in her presence realized that a lifetime of her companionship would send most men to an asylum. It was baffling that someone could have taken such a serious interest in her.

Besides that, I still felt unsettled about our conversation the other day. I'd told her more than I should have, and I did not like it. Tonight, I'd wanted to reaffirm that things had not changed between us. I had perhaps . . . overcorrected. But her behavior just now surely nullified any of my boorishness from earlier.

I returned to the dining room, where the other men were drinking port and discussing some scandal about a lady in a neighboring town. Uncle cast me a curious glance as I sat at the table beside him.

"Is everything all right?" he asked.

I waved a hand. "Fine."

I stewed in my thoughts while the discussion went on. Thankfully, Uncle could tell I was in a mood and did not push me to participate. I eyed Mr. Eastbrook across the table. Marigold's suitor was a dandy if I ever saw one, with his bright clothes and double fob watches. But there was something else about him I did not care for. He was too agreeable. Too eager to please. I knew it was unfair of me to judge that as a failing, but I could not help it.

When we joined the women in the drawing room, I avoided Marigold's piercing eyes and claimed a chair in a far corner. I had no particular desire to play cards or join a conversation, so I picked up a book from a nearby table. *Belinda* by Maria Edgeworth. Awful. It must be one of Iris's. But it could not be worse than enduring any more of this evening. I had just settled into my seat when Uncle's voice called out.

"Pardon me," he said, moving to stand beside Mrs. Penrose's chair. "I also hoped to make an announcement this evening, though perhaps it is not as exciting as Mrs. Cartwell's."

I lowered my book slowly, staring. The room quieted, full of eager expectation.

Uncle held out a hand to Mrs. Penrose, who blushed but stood to take it. "Everyone who is important to us is here tonight," he said, eyes only for her, "so we thought to take this opportunity to share some joyous news."

My stomach sank like an anchor. Blast. Blast, blast, blast.

"Mrs. Penrose has accepted my proposal of marriage," he said, beaming at her. "And I could not be happier."

Cries of surprise echoed through the room. Mr. and Mrs. Cartwell descended on the couple, exchanging embraces and congratulations. Mr. Rogers looked pleased as could be. But of course he was. He was ridding himself of a leech of a sister.

I simply sat, not moving, staring with empty eyes. How could Uncle not have told me? Yes, we'd both been preoccupied in recent days, but this was an *engagement*. Did he think me untrustworthy? Did he know I disapproved? Whatever he thought, I could not stop the stab of betrayal from shooting through my chest. For twelve years, it had just been Uncle and me, and now, in the space of a second, he'd changed everything.

I felt someone watching me and my eyes collided with Marigold's. Her brow was furrowed as she looked at me, as if I was a blurry image behind a dirty glass. I realized I was scowling and carefully masked my expression. Her eyes hardened and she looked away.

It did not signify. I did not care what she thought, and indeed she did not know anything of my suspicions about Mrs. Penrose. I intended to keep it that way until I could somehow end this sham of an engagement.

Tonight, though, surrounded by company, I would have to pretend. It was not my best skill even on a good day, but there was nothing for it. Uncle was looking at me now, concern and doubt written on every line of his face. I forced my lungs to inhale, forced myself to stand. He met me halfway across the room.

"I am sorry I did not tell you sooner," he said, his full voice noticeably quieter. "I proposed yesterday on a whim, and then Meredith wished to tell everyone all together."

On a whim? Who proposed on a whim? But it made sense that Mrs. Penrose would wish to keep it quiet until they could make a grand announcement. Then there would be less of a chance of anyone stopping such a foolish decision.

"No matter," I said, managing a smile even as my head whirled.

"I am happy for you, Uncle."

"Thank you," he said, grasping my shoulder. "It is your opinion I value most in this world. I am glad to know you approve."

I opened my mouth, then shut it again, pulse racing. I did *not* approve, but what could I say? *I am sorry, Uncle, your betrothed is actually a coquette only interested in your fortune.* That would help nothing, not now.

Mrs. Penrose appeared beside Uncle, beaming up at me as she claimed his elbow. "To think we shall be family now, Mr. Gates!"

"Family," I repeated, my smile an icicle. "Yes, I suppose we shall."

"Family does not use such formality," Uncle said, patting her hand. "Meredith, you must call him Tristan."

The very last thing I wanted was for this fortune hunter to use my given name, but I had no recourse. At least Uncle Matthew did not insist that I call her *Aunt*. I spoke before he could make such a request.

"When shall you wed?" My words nearly made me gag.

"Oh, we cannot bear to wait long," Uncle said. "We shall need to have the banns read and allow time to plan the wedding breakfast. But no longer than a month, I imagine."

A month. I'd wasted too much time already. I slipped my hand into my pocket, feeling the shape of the shilling I always kept with me. What was I to do? What would Mother have done, knowing her brother was in the clutches of such a woman?

"That is . . ." I cleared my throat "That is wonderful."

Marigold came up beside Mrs. Penrose, linking her arm with the lady's. "How pleased I am, Mrs. Penrose, that I was the one to introduce the two of you. Why, imagine how long it might have taken you to find one another if not for that fortuitous garden party?"

"Indeed, we are grateful," Mrs. Penrose said, patting Marigold's hand. "And I shall be just as pleased for you when your time comes. Soon, undoubtedly."

"Undoubtedly," Marigold agreed, flicking a glance at me, a glance that assumed I cared who or when she married. I dropped my hand from my pocket, as if she might somehow know what I kept there.

The talk turned to the wedding, the women eager to plan the details. I could not listen and retreated again to my chair and my book. This night had come crashing down around my shoulders. My chest was tight, and every inch of me shouted that I must *do something*.

Again, I felt the itch to tell someone what I suspected. But who? I'd hoped to confide in Mrs. Cartwell, but she stayed at Mrs. Penrose's side all night, the two clearly fast friends. I'd lost that option. Perhaps I could tell Mr. Cartwell and hope that any concern for my uncle, his oldest friend, might outweigh his distaste for me. Yet he too seemed taken in by Mrs. Penrose, laughing at her jokes. Oliver? He was too focused on fun and flirtations to take anything seriously. And obviously, I could not tell Marigold. She would only scoff at me.

I kept myself apart, pretending to read. It was useless. I could not concentrate. Marigold kept laughing, every face turned to her. Somehow she was the center of attention, even when someone else's engagement had just been announced.

That familiar envy crept into my heart. I loved Uncle Matthew, and I was more than grateful for the life he'd given me. Yet I could not watch Marigold without a small ache in my center. She had a loving mother and father. Brothers and a sister. A life anyone would dream of, yet she did not seem to know what she had.

And now she'd orchestrated a wedding that would take away what little family *I* had.

I'd thought Uncle had been content in our shared bachelor-hood. I thought he was like me, that he never wished for anything to change. But if he married, our lives would be altered forever. And *not* for the better.

I squared my jaw. I could not let it happen. I had to focus, plan. I would investigate Mrs. Penrose. I needed to catch her in a lie, or discover more information from her past. And I needed to do it quickly, before Uncle was hurt any worse.

Chapter Eleven

MARIGOLD

THE NEXT DAY, Papa insisted on taking Mr. Eastbrook to the pond, claiming the fish were practically leaping onto the shores, the water was so full of them. I knew what he was about, of course. If Mr. Eastbrook was planning to propose, then he certainly needed an opportunity to speak to Papa in private. Papa winked at me as they left after breakfast, and I grinned into my tea.

"You look strange," Iris said from across the table, tilting her head. "Have your eggs gone bad?"

First Tristan last night, and now my own sister. Was there something inherently wrong with my face when I looked pleased?

"She fancies herself in love," Oliver said, not looking up from his broadsheets. "She will likely look moon-eyed for months."

"My eyes are perfectly fine," I said, taking a sip of tea. "There is nothing wrong with smiling on a beautiful summer morning."

Hawthorne pointed his fork at me. "You are going to make us practice with you again, aren't you?"

"It *has* been a few days," I said innocently.

Groans came from around the table. I set down my tea. "Come now, I need your help more than ever. I must learn how to teach my society if we are to impress at the Lady Patroness's Meeting."

"I had a blister after our last practice," Iris complained. "I have not yet recovered from your . . . *teaching*."

"And I," Hawthorne said, stabbing a sausage, "have no excuse. I simply don't want to."

I turned to Oliver. "What about you?"

He grinned. "Forgive me, sister, but I have far more interesting pursuits today than standing in the hot sun trying to hit a target with an antiquated weapon."

"These 'more interesting pursuits' would have nothing to do with Sylvia, would they?" I said with a sly gaze.

"You dare impugn my honor?" He winked as he stood, taking one last swig of tea. "I am simply going for a ride, and if I happen to see the lovely Miss Halford, then I shall count myself lucky."

"Just marry the girl," Iris grumbled into her toast. "Then you might spare the rest of us your thinly veiled insinuations."

Oliver whipped his gloves at Iris as he passed her. "And here I thought I'd been perfectly obvious."

I turned my beseeching eyes back on my younger siblings as Oliver left.

"Please," I begged. "Our next practice is in three days, and I am still woefully unprepared. What can I do to convince you?"

Iris sent Hawthorne a devious smile. "Oh, I can think of something."

That was how I found myself waiting outside the bakery an hour later. Iris and Hawthorne were inside, spending a good portion of my pin money on tarts, cakes, biscuits, and cheesecakes.

"You shall make yourselves ill," I called through the window. They only giggled and ordered three more Chelsea buns.

I sighed and turned back to the street. I would let them spend all my pin money and more if it would help me in the long run. I had to be ready, and my society had to be ready.

"Miss Cartwell."

I froze. The voice was slick like oil, cold like old tea. I turned to see Lord Beauford approaching, a manservant behind him carrying packages.

I curtsied. "Lord Beauford."

I thought he might simply nod and carry on. At least, I hoped he would. But he came to a very sharp stop beside me, his eyes raking over me in a manner I could only describe as horribly uncomfortable.

"It seems I cannot escape you," he said.

"Pardon?" I squinted at him.

"How interesting that I should come across you in town when just this morning, I heard the most interesting news."

"News?" I tried for innocence. "What sort of news?"

He sniffed. "Do not pretend you know nothing of this plot enacted by Lady Englefield."

I kept my expression neutral. "I suppose you mean the invitation that was extended to my society to shoot at the Lady Patroness's Meeting."

"Ah, you admit it."

"It was hardly a plot, Lord Beauford," I said. "Lady Englefield is free to invite whomever she pleases."

His dark eyes narrowed to slits. "I only find the timing a bit too convenient."

"No more so than Mr. Gates arriving at the fair shoot just as your hand *seized*."

He gave a short laugh. "I do not care what you think of me, Miss Cartwell. But I am concerned by those who think they can trample over my wishes."

Oh, how I had to bite my tongue. What did he know of trampled wishes?

"It is the earl and countess's decision, not mine," I said, forcing my voice to remain even.

Lord Beauford's jaw tightened. "And I will do everything in my power to convince Lord Englefield that they made the wrong one."

He pushed past me, and I nearly let him leave. But then I was struck by an idea, a dangerous, foolish, ridiculous idea, and I could not stop myself.

"Perhaps we might strike a bargain, my lord," I said, mind still tumbling. Was this wise?

"What sort of bargain?" He turned back, trying not to show his interest. But I could see it, in the gleam of his eyes and the angle of his head.

"One based on the result of the upcoming meeting," I said. "My society will be involved whether you wish it or not." I paused, letting him catch up to me. "If I win the prize shoot, you must allow me to join the Sandcliffe Bowmen."

He snorted. "You are not making this at all appealing."

"If I lose," I went on, ignoring him, "then I promise I will no longer shoot at any public meetings, including the summer fair." Even as the words left my mouth, a nugget of dread dropped into my stomach. What was I promising?

But would he even take the bait? Lord Beauford inspected my face, perhaps searching for any weakness. He would not find any; as soon as the words escaped my mouth, I was bound by them. I raised my chin and held his gaze.

"That is an interesting proposition," he mused. "But I do not think you are sacrificing near enough."

I swallowed, my pulse quickening.

He leaned nearer. "If you lose, you will not shoot at any public meetings *and* you will disband your society."

Instinct opened my mouth to refuse. Who was he to demand such a price? I had worked so hard to form my society, and he thought I would simply wager it away on a whim?

But I stopped myself, forcing myself to consider. After all, I was very soon to leave Sandcliffe, married to Mr. Eastbrook. I would likely never compete here again, regardless of this bargain. And while I loved my society and the members, I could not imagine it would continue in my absence. None of the ladies loved archery as I did. It was certainly not a failing of theirs, just a fact. No doubt the society would fade away after I left.

I eyed Lord Beauford, my lungs tight. If I agreed, if I lost in the prize shoot, I would not truly lose anything. But if I won . . . If I won, then I won a victory for every woman ever belittled by a man.

"Very well, my lord," I said. "You have an agreement."

"Excellent," he said, a lazy grin climbing his thin lips. "I only hope you are not too disappointed in the results."

I smiled sweetly. I knew what he was thinking—that he had an ace up his sleeve. He was certain Tristan could beat me.

"You needn't worry for me," I replied. "But I would recommend a bit of practice in the meantime. I do not intend to go easy."

His grin vanished. He said not another word, simply turned and strode away. Uncertainty twinged through me. Had I done the right thing? Had I allowed my confidence to outweigh reason?

"Was that Lord Beauford?"

Iris and Hawthorne emerged from the bakery, holding brown packages and staring after the baron.

"Yes," I said, straightening my back. "Now, come on. We've work to do."

I led the way to our carriage, still not entirely believing what had happened. Mama would groan if she knew how I'd spoken to Lord Beauford—a *baron*—but a baron was still just a man. And a man I could beat, no less.

Now I only needed to figure out how to beat Tristan.

Chapter Twelve

TRISTAN

THE ITCH of desperation worked its way through me the entire day after the Cartwells' dinner party. I had to find a way to spend more time with Mrs. Penrose, to ask her the right questions and catch her in a lie. But I could not profess a newfound interest in her without raising Uncle's suspicions. Luckily, he provided me the perfect opportunity that night at dinner.

"Have you plans for tomorrow?" Uncle asked as he served himself roast chicken.

I paused with a bite halfway to my mouth. "Plans?" I'd learned it was better to know beforehand what I was committing myself to.

He grinned. "No need to be so apprehensive. The Cartwells are planning a picnic on the beach, and extended an invitation to you and me. But seeing as I already forced you to attend a ball and a dinner party in the last week, I thought to let you have a say in it."

I tried for nonchalance. "Will Mrs. Penrose attend?"

"Yes, she has also been invited," he said, watching me closely. "She has mentioned how she loves the seashore."

Of course she did, because *Uncle* did.

"It is no trouble, really," he said. "If you are otherwise occupied, I will pass on your regrets."

"No," I said quickly. "I'll come."

He raised an eyebrow. "You needn't worry yourself on my account."

I knew why he was suspicious. Had I ever willingly promised myself to any social event that did not involve archery?

"I haven't been to the shore since I returned from London," I said evenly. "And Mrs. Cartwell will have an excellent spread, I'm sure."

"True enough." He cleared his throat. "Perhaps you might find an opportunity to converse with Mrs. Penrose. I haven't any desire to force a relationship between the two of you, but I would like to see you grow easier around her, considering she'll be living here within a few weeks."

I swallowed back the words that wanted to pry their way from my mouth. "Yes, I suppose you are right. I know I haven't been very . . . welcoming. But I will make an effort."

He looked so pleased that my heart sank. He was so far gone already. Even if I did manage to prove that his betrothed had nothing but ill intentions, he would still be hurt. That was the last thing I wanted.

"Good," he said. "I shall tell Mrs. Cartwell to expect the both of us. They intend to go later in the early evening, to visit during low tide. I believe they wish to show Mr. Eastbrook the sea caves."

My face tightened at his name, and of course Uncle noticed.

"Has Marigold's beau not made a favorable impression on you?" he asked curiously. "Everyone seems to find him utterly charming."

"Perhaps too charming."

"Too charming?" He looked thoughtful. "Yes, I can see that. But I daresay he is only trying to secure the good opinion of the Cartwells."

"No doubt," I said. "Yet there is something about him I do not entirely trust."

Uncle chuckled. "Shocking, to be sure, that you do not immediately trust a stranger, especially one of whom Marigold Cartwell is so enamored."

"Why should that matter?" I asked, baffled.

"Only that you tend to find yourself opposite her opinion in almost everything," he said.

I gave a short laugh. "That is because she is wrong about almost everything."

Uncle smiled in a way I could not even begin to interpret. "I suppose we shall see."

After catching up on correspondence and business, I spent the afternoon at the target set up in the garden. Marigold liked to insist that she had better technique because of her endless hours of practice. And while she likely did practice more—the woman was *obsessed*—I made a point to regularly exercise my bow. Not just to keep up my form and aim, but because I enjoyed it. The repetitiveness might bore some, but not me. Notch arrow, raise bow, aim, release. Arrow after arrow sunk into the target.

It was an escape. The familiar motions soothed my mind, numbed my worries. It was part of why I'd taken up the sport in the first place, the other reason being that I'd wanted to see if I could beat Marigold. She had been the first of my acquaintance to succumb to the archery fever that swept through Kent years ago. And when she'd proven proficient, I'd decided that I would too. That was how it had always been with us. If I climbed a tree, Marigold would climb it higher. If she could count to one thousand in French, then I would count to two thousand. Neither of us liked being second-best at anything but especially so when the other was first.

I released my last arrow, sending it directly into the center. I grinned. Whatever happened at the prize shoot, I would be ready.

Mrs. Penrose accompanied us in our coach to the beach the next evening. As eager as I'd been to speak with her more, I hadn't any idea how to pose my questions without raising Uncle's suspicions.

Instead, we managed with talk of the fine weather and arrangements for the wedding, both topics I was far from interested in.

When we arrived atop the cliffs, Uncle helped Mrs. Penrose from the carriage and started down the trail that led to the beach. I followed behind, hands in my pockets, trying not to scowl as snatches of their conversation fluttered back to me on the wind. I thought I heard my name at one point, accompanied by a glance from Mrs. Penrose. I met her eyes, wanting her to know I'd heard her. She only smiled and turned back.

The Cartwells had already arrived at the beach, blankets spread over the rocky sand and servants arranging baskets of food. Young Hawthorne had shed his shoes and stockings, playing in the waves while Mrs. Cartwell and Iris argued with slightly raised voices. If I had to guess based on Iris's gestures, she wanted to wade in the water like her twin, and Mrs. Cartwell was having none of it. Mr. Cartwell watched his family with amusement, hands in his pockets, but Oliver was nowhere to be seen. It was not the first time he'd managed to escape a familial obligation.

I trudged towards them, noticing Mr. Eastbrook just down the beach watching the encroaching waves carefully. Clearly he was concerned with keeping his feet dry.

My eyes moved past him without direction. I was certainly not *looking* for Marigold. But I found her all the same.

She stood on an outcropping of rocks that stretched into the breaking surf. She held a hand to her bonnet to keep it from flying off in the ocean breeze, grinning wildly into the sun. Her skirts billowed behind her, spray from the waves spotting her skirts, and yet she did not back away.

Neither could I look away.

I watched as she closed her eyes and raised her chin. Her golden curls whipped about her face as she did not move for a long moment. Then she turned to start back across the rocks—no doubt to rejoin her finicky suitor—and found me staring at her.

So quickly did her face form a scowl that I nearly started. I'd forgotten she was angry with me—that we were angry with each other after our conversation at the dinner party. I turned away, my blood pulsing in my veins, pounding in my ears. I needed to focus on anything besides her. I had a job to do today.

"Good day to you all." Mrs. Cartwell came to greet us, eyes bright. "How pleased I am that you could join us. Especially you, Mr. Gates."

She smiled, though there was meaning in that smile, I thought. She knew this was not my desired way to spend an afternoon. I would much rather be somewhere—anywhere—that did not include other people.

"Tristan Gates at the beach?" came Marigold's unwelcome voice. "What a novelty."

She arrived arm in arm with Mr. Eastbrook. I kept my tone even as I spoke. "I have nothing against the seashore."

She touched one finger to her chin. "Yet I seem to recall a summer not so distant where you vowed never to return."

"I daresay that had more to do with my boots being filled with sand more than any deficiencies of the setting." That had been a particularly childish prank on Marigold's part.

Her lips twitched. "How strange. It must have been an odd sort of sea bird, attempting to build a nest."

"Very strange," I said. "Perhaps the same kind that gathers stockings and shoes."

Marigold narrowed her eyes. It had not been my finest moment, hiding her shoes three summers past. But it had only been done in retaliation for the boots, and I could not deny my delight in watching her storm up and down the beach searching for her things.

"Come, let us find a seat," she said shortly, tugging on Mr. Eastbrook's arm.

Disappointment unexpectedly pinched inside me. She'd so quickly given up our argument.

At least I had been right about Mrs. Cartwell supplying a wonderful meal. We ate our fill of sandwiches and sweetmeats, cold turkey and summer strawberries. It was almost worth the pain of socializing. Almost.

"Now," Mr. Cartwell said after we finished eating, finding his feet and holding out his hand to his wife. "The tide should be low. Let us show Mr. Eastbrook one of the many wonders of Kent."

We all stood, straightening jackets and skirts. I took a steadying breath. I knew what I must do, but I did not relish the task.

"Mrs. Penrose," I asked politely. "Might I offer my arm as we walk to the caves? The rocks can be slippery."

She beamed. "Why, thank you very much, Mr. Gates. How kind you are."

Uncle looked pleased as could be, which sent a twinge of guilt through me. He thought I was doing as he'd asked—making an effort with his bride-to-be. If he knew what I was really about, he would not grin so broadly.

Marigold shot me an odd look as she passed on Mr. Eastbrook's arm, but I ignored her. I walked slowly, pretending concern for Mrs. Penrose's balance when really I wished to allow everyone else to go ahead along the rocky shore.

I cleared my throat. "Allow me to again voice my congratulations to you, Mrs. Penrose, on the engagement. What an unexpected event."

"Oh, to be sure," she said. "I have never felt such happiness."

I watched her from the corner of my eye. Watching a person's expression was crucial to sense if they were lying or not.

"My uncle said you came to Sandcliffe only recently," I said. "Where was it you lived before?"

I knew perfectly well, of course, but I wanted to start with simpler questions.

"Derbyshire," she said, looking out over the deep blue of the sea. "It was lovely country, but nothing as stunning as this."

"So it was the views that brought you to Sandcliffe?"

She laughed, though the sound was a bit tight. "I wish I had the freedom to choose my place of abode based on the scenery. No, I was simply fortunate that my brother chose such a pretty parish to make his home."

"Indeed," I said. "I daresay he shall miss you when you marry."

She lifted one shoulder. "I shan't be going far."

"Not as far as Derbyshire."

"No," she said. "And my first husband lived in Bath. It is a blessing to be close to family, truly."

Aha. This was my chance. "Your first husband?"

Mrs. Penrose glanced at me, her gaze flitting back to the sea upon meeting my peering eyes. "Y-yes. I've been married twice before."

"I must offer my condolences, then."

She cleared her throat. "Yes, thank you."

I thought she might say something more, perhaps change the subject. But she pressed her lips together, staring straight ahead. I hadn't spent much time with Mrs. Penrose, but *quiet* was certainly not her natural state.

We approached the entrance to the sea caves—an uninviting dark archway tucked behind a bend in the shore. To enter, one had to pick their way across the slippery wet rocks near the water, normally covered by the tide. I carefully helped Mrs. Penrose as she lifted her skirts. No matter that she was an opportunist—I wouldn't allow any lady to fall on such terrain. But I would continue with my questions.

"I imagine it must be strange," I said, "to be marrying for the third time. Especially considering some women never marry at all."

Mrs. Penrose was silent, her steps sending pebbles skittering. "Yes," she said, her voice unsteady. "I am aware of my good fortune."

"Did your husband have a line of work?" I asked. "Your second husband, that is."

"No," she said. "He was a gentleman."

"And your first husband?"

A flash of panic crossed her eyes and she looked away. "I would prefer not to speak of him, Mr. Gates, if you would not mind."

My eyes narrowed. Interesting. "Of course. I apologize for prying. I simply wondered if you would be inviting anyone to the wedding."

"No," she said. "No, I do not think so. My brother is the only relation I would care to have present."

I forced my mouth not to climb into a victorious smile. The topic of her previous marriages clearly put her on edge, and it was obvious she had no desire for me—or Uncle, I imagined—to meet anyone from her past. Her charade would not be able to withstand such scrutiny.

"A pity," I said, unable to completely hide my satisfied tone. I was on the right path. I simply needed to tug at more strings until the entire false tapestry fell apart.

"Oh, look," Mrs. Penrose said eagerly as we moved within the shadow of the caves. "We've arrived. Thank you so much for your aid, Mr. Gates."

She smiled and hurried to where Uncle Matthew waited for her in the center of the cavernous opening. I thought she might immediately begin whispering in his ear, no doubt about how I'd made her uncomfortable with my questions. But she only took his arm and listened quietly to his conversation with Mr. and Mrs. Cartwell.

I frowned. Had my questioning been too much? Clearly it had affected her. But I pushed aside the lingering unease. I would do what I must to protect Uncle.

I crossed my arms, looking up at the white roof of the cave, a dozen feet above me. I had visited countless times over the years. The sea caves were popular in Sandcliffe due to their relative safety. Unlike many other caves along England's coast, these did not have dangerous fissures or winding tunnels in which to get lost. But they were dark, especially in the early evening light, which was why two of the Cartwells' servants were now distributing small lanterns among the party.

I took my lantern, resigned to the boredom of exploring the caves, a prospect that had been much more exciting as a child.

"Mr. Gates." Mrs. Cartwell came to my side, glancing over her shoulder as if to ensure no one was listening.

"Yes?" I asked curiously.

She lowered her voice. "Might I beg a favor of you? I'm afraid I'm not quite up to scurrying through the caves as I once was, and neither is Mr. Cartwell. Would you be so kind as to . . . keep a close eye on Marigold?"

I blinked. I certainly hadn't expected *that*. "Keep a close eye?"

She pursed her lips. "Yes. This is just the sort of place a young, courting couple might like, if you take my meaning."

I coughed once. "Can't a servant do it?"

She frowned. "I cannot trust such a task to a servant."

The last thing I wanted was to follow Marigold and her fawning beau around. But Mrs. Cartwell looked at me with such need that I sighed. "Of course."

"Oh, thank you," she said. "What a relief. Even if they do plan to marry, I shouldn't like to start off their lives together with any sort of rumors."

My throat was suddenly tight. "They have an understanding, then?"

"Not yet," she said. "But we expect an announcement from them any day."

I ought to have been filled with jubilation that my greatest rival and irritation from the last decade would soon be gone and married. But instead there was an unexpected emptiness. I could not account for it. Why should such news affect me at all?

I tried to brush it off. I was used to having Marigold around, that was all. Someone to spar with when the winters grew long and dull. Life would be different with her gone, of course. Calmer. More enjoyable.

But despite my rationalizing, the dullness in my chest did not dissipate.

"Thank you," Mrs. Cartwell said with a grateful smile. "I know I am being a worrisome mother, but that is my lot in life."

"You do make parenthood seem appealing," I said. "It is a shock I am not running down the aisle myself."

She laughed. "No running," she said. "There is a special young lady waiting for you, Tristan Gates. You cannot rush love."

When she said things like that, when she smiled with such openness and affection, I had to remind myself she was not my mother. My mother was long gone. But it was hard not to imagine that it was something Mother might have said. My chest filled with that familiar aching pain.

"I only hope this young lady you speak of is also not in a hurry to marry," I managed. "I am not intent on matrimony anytime soon."

"I suppose we shall see," she said. "Love cannot be rushed, but neither has it a timetable."

I wanted to rebuff that nonsense—Uncle and Mrs. Penrose were on a very tight timetable—but she looked over my shoulder and narrowed her eyes. "Ah, there they go."

I turned, and sure enough, Mr. Eastbrook and Marigold were climbing a formation of rocks at the rear of the main cavern. I knew it led to a smaller chamber just beyond, which was still mostly visible to our group. But if they went any further into the tunnels, they would be alone, which was surely their intention.

"After them," Mrs. Cartwell said, giving me a nudge. "Keep a weather eye."

I blew out an exasperated breath and trudged across the sand. If this was what came of accepting invitations to social events, it would be a wonder if I ever left home again.

Then again, I enjoyed teasing Marigold, and this seemed a prime opportunity that I would be foolish to squander.

Chapter Thirteen

MARIGOLD

I KNEW these caves as well as I knew the grounds of Crossdale, and so I knew precisely what I was doing as I led Mr. Eastbrook up the rocks that formed a sort of staircase to the next chamber.

"And where are you leading me, Miss Cartwell?" Mr. Eastbrook said. He was only a step behind, and I liked the idea that he watched me as we climbed. I was wearing one of my favorite day dresses, red and white stripes with rosettes on the sleeves and hem, and I knew it showed my figure to perfection.

I sent a sly glance over my shoulder. "To find treasure, of course. Pirates used to hide their stolen gold in these caves, did you not know?"

"And what if the pirates come back for their treasure?" he asked, playing along with my game.

I grinned. "Then I shall be glad I have you to protect me."

"I cannot say I would last long against a pirate," he said with a laugh. "Perhaps we should have brought your bow and arrows."

My chest warmed. He knew all the right things to say, and in a way that made my skin hum with awareness. If my plan worked, if we stole a moment alone, then I would finally have my first kiss. And, hopefully, my first and only proposal.

We stepped inside the next chamber, each of us holding aloft our lanterns. The late afternoon light had faded behind us, and our candles flickered merrily against the darkness, sending shadows bouncing in every direction.

"Ah," I said, pretending disappointment. "No treasure. And I was so sure."

Mr. Eastbrook's lips curved up, eyes locked on me. "Your eyesight must be poor, Miss Cartwell. The treasure is standing right in front of me."

A thrill ran up my spine as he took my hand and pulled me deeper into the cavern, so that we could not be seen from below. He turned to face me.

"Miss Cartwell," he said, his voice deep and throaty. "That is, *Marigold*, if I may."

"You may," I said, breathless.

"I had been hoping to find such an opportunity," he said, eyes raking over me as if he could not keep them from me.

"And why is that?" I tilted my head up.

He leaned closer. "To have you all to myself."

I nearly melted into a puddle right there, but I managed to keep my knees locked. I tipped my chin upwards as he drew even closer. His lips hovered an inch from mine, and it was all I could do not to rise up on my toes and kiss him first.

"Ah, there you two are."

I jolted, my teeth colliding with Mr. Eastbrook's chin. "Oh!" I exclaimed, holding my mouth as pain flashed through it. Mr. Eastbrook swore under his breath, clutching his jaw.

But I did not care for my pain. I whirled. It was *Tristan*, of course, who stood in the entrance to the chamber with his lantern, an infuriating glint to his eyes. What on earth was he doing here? First, he ruined my moment with Mr. Eastbrook before the dinner party, and now this, my first kiss.

"Is there something you need, Gates?" I snapped. "I do not recall inviting you to join us."

"Oh, no," he said. "I only wished to see this chamber more closely. Fascinating, is it not?" He looked around with false interest, holding his lantern up higher. "Did you know these are some of the oldest stalactites in England?"

I nearly groaned aloud. "Did you know that no one cares?"

He smirked in that way of his, his lips scrunched to one side. "Come, Miss Cartwell," Mr. Eastbrook said, eycing Tristan. Annoyed as I was at the interruption, at least he had finally realized how irritating Tristan was. "I do believe you were going to show me more of the caves."

"Splendid," Tristan said. "We will join you."

"We?"

Iris popped her head out from behind Tristan. "Let us explore together!"

Hawthorne also appeared, climbing up the rocks with a grin. I groaned inwardly. If it had been just Tristan, I would have refused him and marched away. But I could not hide from all of them.

"And a merry party we shall be," Mr. Eastbrook said in amused defeat, though he shot me a meaningful look. That bolstered me. This was only a slight inconvenience. Surely we would find another moment.

There was nothing for it. I sighed, and we started off deeper into the caverns. Iris stole Mr. Eastbrook away from me and peppered him with questions about the sea caves he'd visited in Italy. Hawthorne pretended he did not care but trailed behind, listening all the same.

"I haven't any idea what you are about," I whispered to Tristan as we brought up the rear. "But know I shall enjoy my revenge."

"Don't be ridiculous," he said. "I just saved your reputation. Can you imagine if anyone else had seen you?"

I gave a bark of laughter. "Oh, the horror. I would have to marry the man who was about to propose."

He raised an eyebrow. "Propose? In a dank, dripping cave? How romantic."

"It *was* romantic," I said stiffly. "But you would not know romance if it slapped you across the face."

"Like you are wishing to do right now?"

106

"A lady would never."

"No, but *you* might."

I gritted my teeth. Why was he determined to torment me?

"Marigold, come and see!" Iris was in the passage ahead, and her voice carried back to us in bouncing echoes.

I shot Tristan one last dignified glare before hurrying to catch the others. They stood before a tumble of rocks that lay strewn across the tunnel. Mr. Eastbrook held up his lantern so I could see the dark hole, about the size of my bedroom window, in the otherwise smooth wall. "What is this?"

"It must be a new cave," Iris said eagerly. "It looks like this wall collapsed recently. Isn't it exciting?"

Tristan passed me to inspect the hole, and I wrinkled my nose at the smell of his cologne, intrusive in this small space. He stuck his head inside the opening, holding his lantern aloft.

"It's not another cave," he said, surprised. "It's a mine. Look, you can see the timbers there, and crates and tools and such."

"A mine?" Mr. Eastbrook joined him at the opening. "I did not realize Sandcliffe was a mining community."

"We aren't," Tristan said. "This must be the old chalk mine. I've heard my uncle speak of one that closed a century ago. I daresay we just rediscovered it."

Hawthorne and Iris immediately clamored to see inside, fighting over who got to peek inside first. I was also curious but restrained myself. I wasn't fifteen, after all.

"Let's go inside," Iris exclaimed, her head stuck through the opening. "Imagine what we might find."

"Absolutely not," I said firmly. I might be curious, but I was not a fool. Mama would have my head if I let her youngest daughter go wandering about an abandoned mine. "In fact, we should be getting back. They'll wonder where we've gone off to."

And the sooner we arrived back at Crossdale, the sooner Mr. Eastbrook and I might find a moment together.

"Oh, let us go a little ways in," Hawthorne pressed. "When shall we have the chance again?"

"No," I said, "and I shall inform Papa when we return so that someone might come and fill in this hole. It is dangerous."

"No sense of adventure, Miss Cartwell?" Tristan asked, eyes glinting.

"No sense of self-preservation, Mr. Gates?" I shot back.

Mr. Eastbrook chuckled at our interchange. Iris recovered from her disappointment quickly and dragged him off again, starting back towards the entrance to the caves with Hawthorne in tow. Mr. Eastbrook sent me a look of long-suffering that made me smile.

I took a step after them but stopped when I noticed Tristan was not behind me. He was still peering inside the opening, lantern held high.

"By all means," I said. "Do go in. My life shall be infinitely simpler without you in it."

Tristan did not look my way. "It looks fairly safe. The timbers seem intact, and I cannot see any hint of cave-ins."

"Save for the one you are standing in?"

He sent me a sidelong glance. "I never imagined *you* would shy away from such a challenge."

"Because I value my life."

"Or because you are frightened of spiders?"

I huffed. "Your goading will not work."

"A pity," he said. "I shall go it alone, I suppose. It's more a man's sphere, anyway."

I knew what he was doing. I *knew* it. But his smug voice lit a fire inside me, burning up my former intentions like dry straw. Without thinking, I marched to him, elbowing him aside as I scrambled through the dark, gaping hole. I turned back to him after a few paces, my lantern aloft. "Are you coming?"

He stood staring at me, and oh, it had been worth it to see that look upon his face.

"A man's sphere," I muttered, inspecting the mine tunnel again. "Of all the ridiculous things."

"Come out of there," he said. "You've proven your point."

"No, I don't think I have," I said, moving further inside. "Perhaps if I heard you say just how much braver I am than you, that would help."

Rocks scattered as Tristan climbed through the opening, scowling at me. "I'm not going to say that. Now come back."

"You said it was safe," I said. "Am I not to trust your judgment, then?"

"Marigold," he groaned. There was something in his voice . . . Something that caused a reaction in my stomach. A leap. A twist.

"Very well," I said, more to push away that feeling than anything else. I started back towards the opening, Tristan's face filling with relief.

Then I tripped.

My foot caught on a rock and I went stumbling forward. I threw out my arms, catching myself on a nearby timber, my lantern flickering wildly in one hand.

The timber cracked and shifted.

The earth shuddered.

Then the rocks began to fall.

Chapter Fourteen

MARIGOLD

I SCREAMED. Strong arms encircled me, yanking me away from the rocks, the roaring in my ears, the dust billowing in great plumes. We hit the ground, the air knocked from my lungs as my back collided with hard dirt. This was death. I would not survive, *could* not survive such an onslaught.

I tried to throw my hands over my head to protect myself, but— he was there. Tristan. I could feel his body above mine. Shielding me.

It was over in a few seconds, the awful thudding and tumbling and wrenching of the earth around us. A shifting quiet settled. The sound of my ragged breathing filled my ears. I clenched my eyes closed, waiting for the pain. There would be pain, I was sure. A mountain had come down on top of us. We could not come away unscathed.

But I felt nothing. Nothing but the damp cold, the hard press of rock beneath my back. I blinked, grit coating my lashes. There was light somewhere—one of our lanterns—and it flickered eerily against the dust thick in the air.

"Are you all right?"

Tristan's voice—desperate, tight—spoke directly into my ear. His arms were braced on either side of me, his face too close to mine. I could hear his fear, and yet I could not bring myself to speak, move, anything. What had just happened?

"Marigold!" he said more sternly. "Are you injured?"

"No." I took a deep breath and inhaled dust. I coughed, rolling away from his arms.

"Don't move," he warned, coming to a crouch a few feet away. "You may be hurt."

"I'm fine," I snapped. But I moved gingerly, testing each of my limbs as I sat up. No jolts of pain. Nothing broken. A small cut on my arm, barely visible in the dirt and gloom, but I could not see anything terribly wrong with me.

My lantern was within reach, knocked to its side but somehow still burning. I righted it. Tristan's lantern was nowhere to be seen. I looked back toward where we'd entered.

The opening was gone.

Rocks and dirt—a mountain of it—now stood in its place. Trickles of dirt still ran down the crevices of the mound. I stared, my throat closing over.

We were trapped.

A thud behind me. I whirled, certain another collapse was starting.

But it was Tristan. He'd fallen backwards, sitting and shaking his head, looking dazed. It was only then I saw the blood on his head.

"Tristan," I gasped. I crawled to him, certain I could not convince my legs to support me. "You're hurt."

He touched the back of his head, pulling his hand back to look at the dark red blood staining his palm. "I . . ." He blinked haphazardly. "I think I am."

An unearthly groan surrounded us and I froze. The ceiling suddenly felt much too low. Any second, the whole mine could come down on us. I swallowed hard, fighting the panic. We had to get away from this spot. "Tristan, we must move. Can you stand?"

It took him a moment to respond, but he nodded. He pushed himself to his feet and then immediately staggered to the side. I dove under his arm, steadying him just before he careened headlong into the wall.

"I can do it," he muttered, clearly not in his right mind.

"Of course you can," I said crossly. "I'll be sure to tell them where to find your body."

I wrapped my arm behind his waist, his body a dead weight over my shoulders. Dash it all, he was heavy. I'd thought he was all long limbs and narrow shoulders, but apparently archery had been kind to Tristan, filling in all the muscles he'd lacked as a youth.

I pulled him with me farther into the tunnel, the two of us taking step after awkward step. My pulse raced, my ears straining for any more signs of impending doom. When we'd gone about thirty feet, Tristan stumbled, nearly taking us both down. I locked my knees, gritting my teeth. I couldn't very well carry him.

"Here," I managed, struggling toward the wall. "Sit."

He sat, though fell might be a better word for it. The lantern light had faded behind us and I could hardly see him anymore. I hurried back the way we'd come and fetched the lantern. The candle inside flickered. It was small, meant to last two hours at the most. I tried to take calming breaths as I returned to Tristan. I had to keep a clear head. I could only think about *now*.

"Let me see your head," I commanded, kneeling beside him.

He winced, leaning back against the uneven dirt wall. "Must you talk like that?"

"Like what?" I asked impatiently.

He waved a hand, his movements jerky. "Shrill. Like a bat."

I laughed, a mad, desperate sound that reverberated down the tunnel. "A bat? That is some thanks for trying to help you."

"I don't need help," he mumbled. His eyes closed, and his breathing grew shallow.

My irritation vanished, fear taking its place. He didn't know what he was saying.

"Please let me look, Tristan," I said, forcing my voice to be calm, quiet.

He did not move for a moment, then he exhaled and leaned

forward, pressing his forehead to his arms folded on his bent knees. I held up the lantern and swallowed a gasp. The back of his head was glistening red, soaked in blood.

"Shall I live?" he asked.

My stomach turned. I was not one to be afraid of a little blood. But this was *not* a little blood.

"I . . ." I coughed. "Of course you'll live. Now hush so I can work."

I set the lantern down on a rickety crate and removed my gloves, soiled beyond repair. Then, slowly, gingerly, I turned the back of Tristan's head toward the light. His hair was shorter than most gentlemen wore it, and I could see the gash, nearly two inches wide and seeping blood. He would need sutures, no doubt about it. But I was no surgeon. I had no needle and thread. I would simply have to bandage it and hope the bleeding stopped before . . .

I tore my eyes from the blood and sat back on my heels. I needed a bandage. I patted my sides as if one might magically appear, but I had no shawl, no reticule, no handkerchief. I'd left them at the beach.

Then my eyes fixed on Tristan's neck.

"Give me your cravat," I ordered.

He tipped his head to look at me, eyeing me. "Undressing me already?"

"Hardly," I snapped. "I need to bandage your head or you'll bleed all over my gown."

His eyes flicked to my gown, once bright red and white and now a dreary gray brown. Like my gloves, there would be no saving it. "Forgive me," he said sardonically. "We cannot have that. Perfect Marigold Cartwell has an image to uphold."

"You think now is the time to mock me?" I could not control my voice, how it rose and fell and broke. "It is your fault we are even *here*."

"My fault?" His eyes focused on me. "You were the one who thought it a brilliant idea to frolic through an abandoned mine."

"You taunted me," I shot back. "You goaded me into it."

"Yes, not thinking for one second you were actually foolish enough to *do* it."

I scrambled to my feet, heat pumping through my body. "It seems you do not wish for my help. I have half a mind to leave you here and find my own way out."

"Go on, then," he shot. "I cannot hear myself think with you shouting at me."

I stood there, hands clenched like a petulant child. He was infuriating. Impossible.

But then he winced, his face contorting in pain. He dropped his head between his knees, breathing hard, and I again saw the blood matting his hair. Then I saw more than that. I saw the rips on the back of his jacket, how broken and dirty he was. And I realized why.

Because he'd protected me.

He'd pulled me away from the falling rocks. He'd thrown himself over me, using his own body to keep me from harm. I had a few bruises and cuts, but he—he was truly hurt. He'd suffered a terrible blow to his head. I could tell he was not himself, disoriented and dazed.

I inhaled a steadying breath. This was my fault. I'd been the dolt who allowed herself to get riled up and put both of us into danger.

"I'm sorry," I said quietly. "I'm sorry."

I knelt once again beside him. He lifted his head, and our eyes met. I could not say what I found in his unfocused gaze—disbelief? Confusion? But it did not matter. I was in the wrong and I would not abandon him.

"Your cravat, please," I said.

He looked at me a moment longer, then nodded, sitting back. He tried to untie the knot, but his hands shook and his fingers fumbled. I'd seen this shakiness before, when Hawthorne had fallen from a tree and broken his leg. The doctor had said it was normal when the body was in severe distress, and Tristan's shaking now did nothing to calm the wave of anxiety that choked me. He was truly and badly hurt.

"Let me," I said, my voice thick.

He eyed me, but did not protest, only dropped his hands. I wet my lips, then reached up to find the ends of his cravat. I worked the knot, trying not to move his head overmuch. It was difficult to concentrate, considering how his eyes followed me, intent and piercing. My hands brushed his jaw, rough now at the end of the day, and the contact made me start, heat coursing up my arm.

He stiffened. "What is it?"

"Nothing," I managed, heart pounding. I chastened myself. This was Tristan. Just Tristan. But as I leaned forward to unwind the cloth from his neck, I could not stop myself from stealing a glance at his face. Usually he was careful to keep his emotions hidden, his expressions guarded. But something—our situation, his injury, I could not say—had brought a strange openness to his face.

It was the same face I'd seen for the last twelve years: angled features, long, narrow nose, dark eyes. But now I saw the dimple in his chin, the thick lashes of his eyes. I saw the determined set of his jaw as he fought the pain.

The cravat slipped free, and I sat back, trying to calm my pulse. I could not seem to focus my thoughts. I hadn't been hit on the head with a rock, but perhaps being in mortal peril had the same effect.

"There," I said. "Now, do you have a handkerchief?"

He produced one from his pocket, still surprisingly clean. That was good. I did not wish to press a grimy cloth to an open wound. I folded the handkerchief into a thick square.

"This may hurt," I warned him.

"Go on." His voice came from gritted teeth.

I pressed the handkerchief to the gash. He tensed, but did not speak. Working as quickly as I could, I positioned the middle of the cravat over the handkerchief, holding it tight against his head, then wrapped the ends around his forehead. I tied them in a neat knot just over one ear.

"There," I said. "I should have liked to wash it, but our resources are a bit thin."

He gingerly touched the back of his head, hand still trembling. "I would not have guessed you to be an adequate nurse."

I gave a humorless laugh. "I am far from adequate. But I am all you have, so I shall do my best."

Tristan met my eyes, then looked away. "Thank you," he said, clearing his throat.

I nodded, not knowing what to say. Instead, I also turned away, looking back toward the rock fall. Now that his injury was cared for, as well as I could, we had other pressing concerns.

"What are we to do?" I asked, voice frayed. "We cannot possibly move all that."

"And neither should we try," he said, leaning the uninjured part of his head against the wall. "If we move something, we could bring it all down."

"They will come for us," I said, more to reassure myself than him. "Father will come."

"And your Mr. Eastbrook."

I hadn't even thought of him. "Yes. He will have heard the cave-in and guessed what happened. He will lead them straight to us." I glanced in the other direction, where the tunnel curved into the deepening blackness, the light from our lantern a fading globe around us. "But what if they cannot dig us out? Perhaps we should try our chances at finding the main entrance to the mine."

"I am in no condition to walk," he said. "And you certainly cannot carry me."

I gave a wry smile. "No, but you could've carried *me*. If only I had taken the blow to my head instead."

It was a sad attempt at humor, and he did not smile as he looked straight in my eyes. "No. I would not have that."

I swallowed, unable to look away. "Thank you," I said, throat dry. "For . . ." I could not find the words, and so I gestured back at the cave-in. "You thought far more quickly than I did, and for that, I am grateful."

He shifted his weight. "It was instinct only, I confess. I never imagined myself the hero."

I raised an eyebrow. "So if you'd had longer to think, you might have left me there?"

His mouth drew upward. "At least then I might have some peace and quiet. You do talk ever so much."

Laughter escaped me—a short burst of incredulous laughter. He blinked, then grinned fully, chuckling with me.

"Oh, dear," I said, turning to sit beside him and lean against the wall. "We are in trouble indeed. The two of us together in the face of certain doom. We shall likely kill each other before rescuers find us."

"Then perhaps we might call a truce," he said. "At least until we escape."

"That is easy for you to offer," I said. "You are useless." This was a new experience. Me, *laughing* with Tristan.

"Perhaps physically," he said. "But I daresay you'll be glad I'm here once that candle goes out."

I glanced at the lantern, the flame sputtering weakly. There was only half an inch of beeswax left. "Ah," I said. "So you've noticed."

He started to nod, then touched his head with a grimace. "Best not to do that," he muttered. "But yes, I'd noticed. Yet another reason not to go wandering off in search of the entrance. We could get terribly lost and then have no way of finding our way out or ascertaining danger."

"So we wait." My voice was firm, but I could hear the thread of fear in it. Tristan did too.

"We'll be all right," he said. "They'll find us."

I bit my lip, staring at the lantern's glow. Then I sat up. "Where is your lantern? Did you drop it?"

"Yes," he said. "I was a bit busy saving your life."

"I didn't say it to reprimand you," I said, shooting him an irritated look.

He held up his hands. "Truce."

I blew out a breath. "Yes. Truce. I only asked because if I can find it, we might buy ourselves another hour or two of light."

"Oh," he said. "That is smart."

"No need to sound so surprised," I muttered as I pushed myself to my feet and took up my lantern.

I made my way back toward the rocks, my careful footsteps too loud in the eerie silence. I could hear every breath I took, but thankfully could hear no more shifting of the earth around us. It had calmed, it seemed, for the time being.

Reaching the edge of the cave-in, I raised my lantern, looking for any sign of Tristan's. Shadows loomed behind every great boulder that had fallen, and I tried to be thorough and search everywhere. But I refused to chance moving a single stone. The cacophony of crashing rocks still echoed too closely in my mind.

I found nothing. No lantern. My heart sank.

"Marigold?"

I turned back to see Tristan sitting straight up, searching his jacket pockets.

"What is it?" I called, trying not to shout too loudly, as though a sudden sound would startle the rocks around me.

"I've lost something." He looked over at me. I could barely see his face in the gloom, but his voice held a touch of panic. "A coin."

"A coin?" I repeated, baffled.

"Yes, a shilling. It must have fallen out during the commotion. Can you see it?"

"Do we not have more important things to worry about than lost change?"

"It is *not* lost change." His words were tight. Strained. "Please, do you see it?"

I sighed but found myself examining the ground near where Tristan and I had fallen in the ruckus. It only took a moment—there wasn't much besides the dull brown of dirt. The gleam of the shilling caught my eyes without difficulty.

"Here." I plucked it from the ground and started back towards Tristan. "No sign of the other lantern, though."

He seemed not to care, eyes fixed on me as I dropped the coin into his open palm.

"Thank you." His hand closed around it, his relief clear as his whole body relaxed. I sat beside him again, shooting him a sidelong glance. Why on earth did he care so much for that coin? I'd seen nothing special about it.

But he tucked it back inside his pocket without comment, and the way he avoided my eyes made it clear he did not wish to speak about it.

We sat in silence, broken only by dripping water and our own soft scuffs as we each tried to find a comfortable position. But mines were not made for comfort, and the hard rock was unrelenting.

How long would it take them to find us? The mountain of collapsed rocks was unmanageable for the two of us, especially with Tristan injured, but if Father gathered as many men as he could find, I imagined we might be out within a few hours. Assuming the situation wasn't worse from the other side.

"Your arm."

I started, looking up at Tristan. He was staring at my arm.

I glanced down. I'd already inspected myself and written off my minor injuries, but there was a deep scratch on my arm that looked a bit nastier than the others. The skin was angry and red, blood smeared.

"It's nothing compared to yours," I said.

"But it doesn't look good." He frowned. "Have you anything else to use as a bandage?"

"Not unless I wish to part with my petticoat."

I thought he might offer an acerbic retort, but instead he swallowed hard, meeting my eyes for a split second before breaking away. I stared. Was that a blush creeping along his jaw? I could not trust my eyes, not in this weak light.

"It is fine," I said. "It's hardly bleeding anymore."

But somehow by looking at the injury and acknowledging it, the pain came rearing into focus. It stung and throbbed, feeling like my heartbeat had somehow slipped down into my limb.

"You'll likely have a scar," he said.

I gave a limp shrug. "It is better than being dead."

His lips pulled to one side, as if my answer was not what he had expected.

"You think I would care so much for a little scar?" I asked, genuinely curious.

He paused. "I think you might take offense if I gave you a true answer."

"I am already offended just from that." I brought my knees to my chest and wrapped my arms around them.

He shifted his weight. "It is only that you seem to assign so much importance to the appearance of things."

His words stung, like when a bee had taken a disliking to my cheek the previous summer. That was how I knew there was some truth to what he said. Yes, perhaps right now the thought of a scar did not matter. But once we escaped this wretched place, that would change. I *would* care that I had such a visible scar. I hated that he was right. That he knew me so well.

I inspected him from the corner of my eye. Tristan stared down at his hands, the makeshift bandage around his head a sharp contrast to his brown hair and grimy skin.

"I do not think I'm perfect," I said finally.

"What?"

"Before. You said, 'perfect Marigold Cartwell.'" I gave a short laugh. "I am far from it, and I am fully aware."

"One would not think that to look at you."

I exhaled. "Very well. I admit to some vanity. Is that what you wish to hear? I do not want a scar on my arm, and yes, I *do* generally care how I look to others. There, I've said it, and now you may mock me." I shook my head, my mind trapped in a haze. "I don't know why I'm telling you all this. I think I inhaled too much dust."

"We've nowhere to go," he said mildly. Too mildly. "We may as well discuss all your failings."

"Should we look at your weaknesses next?" I narrowed my eyes at him. "I've quite the list, if you are keen on self-improvement."

He gave a humorless laugh. "Enlighten me."

"You've buckets of pride," I said. "Of course."

"Buckets? That seems an exaggeration."

"You are disagreeable."

"Only when someone disagrees with me."

"You are excessively indifferent."

"I rather think *that* a virtue."

I crossed my arms. He was impossible. "So you have no faults?"

"I did not say that," he responded. "But I see mine very differently than you do."

"Enlighten me."

He did not speak for a long minute. I almost asked him again, but decided to wait him out. I could feel the mood shifting, from one of almost teasing lightness to something deeper. Eventually, he lifted one shoulder, looking straight ahead so as not to meet my curious gaze. "Envy."

I tipped my head. "Envy? What are you envious of?"

His eyes flicked to me, just for a moment, but it was enough.

"Me?" I asked in disbelief.

"Your family," he said simply, and then I understood.

Tristan never spoke of his mother and father, gone before I'd met him. He'd been young when they'd died, only ten years old, and I wondered how well he remembered them. But the tightness in his expression now told me everything.

"I never thought . . ." My voice trailed off, lower than before. "You always had your uncle."

"And he has given me a good life," he said. "I love him, I do. But it sometimes seems you do not know how lucky you are to have a mother and a father, brothers and a sister."

I cleared my throat. What did I say to that? I took a lighter tone. "How did this turn back on *my* failings?"

He frowned. "I did not mean to. Only I know what it is to live without, and it is frustrating that you sometimes seem not to know what you have."

I could not blame him for it. I had no understanding of what it might feel like to be alone in the world. I had always had my family. How could I survive without them? Without Mama's wisdom, Papa's unconditional love, Oliver's companionship, Hawthorne's humor, and Iris's vibrancy?

The ceiling seemed to grow ever lower, and the cold seeped in through my clothes. I shivered. What if . . . what if they could not get to us? What if we died here, trapped and starving? With the very real possibility of never seeing my family again, I found myself softening toward Tristan.

"I can tell you this," I said quietly. "When we are free of this place, I shall never take my family for granted again."

The candle flickered. We both snapped our heads to look at it, a tiny flame fighting for life in a puddle of wax. Bumps raised on every inch of my skin. Tristan was pale, mouth set in a tight line as his eyes met mine. I opened my mouth to say something.

Then the flame went out with a hiss.

Chapter Fifteen

TRISTAN

THE DARKNESS WAS ALL-CONSUMING. I'd been so distracted by our conversation that I hadn't noticed the candle creeping lower. That tiny flame had been all that kept us from this pure black, and now it filled my eyes, crept over every inch of my skin.

Marigold inhaled sharply beside me. She was close enough that I could feel her shrinking in on herself, pulling away.

"I thought we had more time," she whispered, her voice smaller.

"We aren't dead yet," I said, trying to lighten the mood.

"And yet it feels an awful lot like a grave to me."

She was afraid. Of course she was. We were trapped underground with no light, food, water, or any certainty that we would be rescued. Fear hovered over us like a heavy blanket, smothering and inescapable. The wound in my head pulsed in time with my heartbeat. How lucky Marigold was, that her only companion was a dolt with a debilitating injury.

I truly was useless, as she'd jested earlier. I was trying to pretend normality, but it was becoming increasingly difficult. Whenever I shifted my head, blood oozed from my injury. My brain was slow, my eyes flashing with strange lights every few seconds, and my lungs worked hard as my breaths came too fast. But I could not tell Marigold that. It would not help anything to worry her more.

In truth, I was surprised she worried for me at all. Her unexpected gentleness when she'd tended to my head had taken me aback. She'd even apologized, for heaven's sake. If that was not a sign of our true peril, I did not know what was.

The memory of her soft hands undoing my cravat slipped back into my head, faded around the edges. I could only blame my injury for the rush of heat in my chest when she'd worked at the knot, leaning so close I could feel her warm breath on my neck.

I pushed the memory away. She'd helped me. Now I would help her. I couldn't do anything about our situation, but perhaps there was something small I could do for her.

I reached out a hand, searching for hers. I touched warm, soft skin—an arm?

"Wandering hands, Gates?"

I yanked my hand back. "I was *trying* to comfort you."

"Oh."

She was quiet. Then I heard a rustling, and her shoulder brushed mine as she scooted closer. I felt her small, cool hand slide tentatively into mine. I caught my breath. Marigold Cartwell was holding my hand.

"If you tell anyone about this," she threatened, "I will fill your quiver with rose thorns."

"You think *I* want anyone to know?" My words were off balance. She was holding my *hand*. I had been breathing too fast, but now my lungs stalled, the air too warm.

"It will be part of our truce, then," she said. "It is . . . it is only natural to be frightened." She sounded as if she was trying to reassure herself of that fact.

"*I* am the one comforting *you*, if you'll recall," I said.

"Then why is your heart beating so fast?"

My mouth dropped, and I blessed the dark that she could not see. Because it was certainly not fear that drove my heart to pound like a cobbler's mallet.

"My injury," I said quickly.

She seemed to accept that, or at least did not argue further, for which I was grateful. I did not want her prying into what unexpected effect her nearness was having on my body.

We sat in silence for a few long minutes, her hand unmoving in mine. It was not an awkward silence, not really. More of a nothing-to-say silence. Because we both knew what we faced, and our reality was not something that bore more discussion.

I waved my free hand directly in front of my face, eyes wide open. I saw nothing.

"What are you doing?" she whispered.

"Nothing." I dropped my hand. "Why are you whispering?"

I felt her shoulder move up and down in a shrug. "The rats might hear us and come for a snack."

I smiled, though she could not see it.

"Let's keep talking," she said. I felt her turn to face me, as if to see me better. Her knee brushed mine. "I cannot have dark *and* silence."

"Talk about what?" I managed. Yes, talking was good. Anything to distract me from her smooth hand in mine, her heady warmth pressed against my side.

She hesitated. "You could tell me why you are so attached to that shilling in your pocket."

I stiffened, all previous thoughts vanishing. "No."

"Why not?"

"Because I do not want to."

"Please, do not hide your true feelings," she said dryly.

I said nothing, and she sighed. "Very well, then tell me why you do not like Mrs. Penrose."

How was it she managed to pick the two topics I most wished to avoid? "Why don't we talk about something of interest to you?"

"I am interested in Mrs. Penrose," she said, "because I cannot see why you should oppose her match with your uncle."

My head was throbbing, and I closed my eyes, as if that might help. It made no difference, obviously. The oil-slick darkness was the same either way.

"Why will you not tell me?" she asked.

"Because up until an hour ago, we could not speak without bickering."

"A valid point," she conceded. "But I've known Mrs. Penrose longer than you. Perhaps I could help."

"You want to help me." It was not a question but rather an amused observation.

"I am a very helpful person, on the whole." She tugged lightly on my hand. "And I would not mind a distraction from our impending death."

Her words reminded both of us where we were. The cold, the blackness, the gnawing fear that lurked just beneath our calm facades.

"Fine." I blew out a breath. "Mrs. Penrose," I began, "has a past."

"Don't we all?"

"Yes, but not all of us have two dead, rich husbands."

"What?"

I wished I could see her face, but I could imagine it well enough —her blue eyes widening, those pink lips parting. No. I should not think about her lips.

"Yes," I said. "I heard it from a friend. Mrs. Penrose was married twice before, to gentlemen whose fortunes drastically changed after meeting her. Both were ruined financially, and both died."

"So she is a fortune hunting murderess?"

"No," I said, frustrated. "Well, yes, I do think she is a fortune hunter. Not the other part."

"And have you simply asked her about this?" she said. "Perhaps she has a perfectly reasonable explanation."

"I am sure she does," I said. "She cannot have gotten this far without spinning webs all around her. But I should like the truth, which is what I am trying to find by asking questions."

"I think you are being ridiculous," she said.

"Do not hide your true feelings," I muttered, echoing her sentiment from earlier.

"Well, you are," she insisted. "You hear one rumor and decide you know everything about a person. I find Mrs. Penrose to be kind, sweet, and genuine. Is my opinion worth nothing?"

"I haven't decided I know everything." Irritation bubbled up inside me. "I am trying to be objective."

She snorted and pulled her hand from mine, leaving it cold and empty. "Objective? You've been standoffish to the poor woman since you arrived. Don't think I haven't noticed."

"I am only looking out for my uncle."

"And yourself."

"What?"

She shifted her weight. "Mrs. Penrose is fairly young. If your uncle marries, I imagine there will be children. Children who might replace *you* as his heir."

My fingers curled into the sides of my breeches. "I am not so self-centered as that."

"It is a legitimate concern," she said. "No one would blame you."

"I would not put my own fortunes before my uncle's happiness." My voice snapped, though not because she was wrong. I *had* thought of the possibility. Uncle would want children—his own natural-born children. But Marigold had no right to judge me for it. I did not oppose the match because of my own selfish concerns.

Marigold sat quiet, her breathing almost too subtle for my ears. "No," she said finally. "I don't think you would."

Her voice held a new softness, one I had rarely, if ever, heard directed at me.

"I only want to gather all the information I can," I said, somehow keeping my voice even, "before I speak with Uncle Matthew. Surely you can understand that."

"Then perhaps you might give Mrs. Penrose the benefit of the doubt until then," she said.

I sighed. "I suppose I can attempt to be more civil."

"I appreciate your agreeing to the bare minimum."

I let out a low groan. "All the people in England, and I get trapped in a cave with *you*."

"I am not leaping for joy either, you'll notice."

I took a deep breath, trying to calm the agitation that always seemed to claim a permanent space in my chest when Marigold was nearby.

"Perhaps silence is better than talking after all." I crossed my arms and leaned my head back against the rough wall, then immediately jerked it forward when a jolt of pain shot through me. Blast, my head hurt. I could not think straight.

"Fine," she said tightly.

We sat again in silence, one that was most definitely uncomfortable. But of course it did not last long.

"It is so cold," she said. I could hear movement, as if she was rubbing her arms for warmth. She wore only her day dress, with short sleeves, if I remembered correctly. Though it was summer outside, the mine was cold, deep inside the earth.

"Next time you decide to explore a dangerous mine," I said stiffly, "try to bring a shawl."

She gave a hard laugh. "Such helpful advice."

I knew what I needed to do and yet I fought against it. She was the one who had put us in this situation, after all. Why should I pay the price?

Only the thought of what Uncle Matthew would say when Marigold told him I did not offer my jacket made me lean forward and start tugging one arm from my sleeve.

"What are you doing?"

"Trying to be the gentleman you think I am not," I said through my teeth.

"Stop that," she ordered, grabbing my arm. "I don't want your jacket."

"Yes, and then you can go about telling everyone how I was abominably rude."

"Why must everything be a battle?" she asked testily. "I am only being smart. You are hurt. Your body is already in distress. You need the warmth more than I do."

I paused, one arm halfway through. Did she mean it? Was she right?

"Put it back on," she ordered.

I hesitated, then slipped the sleeve back on. It was warm. And now I felt guilty.

"Come closer," I ordered.

"Why?" Her voice held no small amount of suspicion.

"Must everything be a battle?"

She muttered under her breath, but she must have been colder than she let on because in the next moment I felt her move alongside me, her arm and leg pressing against mine. My chest lit up like the fireworks I'd seen as a child. It was exasperating how aware my body was of her every curve, her every movement. The dark only heightened that awareness, my other senses coming alive in a swarm of sparks.

I tried my best to ignore all that, lifting my right arm and sliding it behind her shoulders. Marigold inhaled sharply but said nothing. My hand settled on her elbow, her skin chill to the touch. She *was* cold, far colder than I was. I pulled her closer.

"Is this . . ." I cleared my throat. "Is this all right?"

"Yes," she responded immediately. Was I imagining things or was her voice a touch higher? "It's fine."

We did not speak after that, only leaned into each other, neither of us wishing to admit that we sought comfort as much as warmth.

I closed my eyes, my thoughts swimming in a dark cloud. Surely we would not be here much longer. Uncle Matthew and Mr. Cartwell would do everything in their power to get us out.

I could only hope it would be before Marigold drove me positively mad.

We sat there in the dark, minutes passing with excruciating slowness. I had my pocket watch, but of course there was no point in checking it—I could not see the dials or numbers.

Eventually, Marigold's breathing softened and evened. Her head dropped against my chest, the slightest pressure. My pulse leaped, and I berated myself. How absurd this was. The two of us curled together for warmth.

My head slowly cleared, the pain dimming but not disappearing, and my thoughts sharpened. I wasn't sure I was glad for it. Because now, for the first time, the full desperation of our plight came upon me. We'd heard nothing, seen nothing. No sign at all that anyone was coming for us. Had we made the right choice to stay by the cave-in instead of searching for the main entrance to the mine? But I knew it would have been useless. My injuries had rendered me a stumbling fool, unable to see straight. It never would have worked.

But Marigold might have made it.

She stirred slightly in her sleep, adjusting her head against my chest. Her hair tickled my cheek and I smelled her perfume, that subtle floral that had so affected me at the ball. I held still, not wanting to wake her. Sleep was better than fear. She took a small breath and settled.

My arm tightened around her. It was much easier to feel protective of her when she was asleep and not fighting me at every step.

I was thirsty, I realized. My throat was dry as the sand on the beach, and my stomach held an edge of hunger. The picnic seemed an age ago, with the sun warm on my face and the breeze ruffling my hair. Now the air was still, stale, and damp. What had Marigold said earlier? *It feels an awful lot like a grave to me.*

I could not think that way. Hope was the only way we would survive.

I slipped my free hand into my pocket, curling my fingers around the shilling Marigold had retrieved for me. I tried not to think of the panic I'd felt when I'd thought it lost. I had enough to worry over without thinking of that too.

I closed my eyes and tried to find the peaceful oblivion of sleep.

Chapter Sixteen

MARIGOLD

My pillow was moving.

I found consciousness slowly, my thoughts unfurling like a modiste's measuring tape. Why was my pillow so warm, so firm, and why was it moving up and down in a steady rhythm?

When I realized, I nearly bolted upright. I caught myself just in time, forcing myself to remain still. That miserable blackness of the tunnel found me once again, but I was less concerned about it than I should have been. Instead I was entirely focused on the fact that I was currently curled up against *Tristan Gates*.

My cheek was snug against his waistcoat, my shoulder neatly tucked into his side as if we'd done this a thousand times. And my hand—my hand! It had somehow wandered up his chest and now rested against his open shirt collar. I could feel the smooth skin of his throat and collarbone against my fingertips. My skin flushed, heat trailing along every inch of me.

I could not wake him. He would never let me forget what a position I'd woken in, wound around him like I . . . like I . . . like I *liked* it.

Because I did *not*. Yes, it was warm, and rather comfortable. And yes, Tristan smelled surprisingly good for a man trapped in a mine—

like the spray of the salty waves and sun-warmed grass. Like summer.

But that did not matter. I had to disentangle myself without waking him, or I'd never hear the end of it.

I moved my hand first, listening closely to his breathing as I carefully lifted one finger at a time, trying very hard not to think about where precisely I was touching him. I gave a sigh of relief when my hand was free, but I still had to escape his arm.

I slowly lifted my head, the cool air claiming my warmed cheek. So far, so good.

But when I began to pull away, his arm slipped down my back. He jolted, his hand coming again to clutch me closer. I froze, breath caught in my throat. Had he wakened?

"Marigold?" His voice was drowsy, confused.

"I'm here," I said quickly, using his disorientation to pull farther away. He let me, his arm falling from my shoulders. "Where else would I be?"

Our situation was coming into full focus again. We were still trapped. No one had come. How long had we slept? Minutes? Hours? The dark was impossibly disorienting. It had been early evening when we'd gone into the caves. It could be the middle of the night by now, or the next morning even. I tried to breathe, to remind myself that it would take time. I needed another distraction.

I looked up to where I imagined his face would be in the dark. "How is your head?"

He paused before answering, as if assessing himself. "All right," he said. "A bit better, I think."

"You'll still need to see a doctor," I said. "Once we . . . once we are out."

He heard the catch in my words. "We *will* get out," he said, and his voice was so assured that I found myself believing him. What else could I do? I blinked back the prickle behind my eyes. Dissolving into a puddle of tears would help no one, and would only be a waste of water.

And I was parched, I realized. My tongue was rough, my lips

dry. Even if we were found eventually, we would not survive very long without anything to drink. I could hear water dripping somewhere along the tunnel. It taunted me, but I did not dare venture off. This was an abandoned mine and we were without any source of light. It would only take one wrong step.

As if not to be outdone by my thirst, my stomach let out a ferocious growl. I clutched a hand to my middle, mortified.

"Careful now," Tristan said in a low voice. "I think there's a wild animal out there."

"Quiet," I said, elbowing him. "I cannot help being hungry."

He nudged me back. "No more than you can help talking every minute of the day?"

"Better to have *something* to say than nothing," I retorted, even though I did not entirely believe my own words.

"Ha," he said softly.

I thought he might say something more, but our argument—discussion—faded into silence, swallowed by the blackness that surrounded us.

"Let us sing something," I said suddenly. I had no great musical talent, but I could not bear the quiet. A song would cheer me.

"Sing?" If I could see him, no doubt he would be raising one eyebrow. "You've heard me sing. You must be desperate for distraction indeed."

"Even your voice is better than nothing."

"What if it brings the rats running?"

I smiled. "Perhaps you'd sing better with an audience."

He laughed and it caught me in its wake, tossed me around in his familiar baritone. I would never have guessed that the day I heard a true laugh from Tristan Gates would be the day we faced near death together.

"A game, then," I said.

"Why, are you hiding Spillikins under your dress?"

My face heated, for some reason I could not comprehend. "A gentleman would not ask that, only feign surprise when I produced it."

He made a noise that I thought was perhaps another laugh, but I could not be sure. It was not a sound I was particularly familiar with.

"Do you know any riddles?" I asked.

"I'm afraid not." He paused. "I'd wager you are wishing you were trapped in here with your Mr. Eastbrook. I imagine he'd have dozens of riddles memorized, and no doubt sings like a choir boy."

I opened my mouth to respond, but found I did not have a ready response. Did I wish Mr. Eastbrook was here with me instead of Tristan? A few hours ago, I would have said yes in a heartbeat, but now . . . now I was not so sure. Would Mr. Eastbrook have managed an injury as well as Tristan had? Would he have helped distract me? Kept me warm? Well, likely yes to that last question and probably in quite an enjoyable manner.

I'd gone too long without answering. I had to say something. I cleared my throat. "Heavens, no. I look a fright. I would not wish to subject Mr. Eastbrook to such a sight."

"You do realize it is blacker than midnight in here?"

"Yes, well—"

"And besides," he went on, "if you're to marry this fellow, he ought to know you at your worst as well as your best."

That took me aback. I hadn't imagined Tristan to say something so . . . profound. I cleared my throat. "So it is my vanity at play again?"

"I didn't mean that," he said. "Only that hiding parts of yourself from a potential spouse seems a recipe for disaster. It would be better to discover you don't suit before the vows, wouldn't you think?"

I opened my mouth to respond—what did he know of potential spouses?—but I stopped. I'd heard something. I grabbed Tristan's arm, my fingers digging into his muscled forearm.

He stiffened. "What are you—"

"Hush," I ordered, my voice echoing. "Did you hear that?"

"What?"

"Listen."

We sat still, not breathing. Then it came again. A scrape of rock against rock. And then—a voice! Low and indistinguishable, but a *voice!*

"They've found us!" I scrambled to my feet, using the wall to support myself. "Papa? Can you hear me?"

I began feeling my way along the wall, but Tristan caught my skirt.

"Marigold, stay here," he ordered, tugging me back.

"Stay? But they've come. We need to—"

"We need to do nothing," he said. "We must stay clear until they are through."

I was breathing hard, trembling with excitement, my hands clutching the rock wall. Every bone in my body begged me to run towards the sound. Towards rescue.

But he was right. It was unsafe to be too near.

"Papa?" I called again, my voice hoarse. There was no response besides the shifting of rock. They could not hear me over the noise of their work.

"Sit down, Marigold," Tristan said. "They could be hours yet."

I exhaled a sigh of frustration and found my seat again, already cold in my short absence. But it could not dampen the insatiable glow lighting my soul. They'd found us. We would not be dying in this pit of despair. I closed my eyes, though of course it made no difference. I said a short prayer of gratitude, and a flood of exhaustion and joy and anticipation overcame me. I found myself fighting back tears for an entirely different reason than a few minutes ago.

We listened, every grinding rock and muted shout making my heart lift. I did not know how long it would take for them to reach us, but the nightmare was almost over.

Only, it hadn't been nearly as much of a nightmare as it should've been. If I'd been alone, I would have panicked. But because Tristan had been with me, I'd been forced to keep my head. I'd had someone to make decisions with, someone to help keep the fear and cold at bay.

Tristan shifted beside me, and his hand brushed against mine, which was resting on my knee. He stopped but did not move away. I tried to form a quip, something to make light of our situation. Yet I found I had only one thing I wanted to say.

"Tristan?"

"Hmm?"

"I know you wouldn't have chosen it." I paused. "But I am glad you were here."

A long moment passed. Then came a touch, just the lightest brush of his little finger against mine. My heart stilled, and heat shot through my whole arm. He'd held my hand before to comfort me, but I did not need comfort now. Why, then, was he touching me?

"Marigold," he said, his voice holding a vulnerability I'd never heard from anyone before, least of all Tristan. "I—"

"Marigold?" A muffled voice from the dark.

I sat bolt upright. "Papa!" I knew it was him, that rich timbre. Relief poured through me, so intense I could not breathe. He'd found me. My papa had not given up on me.

"Marigold!" This time my name was a desperate, broken sob, and my eyes filled with hot tears. "Are you all right? Are you hurt?"

"Yes," I croaked back, my throat nearly closed over. "That is, I am unharmed. Tristan is hurt."

"I'm all right, Mr. Cartwell," Tristan called. "Do not hurry on my account. Please be careful and take your time."

Papa chuckled, barely audible through the mountain of debris. "Indeed we will. Both of you stay back to be safe."

"We will," I promised. A few tears escaped, slipping down my cheeks and leaving warm streaks behind. I swiped at them, beaming, as the sounds of rocks being moved once again filled the air. "They came," I breathed.

"You're almost free of me," Tristan said, his tone light.

I realized he'd taken his hand back sometime during my conversation with Papa. And hadn't he been about to tell me something?

But the moment had passed, and I could not help but think it was for the best. There was something about this absolute, impenetrable dark that loosed the tongue and tripped the mind. Neither of us wished to say something we might regret. The sooner we escaped, the better.

A few rocks fell on our side of the cave-in, and a bright beam of light shot across the tunnel. I grimaced and held up a hand to block the sudden glare of light. Tristan reacted more strongly, cursing under his breath.

"Language, Gates," I said. "We are nearly returned to polite society."

"Perhaps polite society could try not to blind us," he grumbled.

I peeked through my fingers. The lantern light pierced through a large gap in the stones, illuminating the still settling dust. I could just make out Tristan's features. He had both hands pressed to his eyes, mouth contorted. Of course. His head wound. No doubt that made the prickling of the light on his eyes that much more painful.

"Tristan?" It was the booming Mr. Raines.

Tristan straightened, dropping his hands even though he still winced. "Uncle?"

"I think we've made a big enough opening," Mr. Raines called. "Can you make it to us without our help?"

"Yes," Tristan said, suddenly agitated. "Please do not send anyone in."

I understood his fear. We were already at risk. There was no need to endanger anyone else.

"We're coming now," I called. I scrambled to my feet, then turned to extend a hand to Tristan. But he'd stood, steadying himself against the wall and looking a bit ill.

"Let me," I insisted, wrapping one arm around his back like I had earlier. He did not protest, which told me everything I needed to know about the state of his head. Slowly, we worked our way through the tunnel, using the flickering light of the lanterns through the gap to guide us. Tristan leaned heavily on me, and my stomach twisted. What if . . . what if he was not all right? What if his injury was more serious than I'd thought?

I let out a long breath. I only had to get him to the opening, and then I could let a doctor worry about that.

As we came closer, a head appeared in the opening—Papa. He was just a dark silhouette against the lantern light. We stepped over a few more rocks, and then we were there.

"Take Tristan first," I demanded. "He needs help."

Hands reached through and grasped at Tristan's arms, helping him climb up and through the opening.

"Careful of his head!" I cautioned. Tristan shot me an exasperated look. I did not care. Let him be exasperated, so long as he was cared for.

Then it was my turn. Papa took my outstretched hand and helped me through. For a moment, I imagined that the rocks began to shake once more. My heart jumped into my throat. But the next moment I was through and in Papa's arms. He buried me against his chest, holding me so tight I thought my lungs might collapse. I did not care. I embraced him just as desperately.

"I knew you'd find me," I whispered.

"Of course," he said, voice raw. "I would be rather a useless father if I didn't."

I spotted Oliver over Papa's shoulder. He watched us with glistening eyes, every inch of his body covered in dirt and grime. When Papa released me, I threw my arms around my brother. He hugged me back.

"Only you would get trapped in a mine," he joked, though his raspy voice betrayed his true emotions.

"You know I love the attention."

He laughed and pulled away. "Well, you shall have plenty of it now, I imagine."

Papa took my shoulders again and inspected me. "Are you sure you're all right? I cannot imagine how you're uninjured."

"Tristan," I admitted. "He pushed me out of the way. That's how he got hurt."

Papa turned to look at Tristan, who was being helped by his uncle to walk the tunnel back toward the sea caves. "He did?"

"Yes," I said, swallowing hard. "I am fairly certain he saved my life."

The tunnel was filled with a dozen men, all of them watching me with beaming smiles, and all looking dirty and worse for the wear. I wanted to thank them, embrace them, but I could barely manage to stay on my feet. The exhaustion from the last day caught me in its claws, and I slumped against Papa.

"Come," he said, wrapping a strong arm around me. "Your mama is waiting."

When we emerged into the main chamber of the sea caves, I blinked. It was daylight, the soft sunshine slipping through the rocky opening. "What time is it?"

"Mid-morning," Papa said. "We worked through the night. Thankfully, Mr. Raines knows a man who had worked in a mine in southern Kent. We fetched him to help us dig you out safely, building supports as we removed rock."

My mind stumbled over his words, barely comprehending them. It hardly mattered. We were out. We were alive.

"Marigold!"

Mama swooped in, embracing me with tears in her eyes. I pressed my face against her neck, smelling her familiar amber perfume and trying not to dissolve into tears yet again.

"She's all right," Papa reassured her. "Just in want of a bath, I imagine."

I gave a weak smile. "Indeed, though a drink might be the priority."

Mama bustled off to find me water, and someone wrapped a blanket around my shoulders. I clutched the edges of the blanket, even that small movement impossibly exhausting.

"Miss Cartwell."

A shadow moved across my vision and I looked up. Mr. Eastbrook stood before me, concern creasing his brow.

"Mr. Eastbrook." I hadn't even thought of him since hearing Papa's voice in the tunnel. How very strange. I hurried to brush back my hair, straighten my dress. Then I heard Tristan's voice from before. *He ought to know you at your worst as well as your best.*

I dropped my hand. It helped that Mr. Eastbrook also looked far from his finest. He was covered in that same layer of dust as all the other men. "How glad I am to see you again. I assume I can thank you for assisting in my rescue."

"Of course," he said earnestly. "Your father and Mr. Raines are to be commended. They worked tirelessly all night, though we helped how we could."

I sent Papa a warm glance where he stood beside a man I did not recognize, gesturing at the tunnel. "I am fortunate to have such protectors."

"Indeed."

I looked back at Mr. Eastbrook. I wondered if he wished to reach for me, hold me like he had for that moment before Tristan had interrupted us. That would be a natural urge, and perhaps even allowed, considering we were nearly engaged. And yet he made no move toward me, clasping his hands behind his back and keeping an arm's length between us. I inspected his face. There was concern there, yes, and relief. But also something else. Something that tightened his jaw and tensed his shoulders.

"Marigold," Mama said, returning to my side and pressing a tin cup into my hands. "Here you are."

I nodded, giving Mr. Eastbrook another smile as he bowed and moved away. Surely his formality was just the after effects of a long night.

I took a long drink from the cup, relishing the cool water against my dry throat and mouth. As I lowered the cup, I spotted Tristan across the cavern, the space lit in hues of gold from the sun. He was sitting on a rock, also wrapped in a blanket, patiently letting Dr. Simmons inspect his head.

Tristan seemed to sense my gaze and looked up. His eyes fixed on mine, intent and alive. In spite of everything—my exhaustion, the history between us—I felt a spark of energy. His lips moved to one side in a half smile and he gave me a nod. I nodded in return.

No one would know what we'd endured together. Whatever Tristan and I were before the accident, we were something different now. And I could not help but be glad for that.

Chapter Seventeen

MARIGOLD

A BATH HAD NEVER FELT SO INORDINATELY wonderful. I'd been trapped in the mine for less than a day but somehow had managed to layer myself so thickly in dust that it took three scrubbings before my hair and skin felt clean. I had several small bruises and scrapes, nothing serious. Only that shallow cut on my arm would leave any lasting mark, but now, in the light of day and the warmth of gratitude filling my heart, I decided I no longer cared in the slightest.

Mama and Iris fussed over me until I finally shook them off by insisting I was tired. I fell into bed, certain I would be asleep in a heartbeat. Yet even though my body begged for rest, after half an hour, it still would not come. I had slept a little last night, I supposed. Against Tristan's chest. Against Tristan's terribly comfortable chest.

I sat up, flushed. I was being ridiculous. I could not allow these thoughts to continue. Yes, Tristan and I had survived something perilous together. No doubt this new bond—or whatever it was— would alter my opinion of him. But I would not be so silly as to think what had happened between us was anything more than survival.

I forced my thoughts in a new direction. Mr. Eastbrook. The

look on his face came back into my mind, that indecipherable tension from when we'd spoken after the rescue. What had that been about? Surely he was just worried for me.

I threw my covers off. I wasn't sleeping and it was only midday. I might as well go and find him, reassure him that I was perfectly well and whole.

I dressed in a simple morning gown and pinned up my hair quickly, not wanting to call my maid for such a small task. Then I peeked my head out into the corridor. Surely Mama would force me back to bed if she found me, so I would need to be stealthy. Where would Mr. Eastbrook be at this hour? It was not yet noon. The library? The stables? I started for the stairs, but paused as I passed the bedchamber that I knew Mr. Eastbrook occupied. I heard the sound of footsteps and low voices from within.

Was knocking on his door too forward? I found I did not care, not after what I'd endured last night.

I knocked and stepped back, touching my hair. The door opened almost immediately, framing Mr. Eastbrook.

"Miss Cartwell," he said, blinking. "Should you not be abed? You've had quite the ordeal."

I waved him off. "I cannot sleep. Forgive my intrusion, but I thought to see if you wished to walk in the gardens? Some sun would do me good."

In truth, I had no desire to ever be in the dark again. I already dreaded the coming night, when the sun sank behind the hills and blackness descended. But I pushed that thought away and tipped my smiling face up toward Mr. Eastbrook.

"I . . ." He coughed, glancing reflexively over his shoulder. "I'm afraid I am occupied at the moment."

"Occupied?" I glanced past him, noticing for the first time the disarray of his room. Waistcoats and jackets hung from the bedposts and chairs, and a trunk sat open in the center of his rug. His valet stood at the chest of drawers, removing a stack of breeches.

I blinked. "Are you . . . are you leaving?"

"Yes, I'm afraid I must," he said, clearing his throat. "Something has come up. Business."

"But you've only just arrived." My lungs were too tight. "I thought you'd meant to stay a fortnight."

Mr. Eastbrook looked down at his feet, avoiding my eyes. "That had been my hope. But circumstances have changed."

I stared at him. What circumstances?

He shook his head. "I wish it might have been different, Miss Cartwell. But you must understand, with things as they are, I cannot stay."

I swallowed hard. "I certainly do not understand. Please speak plainly, Mr. Eastbrook."

He finally met my eyes, his expression truly forlorn. "I mean the undeniable fact that you spent a night alone with another man."

I stood frozen, my heart stopping within my chest. "What?"

He said nothing, only watched me.

"It was an accident," I blurted. "Nothing happened between Tristan and me. Nothing! You must believe me."

He gave a sad, humorless smile. "That is the very worst thing. I do believe you. But not everyone will. The rumors are already spreading."

"Hang the rumors," I said, allowing my anger to color my words, my hands clenched into fists. "What do rumors matter?"

Mr. Eastbrook looked torn. "Miss Cartwell, I am my father's sole heir," he said, his voice weak. "I have a responsibility to my family, my home. I have three younger sisters who will soon be entering Society. I—I cannot allow any hint of scandal to touch my name."

I stepped forward, until only an inch separated us. "Tell me now," I said quietly. "Do you care for me?"

He looked at me, eyes broken and mouth parted. Then he looked away. "I cannot marry you, Miss Cartwell. I am so very sorry."

I moved back, vision blurring. I wasn't crying, I simply could not seem to focus my eyes. I turned and ran, back to my room, back to solitude. I closed the door behind me, bracing myself against the cold wood.

I cannot marry you.

I tried to control my breathing, but my body had spun wildly out of control. I sank to the floor, hands pressed to my chest. Not for one moment during our horrible night in the mine had I given any thought to potential scandal or rumors. We'd been *trapped.* We'd nearly died! And now, because of an accident, my entire future had been snatched away. Mr. Eastbrook would not marry me. He did not want me to stain his name.

I bit my cheek, closing my eyes. Was it true? Was my reputation ruined? I had friends enough, and my family would stand by me. Surely this was not the end of my life.

But the memory of the look in Mr. Eastbrook's eyes told me otherwise.

I sat there, empty and alone, and I cried.

Chapter Eighteen

TRISTAN

WHEN WE RETURNED to Stavely Hall, Dr. Simmons made six sutures in the wound on the back of my head. I bit onto my sleeve, my eyes rolling back. The pain was awful, but it was the tugging and pulling of my skin that made me gag. The doctor was thankfully quick in his work and soon finished.

"Would you like a dose of laudanum before I go?" he asked, buckling his medical case.

"No," I said. "No, thank you." I wanted a clear head. I could manage the pain.

He sent me an odd look but did not question me. He bid Uncle Matthew farewell and quit the room.

Uncle crossed his arms, coming closer. "You are sure you do not want the medicine?"

"Quite." I touched my newly bandaged head and winced. "I only need some rest and I'll be fine."

He nodded and clapped me on the shoulder. "I am glad you're all right," he said quietly. "I . . . well, it was not an easy night. We did not even know if either of you were alive."

I swallowed. The knowledge that he, and so many others, had spent the entire night in an effort to rescue us was humbling. "Thank you for not giving up."

He shook off his soberness—it never lasted long—and grinned at me. "I daresay you wouldn't have survived much longer, trapped with Marigold."

For a moment, I almost admitted the truth—that it hadn't been so terrible at all. But I knew how it would sound to Uncle. Instead, I forced a laugh. "To be sure."

He patted my shoulder once more and turned to leave. "Get some rest. I'll check on you in a few hours."

"I'm not a child," I said with a wry smile.

He fixed me with a serious look as he paused at the door. "You are *my* child, Tristan, and I won't hear otherwise."

He closed the door behind him, and I stared at it, my eyes suddenly blurry. I blinked and looked away. Uncle rarely said such things. Neither of us were ever eager to share our emotions. But the events of last night had changed so much.

My opinion of Marigold most of all.

I gingerly lowered myself to my bed and settled the side of my head on the pillow, rubbing one hand over my face in weariness. I'd told Marigold far too much. Would it change things between us?

And did I want it to?

No. No, things would go back to how they always had been, and it would be for the better. We'd bicker and compete. She'd marry Mr. Eastbrook and become an erstwhile fixture of my life, our paths only crossing when she visited her family in Sandcliffe. It was how it should be.

Yet as I drifted off to sleep, my mind clung to one memory—the feel of Marigold's small hand entwined with mine.

～

I woke a few hours later, feeling both better and worse. My body had lost that weight of exhaustion, but my head pounded terribly. I debated going back to sleep just to escape the headache, but night would be descending soon enough. I didn't want to spend half the night staring up at my ceiling, pretending not to think of Marigold Cartwell.

I dressed slowly, careful not to exacerbate my injury, then went in search of Uncle and hopefully some dinner. Cook must've been feeling nostalgic—I thought I recognized the smell of mutton pie in the air, my favorite as a child.

The door to Uncle's study stood ajar, and I could hear the sounds of his footsteps inside, back and forth. I frowned. He was pacing. Uncle never paced.

I stepped to the doorway. Uncle was near the window, hands clasped behind his back. I knocked softly and he spun, his eyes wide.

"Tristan," he said, his voice agitated.

"What is wrong?" For a moment, my mind strayed to horrible possibilities. "Is Marigold well?" That was the only thing I could think of, that she had suffered some ill affect from our night trapped in the mine.

"She is well." He shook his head. "Physically, at least."

My heart skipped a beat. I took a few steps forward. "What does that mean?"

Uncle let out a long breath, raking a hand through his hair as he came closer. "I did not think it would come to this. That is, I worried, but it seemed unlikely considering how intent he seemed."

I grabbed his shoulders. "Uncle, you are not making any sense. Who are you speaking of?"

He met my eyes, his mouth pressed into a thin line. "Mr. Eastbrook. He left."

"Left?" I stared at him. "Why?"

"Is it not obvious?" Uncle exhaled. "He is a coward. He cares more about what people might say than for the woman he'd planned to marry."

My mind spun. I pulled back.

"He has abandoned Marigold," Uncle said softly.

Mr. Eastbrook, abandoned Marigold. Because . . . because of what had happened. Because of *me*.

I turned away and shook my head, which only aggravated my

injury. "You cannot be sure. Perhaps he had other reasons for leaving." Desperation clawed at my voice.

"Mr. Cartwell came himself to tell me."

My eyes flashed back to his face. Marigold's father had come here? "Did he . . . ?"

Uncle raised one hand. "He said nothing of you."

It was not surprising. Mr. Cartwell wouldn't want me as a son-in-law, and Marigold certainly would not have sent him.

"He did not insist upon anything," Uncle said. "He only wanted to tell me the news. However . . ."

I rubbed my forehead. "I do not like the sound of that *however*."

Uncle said nothing for a long moment. Then he sighed. "Tristan, you know what you must do."

I stiffened. Did he mean what I thought he meant? My stomach clenched.

"You must offer for Marigold," he said.

A violent panic tore through my chest. I gaped at him. "You cannot be in earnest."

"I am entirely earnest," he responded, leaning his hands on the back of an armchair.

I shook my head wildly. "We would be miserable together. Surely anyone can see that." Uncle's eyes narrowed, but I went on. "I'm only two and twenty, Uncle. Far too young to be married and settled. I cannot—"

"Tristan." Uncle gripped the chair so tightly his hands turned white. "You know it is her reputation that will suffer the most. An unmarried woman, alone with a man for an entire night? The rumors, no matter how untrue, will ruin her. Her prospects will vanish, especially now that Mr. Eastbrook has run. I've seen it before. No, you must do the honorable thing."

I stood stock still, my eyes unseeing. Uncle had never pressed me like this. That, more than anything, revealed the seriousness of our predicament. But propose to Marigold? Marry her? Just the thought of it made my head pound harder. "Think about this, Uncle. Please. You know the both of us. You cannot mean to say that our best option is to spend the rest of our lives driving each other mad?"

Uncle softened his gaze. "I do know the both of you. Certainly you have your differences, but what couple does not? Perhaps you might even find happiness."

My eyes flashed to his. He could not be serious. "And what do you know of happiness in marriage? You don't even know who *you* are marrying!"

Uncle froze, staring at me. "What did you say?"

I stared back at him. I hadn't meant to say that, but it was too late now. The words spilled from me. "Mrs. Penrose. The things I've heard about her. If you are so concerned about a lady's reputation, perhaps you might start with the one you intend to meet at the altar."

I turned and strode from the room. My face was hot. I needed air. I threw open the front doors and clattered down the steps. The air had turned chilly, grey clouds low on the horizon.

I kicked the pebbled drive, sending out a spray of white rocks. Then I cut across the lawn, my boots shiny with newly-fallen rain. I did not want to think. I wanted to escape. I considered going to the stable for my horse, but then I would have to wait for him to be saddled. No, this was better. Me wandering the wind-driven land-scape, like some tragic Gothic hero.

I gave a laugh, a wild sound, and crouched to my haunches there in the middle of the lawn, dipping my pounding head between my knees and lacing my hands behind my neck. I swore I could feel every suture. I tried to breathe through it, the pain I'd stubbornly insisted upon, but all I could hear was Uncle's voice, echoing endlessly. *Offer for Marigold.*

How could I propose to the woman who had been my nemesis from the moment we'd met? I could count on one hand the number of civil conversations we'd ever had—and most of those were from last night in the cave, when we *had* to be civil to survive. And while those exchanges had also been unexpectedly sincere, it would be foolish of me to assume we could ever maintain that sort of relationship. Our history spoke for itself.

I groaned, from the pain in my head and from the pure impossibility of it. Marigold and me. It would be a nightmare.

And yet I knew. I knew deep in my bones that Uncle was right. I was a gentleman, and I had to take responsibility for what had happened, no matter that we'd simply been in the wrong place at the wrong time—victims of an unlikely accident. I was duty-bound.

I raised my head, staring at the grass waving in the wind. I had to propose to Marigold Cartwell.

Chapter Nineteen

MARIGOLD

I RAISED MY BOW, arrow pulled taut to my ear. I released and the arrow flew, striking the outermost circle of the target.

I lowered my bow, glowering. None of my other two dozen shots this evening had done any better, and my waist pouch was now empty. I was using my favorite bow again, but it seemed to make no difference in my shooting. I strode across the grass, ignoring the wind and light raindrops, and began yanking the arrows from the target.

"Botheration," I muttered under my breath. I'd never shot so poorly. I pulled the last arrow free and turned, planning to return to my place and shoot again. But I stopped, nearly dropping my entire bundle of arrows.

Tristan stood there, hands in his pockets, watching me with a pained expression. His hair was damp with the misty rain, curling around his ears, and a new bandage was wrapped around his head, a strip of pure white. He wore no jacket over his rain-speckled shirt-sleeves. My pulse quickened.

"I've been expecting you," I said, raising my chin.

He gave a low, humorless laugh. "Seeing as I only just decided to come, I find that difficult to believe."

I *had* been, though. In the midst of my foolish crying over Mr.

Eastbrook earlier this afternoon, I'd seen Father slip away. I'd known where he'd gone. And I knew why Tristan was here now.

"Men are entirely too predictable." I walked back toward him, working to place my arrows back in my pouch.

"Apparently not your Mr. Eastbrook."

A flash of pain burned through me. I stopped, my feet frozen to the earth. I said nothing.

Tristan blew out a breath. "I am sorry. I should not have said that."

I clenched my jaw, returning to my task of sorting out my arrows by the color of their feathers, which designated what distance they were best suited for. "Mr. Eastbrook made his choice," I said finally, unable to look him in the eye. "I do not blame him for it."

Nor did I hate him for it. It would have been different if we were engaged, but we'd had no understanding. He had more than just himself to think of, his family and sisters. I understood it, but that did not make the misery any more bearable.

Tristan choked on a laugh. "You cannot mean that. You have every right to blame him. The man has no integrity and ran at the first sign of trouble."

"Then I should count myself lucky," I shot back, "that I did not yoke myself to him for life."

Tristan did not speak, and I forced myself to look up at him. His eyes locked on mine, desperate and dark.

"Marigold," he said, his voice gravelly.

But I did not want to hear what he would say. Out of duty? Out of pity? I tore my gaze away, grinding my feet into the damp earth as I found my shooting stance. I nocked an arrow and drew my bow.

"Marigold." His voice tugged at me, unwinding me. I ignored him. I released the arrow. It flew off into the mist, missing the target entirely.

"Of course you would see that," I muttered, reaching for another arrow.

"Marigold, look at me."

"I don't want to look at you."

"Why?"

"Because you are going to propose."

Silence.

I closed my eyes. I'd been right.

"What else am I to do?" he said, frustration coloring his voice. "It is the only solution."

"No," I said, though my words held no surety. "I shall be a spinster aunt, doting on my nieces and nephews. I am perfectly content not to marry at all."

"*That* is not true."

I finally shot him a sharp look. "We spend one night together and you think you know me so well?"

"I've known you since you were seven years old," he countered. "So yes, I am certain that is not the life you want. You want a home of your own. You want a family."

"And having that life with you would be better than one as a spinster?" I gave a mirthless laugh. "Tristan, we *despise* each other!"

He narrowed his eyes. "Despise is a strong word."

I paused. He was right. Though he sometimes made me so furious I could not think, I did not despise him. Especially not after last night. But it still did not solve our problem. "We would be unhappy. We argue constantly. Tell me truly, do you wish to marry *me?*"

How was it I'd asked a similar question to two men in the same day?

"No," he said, his voice quiet. "No, I don't. But if I do not, you shall be ruined and I shall be judged for ruining you."

"So it is your masculine pride which drives you," I said. "Believe me, I will bear the scorn of Society, not you." Which was another issue entirely. The injustice put a sour taste in my mouth.

He groaned, arching his neck back. "You are not listening to reason!"

"Try being reasonable."

He scrubbed a hand over his face, and I tried very hard not to notice the shadow on his jaw, unshaven since yesterday, no doubt. Then his eyes fixed on the bow in my hand.

"Fine," he said. "Let us make a wager."

I blinked. "What?"

"You like a competition." He tugged the bow and arrow from me. "If I hit the center, we marry."

I gaped at him. "You cannot be serious. I will not base my future on something so . . . so . . ."

"Unpredictable?"

I scowled. "You won't make it. The wind is too strong. I've been shooting for hours and haven't hit the center."

"Then there is no risk." He raised my bow.

I opened my mouth to protest, but nothing escaped. *Did* I want to stop him? Because I knew he was right. I wanted children. A home of my own. But now if I ever hoped to gain those, I would have to marry him. And I could not for the life of me make such a decision.

Ought I leave it up to fate?

"You'll miss on purpose," I said, more to hide my uncertainty than anything. "You don't want this any more than I."

He ignored me, assuming that infuriatingly perfect shooting stance of his. He squinted as he aimed, the muscles of his shoulder taut beneath his damp shirt. There was no possible way he could hit the center.

He pulled the string tighter and—

CRACK.

Tristan jolted back. I gasped even as the bone-numbing snap echoed in my ears and splintered wood flew past me.

Then I stared. My bow had broken, just below the handle. My stomach wrenched, and I thought I might be sick.

Tristan stood there, unmoving, then bent to pick up the jagged end that dangled from the string. He turned to face me, holding out the pieces in utter bafflement.

"My bow," I said dumbly.

"I am sorry." He was aghast.

I snatched the pieces from him, my hands shaking. "You know better than to handle a lady's bow."

I'd chosen this particular bow today for a reason. It was the same one I'd beaten Tristan with at the fair two years ago, when I had first proven my mettle. I'd needed the reminder that I was strong. That I could do hard things. And now my bow was shattered, useless in my hands. I gripped the wooden fragments tightly, as if they tethered me to reality. If I released them, surely I myself would shatter into a million pieces.

"I did not mean to." He did not meet my eyes, staring at the remains of my bow. His voice had a boyish humility to it, contrite. I did not care.

"I might believe such a thing if this was your first time taking up a bow." I could not stop my voice from snapping at him. Even a novice archer knew not to shoot with another's bow. Each bow was made specifically for that person, taking into account their height and strength. My anger flared, my disbelief vanishing in its wake. Tristan should never have touched mine. He was too strong, too tall. "And you tout yourself as the foremost archer in Sandcliffe."

His eyes finally met mine and narrowed. "It was an accident. Forgive me if my head is not entirely functional yet. I was nearly killed yesterday saving your life."

I gave a harsh laugh. "So this is how it would be? You will remind me every hour how you saved my life? What a future to look forward to."

He threw his hands into the air. "Blast it, Marigold. Why is everything so difficult with you?"

I wanted to cut back at him. But I held my tongue, miraculously. I stared at my broken bow in my hands, one thumb tracing the ragged edge. I took a few long, deep breaths, trying to find some balance in my ever-shifting world.

I set my jaw as I looked back up at him. "We questioned Fate, and it answered." I held up the broken bow. "Is there no more clear omen than this? We *cannot* marry."

He stared at me. "Is marrying me such a horrible prospect that you must rely on superstition to avoid it?"

I remained quiet, which was answer enough for him. His face hardened, his eyes taking on an unfamiliar glint. Then he turned and walked away, not looking back even once as he disappeared into the trees.

I carried the broken pieces of my bow inside. Papa had bought me an Ascham cupboard for my fourteenth birthday, and it stood beside the door to the garden. I stopped before it, numb from the cold and from the look in Tristan's eyes as he'd left. What had it been? If I did not know better, I would have thought it was hurt. But in the twelve years I'd known him, I'd never seen such a thing from him. Tristan Gates held himself apart, above. He did not dally in something so foolish as *emotions*.

I dried my things carefully, placing the arrows one by one into the slots, my glove and brace onto the shelf above. The mindless task soothed me, even just for a few minutes. Then I carefully leaned the remains of my bow against the inside corner of the cupboard. There would be no throwing it out, no matter its state. It was a reminder of everything I had done, and everything I could do, and I needed that now more than ever.

When I closed the cupboard door, Mama was waiting. She stood down the hall, hands clasped before her, eyes red.

"How much did you see?" I asked wearily.

"All of it," she admitted. "I was watching you shoot when he came."

I bit my lip, holding my elbows. "I suppose you are very disappointed in me."

"Oh, darling." She came to me, taking both my hands in hers. "Of course I am not."

"But you do want me to marry him."

"I would never presume to make such a choice for you," she said softly. "It is your life."

I closed my eyes. "Then I cannot help but hope that we are making too much of this. I have friends enough. Surely things are not so dire."

Mama's hands tightened around mine. "I wish I could hope for that. But Mr. Eastbrook . . ."

"His opinion does not mean everything, does it?" I peered into her eyes.

She shook her head. "Society will see what it wants to see. And if they see a respectable gentleman turn tail and run, then they will draw the only conclusion they wish to."

"That the lady in question is compromised."

She sighed. "Yes."

I took a shuddering breath, trying once again to hold the tears at bay. "It is so unfair, Mama," I whispered.

She pulled me into her arms. "I know, Mari. Heavens, I know."

She held me, and I pressed my eyes closed, as if I could hide from life and all of its problems. In the arms of my mother, I could almost pretend I was a child again and that she would shield me. But she could not save me from this.

"I know that Tristan can be difficult," she whispered into my ear, "but he is a good man, and clearly he possesses far more honor than Mr. Eastbrook." She pulled back and gave me a small smile, tugging on one of my curls. "For what it's worth."

I had no response to that. It was not Tristan's honor I was concerned about—it was *everything* else. Our inability to speak without bickering. His arrogance and aloofness.

Mama kissed me on the cheek. "Your father and I will support you no matter your decision. But you must be certain. This affects Tristan's life as much as your own. Please, be careful as you consider."

She left me then, her hand slipping silently from mine.

I went to my room, closing the curtains and curling up in bed, though my dress was damp. It was foolishness. Insanity. Tristan and

I could not marry. And yet everyone besides me seemed certain it was the best option. Was I the one in the wrong?

No, I decided. I would not be cowed by false rumors into a loveless marriage. Nothing *had* happened between us. I would cling to that truth and hold my head high. Tristan had done his duty. Society could expect nothing more from him than that.

I would ride out this storm. Soon enough, the waves would calm and the sun would shine again. There would be some other scandal for people to sink their teeth into and everyone would soon forget about me.

I hoped I was not lying to myself yet again.

Chapter Twenty

TRISTAN

I STALKED HOME, the rain falling harder now, wetting the shoulders of my shirt and dripping down my face. She'd refused me. I hadn't even spoken the actual words, and still she'd rejected me.

It should not hurt. It should not burn my chest like a glowing ember. *I did not want to marry her*, I reminded myself. But the fact that Marigold would choose *anything* but me . . . . A man could only endure so much.

At least I could report to Uncle that I'd done it. I'd asked. If Marigold wished to throw her life away, then at least Society would not blame me for it.

But my rationalizing did little to loosen the squirming knot in my stomach, or silence the little voice that repeated that this was all my fault.

When I arrived home, I expected to see Uncle waiting for me. He did not like to leave conflict to simmer—he preferred to face it head on and force a solution. But there was no light emanating from his study, or from underneath his bedroom door. It wasn't possible that he could have gone to bed already; it was not yet six o'clock.

I paused in the corridor. Had he gone to call upon Mrs. Penrose? Had my accusations against her been enough to stoke his suspicions?

My head ached. I stumbled inside my room, dropping to my bed without undressing. My body had been pushed to its limit. I needed to not think of Marigold or Mrs. Penrose or Uncle Matthew.

I needed to sleep.

~

I woke to a knock on my door. I sat up too fast and winced. How long would it take before my head felt normal again? This was deucedly annoying.

"Tristan?" It was Uncle.

"Yes?" I managed to open my eyes a slit. It was light outside. Morning.

"May I come in?"

I closed my eyes again. I couldn't avoid him forever. But neither did I feel like having a *tête-à-tête* about Mrs. Penrose so early in the morning. Or ever.

I exhaled and threw off my covers, going to open the door. Uncle stood there, hands clasped behind his back. I tried to interpret his expression. Was that anger in his eyes, or concern? I'd never been good at reading people.

I gestured him inside and he closed the door behind him. I dropped into the armchair beside the empty fireplace.

"How is your head?" he asked, his voice careful.

"Fine." I spoke in a detached tone.

He nodded, looking away. "You went to Crossdale last night."

He said it as a matter of fact. Had Marigold told everyone of my proposal, laughing at me as she recounted it? Well, she probably hadn't laughed. I'd broken her bow, after all.

"I did."

"What did you say?"

I looked up at him. "I'm sure you've heard."

He shook his head. "I haven't. I only assumed you would go once you had a chance to think."

160

I swallowed. "Then you will be disappointed to hear there won't be any wedding vows in our future."

"Oh." Uncle stood still, staring down at his feet.

There wasn't anything else to say. I knew he was fond of Marigold, and even if our marriage had been forced upon us, he would have been pleased to join our families. Though he would likely be the only one.

Perhaps save for Mrs. Cartwell. Would she have wanted me for a son-in-law? I shook off that thought before it could cause any more pain.

"I am sorry, Tristan," Uncle said quietly. "I am. I would not have you suffer this."

I stood and went to my wardrobe, sorting through my clothes for clean shirtsleeves and breeches. "It's done with," I said. "She made her choice."

"If it is any consolation," he said, "I think that choice was based on her own stubbornness and pride. Because I know, beyond everything in this world, that any woman would be blessed to have you."

My hands paused in their work, but I said nothing. Yesterday, I'd shouted at him, insisted he knew nothing of marriage and love. Why was he being so kind?

Uncle's footsteps moved to the door. "Will you dress and come downstairs, please? I think we have some things to discuss."

I cleared my throat. "Yes." I had no doubt what he meant.

He left and I dressed quickly, though changing the bandage on my wound took a few minutes more. Eventually, I made my way down the stairs to Uncle's study. I pushed the door open, then froze.

Mrs. Penrose sat near the desk. She stood upon my entrance, wearing a blue pelisse, gloves, and a bonnet, her reticule swinging from her arm. What was she doing here?

"Tristan. Come, sit." Uncle rounded his desk, gesturing me to sit beside where a tray of tea and toast had been set on the desk. "Eat something."

I slowly moved to the chair, eyeing Mrs. Penrose as I went. She did not smile, only watched me with wary eyes. Good.

"I'm not hungry," I said, sliding the tray aside.

Uncle frowned but did not protest.

My gaze flicked again to Mrs. Penrose before returning to my uncle. "Might I ask what it is you wanted to discuss?"

Uncle and Mrs. Penrose exchanged a look I could not begin to interpret. He sighed and sat beside me, leaning forward to balance his elbows on his knees.

"Yesterday," he began, "you said something about how I did not know the woman I was marrying."

I stiffened. "Yes."

"Well, I wanted to make it clear that I am not some lovesick fool swayed by the first pretty face to come my way." He smiled at Mrs. Penrose. "Though it is a pretty face indeed."

My stomach twisted. Why was he treating this so lightly?

Mrs. Penrose did not smile at the compliment, her face creased with worry. She moved to the edge of her seat, clutching her reticule on her lap. "Your uncle came to me last night," she began, her voice tremulous. "He told me what you said, and together we surmised that you must have learned something of . . ." She took a deep breath. "Of my past."

I sat back in my chair. "I heard some things from a friend."

"Shall I guess?" she said. "I am a fortune hunter, stalking foolish old men in their dotage with the intent to inherit their fortunes upon their deaths."

I fought to keep my mouth from dropping open. I glanced at Uncle, but his eyes were fixed on Mrs. Penrose's. I squared my shoulders. If he wanted to face this head on, then so be it. "Yes," I said. "That is precisely what I heard."

She nodded, looking down at her lap. "I am not surprised in the least. People can be cruel."

"Do you mean to say there is no truth to the rumors?" I asked, narrowing my eyes. "You told me yourself you'd been married twice."

"Yes, I did," she said. "I never lied to you, Mr. Gates." She paused, taking a long second to collect her thoughts. I drummed my fingers on the arm of my chair, watching her closely. She looked nervous, to be sure, but also assured in a strange way.

"I married later in life," she said. "My parents were growing old and I was desperate to support myself when I met my first husband." She paused. "He was not a good man. He was . . . unkind to me."

Uncle's hand, resting on his leg, clenched into a fist.

"I endured years of living under his thumb, and that of his wretched mother." Mrs. Penrose's eyes flashed, the first sign of anger I'd ever seen from her. "When he died, it was only a relief. I thought he would leave me the house. But when the solicitor read the will, I could not believe it. My husband had left me nothing."

Her voice cut out, and she took a deep breath. "My own parents had since died. My brother was a poor vicar. He could not hope to support me. I had nowhere to go."

I tried to school my features. I did not allow any of my reactions to appear on my face. And yet my mind spun. This was not at all what I'd expected.

"But I had a friend," she said. "My father's old business partner. He was quite a bit older than I, but he'd always been fond of me, more like an uncle than anything. He wrote to me and proposed a plan: a marriage between us, on paper only. He had heard my troubles and wanted to help."

Mrs. Penrose now smiled, a soft, small smile. "I accepted. We had a wonderful year together, a year of simple friendship. Upon his death, he left me a tidy sum, enough that I could be modestly independent for the rest of my days."

I blinked. "But you came to live with your brother."

"Not for money," she said. "For company. When he attained this parish, he immediately wrote and invited me to live with him." She shot Uncle a significant look. "He is still a bit put out with *you*, stealing me away."

"Because I did steal her away," Uncle told me. "I fear you've got it into your head, Tristan, that Mrs. Penrose set her cap at me and my fortune. But she has no need of my money, and indeed I was the one to pursue her. It took quite a bit of convincing for her to give up her disinclination for another marriage."

I stared at the rug, at the intricate woven design. I tried to find some flaw in her story, some inconsistency that proved she was lying. But I found nothing.

"And the rumors I heard?" I asked, though my voice held little force.

Mrs. Penrose sighed. "My mother-in-law from my first marriage has never been quiet about her loathing of me. She has many influential friends. I daresay she is the source of the falsehoods, though I cannot be certain."

She met my eyes, spoke in a clear, firm voice, and did not shy away from details. There were no signs of lying in Mrs. Penrose's visage, because, of course, she *wasn't* lying. I sat back in my chair, thoughts wheeling in my head. How could I have been so stupid to have trusted in a rumor? I'd been wrong. Horribly wrong.

"I—" Shame filled my chest, and my voice broke. "I clearly have misjudged you, Mrs. Penrose. You must understand that I was only trying to protect Uncle Matthew."

"Protect me." Uncle scoffed. "My boy, I have been warding off greedy women since before you were born. I think I know a diamond when I see one."

Mrs. Penrose blushed, her smile returning.

"Truly," I said, more quietly. "I am sorry. I was so eager to believe the worst of you that I did not allow you a fair chance. I hope this will not hurt your opinion of me too much."

Her eyes softened. "No. Indeed, I am grateful Matthew has such a loyal nephew. And I am glad to tell you the truth. My past is not something I enjoy discussing, but we . . ." She took a deep breath. "But we are to be family now, and I think it right that you should know."

Family. A vision slipped into my mind, of Mama kissing my

forehead as she read to me, of Papa glancing over his ledger to smile at me.

No. I forced the painful memories away. Uncle was my family now. And I had to accept the fact that Mrs. Penrose soon would be too.

"Yes," I said, my throat dry. "Family."

Mrs. Penrose excused herself soon after, giving me one more gracious smile as she left, and when the door closed behind her, Uncle turned to me.

"Are you satisfied?" he asked. There was no malice in his question, only steadiness.

I nodded. "I think I owe you an apology as well. I should not have doubted you."

He sighed. "You did not doubt *me*. You simply assumed the worst and insisted it be so."

I slumped back in my chair. He was right. He was always right. "I wish I wasn't like that." Why could I not be sunny and optimistic and cheerful?

Uncle shook his head. "I would not change you for the world, Tristan. You are who you are because of the life you've lived, and I love you for it."

"But?"

He smiled. "But there is no harm in looking on the brighter side of life every now and again."

He clasped my shoulder and left. I wished he had stayed. I did not want to be alone with my thoughts just now.

I had realities to face. Mrs. Penrose was not, in fact, trying to steal Uncle's fortune. She would be marrying him. And glad as I was that she was not duplicitous, I now had a new problem. I recalled Marigold's words from the mine, spoken to me from the darkness.

"If your uncle marries," she'd said. "I imagine there will be children. Children who might replace *you* as his heir."

Mrs. Penrose could not yet be forty years of age. She was young enough to bear a child. I did not care for the money, but would that child replace me in my uncle's affections?

I pushed that thought aside. There I went again, thinking the worst of things.

But like Uncle had said, I was who I was for a reason. And the thought of depending on anyone for *anything* pricked my very soul. I would work harder, I decided. I would be vigilant in my investments and ensure I had no debts. Only then could I secure my own future, independent of any inheritance from Uncle.

It was better that way. Safer.

Safer.

Chapter Twenty-One

MARIGOLD

THE DAY FOLLOWING Tristan's proposal, I threw myself into work for the Lady Archers of Sandcliffe. I wrote the bylaws, compared subscription fees imposed by similar societies, and sent inquiries to various modistes regarding our shooting costumes. It would be a boon to any modiste who secured our account, as every member would need to visit the same dressmaker to ensure complete coordination among our set.

I did not speak of what had happened with Tristan, and neither did any of my family. I pretended nothing was amiss. If one pretended long enough, the pretense became reality. At least, that was what my stubborn pride insisted.

In any case, I did not have time to wallow. The Lady Patroness's Meeting was only three weeks away, and I still had to teach the majority of the ladies in my society how to shoot.

Three days after the incident in the mine, I rose early, intent on seeing to every detail of today's scheduled practice. The food, the arrangements, everything must be perfect. Once the members arrived, we would laugh and shoot as we had before. Everyone would forget what had happened, and life would return to normal.

Mama, Iris, and I waited on the terrace, prepared to greet the ladies as they arrived. I'd arranged for chairs and tables to be scattered about the space, plenty for everyone who had previously attended. As the minutes ticked past, however, my forced optimism began to fade. There was no crunch of carriage wheels on the front drive, no friendly voices at the door.

"Perhaps everyone is running a bit late today," Iris mused, sitting beside me.

"Yes," Mama agreed quickly. "Or perhaps a tree fell and blocked the road. Surely they will be here soon."

"Surely," I echoed, grasping at her words. I could understand some ladies being hesitant to attend, but what about my friends? Where were Cora and Sylvia?

I heard footsteps in the house and I straightened, turning to the garden door. Hope filled me until Oliver stepped out onto the terrace. My heart dropped. Just Oliver.

"I've never seen a group of people so displeased to see me," he said, crossing to join us.

"Well, you are not a legion of women intent on practicing archery," Mama said, casting a meaningful look at me.

Oliver glanced around, seeming to realize for the first time that there ought to have been two dozen other women on the terrace with us. His expression tightened. He and I had yet to speak of Mr. Eastbrook's departure. Since that day, he'd carefully kept to himself, watching me like I was made of delicate glass. What did he think of his friend abandoning me? I could not help but wonder if he felt responsible for the whole affair. He had introduced us, after all. But of course I did not hold Oliver in any way responsible. In fact, I preferred if we never spoke of it again.

That did not seem likely, however. Not with irrefutable proof of my ruined reputation right before my eyes.

I took a deep breath, and Mama patted my hand. "They'll be here soon enough."

Movement caught my eye. A figure rounded the back of the house, hurrying across the lawn in a dark blue walking gown and straw bonnet. I stood immediately, already smiling.

"Cora!" I called, waving.

She saw me and returned the wave, though her own smile soon faded when she took in the empty chairs and tables.

"Where is everyone?" she asked when she reached us. She peered around, as if the other ladies were hiding in the hedges.

I swallowed. "This is it, I'm afraid."

Cora blinked. "No one else has come?"

I could not find the words. I sat abruptly and buried my face in my arms on the table. I did not cry—I simply could not stand the sight any longer.

"Oh, Mari." Cora dropped into the chair beside mine and rubbed my back. "I cannot believe it. I was sure *some* would still come, even if . . ."

"Even if what?" Oliver asked quietly.

Cora paused. "Well, everyone has heard what happened. Or what they think happened."

"And now they all believe I am a trollop who seduces men in caves?" I said, my voice muffled by my arms.

"No," Cora said, horrified. "That is, certainly the rumors are awful. But not so dreadfully worded as that."

I peeked up at her. "But you are here. You came."

She swallowed. "I must admit it was not easy. My mother forbade me to come. That is why I am late—I had to sneak past half a dozen servants."

"You came without her knowing?" Oliver stared at her.

She looked up at him, all sincerity. "I know how important this is to Mari."

Oliver grunted and turned away. Cora sent me a confused look.

"Sylvia has not come," I said softly.

Sylvia had sent a note the day after the incident, inquiring after my health and assuring me she would visit soon. I'd been so busy preparing for today's practice that I hadn't noted her continued absence. Not until it was unavoidably obvious.

"Surely she forgot," Mama said, trying to fix things as she always did. "It cannot mean anything."

"It means everything," Iris said darkly.

I stood and moved a few paces away, wrapping my arms around myself.

"It is ridiculous," Cora declared. "Why should any of them believe a rumor when they know you so well themselves?"

"The *ton* sees what it will see," I said in a detached voice, echoing Mama's words from the other night. She had been right—Society would not forget.

This was a fool's errand. No one was coming.

I pressed my lips together. This was far worse than I'd imagined. I'd thought perhaps we'd lose a few members, but all of them? If I had no members, I had no society. What was I to do, show up to the prize shoot alone? What would become of my deal with Lord Beauford? I'd made that deal—to give up my society and competing in the fair should I lose—because there had been little risk. I was planning to marry Mr. Eastbrook and leave Sandcliffe. But now . . . now I had nothing. No society. No husband. No future.

I turned to face them, Mama and Oliver, Iris and Cora. All of them watched me with varying expressions of worry and apprehension.

"Well, there is no need to prolong this awfulness," I said, attempting a smile. "Shall we put the terrace to rights?"

"Mari," Mama said, her voice sympathetic.

"No need for that," I said briskly. "What's done is done and I simply have to face the facts." I looked at Cora, trying to hide my hopelessness. "You had better go. I wouldn't like for you to be in trouble on my account."

She hesitated, then nodded and stood. She knew I needed space, and I loved her for it. "I'll try to visit soon."

Cora kissed my cheek as she passed, and left the same way she had come. Mama let me be, taking Oliver and Iris with her as the servants began clearing away the food and collecting the chairs.

I closed my eyes. I could not find a solution. Perhaps, with enough time, I could fix this. I could repair my reputation, convince Society that I was not wanton and ruined.

But I was being foolish. There was no guarantee I would ever be anything but a social pariah. What if no man ever wanted me again? And what of my family? I was not the only one who suffered the effects of this scandal.

I glanced over my shoulder, watching as Iris disappeared inside the house with Mama. Iris was fifteen now—she would enter Society in a year or two and the *ton*'s memory was long. My shame would taint her future. I was understanding better and better why Mr. Eastbrook had left, what with his younger sisters depending on him. I could not abandon Iris to such a fate. She did not deserve it.

Besides that, the prize shoot was fast approaching. Certainly Lord Beauford had already heard the rumors about me. What if he wrote to Lord and Lady Englefield and told them? They might withdraw their invitation entirely.

I took a deep breath. There *was* one way. One way to stop the rumors, one way to recover my reputation in time for the prize shoot. One way to save Iris's future. One way to find any scrap of the life I had once imagined for myself.

And there was no point in putting it off a second longer.

"I'm here to see Mr. Gates," I told the footman who answered the door at Stavely Hall an hour later.

He stared at me. No doubt he'd heard all the rumors, possibly even knew about me rejecting Tristan. But he said nothing, only allowed me inside and closed the door.

"He is in the game room," the footman said. "Shall I . . ."

"No, thank you," I said, handing him my bonnet, pelisse, and gloves. "I know the way."

He looked uncertain, as if he should not allow me to visit Tristan unaccompanied. But then, I was already a ruined woman. What could it hurt?

I strode down the hall, my skirts swishing about my ankles. My heart rose into my throat as I tried to decide how to go about this, but by the time I arrived at the game room, I still hadn't formed any plan. I would have to improvise.

A loud crack came from inside the game room, and I jumped. What on earth? I peeked inside the open door. Since the last time I'd visited this room, an enormous oak billiards table had been erected near the bay of windows. Tristan stood beside the table, cue stick in hand. His hair was as neat as ever, even beneath the narrow, white bandage still wrapped tightly around his head, but he was dressed casually in his shirtsleeves with his waistcoat undone and cravat loosened.

I swallowed, pulling back slightly so he could not see me. My eyes traced the lean angles of his shoulders and arms, no longer hidden beneath his jacket. His sleeves were rolled up to his elbows, exposing muscled forearms as he bent with his billiards cue to line up his shot.

Those familiar brown eyes—usually narrowed at me—now squinted in concentration, and I could not help but notice the definition of his jaw. How odd. I'd never looked at him in this way, as a woman contemplating a man. He had always just been Tristan, the irritating, unapproachable neighbor boy.

He made his shot, the balls cracking together again. The red ball he'd been aiming at flew directly into the netted pocket, and Tristan straightened with a pleased expression.

I pulled back my shoulders. Now was as good a time as any to ruin his day.

I swept into the room. "Have you given up on archery, then?"

He jumped, nearly dropping his cue stick. He caught it in fumbling hands, then stared at me. "Marigold?"

I ran one finger over the green wool baize of the billiards table. "I admit, I hadn't pegged you as a billiards man. It seems too small a game, don't you think? Rather a step down after a prize shoot."

His eyes followed me as I picked up a white ball, tossed it, and then caught it again.

"I was playing with that," he muttered, turning to chalk his cue.

I set it back down right where I'd taken it. "There. Now you may continue winning against yourself."

"Is there something you need?" he asked, his voice dull.

I wet my lips. I'd known he wouldn't be happy to see me. Our last conversation had not been . . . pleasant. This would be no easy task.

"I wanted to . . ." I stopped, my tongue suddenly heavy. The right words would not come, which was a new experience for me. But how did one voice such a singular and peculiar request? I tried again. "That is, I'd hoped you would . . ."

"I cannot read your mind." He turned back. "You shall have to speak clearly."

I took a deep breath. "I want you to propose again," I blurted out.

He froze, cue clutched in his hands. His eyes slowly lifted to mine. "What?"

"I want you to propose marriage again," I said. "To me."

He gave an exhale of disbelief. "*Why?*"

"Because I have changed my mind."

His eyes darkened. "That is not something to joke about."

"I am *not* joking."

He shook his head, going to the pocket and retrieving the red ball. "Forgive me, but have you not considered that I might also have changed my mind within the last few days?"

My stomach tightened. Had he?

"A proposal does not last indefinitely," he said, setting the ball on the table and leaning over to line up his shot. "I am afraid mine has expired and I will not be issuing a new one."

He focused all of his attention on his aim, and now I realized why he'd been so irritated the other day when I refused to stop shooting. It was blastedly annoying to talk with someone who couldn't be bothered to look at you.

I strode to his side and plucked the cue from his hands.

He jolted upright. "What are you—"

"Shall we have a wager, Gates?" I said, balancing the cue between my hands.

He blew out a breath. "Don't be absurd."

I ignored him. "If I make this shot, you must propose again." Except I would be far better behaved and not break his cue.

He stood still, and for the first time, he seemed to really look at me. He settled that intense gaze upon my face, as if trying to see beyond my stiff expression. "What is this about, Marigold?"

"I . . ." I swallowed. I had to tell him, didn't I? To convince him? "I have come to some difficult realizations."

He said nothing, only waited.

"I held another practice today," I said. "For my society."

He raised an eyebrow. "And?"

"And no one came."

"No one?" He looked startled.

I shook my head, unexpected tears pricking at my eyes. I turned my face away. "Cora came, angel that she is. But no one else. I'd thought—I'd *assumed*—that rumors would not mean so much to those I called friends. But I suppose nothing is assured when one's name is akin to mud."

I tried to find any amount of anger, but there seemed to only be room inside me for pain and sadness. Sylvia and I had been friends for years. She was flirty and flighty, to be sure, but I had never doubted her integrity. That was what hurt the most. I'd counted on her, and she had proven to be nothing but a fair-weather friend.

"So you want to marry me simply to save your society?" he said in disbelief.

I blew out a breath of frustration. "Of course that is not the only reason, or even the most important. I also must think of Iris, of how my actions have affected her prospects. I cannot be responsible for ruining her future. I would never do that to my sister."

Tristan said nothing for a long moment, so long that I turned back to ensure he hadn't, in fact, left the room. He stood there watching me with the most peculiar expression. Finally, he cleared his throat. "Take your shot."

His words pierced through me. Did he mean it? I eyed him, but he seemed sincere, his mouth set in a serious line. I hesitated, then moved to the edge of the table where he'd been leaning a minute before. I examined the shot. It was an awkward angle. I'd played billiards all of once, at my cousin's home in Dover. I hadn't had an immediate talent for it, so I'd written it off.

I certainly had no chance of making this shot now, but I set my jaw and positioned the cue stick as I'd seen Tristan do. My hands were trembling, as if my body already knew how much depended on this shot. I tried to aim, though I truly had no sense of how it was done, then I took a deep breath. I drove the cue forward.

The white ball flew across the table, glancing off the red one I'd aimed for—and sending it directly into the corner pocket. It thumped in, the finality deafening.

I stared. I'd made it.

Tristan's mouth hung open, and he blinked.

"There," I said with a confident nod, as if I'd known all along I would make it. "Fate agrees with me this time."

"Fate?" He shook his head. "That was pure luck."

"Yes, how lucky am I," I said wryly.

"It is almost as if you do not wish me to propose." He turned, as if to move away. I grabbed his hand. He stopped.

And there we were again, holding hands. They came together as if they'd never been apart, his skin warm against mine. I stared down at our hands. His was so much larger than mine, tan and strong. I looked up to find him already watching me. I took a steadying breath.

"I am sorry, Tristan," I said quietly. "Sorry for what I said to you the other day. You were doing me a kindness, and I refused to listen. That was unforgivable."

His fingers tightened almost imperceptibly around mine. "And yet," he said with a resigned sigh, "somehow I find myself forgiving you."

I pressed my lips together, waiting.

He sent me a discerning look, as if trying to see through a thick fog. "You are sure this is what you want?"

No. It wasn't what I wanted. We both knew that. And yet it was what must happen.

I nodded.

He blew out a breath, running his free hand through his hair. "Blast it all." He closed his eyes. "Best do it properly so you've no complaints."

Tristan turned to face me fully, and he raised my hand between us. "Miss Marigold Cartwell, will you—" He cleared his throat, giving his head a slight shake. "Will you marry me?"

A girl imagined those words countless times in her life. *Never* had I imagined them spoken by Tristan, and never had I imagined that it would send an unfamiliar jolt throughout my body.

Even though I was the one who had forced him to ask again, still I hesitated. This was the rest of my life, decided in a moment. I looked up at him, at my own turmoil reflected in his eyes. The eyes of the man I would marry.

"Yes," I managed, my voice squeaky. "Yes," I said more firmly. "I will marry you."

We stared at each other a long moment, as if neither of us could believe what had taken place. Were we truly engaged?

"Well, that's that." He nodded, as if this was a business transaction and nothing more. He made to pull away, but I held tight to his hand, narrowing my eyes. I was not just one more thing on his list.

"Do you not wish to call for the doctor?" I suggested innocently.

"The doctor?" He furrowed his brow. "My head is fine."

"Is it?" I allowed a small smile to find my lips. "I recall you saying that if you ever proposed to me, it would be due to a fit of madness."

He let out a short laugh, and suddenly the room felt brighter, more airy.

"We cannot rule out the possibility," he said. "It *was* a serious injury. Perhaps this is all an invention of my muddled head. A wild dream."

"A daydream, Gates? Of me? I hadn't any idea you felt that way."

I was toying with him and he knew it. A gleam of mischief flashed in his dark eyes. He moved closer, so our joined hands met his chest and our faces were only a few inches apart. "I daresay a man is allowed to dream of his newly betrothed."

A pleasant shiver ran up my back, and my lips parted as I stared up at him. He was trying to unnerve me, clearly. We were playing a game, another in this long string of competitions between us. And yet, the way my hand pressed against the thin muslin of his shirt reminded me too much of our time in the mine. His warmth, his scent, his voice—they were all so vividly familiar to me, in a way no man's ever had been before.

I broke. I pulled my hand from his and stepped back. I expected a look of victory to cross his face, but instead his features only rearranged themselves into that careful, unconcerned expression he always wore. As if this was just another day. As if I was just another girl.

I wasn't. I was his future wife.

I tucked my hand behind me, not wanting him to see as I rubbed it with my other hand, trying to distill the lingering warmth he'd left upon my skin.

"We ought to share the news," I said briskly. "Everyone will be pleased, no doubt."

"Pleased?" he echoed. "Uncle will be beside himself. I can hear him already. 'We will both soon be married men!'" He attempted an imitation of Mr. Raines's deep, booming voice, and I smiled.

"Are you reconciled to him marrying Mrs. Penrose, then?" I asked. "Or are you still determined to break them apart?"

"I never wanted to break anyone," he said, though with less steel than he normally would have. "But I . . . yes, I am reconciled. I learned that I was wrong in my assumptions about her."

I raised an eyebrow. "You are admitting you made a mistake?"

"Not all of us have as much pride as you, Marigold." He went to where he'd thrown his jacket over an armchair. Shrugging into it, he came back to me as he buttoned his waistcoat. My eyes followed his every movement, his fingers quick and efficient over the fabric-covered buttons.

"Are you ready?"

I snapped my eyes to his, though they begged to watch as he tightened his cravat. It too easily provoked the memory of removing his cravat in the mine, my hands brushing the roughness of his jaw.

"Yes," I said too quickly.

As I followed him from the game room, a cacophony of thoughts rang through my head. But the loudest of all was also the most ridiculous.

Why, on this of all days, did I have to discover how absurdly attractive Tristan Gates was?

Chapter Twenty-Two

TRISTAN

UNCLE WAS NOT in his study when we went to find him, and a maid informed us he had gone to visit a tenant.

"Pity," Marigold said, collecting her things from the footman. "I should have liked to see his face when we told him. I daresay he'll soon like me more than you."

"He already does," I muttered.

She grinned, and my stomach did the oddest flip at the sight. "I know."

She swept past me, tying on her bonnet. I stared after her, still not sure my mind had caught up to this afternoon's events. We were engaged. *I* was engaged—to Marigold Cartwell.

I could not account for it. When she'd arrived today, my pride had still been wounded from her rejection a few days ago, and I had been resolved in my course. That is, until . . .

Until she'd spoken of her sister. Until she'd almost cried when telling me that no one had come to her practice. Marigold, crying. She always seemed to have the upper hand, but this time, she just seemed . . . alone. Frightened.

What else was a reasonably well-mannered fellow to do? I'd let her take the shot.

I'd let her take the shot, and she'd made it.

Confound it.

I followed her down the front steps. "Do you wish for me to accompany you to tell your parents?"

I hoped she would refuse me. I hadn't faced either of her parents since our rescue in the cave, and I'd wanted to continue that avoidance for as long as possible. After all, I was the man who had ruined their daughter's reputation and her future with Mr. Eastbrook. And even though our engagement was the necessary next step, they still could not be wholly pleased at the prospect of me as their son-in-law.

Marigold stopped before her carriage, her driver waiting to help her inside. She frowned, thinking. "No, I should like to speak to them on my own."

"Ah," I said, hiding my relief. "I am disappointed, to be sure. But whatever you think is best."

She cast me a despairing look. "We are not married yet, Tristan. You needn't take such a tone."

I tipped my head. "Tone?"

"It is how my papa always sounds when he is placating my mother," she said, pulling on her gloves. "The tone of a long-married couple."

"We've known each other more than a decade," I said. "We have quite the lead on most newly engaged couples."

"I do not know if our extended acquaintance is an advantage in this case," she said, setting one foot on her carriage's step.

I moved forward without thinking, and when she reached for the driver's hand, it was mine she found waiting instead. She started, and her wide eyes met mine. I helped her inside, her hand barely skimming mine, and my pulse sounded in my ears. I held her hand a moment longer than necessary. I wasn't exactly sure why. Only that I liked how she was looking at me, surprised and pleased all at once.

"Thank you," she murmured as she sat and arranged her skirts, taking her eyes from mine. "Perhaps my mother is right and there has been a gentleman hiding in you all this time."

The driver stepped forward to close the door, but I waved him off and took hold of the door myself, though I did not close it yet.

"We are engaged," I said, my voice steady and sober. How permanent that word sounded. "I intend to take such an obligation seriously."

"An obligation," she said. "How romantic."

"Romantic?" I fixed her with my gaze. "You still want romance even after what happened with—"

I stopped short as hurt flashed in her eyes.

"No," she said sharply. "I don't want romance. Good day, Mr. Gates." She leaned forward and tugged the door closed. The carriage started off, and I was left staring at the plume of dust in its wake.

I blew out a breath. Now I knew why Uncle had avoided remarrying for so long. I could not think of any compelling reason a man would willingly enter into the entrapment of marriage.

Uncle Matthew arrived home an hour after Marigold's departure. I waited in his study, and when I heard his familiar weighted steps, I stood.

He stopped in the doorway. "Tristan? What are you doing in here?"

I set my jaw. Better to have it over and done with. "Marigold came here today."

His eyes widened and he opened his mouth to speak, but I continued before he could. "She has changed her mind." I braced myself. "I proposed, and she accepted."

Uncle stared at me. "She accepted," he repeated, as if it was something he'd read in a letter.

I nodded, unable to form any more words.

"She accepted," he said once again, trying to gauge my tone. "I . . ."

I sighed. "It is all right, Uncle. You can be pleased."

He shook his head. "I cannot be pleased if you aren't."

This, I hadn't expected. Of course, Uncle was always sympathetic, but I truly thought he would be thrilled at the prospect of me marrying Marigold. She was the daughter of his oldest and closest friend, after all.

I sat again, leaning forward and clasping my hands between my knees. He found the armchair beside me. "It is not ideal," I admitted. "But I had intended to marry someday. And Marigold is not . . ." I paused. "She is not the worst prospect I could have found."

Uncle straightened, a familiar gleam coming into his eyes. "You don't say."

I shot him a shrewd look. "I am not falling in love with her, Uncle. I only meant that she has a sizable dowry and excellent connections. From an objective standpoint, she is a tolerable candidate."

"Tolerable candidate." He scoffed. "I hope you do not speak like that around her."

I winced. I'd done worse—I'd called her an obligation.

Uncle sighed, leaning forward. "Tristan, far be it from me to tell you how to manage your affairs, but perhaps I might offer some advice."

I straightened. "Of course."

His face softened. "In accepting your offer, Marigold has lost more than you can imagine. A girl like her dreams of courtship and a love match. And instead she has . . ."

"Me," I supplied.

"And you can be sure I will remind her that she is fortunate indeed," he said, ever loyal. "You are both good people trapped in a difficult situation. Perhaps there is a way to make the best of things."

"Such as?"

He smiled. "Try."

"Try what?"

"*Try*," he said again. "Try with Marigold. She deserves a courtship. She deserves flowers and poetry and carriage rides."

I frowned at him. "I am *not* writing her poetry."

He gave an indulgent laugh. "Then make her a bouquet of arrows. You know her better than most."

"Try," I repeated. Would Marigold even welcome such gestures from me? Or would it only remind her of all she'd lost? And yet I'd seen the surprise in her eyes when I'd helped her into the carriage. She hadn't imagined I could be thoughtful or . . . *romantic*.

I wasn't sure I could be either. I wasn't like Mr. Eastbrook or any of the shining gentlemen in London. But I'd liked surprising her at the carriage. Could I do it again? The challenge lit up inside me.

"You never know," Uncle said. "It cannot hurt to make an effort. At the very least, you might enter into the marriage as civil friends. At best . . ."

I knew what he was suggesting, and I sighed. No matter that Marigold made my head spin in every possible way, there would be no falling in love. There was too much between us, and in our past. But friends? Perhaps he had the right idea of it.

I cleared my throat. "I can promise to try," I warned him. "Please do not expect too much."

He held up his hands in surrender. "I would not dare to."

But I could see it in his face. He was already hoping.

I knew better. A love match between Marigold and me? It was absurd.

Absolutely absurd.

Chapter Twenty-Three

MARIGOLD

I BIT my lip as Mama embraced me, my head still whirling with the reality of what I'd told them. Papa sat silently, face an impassive mask as he looked on.

Mama did not say anything as she held me. We both already knew why I'd made my choice. When she pulled away, she touched my cheek. "He's a good man," she said quietly.

I could only nod. I knew that. And it *was* reassuring. I'd seen a variety of matches during my Season in London, and while many of them had been for love, some only married for wealth or status, for recognition or advancement. But no matter the reason, with so short an acquaintance afforded by the Season, a lady did not often know what sort of man she was really marrying. At least I knew Tristan, whatever that counted for.

Mama smiled then. "We shall have a lovely time gathering your trousseau, I think. And you'll need a dress for the wedding. I ought to write Madame Lavigne now and inform her."

I could not help a smile myself. Mama loved a party, and she was a master of organization. I was glad to give her that, even if I could not give her the image of a beaming, blushing bride.

She patted my cheek then went to the writing desk in the

corner, no doubt to begin her preparations. Papa stood and approached me slowly.

"You know I've never much liked Gates," he said, his voice low so Mama could not hear.

"That makes two of us," I said, attempting a light tone.

He shook his head. "I know this is the proper thing, but if you do not wish to go through with this, we would understand, Mari. You know we will stand by you."

"I do know." It was comforting, in a strange way. But I would not ask it of him, or Mama or Oliver or Iris or Hawthorne. I had to be resolved in my course or I would go mad imagining the possibilities.

"He *did* save you from the cave-in," Papa said resignedly. "Showed some fortitude. I suppose that is a point in his favor."

"I am sure he will be interested to hear of this point system," I teased. "You ought to tell him of it at our next dinner."

He chuckled, leaning forward to press a quick kiss to my brow. "Do not tempt me."

I retreated to my room soon after. It was exhausting, pretending that I was perfectly fine. Pretending that I had any control over my life. Because in reality, I was drained and afraid and overwhelmed. Had I made the right choice?

I could not doubt myself. Doing so would only add to my torment. I simply needed to forge ahead and do my best.

I sat on the window seat that overlooked the formal garden, flowers in full bloom and topiaries carefully trimmed back. If I hadn't just given Mama a wedding to plan, she would no doubt be bustling around below me, weeding and watering her prized blossoms. It was a lovely view, but my eyes did not see it, wandering instead to the north where Stavely Hall resided beyond the pond and the wooded hills.

Tristan's face danced in my memory, from when he'd helped me into the carriage. I certainly hadn't expected such a gesture. But then, he hadn't been raised in the wilds. He knew how to behave, even if he generally refused to.

A knock came at my door—a familiar four taps.

"Come," I called.

Oliver's head poked in. "Mari, what is this I hear about you marrying Gates? Mama swears it is true, but I cannot believe it."

I gave a wry smile. "There are so many rumors about me, it is difficult to know what to believe."

"Mari," he warned, coming to lean his shoulder on the window frame.

I gave a resigned sigh. "It is true."

He gaped. "But you hate him."

"I also hate fish, but Mama insists it is an acquired taste," I said. "Perhaps Tristan will be the same."

"Do not jest, not now."

I closed my eyes and leaned my head back. "Ollie, I am tired of having to convince everyone, especially myself, that this is a good idea. Please, let it be."

He was quiet, then the cushions shifted as he sat beside me. "I am sorry," he said. "I am sorry for everything."

That, more than anything, made me want to cry. Oliver was rarely anything but lively and teasing, never taking life seriously if he could help it. But now his lips twisted to one side as he stared out the window, his jaw tight.

"It is not your fault," I said quietly.

He gave a dry laugh. "I was the one who introduced you to Eastbrook."

"That is true," I said, as if just realizing. "In that case, you are entirely to blame. I feel much better."

He returned my grin, but neither of our smiles lasted long. He dropped his gaze, scuffing his boot along the floor.

"I am sorry about Sylvia," he said.

I sighed. "That is also not your fault."

"No," he said. "But I thought I knew her better than that."

"So did I." My heart clenched.

We sat in silence for a long moment, then he shook his head. "Tristan Gates," he repeated. "I would never have imagined."

"Believe me when I say I have considered all the options."

Oliver looked at me, his eyes more sober than I had ever seen them. "What if Eastbrook hadn't left? If you had the choice, right now, between him and Gates . . ."

If anyone but my brother had asked me, I would have waved off the question. But I did not. I considered it seriously. I'd fancied myself in love with Mr. Eastbrook. Well, perhaps not *in love*, but well on my way. There had been little doubt in my mind that we would have had an excellent life together. He was everything I'd wanted in a husband: handsome, charming, established.

But Tristan . . . Tristan was infinitely more complicated. So contrary and always determined to prove himself right. He did not have a romantic bone in his body, evidenced by his comments today after he'd helped me into the carriage. He'd been in disbelief, as if wishing for romance was akin to wishing for a pot of gold.

I sighed. I was being unfair. He *did* have good qualities, difficult as they were to see sometimes. He had saved me in the cave. He'd done the honorable thing and proposed, even after I'd treated him poorly.

But if I had a choice?

"Mr. Eastbrook was everything I had wanted in a husband," I said quietly. "But I cannot waste time pining for a man who does not want *me*."

Oliver did not push me further. He sat beside me for a time as we stared out the window together, and I was glad, for once, for silence.

I allowed myself the rest of the evening to mope, but by the next morning, I was already planning my next move. I was engaged, and now I had to ensure that everyone in Sandcliffe knew it. Word would spread quickly, of course, but I needed a wildfire of gossip if I was to save my society. The members had to know I was engaged, that I was soon to be married, and that it was perfectly proper to attend my society practices once again. But how?

The answer came at breakfast, when Mama mentioned the upcoming public assembly in two days' time. I straightened, latching onto her words. Of course! A public assembly. Tristan and I could attend together. Everyone would see us, and everyone would know what I needed them to know.

The problem was, Tristan detested balls. His appearance at the Halford's ball a few weeks ago had been as rare a sighting as a comet. But I needed him. Had he meant what he'd said, about taking our engagement seriously? Well, *he'd* used the word "obligation," but I tried not to think of that.

After breakfast, I penned a note.

My dear Mr. Gates,

I knew that would irritate him, which made me smirk.

Now that we are engaged, I hope you will forgo your usual avoidance of anything diverting or enjoyable and accompany me to the upcoming public assembly. We shall need to show a united front if we are to withstand the worst of the rumors.

Your affianced,
Marigold Cartwell

I sent the note and received his response only an hour later as I practiced the pianoforte. Surprised, I unfolded the paper.

Miss Cartwell,

Must I?

T. Gates

I smiled, the smallest tugging of my lips. I could just see him writing it, sighing dramatically as he envisioned an evening of torturous dancing and twittering gossips.

Mr. Gates,

I promise I shan't abandon you to Miss Kingsley. If you would be so kind as to inform me of the colors of your outfit, I shall dress to match so we may look the part of a perfectly happy couple.

Most truly,
Marigold Cartwell

His response, even quicker this time.

Miss Cartwell,

I always look perfectly happy, so it will appear most natural, I think. If I agree to come, then you must promise me your first set and the supper set. There is little point in dancing with anyone else.

T. Gates

Then, in a post script so small I had to squint to read it:

I will wear blue.

I lowered the note, curiosity uncurling inside me. Blue was my favorite color, and I was certain he knew it. It was the color I used to paint my initials on my arrows. Was that why he'd chosen it?

No, I told myself. Tristan Gates would never have such a sentimental thought. He was too pragmatic to entertain that sort of triviality.

But still I folded the note carefully, stacking it with the first, and tucked them into the drawer of my writing desk. It was as close to a love letter as I was ever to get.

When the evening of the assembly came, I dressed with care. This was not a night to fade into the background. I needed everyone's eyes on me. I wore my sky-blue muslin, the one with a flounced lace hemline. A diamond pendant hung at my neck, matching bobs in my ears, and a white feather billowed from the top of my intricately braided coiffure. I looked in the mirror, feeling the burst of confidence that came when I felt particularly well put together. I would need that confidence tonight when I faced all of Sandcliffe's high society.

Including Sylvia.

I had yet to see anything of my friend. But she would be there tonight—she had to be. Sylvia never missed a ball, and I was determined to speak with her. I wanted to know, from her own mouth, why she had not come to my practice.

I pulled on my gloves, hesitating a moment as my eyes caught on the thin pink line of my still-healing cut. For half a second, I hated the sight of it, marring the smooth skin of my forearm. But then I set my jaw. That scar meant I had survived. That I had people who loved me enough to dig through the night to reach me. I decided right then that every time I noticed my scar, I would say a prayer of gratitude for each and every blessing that I had.

When I descended the staircase, Mama, Papa, and Oliver waited for me. To my surprise, Mr. Raines also stood near the front door.

"A vision, Miss Cartwell," Mr. Raines declared. "You shall break every man's heart tonight when they learn you are taken."

"I am quite sure most already know," I said drolly as I stepped to the marble floor.

"It will be a relief to me," Oliver said. "I shall finally have a respite from all the gentlemen wishing to get to you through me. It has been an exhausting task over the last two years."

I shot him a mock glare, then turned back to Mr. Raines. "Where is Tristan? I thought we planned to meet at the assembly rooms."

He nodded toward the front door. "He is outside. He thought that arriving together might provide a stronger entrance."

Hmm. He was right. I should have thought of it myself.

"Well, shall we?" I said. "We don't want to be late because Oliver spent too much time on his toilette."

I led the way out the front door, followed by Oliver's protests and Mama's laughter. Tristan sat on the stone steps, black hat in his hands as he gazed off towards the lowering sun, the sky a swath of red and gold. When he heard us coming, he hurried to don his hat and find his feet, brushing his breeches as he turned to face us. As promised, he wore a dark blue waistcoat with his dark jacket. No bandage was wrapped about his head tonight, which I hoped meant his injury was healing well.

He froze when he saw me, face blank as his gaze traveled the length of me, then jumped back to meet my eyes.

"Good evening, Mr. Gates," I said pointedly.

He blinked as if to clear a fog, then looked away, hands tugging at his jacket. "Miss Cartwell," he said, his voice gruff.

Was it because he liked how I looked, or the opposite? I sighed. Mr. Eastbrook would have offered the perfect compliment.

No. I took myself firmly in hand. That was a dangerous thought. Mr. Eastbrook was not here, and there was no use comparing.

"Now," Mr. Raines said, clapping his hands once. "How shall we divide up?"

Two coaches waited in the rounded drive, Mr. Raines's and

ours. There were six of us, and it made sense to divide equally. But I saw my chance.

"If I may be so bold to request it," I said, "I had hoped to ride with Mr. Gates alone."

Tristan stiffened, though he did not look at me.

"There is something I wished to discuss with him," I said sweetly. "Assuming such an arrangement is agreeable."

I could see the consternation on everyone's faces. Technically, Tristan and I were engaged. But I knew I wasn't the only one who struggled to comprehend that this was *real*. The instinct to demand a chaperone was fighting on Mama's face, and Papa simply looked baffled.

Mr. Raines, however, laughed. "Of course," he said. "Let the young couple have their time together."

Tristan shot his uncle a glare, though I could not say if it was in response to his abandonment or to the insinuation in his words.

Mama sighed. "Very well. I suppose nothing worse can come of it."

The four of them headed to Papa's coach, and I turned to Tristan. He sent me a wary look. "Have I done something wrong? Are you planning to scold me in private?"

"Of course," I said, moving to the coach. "What is marriage if not a series of lectures?"

"To love and to lecture," he muttered as he followed me.

He helped me inside, and I made certain not to breathe as he did so. I did not want his scent in my head, muddling my thoughts.

It was a foolish plan, because as soon as he entered, he sat right beside me on the forward-facing bench. I couldn't very well hold my breath for the entire three-mile drive into town.

Tristan knocked on the ceiling and the coach started forward. Then he turned to face me, so close I could see the fine, dark lashes of his eyes in the fading sunlight.

"Well?" he asked.

I cleared my throat. Focus. "I thought we might discuss how we intend to act tonight."

He raised an eyebrow. "I intend to act as I always have."

"Like you have better things you could be doing with your time?"

"Precisely."

My lips twitched. "Perhaps you might relinquish your superior glare for one night."

"Why?"

I hesitated. This was a bit awkward. "My main purpose tonight is to convince everyone, the ladies especially, that we fully intend to marry. If we can do that, then perhaps my archery society might have a chance to survive."

"Of course we intend to marry." Tristan sent me a blank look. "Why should tonight make any difference?"

I coughed. "I'd hoped that we could be . . . convincing."

His expression did not change for a long moment, then he tilted his head, regarding me curiously. "You want us to pretend this is a love match."

"No, not a love match," I hurried to say. "Only, I expect people will find it difficult to trust our engagement if we argue and scowl."

"Should you like me to flutter my eyelashes like a love-sick milkmaid?"

"No," I said with a sigh of long-suffering. "I daresay that would be a bit obvious. But perhaps if we can come across as satisfied? Content in our lot? I think that might be enough."

Tristan did not look away, and his gaze sharpened. "This is important to you."

Not a question, but a statement of fact.

"Yes," I said simply.

He nodded. "Very well. I shall play the besotted husband-to-be."

I fought a smile. "You need not be besotted."

"Oh?" he said. "I suppose there is no use for this flower, then."

To my utter surprise, he bent and produced a white rose from beneath the bench. A blue velvet ribbon trailed from the stem. My mouth dropped.

He'd brought me a flower.

"A pity," he said, twirling the stem in his hand. "I asked the gardener for the finest blossom in the garden. But I shall tell him you did not want it."

I'd received bouquets before, towering displays of wealth and elegance. Mr. Eastbrook especially had been fond of sending me marigolds after we spent an evening together in London, though they'd never been a particular favorite of mine, oddly enough.

But there was something in this gesture, this simple rose. Perhaps it was the realization that he'd gone to the garden with the express purpose of getting it for me. Or perhaps it was the blue ribbon, tied just so beneath the spreading petals. Blue again. He had to mean something by it.

"No." The word escaped me in a breathless rush. "No, I want it."

His eyes met mine, reflecting the vibrancy of the setting sun. He handed the rose to me, and I took it. No thorns pricked my skin— he'd gone to the trouble of removing them all.

"Thank you," I said softly.

He cleared his throat. "You are welcome."

Silence reigned for a long minute, though it was a quiet filled with meaning. I could not recall ever having such a conversation with Tristan. Had we ever spoken without quarrelling? I cast him a sidelong glance. He was stealing a glance at me. We both looked away quickly, though my skin heated like I had a warming brick at my feet.

"So," he said, shifting his weight. "Your society. Do you think you can train them up in time for the prize shoot? It is only a few weeks away."

"Is it?" I said indifferently. "I was unaware."

His lips pressed together as if fighting a smile.

"But yes," I said. "Provided we can put on a good show tonight, I am hopeful to resume practices in a timely manner."

"Shall the ladies prove competitive?" he asked. "I imagine it is disheartening shooting against you at every practice."

I peered at him. "Is your head still hurting?"

He blinked. "My head?"

"Yes," I said. "First, you bring me flowers, and now you are complimenting me. I can only assume your injury is the cause."

"I brought you *one* flower," he defended. "And it wasn't a compliment. It was simply an observation."

"A complimentary one."

He blew out a breath of exasperation. "I was only trying to—" But he stopped.

"Trying to what?" I asked curiously.

"Nothing," he said, his voice short. "Let us return to the subject at hand."

I eyed him but decided not to press further. "My ladies will be ready. You needn't worry." I paused. "Well, that is not precisely true. You do need to worry, since you will be shooting against me at the tournament."

"It has never worried me before."

"Save for two years ago?"

He crossed his arms. As much as he'd bragged about his victory last year, I'd certainly boasted equally so the year previous. "Two years is a long time to have gone without a victory."

"Because we only compete once a year," I pointed out. "Otherwise our lists of victories would look quite different."

"Perhaps."

The corner of his mouth drew up, and I found myself utterly distracted. I'd noticed a great deal about Tristan lately—his lean, strong figure, the defining cut of his jaw—but this was the first time I'd focused on his lips. They were . . . fascinating. His eyes and his stony expressions always hid most of his emotions, but his lips were a different matter. They betrayed him, his humor or anger, and I found myself wondering what sort of other things they could do.

I came to myself, my cheeks prickling with heat, and tore my eyes from him. Had he noticed my preoccupation? I was an absolute ninny, staring at him like that.

"Still," I said, forcing my gaze straight ahead. "You will likely wish to practice more in the coming weeks. Your luck can only hold for so long."

"Luck?" Now he laughed, and there was something in the sound of it. A lightness I'd never heard from him. "I suppose you mean my natural talent and skill."

"You are stronger, that is all."

"You've been admiring my figure as I shoot, have you?"

"Ha," I said haughtily, fighting a blush. "I am too busy practicing because I actually have to work for what I want."

His smirk vanished. "What?"

"Yes," I said firmly. "You have an unfair advantage, but I will not let it deter me."

He made a sound but not a laugh. A laugh was not so dark. "No. I meant, do you think you are the only person who has to work for what you want?"

I was taken aback. "No, not at all."

"And yet, you said it."

"I—" I shook my head. "You are twisting my words."

"No, I heard you quite clearly," he said. "Never mind that not everyone has the time or opportunity to devote themselves obsessively to a simple game of sport. But heaven forbid anything stop Marigold Cartwell from getting what she wants."

Anger lanced through me, followed closely by hurt.

"You are one to speak," I snapped, "living the pampered life of a gentleman."

"Hardly," he said. "I've supported myself since I left Oxford."

His response surprised me so much, I only stared, unable to respond. I'd always assumed Tristan lived off an allowance from Mr. Raines.

It was at that opportune time—or inopportune, I could not say —that we arrived at the assembly rooms. Our coach jolted to a stop before the wide and well-lit doors, and the footman who had accompanied us lowered the steps and opened the door.

We sat without moving, then Tristan exhaled and descended the steps. He held out his hand to me, his fingers flat and uninviting.

I did not want to go. I'd been full of purpose earlier, determined to face my troubles and vanquish them. But how was I to vanquish the man I was to marry? Why had I thought anything could change between us? No, Tristan would always be cynical and hard, a rock with rough edges and broken points.

But even if there was no chance of love between us, the reality was that we would be married. And I could not face a marriage of constant quarrels and bitterness. I could not.

"Marigold," he hissed, glancing to his left. "There are carriages behind us."

I did not move. No doubt he thought me dramatic and obstinate, but I was not waiting in order to provoke him. No, I simply had to decide. I had to decide if I was angry or not.

I looked at him, trying to read behind the wall in his eyes. Why had he reacted the way he had? There was more to his words.

How I wished we could be like Mama and Papa. They did not always agree on everything, of course. But it was how they disagreed that made the difference. They sought to understand one another's perspective from a point of love, and from there compromise inevitably came.

But the trouble was, Tristan and I did not love each other. We did not even like each other most days. How would I find the patience and desire to understand him?

At present, it was not difficult to see what he wanted. He glanced again at the line of carriages waiting behind us, lips dipping into that familiar scowl as he held his hand closer to me.

I looked down at the white rose still in my hands. Though he might deny it, I knew it was a symbol of *something*. Perhaps a small, barely-there hope for the future.

I had to have hope as well.

I placed the rose on the seat of the coach and slipped my hand into his.

Chapter Twenty-Four

TRISTAN

MARIGOLD FINALLY GAVE me her hand, and I wasted no time in tugging her from the coach and shutting the door behind her. Heads were peering out of the coaches waiting in line, all wondering what the delay was.

Just Marigold Cartwell, I thought. Proving yet again why this engagement was doomed from the start.

I led her to stand beside the open door to wait for the rest of our party. I said nothing, only stared into the darkening sky, my lips pressed together.

Marigold did not speak either. I resisted the urge to look at her, to guess what was in her mind. No doubt she was angry. She did not like to hear hard truths, and my words had been hard.

Too hard.

I shook that off. It was nothing I hadn't thought a thousand times.

The other coach pulled forward as ours departed. Mr. and Mrs. Cartwell smiled at each other as he helped her descend the steps. How did they attain such easy happiness? Nothing about Marigold was easy.

"Shall we?" Uncle said, coming even with us. He raised an eyebrow, as if to ask how our ride had been. I nodded without expression. His mouth dipped into a frown, and he shot Marigold a curious glance. But she forced a smile and pulled on my arm to follow after her parents into the assembly hall.

The dancing had yet to start, but couples milled about the parquet dance floor as the musicians tuned their instruments, a harsh discord that drilled into my head. As we entered, heads turned and whispers flew like arrows. I set my jaw. I hated any sort of attention, let alone being the center of a scandal.

Marigold's expression remained smooth and pleasant, as if this were any other ball. But she clutched my arm tightly, and her steps held the slightest hesitation. Had this been a good idea? Facing Society all at once now seemed inexorably stupid.

The first dance was called, and the crowd turned away from us. Dancing with Marigold was the last thing in the world I wished to do, but I was a man of my word. I began leading her to the dance floor.

She stopped, holding me back. "Tristan, wait."

"What is it?"

She looked up at me. "I don't want to dance."

I nearly groaned. "Was this not the purpose of coming? To make a show for everyone?"

"It was." She swallowed hard. "But there are more important things."

"Such as?"

There was a new hesitancy in her eyes, which made me turn towards her. Marigold was not a hesitant person. She plunged full ahead with everything in her life. Why was she wavering now?

She took a long, deep breath, then met my eyes, her chin strong. "We are to be married, Tristan," she said softly.

"I am quite aware." I spoke in a stiff, clipped tone.

"And I do not want to dance," she said, "until we learn to *talk*."

I examined her face, looking for any sign she was not sincere. But she met my inspection with a willful gaze, not caring that everyone around us still watched and whispered.

I did not care either. I never had. But Marigold did. And the fact that she ignored them, and that she was refusing to dance when it was fully expected of us . . .

"All right," I said, and my voice held a hoarseness that I hadn't anticipated. "Come with me."

I took her hand and led her up a set of stairs to the balcony that overlooked the dance floor. It was perfectly proper, since we were still in view of the entire hall, but it afforded us some privacy from the listening ears.

On the balcony, Marigold took her hand from mine and leaned her elbows on the railing, looking down on the dancers who now dipped and wove in time to the music. I stood beside her as my pulse tripped along. I hated not knowing what this conversation would hold.

"What you said in the coach," she said, not looking at me. "Is that truly your opinion of me? That I am spoiled and always get what I want?"

She spoke in an even tone, trying to hide her emotions, but I heard the layer of hurt hidden in her words. Guilt pooled inside me. I'd known when I'd spoken that I was being too cruel. And this coming after I'd already accused her of vanity while trapped in the cave.

I hesitated, but there was no use denying it. I'd said it. "Sometimes."

She nodded, having expected my answer. "I see. And what do you think the other times?"

I considered that. I had to be truthful. She would see right through me otherwise. "You care too much what others think of you. You enjoy attention, for reasons I cannot begin to comprehend. You are stubborn and overconfident."

"Is that all?" she said with a tight laugh.

But I wasn't finished. I leaned on the banister beside her, our arms nearly touching.

"You are determined," I said softly, my voice just barely audible above the strains of the violins. "You are talented. You love more fully and deeply than I can ever imagine. It terrifies me, in fact. I don't think I've ever loved anyone the way you love."

I hadn't any idea where this was coming from. I'd never allowed such thoughts to evolve fully in my head, but that did not make them feel any less true in this moment. I'd watched Marigold with her family for years. There was nothing she would not do for any of them. Her love and passion drove every one of her actions, including marrying me. I knew she would do that and more to save her sister's future.

Marigold stood still, head bent downward as she listened. "Do you mean that?" she whispered.

I exhaled. "I do." I shook my head. "I am sorry, Marigold. I should not have said those things in the coach."

"Why did you?"

"I . . ." I stopped, then rubbed the back of my neck. "Do you remember when we met?"

She scrunched her lips to one side. "Vaguely. I was only seven. I do recall my parents telling me to be kind, since you were mourning."

"Uncle brought me to Crossdale to meet your whole family," I said. "You were . . . awful."

She pulled back. "I was not!"

"You were," I said, fighting a smile. "You insisted on taking me for a tour of the house and spoke without ceasing for nearly an hour. You plied me with questions."

Her eyes held a gleam of amusement. "Only because you refused to say *anything*. You were so terribly sullen and rude."

"I was," I admitted. "I did not want to be there. In fact, the last thing I wanted then was to have such a bright, happy family paraded before me."

Her face softened. "Oh."

It was unnerving, speaking of such things here at this glittering ball, with a hundred people watching us. I cleared my throat, turning and leaning my lower back on the banister. This way I did not have to see the sly eyes peering up at us.

"Is that why you acted as you did?" she asked. "I thought I was being welcoming, but you seemed to hate me."

"I did not deliberately choose to hate you," I said, crossing my arms. "All I know is that as a ten-year-old boy, I thought you were haughty and frivolous, and I've never tried to change my own mind."

"Until we were trapped together in a mine," she said. "And an engagement."

"Yes." I twisted my lips. "I am sorry for it."

She sighed. "It is not as though I have been entirely innocent. A feud always has two sides. I knew you did not like me, and no one had ever disliked me before. Part of being spoiled, I suppose."

I grimaced at her word choice, once again feeling the prick of guilt as she went on. "Perhaps you did not make a deliberate choice, but I did. I decided I would dislike you even more than you disliked me. I told myself you were just a cold-hearted nuisance. It was the only way I could make sense of your behavior."

"I haven't much changed since then," I said.

I felt a soft brush on my arm. Marigold had moved closer so that our shoulders touched. I stopped breathing, not daring to look at her. We faced opposite directions, but that bare connection between us sent a charged energy through my body.

I'd never felt anything like it before.

"You've changed more than you think," she said. "The Tristan from twelve years ago would never have given me a flower."

I was so distracted by her warmth next to me, by the way one of her golden locks curled down her slender neck, that it took me a moment to respond.

"He might've," I managed. "But there would have been a spider in it."

She laughed, and my chest flared with heat.

"Indeed." She looked up at me then, those blue eyes glittering in the candlelight. "Why can we not go one day without bickering?"

I shrugged. "We both hate to be wrong. It is understandable."

"But is it fixable?" She turned, leaning on one elbow to face me.

"You said you take our engagement seriously, Tristan. I want to as well. Perhaps it is time to stop assuming the worst and instead try to see each other for who we are, rather than who we *think* the other is."

I mulled that over. She was right. Both of us so often jumped to conclusions, always wanting to be one step ahead.

"I imagine it will take some practice," I said. "A decade of bad habits will be hard to break. But . . ." I paused.

"But . . . ?" she prompted.

"But I don't want to quarrel either," I admitted. "We had little choice in this engagement. But we can choose how we continue in it."

Marigold bit her lip, and my eyes sank to where her white teeth nipped the pink softness. I swallowed hard, and tried to focus my attention anywhere else.

"Let us declare another truce," she said. "But a permanent one, instead of one for survival."

"I would argue that this is simply a survival of a different sort."

"True enough." She cast a glance over the dancing below. "I daresay bets are already being placed as to whether or not we even make it to the altar."

"Well," I said, leaning forward until our faces were only inches apart. "If there is something we both cannot resist, it is a challenge."

Her perfectly rounded lips curled up. "Indeed."

We stood so close that I could see the smallest of freckles near her left eye, could feel the warmth that seemed to emanate from her skin. She smelled like a garden after a rain.

"We shall be allies, then," she said, a bit breathless. Or perhaps I was imagining things. "It will be us against them."

"Save for on the archery range."

She smiled again, and to my surprise there was no malice or edge to it. It was the smile she gave everyone else, the smile she'd withheld from me as long as I'd known her.

"Well, of course," she said. "We must keep things interesting, after all. What would we be without a little competition?"

"Normal?"

Marigold exhaled a laugh. "Boring, I think." She pushed away from the railing. "Now then, I believe you promised me a dance."

She took my arm, so naturally one would think we'd done this dozens of times. Awareness swept up my arm as her gloved fingers curled around my forearm. I had to look away from her, from her dazzling smile and bright-blue eyes. It was too much, like staring into the sun. And the sun burned, I tried to remind myself. She'd burned me before, countless times.

But I knew this time was different. *We* were different. Anything was possible.

The thought was electrifying—and terrifying.

Chapter Twenty-Five

MARIGOLD

THE DANCE PASSED in a blur of music and faces. I tried to ignore all the curious glances while also remembering the steps of the dance, smiling as if I was perfectly content.

Surprisingly, that last task was not as hard as I thought it would be.

I glanced at Tristan across the line of dancers as we waited for our turn. He was watching me already and offered a small smile. I'd never spoken with him like we had on the balcony. We had been honest with each other, almost painfully so. His words had struck a dissonant chord within me, and though I'd felt truth in them, it certainly wasn't pleasant.

But somehow knowing what he had thought made it easier to disassociate myself from that girl. She was who I used to be. Before the scandal. Before Tristan.

Now I had a chance. We both did. We could start over, be the better version of ourselves. We'd promised to try and to trust, and I had to do my part.

When he took my hand to lead me through the movements of the dance, there was a new vitality between us. Tristan wasn't an accomplished dancer, not like many of the gentlemen with whom I'd partnered during the Season. But it did not matter. My emotions were still flowing strong from the raw, real words that had stretched between us, and every touch of his hand and brush of his eyes sent a stirring through my bones.

Mr. Eastbrook had made me feel warm and giggly, a girl in the first blush of love. But this feeling was stronger, deeper—and more complicated. Which was not at all surprising, considering the mercurial nature of my relationship with Tristan. No doubt these feelings were simply a natural reaction to the strain of the past few weeks.

When the dance ended, I curtsied to Tristan, who bowed in return. We remained facing each other as the other dancers applauded and moved from the floor, my heart skipping a beat.

Then he extended his arm. I took it, and the spell was broken.

"Are you ready?" I asked as he led me to the outskirts of the room. "We must convince an entire ballroom that we are perfectly proper, and we have only a few hours in which to do it."

He sighed. "I am at your service. Should you like me to flirt and shower you with compliments?"

"Well, we cannot appear *too* happy with the engagement," I said. "Else everyone will believe something actually did happen in the cave."

"What sort of something?" His lips twitched.

He thought to make me blush. I raised my chin. "Something decidedly less innocent than holding hands."

"Yet I recall a bit more than holding hands."

Memories lit up my mind like a lantern in the dark—his strong arm curled around me, pulling me close for warmth, my hand against the smooth skin near his open neckline.

So much for not blushing. My cheeks tingled, no doubt bright red. "Quiet. Someone will hear and then this charade will be pointless."

"Very well," he said with a sigh of long-suffering, even as his eyes danced. I turned away with a smile.

A smile that vanished as soon as I met the eyes of Lord Beauford, shining darkly from across the assembly hall. He watched me through narrowed slits, holding a glass of what I suspected was not the lemonade being served at the refreshment table. A baron could do whatever he pleased.

Though he did not look pleased now, as his gaze flitted to Tristan beside me and his scowl deepened. I could easily guess why. Tristan was in *his* archery society. He was the baron's ace, and now he was betrothed to me. That could not sit well with Lord Beauford, but it sent a surge of audacity through me.

I tightened my hold on Tristan's arm and sent Lord Beauford a superior nod. He only threw back his drink and strode off without another glance.

"Your mother wants us," Tristan said, apparently not seeing my interaction with the baron.

I followed his gaze to where Mama stood beside Mrs. Atherton, waving us towards them. Cora was just behind her mother, eyes wide. I'd written to her of my engagement to Tristan, of course, though I could not be certain the letter had made it to her. I would not put it past Mrs. Atherton to confiscate a letter from me, ruined woman that I was.

I understood Mama's intent immediately. If we could convince Mrs. Atherton that I should be forgiven of my scandal, then many would hurry to follow her example. And I would hopefully have my friend back.

"Prepare yourself," I warned Tristan.

He narrowed his eyes. "I'm not afraid of a society matron."

"Silly, silly man," I said with a sigh as I led him over.

"There you two are." Mama greeted us with an overly cheerful voice. "I was just telling Mrs. Atherton about your wedding plans."

"Indeed," Mrs. Atherton said, eyes like a hawk. "Three weeks away, is it?"

Mama was already in the thick of planning, though I was only vaguely aware of the date: the Sunday following the Lady Patroness's Meeting. The two events loomed in my future like dark clouds. They could either storm and rain and rage, or they could dissolve into a beautiful summer day. I was almost afraid to hope for the latter.

"Yes," I managed. "We are both looking forward to it."

My left arm was already looped through Tristan's, and I laid my right hand along his forearm in a somewhat possessive manner. He tensed, glancing at me for a half second before looking away. My heart ticked a little faster.

"Oh?" Mrs. Atherton watched us with skeptical eyes. "It is rather soon. I had not imagined you would be so eager a bride, considering . . ."

I cleared my throat. "We are quite resolved. There is no reason to delay, I think."

"Quite right," Mrs. Atherton said, taking a sip of her lemonade. "Better to have it decided and done with." She fixed her eyes on Tristan. "You must be pleased. To emerge from such a . . . such a *situation* with a wife like Miss Cartwell."

Never mind that I had refused him initially, or that I had begged him to propose the second time. I glanced at him from beneath my lashes. What would he say?

Tristan offered a smile, restrained and cool. "Pleased as punch."

I tried not to frown. I'd told him not to shower me with compliments, but a little enthusiasm would not go amiss.

Mrs. Atherton nodded, her eyes squinted as she decided our fate. Cora stood nervously beside her mother, having said nothing during the conversation. It was unlike her, but given Cora's tendency to blurt out her thoughts, she also knew that staying quiet was for the best.

"Hmm," Mrs. Atherton said. "Well, I am glad to see you both seem set on your course."

"Indeed, we are," I said.

"Good." She turned to Mama. "Do let me know if you need any referrals for her trousseau. It shall be needed in a timely manner, no doubt, and you might require multiple modistes to complete it."

She droned on, but I did not listen. My heart lifted. It wasn't done, not yet, but for once, it seemed like I was on the correct road.

Cora grinned at me, then tipped her head away from the group. I slipped my arm from Tristan's, and he snapped his eyes to mine. I nodded at Cora, and he relaxed as I moved to stand beside her. I needed a moment with my friend.

"I shall be at the next practice," Cora whispered, taking my arm. "You can depend upon it."

"I already depend on you far too much," I said. "But thank you." I squeezed her arm.

She glanced again at Tristan. "Heavens, Mari, I cannot convince my mind to accept it. You are engaged to *Tristan Gates*."

"Am I?" I said wryly. "I hadn't noticed."

She sent me a reproachful look. "You'll notice in three weeks, I'll wager."

My stomach took a tumble. Three weeks, and I'd be married.

"Yes, well, it is your fault," I said quickly. "I was so lonely in your absence, I would have accepted anyone."

That made her laugh, though she shook her head. "Nothing like scandal and desperation to start an engagement." She sobered again. "How are you really?"

I pressed my lips together, turning to watch the dancing. "I'm all right," I said quietly. "Better than I might have imagined a few days ago."

"I am glad," she said sincerely. "I want only happiness for you, Mari."

I squeezed her hand but could not manage a response. It was what everyone kept saying, that they hoped we could find happiness. Perhaps if enough people collectively hoped for something, it might come to pass.

"Have you spoken to Sylvia yet?" Cora asked, voice soft.

The world tilted slightly. What with my conversation with Tristan, and our dance, then Mrs. Atherton, I had quite forgotten about Sylvia.

"No," I said. "I haven't seen her tonight, and neither has she come to visit me."

Cora sighed. "I tried to see her yesterday, but she was not at home. Or, at least, that is what her footman told me."

"Cora, dear," Mrs. Atherton called out, apparently finished conversing with Mama. "Come with me."

Cora sent me a resigned smile. "We'll speak more soon," she said, and followed after her mother.

I rejoined Mama and Tristan. "Do you think we succeeded?" I asked her.

"Oh yes," she said, eyes alive. "You did wonderfully, my dear. You've a deft hand."

She winked and moved off to join Mrs. Vale, another member of the ladies' society, no doubt to spread the word of Mrs. Atherton's approval.

"She's right," Tristan said. "You managed that well."

I looked up at Tristan, surprised. He kept his face impassive, but there was a touch of something new in his eyes. Respect.

"Sometimes restraint is the best course." I did not think I would grow used to Tristan complimenting me.

He gave a half smile. "Not a strong suit of mine."

"It needn't be," I said, "now that we are working together."

"An excellent point. I shall stop trying altogether."

I laughed, and he smiled fully. A group of ladies to our right took notice of our interaction, turning to each other to whisper. My smile faded. Did we look as if we were enjoying each other's company too much? That could lead to more rumors, which was precisely what I was trying to avoid.

The problem was, Tristan was not terribly difficult to be around when we weren't picking each other apart. And when he smiled like that, like he enjoyed my company too, it seemed laughable that I'd gone so many years without noticing how attractive he was. He was so handsome, I had to remind myself to breathe.

I forced my eyes from him and my gaze immediately caught on someone else: Sylvia. She stood across the room, her beaded dress glittering in the candlelight, a beautiful, rich red. But she wasn't dancing, simply watching the crowd with a frown. I'd never seen Sylvia without a partner at a ball.

She looked my way and froze, staring at me. I stared back, my stomach a block of ice. What would she do?

Sylvia broke our gaze, turning away and moving towards the open door. A sudden burst of determination claimed me. Did she think she could avoid me forever? I looked up at Tristan. "I'll return in a few minutes."

He frowned. "Where are you going? Miss Kingsley is already circling."

I grinned. "You're an engaged man now. Use that to drive her away."

"I do not think she will care," he grumbled but let me go. I hurried after Sylvia, who had already disappeared through the door. I reached the corridor, lit by sconces along the walls. The retiring room was around the next corner. If I could catch her alone, perhaps we could have a real conversation about what had happened. Perhaps she did have a reason for not coming to the practice.

I was about to turn the corner when I heard voices. Voices I knew. I stopped.

"Oliver, what are you doing here?" That was Sylvia's silken tones.

"Since you've been avoiding me, this was the only way to speak with you." Oliver's voice was hard.

Sylvia had been avoiding Oliver as well?

"I've been terribly occupied lately," she said. "I am sorry for it. Perhaps next week, we might—"

"I think we can speak plainly," Oliver said. "You haven't been busy. You've been afraid."

"Afraid?" She laughed nervously. "Afraid of what?"

"Of Society," he responded. "Of doing what's right."

Sylvia said nothing, and I could only imagine her face. Oliver rarely spoke like this, so severely, and never to her.

"Marigold needed you," he said. "She needed you and you abandoned her."

"No," she protested. "That is, of course I wanted to come to the practice. But you must understand how it would affect—"

"I do understand," he said. "I understand that keeping the high opinion of others is more important to you than loyalty to your friend."

She sniffed. "You are being ridiculous. It was just one practice."

"Then why haven't you come to see her?" he asked. "Why haven't you spoken to her tonight?"

Two excellent questions, in my opinion. I craned my ear closer to hear her answer.

A long beat of silence. "What would you have me do, Oliver? Destroy my reputation along with hers?"

"I would have you be the person I thought you were," he said with an edge of sadness.

"Do not pretend such self-righteousness," she snapped. "If she was not your sister, you would make the same choice."

"No," he said. "No, I do not think that I would. And it tells me everything I need to know about you."

His retreating footsteps echoed down the corridor. I leaned heavily on the stone wall, tears clouding my vision. Tristan had been right, what he'd said in the cave. I *did* take my family for granted. Never had I thought Oliver would be such a fierce protector, especially not against Sylvia.

But my tears were not just for him. They were half tears of pain. Sylvia's words echoed in my mind. *What would you have me do, Oliver? Destroy my reputation along with hers?*

I was so distracted that I did not hear her footsteps until she rounded the corner. She jolted to a stop as I straightened. I held my chin high, keeping my watery eyes fixed on hers.

Sylvia opened her mouth, glancing back the way she'd come. She had to know I'd overheard. When she looked back at me, there was regret in her eyes, but also resolve. She tore her gaze from mine and hurried away.

My heart limped, broken and bruised. That was how a friendship ended.

I allowed myself a few minutes to dry my eyes and pinch my cheeks, hoping to distract from the puffy redness around my eyes. But I failed, based on the sharp look on Tristan's face when I rejoined him.

"What's happened?" he asked.

"Nothing," I said with false brightness.

"You've been crying." He had no tact whatsoever.

My first impulse was to push him away, protect myself. But I took a deep breath and reined in my misguided anger.

"I—" I swallowed. I did not think I could tell him all the details. "Sylvia," I said simply.

His jaw tightened as he turned to glare at Sylvia across the room. She did not notice, since she had carefully kept her back to me.

"She is a blockhead," he declared.

A surprised laugh burst from me. "Tristan!"

"Well, she is," he said unapologetically. "Friends are not so easy to come by. She should not treat you so."

His words touched me, plain as they were. I slipped my arm through his, pulling myself against his side. "Thank you."

Tristan glanced at me, his expression suddenly uncertain. "Do you . . . Would you like to dance again?"

I raised an eyebrow. "Would *you*?"

He nodded toward Sylvia. "If it would help you forget *her*."

Another kindness.

"Yes," I said. "Let's dance."

Chapter Twenty-Six

MARIGOLD

IN THE DAYS following the ball, I visited every member of the Lady Archers of Sandcliffe and extended an invitation to the next practice. Many were still hesitant, but that was better than the ones who pretended they were not at home. There were a few, however—Miss Weston, Mrs. Vale and her daughter, Eliza, Mrs. Mifflin—who seemed perfectly happy to accept the compromise I'd offered: an engaged hostess free of scandal in exchange for their continued membership.

My plan worked, for the most part. Nearly all the members agreed to return for the next practice. I tried not to let any hurt feelings I might have interfere with my aspirations. These women were subject to the same rules of Society that I was, after all. Reputations were fragile things and could determine so much of a lady's life. I would welcome back anyone who was willing to come.

There was only one member I did not visit. Sylvia. After much debate, I finally resolved to send her a written invitation, cool and cordial. She'd hurt me, but if she came, then I would perhaps lean towards the idea of forgiveness. Even then, forgiveness was one thing. I did not think I could ever fully trust her again.

For those few days, I kept busy with my visits and preparations for the upcoming practice. But there was a part of me that was constantly distracted. Whenever a knock sounded at the front door, I jolted up, wondering if it was Tristan, come to call on me. When I went to town, I thought I saw him out of the corner of my eye, and an unfamiliar warmth flooded me before I realized it was a different tall, brown-haired gentleman.

So when Tristan did not come, when I did not see him, I struggled with the unexpected disappointment. What was I hoping for, precisely? Just because we'd called a truce did not mean he wanted to spend all his time with me.

But it would have been nice to know he was thinking of me.

It did not matter, I decided. I did not have the time, and besides, we would be married soon enough. I ought to enjoy my last weeks of freedom.

I awaited the next society practice with nervous apprehension, worried that some of the ladies might change their minds, but they came. They cast me curious, indiscreet looks as I greeted them on the terrace, but they came. Now that I was engaged, there was no reason to further offend either me or my family, and at least a few of them seemed to truly enjoy shooting. Besides that, I knew they were all desperately curious. I prepared myself to field questions about Tristan, the engagement, and our night trapped in the cave.

To avoid these conversations as much as possible, I immediately escorted each arrival to the prepared targets, showing them where they might shoot and suggesting a few exercises to warm their muscles.

I wandered among the ladies, trying to spread myself among them as best I could. It was just as difficult as our first two practices. I was only one woman, and there were close to twenty women trying to shoot all at once. With so little time between now and the Lady Patroness's Meeting, how on earth would I be able to help them adequately prepare?

When Cora arrived with her mother, I went to meet her on the terrace. She embraced me with a beaming smile while Mama greeted Mrs. Atherton.

"I told you I would be here," she said, pulling back. Her quick eyes darted over the crowd. "Sylvia?"

My heart clenched and I shook my head. "Part of me thought she might come, but . . ."

My voice trailed off and Cora tipped her head. "What?"

"I saw her at the assembly." I swallowed. "She and Oliver had an argument."

Cora stilled at my words, staring out over the lawn. "They quarreled?"

"Yes," I said. "You mustn't tell him I overheard. He has been abnormally quiet since."

"Indeed," she said, though her voice had faded somewhat, as if she was not truly listening. Then she focused again on me. "What did they argue about?"

My eyes blurred, and I looked away. "I think you can guess."

We stood quietly for a long moment before Cora spoke. "So she will not come?"

I shook my head. "She made her choice."

Cora squeezed my arm. "The wrong one," she said, her voice soft.

I straightened. I needed to put this behind me. I had plenty to still be grateful for. "Never mind all that. I am ridiculously happy you are here. Heavens, I've missed you."

"You are simply glad for any warm body in a dress," she said with a laugh. "Lucky for you, I'm a decent shot as well."

I gave a laugh. "Is my desperation so obvious?"

"Just to me." She linked arms with me. "Do not worry. I have full faith in you."

"If only I could have half your confidence," I muttered.

She waved that off. "Come, tell me more of your wedding plans." She was an expert in distraction.

I lifted one shoulder in a small shrug. "Mama is taking care of all that. I am too focused on the prize shoot."

Cora blinked. "Gracious, Marigold, I know you are competitive, but this is your wedding we are speaking of."

"A wedding to stave off scandal," I countered. "It is not as though I am eagerly counting down the days. Trust me, neither of us wishes for it."

Cora's eyes focused on something behind me. "Are you so sure?"

I tipped my head. "Of course I am. We've always loathed each other."

"Then why is Mr. Gates currently standing on your terrace?

I whipped my head around. Sure enough, Tristan had stepped out onto the stone terrace, tightening his cravat as he eyed the sea of women before him uneasily.

"I . . ." I shook my head. Why was he here?

"You had better go see what he wants," Cora said, her smile mischievous.

With an exasperated look, I left her and moved toward Tristan. His face was tight, his eyes guarded as he observed the ladies on the lawn. But when he turned and saw me, his face relaxed slightly. "Miss Cartwell."

"Mr. Gates." I bobbed a curtsy. "Have you come yet again to spy?"

His eyes narrowed. "I did not come to spy the first time."

"Hmm," I said. "I've yet to be convinced of that, especially now that you've arrived once more during one of our practices."

"Last time was accidental."

"And this time?"

He paused. "I came quite intentionally this time."

My heartbeat ticked a bit faster. "Oh? I am intrigued, especially since I've seen nothing of you since the ball."

He eyed me. "Did you *want* to see something of me?"

I cleared my throat. Why had I said that? "I only imagined we might need to discuss wedding preparations."

He sent me a quizzical look. "I did not think I would be particularly useful in that regard. That is better left in your mother's capable hands."

"Of course." I tugged at the sleeve of my gown. "So why is it you came today?"

Tristan shifted his weight and clasped his hands behind his back. What was this reaction? It almost seemed shy. But that was never a word I'd ever use to describe Tristan.

"I . . ." He coughed. "I brought you something."

I squinted at him. "You brought me something."

"A gift." He nodded back the way he'd come, through the garden door into the morning room. "It's just in there."

I followed him inside, trying not to show my interest. What would he have brought me?

He went to the sideboard beside the door, fetching whatever he'd left there, then turned back to me. In his hands was a beautiful bow, its shining, polished wood reflecting the gentle summer light.

"I thought," he said, not meeting my eyes, "that I should probably replace the one I broke."

I stared at the bow. It was beautiful, to be sure. I'd never seen such exquisite craftsmanship. Yet I stared for another reason. Just by looking at it, I could tell that this bow was the perfect size for me. But that was impossible. Bowyers needed a person's exact measurements in order to craft a bow of the right dimensions. That was why a person should only shoot their own bow—so much depended on their height and strength.

I met Tristan's eyes. "How—"

"I asked your mother for your measurements." He spoke quickly, no doubt embarrassed to be discussing a woman's figure.

"But how did you manage it so quickly?" I shook my head. "I commissioned a bow after . . ." I cleared my throat, and he looked at the ground. "But it will not be finished for another fortnight."

"I have influence with a bowyer in town." He shrugged. "I convinced him to put aside other commissions and work on this first. I knew you needed one."

"I did. That is, I do." I stepped forward. "May I?"

He presented it to me, and the moment I took the bow by the handle, I knew this was a weapon of impeccable balance and soundness. I ran my hands over the smooth, curved yew. "It is stunning, truly. Who is your man? I hadn't any idea there was someone with such talent in Sandcliffe."

He grinned. "His name is John Coultry. I'd been keeping him a secret, but since I have recently invested in his shop, it would be foolish to keep such information to myself."

I looked up at him. "You're an investor?" Somehow that fact was more surprising than that he'd been hiding the best bowyer in Kent away from me. I'd never really considered what Tristan Gates did with his time. If someone had asked me a few weeks ago, I would have said that he sulked about and thought of insults to use the next time he saw me.

Tristan nodded. "My father was a successful barrister and left me a small inheritance when he died. Nothing grand, but it was enough to help me start. I've invested in a dozen businesses over the last few years."

I focused my eyes again on the bow, pretending I was not nearly as impressed as I was. "Is that what you meant when you said you've supported yourself since you left Oxford?"

I saw him nod from the corner of my eye. "It is admittedly a fair bit of work for such small gains, but it's enough." He paused. "Well, it *was* enough."

I followed his thoughts. He hadn't planned on supporting a wife and family for years yet. And his uncle was in the peak of health, so an inheritance would not be forthcoming for decades.

I bit my lip, trying to phrase my next words carefully, knowing they were important. "I don't mind living simply, Tristan," I said. "And we'll have my dowry."

"Your dowry will remain untouched," he said firmly. "I'll find a way."

I nodded, looking up at him. He watched me apprehensively. I ran my hand once again over the curve of the bow. Besides the members of my immediate family, no one had ever given me such a thoughtful gift. Certainly not a man.

"It is beautiful," I said in a soft voice. "Thank you."

Without thinking, I took a step forward and rose onto my toes, balancing myself with one hand against his broad chest. My lips found the curve of his jaw, smooth and smelling of soap from his shave that morning. The scent filled my head, sending a fluttering to my stomach. For the briefest of seconds, something inside me clamored to move to the right, to let my lips wander to his.

I quickly pulled back. What had come over me?

But he did not look offended in the least. In fact, he stared at me, his mouth parted, with an intensity in his eyes that I'd only ever seen during prize shoots. It did nothing to calm the spiraling warmth underneath my skin.

He swallowed, his gaze dipping to my lips. "You are welcome," he said, voice gruff.

I could not lie to myself, not in this moment. I wanted to kiss him, and, if my womanly senses were not entirely off the mark, he wanted to kiss me back.

But that was preposterous. I did not even like Tristan. Hadn't he called me spoiled just a few days ago? Although, that had been my own word. And he'd also said those other unexpectedly kind things. *I don't think I've ever loved anyone the way you love.*

I calmed my racing heart. This was nothing. He'd given me a lovely gift, and I was assigning too much importance to it. We had called a truce, that was all.

"I do think I shall like being allies with you," I said lightly. Though the bow was not yet strung, I held it up as if I was preparing to shoot. "First a flower and now a bow. If you continue on this way, I shall expect a racehorse next."

Amusement flashed in his eyes, though he kept his mouth pressed into an even line. "I'm afraid that is beyond my area of expertise."

I lowered the bow with a smile. "A pity. I did so want to win at Newmarket."

"You shall have to settle for this paltry bow."

I shot him a look of reprimand. "It is quite the loveliest bow I've ever seen. Better than my old one, certainly."

The corner of his lip curled up. "I know."

I narrowed my eyes. "Then do you also know that in order to truly replace the one you broke, you shall need to lose to me at the prize shoot?"

"What do you mean?"

I rested the bottom of the bow on the thick rug, still admiring its fine lines and glossy surface. "That was the bow I used when I won against you two years ago."

"Oh." He rubbed his jaw. "Now I feel even more like a brute."

I softened. "It doesn't matter. I was only teasing."

He still looked a bit tortured, so I changed the subject. "I had better return to the ladies. No doubt they're wondering where I got off to."

He nodded. "Their fearless leader."

"Hardly." I glanced out the window to where I could see a few ladies shooting. They were just thirty yards from the target, but none of their arrows had pierced beyond the outer rings. "I hate to admit it, but I think I have taken on too much. There is so much potential here, only I haven't the time to tutor them all individually."

For a moment, I considered telling him about my wager with Lord Beauford. But what would he say when I admitted to wagering away the fate of my society? I'd been unbelievably foolish. Tristan would certainly think badly of me, and I could not bear that.

If I lost the wager, though, he would find out eventually, when I no longer competed at the summer fair. My heart twinged. I couldn't allow myself to think of what I might lose, not when it sent panic through my veins.

Tristan interrupted my thoughts. "Perhaps I could help."

My eyes flew to his. "What?"

"Help with your society." He lifted a shoulder. "I know a few things about archery. I might be of use."

I examined his face, but he looked perfectly sincere. Eager, almost, as if he wanted to prove himself.

"I'm not sure that is a good idea," I said, though my head was shouting at me to stop talking. Tristan was the best archer in the area, aside from myself. I should be falling over myself to accept his help.

He crossed his arms, leaning forward. "Do you think I am attempting to spy again? Perhaps organize a coup?"

"*Now* I am." I managed a tight smile.

He eyed me. "You're thinking of Lord Beauford."

I sighed. "How can I not? He would be furious if he found out."

Tristan smiled, a dangerous flash of his teeth. "You let me worry about the baron." There was an undertone to his voice that made a shiver race across my skin.

I chewed on my lip. "I hate to ask it of you. It would be something of a commitment. I am hoping to hold practice three times a week until the meeting."

"Fortunately for you, I am an expert on commitment," he said. "As of a few days ago."

I could not help a grin. It would be an incredible boon to have someone of his skill here to help. And besides that, I was realizing that I was not terribly upset at the idea of spending more time with him.

But I would have to guard myself better next time. I couldn't very well go around kissing my betrothed.

Looking up at him, I set my shoulders. "I should like to take you up on your offer," I said. "Thank you."

"It is no trouble," he said. "And it will give me the opportunity to watch you practice and discover all your tricks."

"Ha," I said dryly. "It is no illusion, Gates. I am simply better than you."

His eyes gleamed. "I suppose we will see."

I lifted my bow again, a thrill of excitement pulsing through me at the thought of shooting it. "Come on, then. We've work to do."

Chapter Twenty-Seven

TRISTAN

I FOLLOWED Marigold back out into the bright daylight, my already warm face now blazing under the sun. My mind stumbled over itself like a newborn colt. Why had I offered my help? I knew it would bring me a world of trouble with Lord Beauford.

But when Marigold had kissed my cheek, her shallow breath against my ear and her hand on my chest, I seemed to lose all ability to form rational thought. I would likely have agreed to anything. I was fortunate, really, that this was all I'd trapped myself into.

I shot Marigold a sidelong glance as we walked and caught her admiring the new bow. I grinned. I'd known she would like it. Uncle had given me the idea, with his bouquet of arrows suggestion. That had been absurd, of course, but it had led to me stopping at Coultry's shop the day after the assembly.

"You want me to make a lady's bow," he had said slowly, eyeing me as if I'd asked him to help overthrow Parliament.

"Yes." I'd been impatient. Uncomfortable. "And I shall need it sooner rather than later. Three days, if you can manage it."

"I can," he said. "Though your request does beg the question as to *why* you are commissioning a woman's weapon."

"A wedding gift," I said, my voice short. "For Miss Cartwell."

"Ah." Coultry nodded sagely. "You are wooing her."

"I'm not—" I stopped myself. "I don't need to woo her. We are already engaged."

He raised one eyebrow. "She is a lucky woman, to be sure."

"Just make the bow," I said irritably, handing him the slip of paper on which Mrs. Cartwell had written Marigold's measurements. "And have it ready in three days' time."

When he'd delivered the bow this morning, I'd stared at his creation. It was a stunning weapon.

"Have you been holding out on me, Coultry?" I asked, examining the curved wood from every angle. "This is spectacular work."

He crossed his arms and leaned against the fireplace. "I thought my very best would be necessary, considering."

I looked up at him. "Considering what?"

Coultry nearly smiled. "Considering you shall need all the help you can get to convince Miss Cartwell she ought to go through with the wedding."

I laughed. "No loyalty among friends?"

"Oh, but we are business partners," he said. "Only brutal honesty here."

I set the bow down on the table. "Excellent. Then you won't be put off when I tell you I expect you to attend the Lady Patroness's Meeting. You have no excuse, since the public is invited to watch. This is your chance to meet a good portion of Kent's archers. Its *wealthiest* archers."

Coultry considered that. "Very well," he said with a grumble. "But I'll not be kissing anyone's boots. It was bad enough delivering Lord Beauford's bow the other day."

"Oh?" I shot him a curious glance. "How did he like it?"

He crossed his arms, face tight. "He said the work was acceptable. Acceptable! As if it wasn't the finest bow I've ever made."

"Forgive me," I said, once again lifting Marigold's bow, "but I thought this was the finest bow you've ever made."

His mouth twitched. "Well, I could hardly tell you I made your fair lady the second-best bow. I'd have no peace from you."

I'd laughed, because it did not matter. All that mattered was that he had delivered an incomparable piece of art. It had been well worth the secrecy and the wait, watching her eyes glow with appreciation when I'd handed it to her.

And that kiss on the cheek had not been a terrible reward either. Perhaps I should buy another dozen bows.

After Marigold called the ladies' attention and explained that I would be helping them practice, I was met with everything from tight, polite smiles to distrustful glares—I had, after all, been the center of a reputation-ruining scandal. And I hadn't been the most likable fellow prior to that, besides being a member of the Sandcliffe Bowmen, their competition. What had I gotten myself into?

I spent an hour in the hot July sun observing and offering advice, showing the women how best to stand, how to angle their heads in order to aim, and how to notch the arrow more efficiently. Not many of the women were proficients—most had only learned the basics because it was one of the few sports acceptable for ladies. But Marigold was right. There was potential here. I could see it in their sharp eyes and patience, their willingness to listen and learn.

As I worked, my eyes continually wandered to Marigold, searching her out among the flowered bonnets and light muslin dresses. It wasn't difficult to find her, since laughter followed her wherever she went. The ladies liked her, the scandal notwithstanding. She made it look so easy to have friends, to laugh and converse.

But for the first time, it was not envy that crept inside my chest. It was . . . pride? After all, if I had to marry, perhaps it was good I should marry someone like Marigold. She navigated conversations and Society like a sloop amongst bulky merchantmen. If I wanted to grow my investments and continue to thrive, then she could prove a valuable asset.

Of course, that was not the only reason I watched her. After a while, she took up the bow I'd gifted her, strung it, and moved to an available target. And then I could not keep my eyes from her.

When Marigold shot, it was almost indescribable. She left

nothing to be critiqued in her stance or technique, but it was more than that. There was a grace to her motions that I could never achieve. Her arms, lithe and strong, raised the bow and drew back the arrow. She bent her slender neck as she aimed, and I tried to be gentlemanly and not let my eyes linger on the curves of her figure. I did not entirely succeed. But, if this was not an advantage of being engaged to her, then what was?

"Mr. Gates?"

I started, quickly looking at Mrs. Cartwell, who I'd been helping with her aim. "I am sorry," I said. "I was distracted."

Mrs. Cartwell's mouth twitched. "Clearly."

I followed her gaze back to Marigold. Had I been so obvious? "I was only observing her technique."

"Of course."

What was I to say to that? I cleared my throat, pretending to be fascinated by a passing bee. Mrs. Cartwell had a mother's eyes. She saw everything.

Her voice softened. "I can tell she loves the bow. I am glad you thought of it."

I shrugged that off. "I broke hers. It was only right."

Mrs. Cartwell smiled and turned her attention to the target, raising her own bow. Her form was good, though I could expect nothing less from Marigold's own mother. But there was always room for improvement.

"Try bending your left wrist a bit more," I said, my voice brisk.

She did as I said, aimed another moment, then released the arrow. It hit the red ring, her best score so far.

A few of the ladies nearby applauded, and some even sent me appraising, if not approving, glances. Mrs. Cartwell beamed as she turned back to me.

"How helpful you are, Mr. Gates," she said, her voice a touch too loud. "Thank you very much."

My lips twitched. "It is my pleasure, Mrs. Cartwell."

But after that, the others did not seem to mind as much when I stopped beside them, watching and offering small suggestions. And, if I did say so myself, I thought I noticed a marked difference in the amount of points by the end of the practice.

So did Marigold. She came to find me as the ladies were taking their last few shots, all of them far more cheerful than when they had arrived.

"My goodness," she said, crossing her arms as she watched them. "I'd never thought to see such improvement within the space of an hour."

"You were right," I said. "They have talent."

"And an excellent teacher."

"You needn't fish for compliments."

She snorted. "I meant you, you duffer."

I shrugged, trying to remain indifferent, but I was pleased. The Sandcliffe Bowmen were vastly different from this group. The men were all certain they had the best method, the best technique, the best equipment, and no one bothered to learn from each other or try anything new. Most of them were decades older than I and firmly set in their ways.

But these ladies . . . . Many were young, still unmarried or newly so. They were eager and excited, and no doubt thrilled at the prospect of competing in a real prize shoot. If they could continue their practices with the care and determination they'd shown today, they would quickly become real competitors.

Still, I did not wish to give Marigold false hope. There would be several societies at the Lady's Patroness's Meeting, and I knew better than anyone how skilled Kent's archers were. It would not be easy.

Our conversation died away, and silence gaped between us as we watched the archers retrieve their arrows. I shifted my weight, sending her a sideways glance. Now was as good a time as any.

I cleared my throat. "I must admit that I did not come today just to bring you your bow."

"Oh?"

"I have been tasked with asking you something."

She turned towards me, eyes curious. I hesitated. There was a reason I'd been putting this off. "Uncle has offered the use of the dower house at Stavely Hall."

Marigold blinked. "For what?"

Would she make me spell it out? "For us to live in. After we marry." The words clung to my mouth like molasses, reluctant and slow.

"Oh." She flushed red. "I hadn't . . . That is, I have been so focused on the society, I haven't considered . . ." Her voice trailed off.

I tried to soldier on. "Have you seen the cottage?"

"Yes," she said quickly. "That is, it has been years, but I recall it to be a pretty house."

"It is small," I reminded her.

Marigold's eyes flicked to mine, her cheeks still pink. "We shall be in close quarters, then."

My skin felt too hot, like I had the start of a fever. It seemed impossible that we were discussing this—living together in a cottage not a mile from here. Breakfasting in the morning, bumping into one another throughout the day. Not to mention the nights, a subject I well and truly did not wish to examine at the present.

"Are you certain?" I asked. "I can look elsewhere, if you are not keen on living so near my uncle."

"I quite adore your uncle," she said with a small smile. "Besides, I should like being close to home. I can visit Mama and Iris and complain of my boorish husband."

I coughed. Husband. That word did not belong to me. It was utterly foreign, and my mind rejected it outright.

"Yes. Right then," I said, too quickly, taking a step back. "I will tell Uncle we accept. And I shall see that it is cleaned and readied for you. For us, that is."

She eyed me strangely. Did she not feel the discomfort I did? This was a firm reminder that these were not normal circumstances. Generally, engaged couples spoke of their future arrangements with excitement. Not uncertainty and, yes, some alarm.

"Very well," she said. "And truly, thank you for today." She paused, looking up at me through her lashes, almost shyly. That was a word I'd never used to describe Marigold Cartwell before. "Our next practice will be on Thursday. Will you—that is, might you be available to come again?"

Was that hope in her voice? And if it was, did she want Tristan the teacher, or *me*?

"Yes, of course." I straightened my back. "I enjoyed myself, to be honest."

"Do not let Lord Beauford hear you say that," she warned.

"He is not my master," I said. "He cannot control whom I choose to spend my time with."

She sent me a careful look but said nothing. We both knew I was not speaking the truth—Lord Beauford had more influence than either of us wished to admit. If I displeased him, he certainly could find a way to exact his revenge.

I arrived at Camberwell Court the next afternoon, bracing myself for the worst. All I wanted was to practice, perhaps hawk Coultry's wares a bit and send him some business. But there was no doubt in my mind that Lord Beauford would have heard of my appearance at the lady's society yesterday. He had ears everywhere.

But I would not be cowed. I had every right to spend my time how I wished, with *whom* I wished. Besides, I was engaged to Marigold. He could hardly punish me for helping her. I hoped.

Thomas Lawrence stood near the garden door as I arrived, tightening his shooting glove. "Mr. Gates," he greeted me. "I wasn't sure you would come. You had something of an eventful week. I hope you are well?"

He spoke kindly, without censure or prying. But still, my mind immediately went blank. Why were basic conversation skills so beyond me? I coughed, buying myself a moment. What would Marigold say?

"Yes, thank you," I managed. I barely contained a wince. Well, she certainly would not have said that.

He examined me. "You seem to have survived your ordeal relatively unscathed. That is a blessing, to be sure."

"Unscathed might not be the right word," I said wryly. "I *am* engaged, after all."

He laughed, and I tried not to feel too pleased about that.

"Yes, but to Marigold Cartwell," he said. "Any other man would count himself fortunate beyond belief. Though I daresay it is different with the two of you, what with you being lifelong rivals."

It took me a moment to respond. I'd so long thought of Marigold as the last woman I would wish to marry that it was a strange adjustment to this new idea of her. It was becoming abundantly clear to me that if she had not married Mr. Eastbrook, and if she was not engaged to me, she would likely be the most sought-after lady in all Kent.

I chose my words with care. I wanted to trust Thomas. "In truth, I think I am coming to realize that perhaps I did have a great deal of luck. Marigold is . . ." I shook my head. "Well, she is something."

He clapped me on the back, smiling broadly. "I could not have said it better myself. Just know that we are all horribly envious of you. I wish *I'd* thought to trap myself in a mine with her."

I began to protest, until I realized his eyes danced with mirth. He was jesting with me.

I allowed a small smile. "It is the only way to find a wife of quality these days."

He laughed again. "Oh, I do look forward to hearing your tales of marriage. Perhaps you'll be able to offer this bachelor some advice."

What advice could *I* possibly offer? This engagement wasn't the result of any effort of mine. I hadn't courted and wooed Marigold, convinced her to love me. No, it was a patched-up betrothal to avoid scandal and ruination. And so far, I was terrible at being engaged. I could not imagine I would be any better as a husband.

Husband. That blasted word again. It was never a role I'd wanted or envied. I was used to caring for myself. How was I to also provide for a wife and family? Well, that was assuming there would *be* a family. There were certainly signs that Marigold was coming to tolerate me—that kiss on the cheek was key evidence—but I could not allow myself to hope for more. I was not her first choice, not by a mile. She had only accepted me because she had no other option, and I would be a fool not to remember that.

I opened my mouth to respond to Thomas, but a heavy hand clamped down on my shoulder. I turned to find Lord Beauford standing behind me, his eyes unreadable.

"Mr. Gates," he said coolly. "There is an open target. Won't you shoot with me?"

Requests from the baron were never actual requests. They were commands.

"Certainly," I said.

Thomas sent me a sympathetic look as I followed after Lord Beauford. No one liked shooting against the baron. Either his opponents were too intimidated to shoot well, or they lost on purpose. I was the exception. I would shoot my best, no matter my opponent.

We set our quivers on the grass and I set to stringing my bow, perfectly content to shoot in silence for as long as Lord Beauford would let us. Unfortunately, he had other plans.

"Mr. Gates," he said, his eyes sharp. "I understand I am to congratulate you on your engagement."

"Thank you," I said, not looking up from my bow. "It was sudden, to be sure, but we are making the best of it."

"Marigold Cartwell," he mused aloud as he rifled through his arrows. "Of all the eligible young women in Sandcliffe, how amusing that *she* should be your future bride."

I remembered saying something similar when we'd been trapped in the cave. Of all the women, I'd been trapped with her. But it was beginning to feel very different from the curse I'd thought it then.

"Yes," I said evenly. "Amusing."

"I also heard," the baron went on, "that you were present at a meeting of the ladies' archery society yesterday. I could not believe such a thing. I laughed to hear it."

I was certain he'd done no such thing. No, his face had likely turned red, his eyes bulging like they did when he missed a shot.

"I did attend." I spoke without deception or emotion. Let him think of my words what he would. "I plan to return again, in fact. I offered Miss Cartwell my help in instructing the members."

He nearly choked. "You are *helping* them?"

"Indeed." My bow strung, I took an arrow and nocked it, raising my bow. "Their society has a great deal of potential."

He remained silent as I aimed and released. My arrow hit the inner red ring. A good start.

I stepped back and waved Lord Beauford forward, but he narrowed his eyes, clutching his bow in one hand.

"My lord?" I was perhaps enjoying this too much, watching him try to hide his shock and outrage.

He took one step forward. "I cannot say I like the thought of you fraternizing with their society."

"Fraternizing?" I echoed. "This is archery, my lord, not a war. I am interested only in competing."

"Then perhaps you might take care that you do not offend the society you already belong to."

"There are no rules against it."

Lord Beauford tightened his jaw. "Not yet."

We both knew he could throw me from the society faster than a drunk tossing back an ale. Yet we also both knew I was the best archer he had. With the Lady Patroness's Meeting fast approaching, and Marigold's society posing a bigger threat than he'd anticipated, he could not risk losing me.

Lord Beauford moved to take his shot, pulling back his arrow with strong, smooth movements. He was a good shot, I had to admit. Yet not much could make up for natural talent, which Marigold and I both had. It would come down to the two of us, as it always had.

But for once, I was not excited to discover who the winner might be.

The baron released his arrow, striking close to the skirt of the target. He made a noise of frustration, and I hid a smile. The perfect reminder that he needed me.

He turned to prepare another arrow, allowing me to take his spot. But then he spoke before I could shoot.

"I recently learned you are Mr. Coultry's benefactor," he said, his words smooth and unbothered as if we had not just had a tense discussion.

I paused, my arrow nocked but not yet raised. "Yes, indeed I am. I invested with him a few months ago."

He prodded the tip of his arrow, not looking at me. "I have commissioned a bow from him. I have yet to use it, but I have heard only praise of his work."

I furrowed my brow, not sure why he had turned the conversation in this direction. "His work is of the highest quality. I am sure you will be pleased."

"I hope so," he said, his voice low. "I would hate to be disappointed. Because I could never let my friends and peers patronize an inferior establishment. I would certainly warn them off should I find I am displeased."

I froze. That was his angle. That was why he'd brought me here to talk, so he could issue his indirect threat.

I turned to look at him, wariness filling every inch of my body. "What is it you want, Lord Beauford? I would hate for us to misunderstand each other."

He held up a hand, as if I were overreacting. "Now, now, no need to shore up your defenses. I simply want to ensure the longevity of this society, of its traditions and bonds. If a woman were to defeat us at the prize shoot, it would prove ruinous." His expression hardened, and those dark eyes focused on me meaningfully. "We *must* win."

Ah. He imagined I was defecting and wanted to ensure that I

would still shoot for his society. In order to do that, he threatened not only my investment but the livelihood of my friend. And should Lord Beauford spread rumors that Coultry's work was somehow wanting, then it was almost a certainty that his business would fail.

I gritted my teeth, trying to tamp down the rising anger in my chest. I'd dealt with men like Lord Beauford before, but never had they had so much power over me. He knew I would give in, and the gleam of satisfaction in his eyes made my teeth clench.

I wanted nothing more than to walk away, to refuse him outright. But I did not. Not with Coultry and his family in the balance. Their lives would be ruined, and I could not let my pride be the cause.

"You needn't worry about that," I told him, my voice empty and hollow. "I might be engaged to Miss Cartwell, but I still plan to win the prize shoot."

It was what I had intended to do all along. But it made my blood boil to think of handing him the victory. My win would not be mine. It would be the baron's, because my talent, my skills, belonged to him.

"Good," he said, turning to raise his bow. "And if you should happen to see or hear anything of consequence when you are *helping* the ladies' society, then of course you must report it to me directly. Your loyalty must be first and foremost to the Sandcliffe Bowmen."

I gripped my bow so tightly I thought it might shatter into splinters. Why should he have my loyalty? What had he ever done for me?

The baron released his arrow, then turned to me with hard eyes, waiting for an answer.

I managed a tight nod but could not speak through the hot anger in my throat. He seemed satisfied with my nod and called for his servant to run and fetch his arrows from the target, because of course a *baron* could not be expected to do something so low.

I watched him leave, eyes narrowed. He had me pinned for now, but if there was anything I knew, it was that life had a way of catching one off guard. And if anyone deserved a storm of misfortunes, it was the Baron Beauford.

Chapter Twenty-Eight

MARIGOLD

THE NEXT FORTNIGHT passed in a whirl of practice, practice, and more practice. Whenever my society was not meeting, I was practicing on my own, tempting the weather to do its worst. I could not guess what the day of the prize shoot would bring, but whether there was wind and clouds, or too-bright sun and heat, I would be ready.

And so would my ladies. Our meetings had increased in frequency, with many members—Miss Weston and Mrs. Vale in particular—clamoring to practice daily until the prize shoot. They had caught the archery fever, and it was a singular thrill to stand on one side of the line of archers as they shot. To share my love for the sport with them was a pleasure I could not have anticipated.

The ladies improved with every practice. I had started them at shorter distances, thirty or fifty yards, but most quickly graduated to the hundred yards we would be shooting at the prize shoot. That meant lighter arrows, different techniques for drawing and aiming, and even more for me to teach them.

But I wasn't alone.

Tristan came to every practice. Every single one, even when we increased them from three times a week to daily. Not once did he give his excuses or act bothered by the fact that I was clearly taking advantage of his skill and knowledge. Beyond that, he stayed and consulted with me after every practice, and we made plans for the next day: who would benefit most from our focus and what we might teach. As was to be expected, we did not agree on everything. We squabbled over whether Cora should shoot with longer arrows —I thought yes, he insisted no—and argued about the best methods for managing wind.

But somehow, even when we disagreed, I never wanted him gone. Every day after he left Crossdale, my chest always felt a bit empty. Incomplete.

I watched him often at our meetings, my eyes continually drawn to him. He had a seemingly unlimited amount of patience and the ability to notice and correct mistakes that even I missed. I had to admit—if only to myself—that between the two of us, Tristan was the better teacher. Perhaps one day I might tell him that, *if* I decided it would not puff him up overmuch.

When the ladies saw almost immediate improvement upon implementing his suggestions, they began to regard him differently. They grew more comfortable around Tristan, and, perhaps even more surprisingly, *he* seemed comfortable around them. A strange camaraderie formed from the exchange of jokes and teasing during our meetings.

I was pleased, of course. Every day brought incremental progress to the members, and I would be a fool not to be grateful for Tristan's help. If only I wasn't so . . . so . . . *unbalanced* because of my own feelings toward Tristan. Every time his eyes met mine across the lawn, lightning darted up my spine. I had to look away and catch my breath.

This distraction, this *attraction*, was too confusing. If I did not know any better, I might've believed Cupid had shot me with his arrow, enchanting me with mystical, uncontrollable desire. It did not help that as the date for the Lady Patroness's Meeting crept closer, so did our wedding. Mama had been busy planning the wedding, stealing me away for dress fittings and sorting through my things to pack for the dower house. But I preferred to focus on archery. It was far less frightening than imagining myself married to Tristan. Every time I did, an uncomfortable heat swept me from head to toe.

Married. I would be married. I would be a wife. And Tristan would be my husband. It seemed that no matter how many times I thought it, I could not quite reconcile myself to that reality.

Today, our last practice before the prize shoot, I was standing near the line of ladies shooting, observing their technique. Or, at least, that was what I meant to be doing. I found myself sneaking glances at Tristan instead, who stood on the opposite side of the line. He was helping Miss Weston adjust her grip on the arrow, and I fought a flash of jealousy. It was ridiculous. He and I were engaged. But *I* wanted to be the one close to him, wanted to be the one whose fingers he brushed.

We hadn't so much as touched each other since I'd brazenly kissed his cheek, and that was to be expected. We were engaged, not in love. But as I watched his strong, capable hands moving over Miss Weston's—who looked red as a rose—I could not stop myself from imagining what it felt like to have his hand graze mine, to have his intense gaze fixed on me, his lips a breath away.

I shook myself, my face heating. We had spent a night together, for heaven's sake. We'd slept practically entwined with one another, but now the thought of a mere touch was enough to send me into a swoon?

"Marigold!"

Mama was calling for me and I turned, certain that my thoughts were written all over my face. But she nodded meaningfully to where most of the ladies had gathered near the terrace steps. I usually ended each meeting with an encouraging speech.

I nodded and swept forward, keeping firm control of my eyes even as they fought to glance at Tristan, standing behind the ladies. I climbed the steps and faced my society, a sudden burst of pride and excitement overcoming me. With the improvement I'd seen in the last fortnight, I knew we were as prepared for the Lady Patroness's Meeting as we could be. We would do well, and I would revel in the shock on Lord Beauford's face when he watched us. Though not as much as I would enjoy seeing his face after I won first prize.

Except, I still had to beat Tristan. I wasn't nervous for anything but that, the final round where we would undoubtedly face each other. It was frighteningly possible that he could beat me. And if he did, I would lose everything I'd worked for in the last few weeks. All for a foolish wager. Regret pulled at me, not for the first time. *Why* had I agreed to Lord Beauford's terms? Would he truly make me disband my society if I lost?

I pushed that thought away and forced a smile to my face as I prepared to address the ladies.

"What a thrill I had watching you all today," I said. "How far we have all come, and in so little time. I daresay everyone at the prize shoot will be astonished by the quality of the Lady Archers of Sandcliffe."

"Mr. Gates, at least, will have some warning," Mama quipped, winking at Tristan.

The ladies chuckled good-naturedly and Tristan held up his hands. "I should not wish to compete against any of you. I know far too well what you are capable of."

"Perhaps we ought to dress him in our colors," Cora suggested mischievously. "Surely we can have a new shooting costume made up for him in time."

That won another laugh. Every society had their own colors and costumes, though, as was custom, they all included green. We'd commissioned shooting outfits in a rush for the prize shoot, and the thought of Tristan wearing our forest green jackets and fawn waistcoats made me smile.

"I wouldn't look very nice in a gown," Tristan said, the corner of his mouth turned up. "I am sorry to disappoint you all."

Everyone laughed again. Who was this man, jesting with the same group of women who only two weeks previously had not trusted him as far as they could throw him? I would never have thought it possible. Tristan had changed so much. Or perhaps it wasn't that he'd changed, but that I'd grown to understand him better.

And the more I understood him, the more I liked him.

The ladies left soon after my speech, conversing excitedly in small groups. Iris was again pestering Mama, trying to convince her to let her attend the prize shoot tomorrow, but Mama held firm. Iris was not yet out in Society, she reminded my sister, not to mention that Iris had not been included in the invitation to stay at Highstead Castle that Lady Englefield had extended to our family.

Tristan stood speaking with Mrs. Vale, but I wanted to shoot more. I hadn't had much chance during the practice, occupied as I'd been instructing the others—and stealing glances at my betrothed.

I found my bow and moved to the targets. I did not know if it was because of the fine craftsmanship of my bow or all my practice, but I was shooting better than ever. Steadier. Calmer.

As I raised my bow, I heard Tristan's steps approaching from behind. I knew it was he without looking—I'd grown attuned to his presence. I aimed, countering the breeze by moving the tip of my arrow half an inch to the left. My heartbeat sounded in my ears, constant and reassuring. I exhaled and released.

The arrow struck the gold center, so close to the middle I might have won a prize if this were a real shoot.

"Confound it," Tristan said from behind me.

I looked over my shoulder with a grin. "Are you terribly intimidated?" I asked, already reaching for another arrow. "Or perhaps wishing you had not bought me this bow?"

"I wished it the moment I gave it to you," he muttered under his breath, stepping forward to better see the target. He shook his head. "I do believe that is dead center."

"I suggest you accustom yourself to such a sight."

He crossed his arms. "Oh, I see it often enough. You forget that I practice as much as you do."

"I doubt that. You spend all your time here with us." I swallowed as I nocked my next arrow. He'd sacrificed a great deal over the past weeks. Had I ever truly thanked him for it? "I'm afraid we've taken up too much of your attention. You might have spent all this time preparing for the shoot."

Fabric rustled behind me, as if Tristan shrugged. "It has not been a waste. Teaching only increases one's own knowledge." He cleared his throat. "Besides, it has not been as tortuous as I might have thought."

I lowered my bow, turning to stare at him in exaggerated astonishment. "Gates, are you admitting you enjoy my company?"

"*Your* company?" he repeated. "Hardly. You know I come solely to see Mrs. Mifflin."

I only just contained a laugh. Mrs. Mifflin spent every practice wandering about with her cane, calling out every now and again to insist someone tell her what was happening.

"Shall you call off our engagement and elope, then?" I said, pretending seriousness. "She has quite the fortune from her late husband."

"Oh, yes," he said. "I am already plotting our route to Gretna Green. I hear Scotland is lovely this time of year."

"You two shall be perfectly happy together, I have no doubt."

We eyed one another, both fighting laughter. He broke first, a snorted laugh escaping him.

"I won," I crowed.

He shook his head, though his mouth still curved upwards. "Always a game with you."

"Anything to win," I said. "Competition is the spice of life, as they say."

"I do not think that is the correct adage."

I grinned. "It should be."

He narrowed his eyes, moving closer. "Shall we even the score, then?"

"What do you suggest?" My heart ticked faster.

His eyes raked over my face. "How long has it been since you've gone roving?"

My chin pulled back. "Roving?"

"Yes, roving," he said, amused. "You go about the countryside selecting marks in turn. Whichever arrows land within five low lengths of the mark—"

"Quiet, you." I shot him an exasperated look. Of course I knew what roving was. "It has been . . . oh, years, I think." I tried to remember the last time I'd gone. I used to love it—tramping about the countryside, dirtying my hem and tangling my hair. It was so freeing. Why had I given it up? I certainly hadn't meant to. I'd just become distracted, obsessive. It was the same with my love for the beach. I escaped often to the sea as a girl, but it had fallen by the wayside as I'd grown older. I'd prioritized so many things that now did not seem important in the least.

He quieted, his face sobering. "It has been years for me as well. I daresay we've been a bit too focused on target shooting."

Too focused on defeating each other, is what he really meant. And I could not disagree.

I looked at the target across the lawn, my center hit now seeming to mock me. Yes, I'd grown proficient at target shooting, but I'd lost much more. The pure joy of shooting.

"Let's go," I said, facing Tristan with determination. "Let's go now."

His eyes glinted. "I'll fetch my bow. Meet me at the hedgerow near the Markhams' farm."

He immediately set off towards Stavely Hall, and I sent a maid to inform Mama where I was going. I left my quiver on the terrace, placing a dozen yew arrows in my waist pouch. Roving did not require a mass of arrows like target shooting, and I wanted to travel light. I quickly checked all my equipment, then I started off, winding through the alder trees and brush until I met the hedge that surrounded the wheat fields, growing gold in the summer heat. I followed the hedge east, knowing I would eventually meet Tristan coming the opposite way.

Sure enough, not ten minutes later, I spotted him striding toward me, bow in hand. The breeze ruffled through his hair, throwing those normally neat locks into casual disarray, and he moved effortlessly, his body lean and strong. My eyes lingered on his shoulders and trim waist. I knew from watching him shoot for the last few years that his jacket hid well-conditioned muscles. I simply had never imagined finding myself appreciating his hard work so very much.

My neck and face heated, and the sudden realization that our wedding night was only days away did nothing to help the quickening of my pulse.

"I was thinking," he said as he approached, thankfully not noticing my red face. "We ought to have a prize for the winner. I'd like to know what I am playing for."

I coughed. "Shall we say a boon?"

"That is frightfully unspecific," he said, slipping his bow over his shoulder. "Heaven only knows what sort of favor you might ask of me."

"So you rightly assume I will win."

"I said *might*," he corrected.

"And here I thought we'd begun to trust one another," I said. "Do you really think I'd choose a favor disproportionate to the value of winning?"

"Without question."

I grinned. "Then you will simply have to hope you come out victorious."

He returned my grin. "Hope has nothing to do with it."

He chose the first mark, a fallen, moss-covered log. It must have been two hundred yards away and I relished the challenge. Roving was quite different from target shooting. While the intent was still the same—shooting one's arrow as close to the mark as possible—the methods were vastly different. The distance was greater, and landing an arrow within even five bow lengths of the target was considered a point. We each had seven shots per mark, and I'd made sure to bring my long-distance arrows—lighter and blunt, so they could be more easily extracted from whatever they hit.

I shot first, curious to know how my new bow would hold up under the additional stress. But I needn't have wondered. My first arrow flew straight and true, sliding to a stop in the grass only a few feet from the log. The rest of my shots were nearly as good. Heavens, I loved this bow.

After I finished and Tristan shot his seven arrows, we walked to the log and measured five lengths of our bows. Four of my shots counted as points, and three of his.

"Are you rethinking your challenge?" I teased as I cleaned the tips of my arrows on the tassel at my waist and placed them back in my pouch.

"Not in the least." He looked completely unruffled. "This is a long game, Mari."

My fingers fumbled over my arrows, dropping one to the grass. He picked it up for me with an amused look and I mumbled a thanks as I took it.

He'd never called me Mari before.

A dozen people or more called me that. But not him. Never him.

I gave my head a shake. It was just a name. But he said it with such intimacy, such ease, that I was nearly undone.

And if him saying my name undid me, I could only imagine what a kiss might do.

Chapter Twenty-Nine

TRISTAN

MARIGOLD WAS ACTING STRANGE.

She still spoke normally, with that teasing thread to her voice. But I caught her looking at me with odd expressions, as if I had food on my face. And she was so jumpy. When I'd handed her the arrow she dropped, she took it without meeting my eyes.

She must be nervous. She had a great deal to be nervous about, after all. The prize shoot was tomorrow. And our wedding . . . .

I swallowed. Less than a week remained until we would be married. Until we were husband and wife.

I shot her a sidelong glance as we both smoothed the feathers in our arrows before placing them back in our pouches. Did she think of our wedding at all, or was she so focused on preparing for the prize shoot that marriage was an afterthought?

And if she *did* think of our wedding, was it with dread?

Because that was not how I felt. Not anymore.

These last weeks with Marigold had been . . . well, I could not adequately describe them. But I found that now I regretted all the years I'd spent thinking of her as I had. She wasn't spoiled or superior. She was far from it. She was confident, yes, and she knew just how to push me to the brink of aggravation, but I'd also seen the parts of herself that I hadn't known existed in our twelve years of acquaintance. Her dedication and determination. Her intelligence and good humor. She cared so deeply—for her family, for her friends, for her society.

Did she care for me too?

I cursed myself for wondering, for wishing. Marigold and I had been forced into this marriage, and we had such a history. I could not fool myself into thinking that so many years of competitiveness, snide remarks, and hard feelings could be put aside that easily. Especially not when she had been all but engaged to another man just three weeks ago. She would never have chosen me if there had been any other path forward.

If we could enter this marriage on good terms, as friends, then I would have to be satisfied with that.

But my mind raced to the next worry without my permission. Because what on earth did married friends do on their wedding night?

"Are you ready?"

I jerked my head up. Marigold had stopped, eyeing me. And here I had just been thinking how *she* was acting strangely.

"That spruce tree there," she said, nodding to our left. The tree stood across a meadow of golden grass, nothing impeding our view of it. "The next mark. You go first this time. Perhaps you'll do better if you do not see how well I do."

"How thoughtful."

I did not much like the idea of her observing me as I shot, not if she watched me as closely as I watched her. Because, as I was finding, the closer I looked at Marigold, the better she seemed. But I wasn't sure I would hold up to the same scrutiny.

I raised my bow and aimed, releasing the arrow too quickly. It darted off to the left, and I lowered my bow, exasperated.

"Do that again," Marigold said, coming around to my right side.

"Actually, I'd like to avoid that." I nocked another arrow. "I am trying to win, you know."

"Just shoot again," she said, hands on her hips. "I want to see something."

Wonderful. Now she was watching me even closer.

I cleared my throat, aiming carefully. When I released, my arrow flew straight, sliding to a stop directly before the tree.

I turned to send her a boastful look, but she hadn't seemed to notice my shot, her eyes focused on my right hand.

"As I thought," she said. "I hadn't noticed before. I never stood close enough."

"Close enough for what?" I took another arrow.

"Your right hand," she said. "You hold the arrow too far up your fingers."

"I beg to differ." I raised my bow and drew back the arrow. "I've shot this way for years and seem to do perfectly well."

"You could do better." She stepped forward. "Here, let me show you."

I froze as she brushed against my side. Her fingers, feather light and deft, carefully adjusted my grip around the nocked arrow, pulling them back so I barely had any grasp at all.

"There," Marigold said quietly, her voice in my ear, her breath caressing my neck above my cravat. Her hand settled on my shoulder, warm even through my jacket. "Holding it this way allows you to remove your fingers more quickly from the arrow. It will fly true. Go on, try."

Blast it all. She expected me to aim with her standing right there?

"There is a reason I do not shoot this way," I said, managing to keep my voice calm. "My grip is too tenuous. I'm not in control."

"So don't be in control."

I turned my head an inch to look at her. Her eyes sparkled, her lips pulled upwards into a tempting bow. The moment stretched between us, and I very nearly tossed my bow aside and kissed her right there. It was easy enough to imagine, the feel of her skin, the taste of her mouth. Something slipped into my chest, warm and engulfing and unfamiliar.

"Go on," she said again, a bare whisper.

Go on and kiss her?

I caught myself just in time. She meant my shot, clearly.

I turned back, berating myself. Did Marigold know what effect she had on me? She was not a flirt, not like Oliver or Sylvia, but she had to know what her words and nearness did to my determined coolness.

I swallowed hard, aimed again, and released. My arrow struck the tree.

"You see?" Marigold said in triumph.

She stepped away, and I could finally breathe again. I rolled my shoulders, imagining I still felt her hand there. "I maintain that my score will still be better overall if I use my normal grip. Less risk."

"It is possible," she said. "But it's not nearly as much fun."

"And is fun now more important than winning?"

She grinned. "Today it is."

I narrowed my eyes. "Almost you convince me. But I am quite certain you only wish to toy with my mind. Make me change my strategy right before the prize shoot."

She winked. "Anything to win, Gates."

I shot my remaining arrows using my normal grip, and I did do well. I estimated that at least five of my seven arrows would count as points.

"Hmm," she said, leaning on her bow as she scrutinized my arrows. "A fair showing."

"As I said." I gestured her forward. "The floor is yours, madam."

Marigold stepped forward, regarding the tree for a moment before she raised her bow. She drew back the arrow, her movements fluid and elegant. She released her arrow, and it soared away, landing a foot from the base of the tree. She shot me a triumphant look over her shoulder, brilliant blue eyes challenging me. The wind tossed her curls about her face, a golden halo.

She was beautiful.

I'd always known she was. It had irked me before, but now it unnerved me. This stunning creature was to be my wife, and I felt a bumbling oaf in comparison. Such was her poor luck.

She continued shooting, and I watched her right hand. She held the arrow as she'd shown me, but since she had clearly practiced it for countless hours, I saw no disadvantage to the more tenuous grip.

"Well done," I said when she lowered her bow after her seventh shot.

"Thank you." Marigold smiled. She'd known I was watching her technique but said nothing.

"Shall we?" I gestured toward the tree and we started across the meadow together, wading through the knee-high summer grass.

"I nearly forgot to ask," she said, holding her skirts in one hand, her bow in the other. "Mama wishes to know if any of your family will be attending the wedding breakfast."

"My family?"

"Yes," she said. "Have you any cousins or distant relations we should count on?"

I frowned. "No. It will just be Uncle and me."

"Oh." She quieted, the only sound the soft press of our footsteps in the grass, the twitter of birds.

I felt the need to explain, lest she think me rude. "Uncle Matthew was my mother's only brother. My father had no siblings, and none of my grandparents live."

"Oh." Her voice was sadder this time. "I am sorry for it." She looked down at the bow in her hands. "I wish I might have known your parents."

"I would have liked that as well." My throat seemed to have closed over, making my words raspy and harsh. "They were . . . they were good people."

I unconsciously touched my jacket pocket where I kept the shilling. Marigold's eyes missed nothing, following my movement.

"The shilling from the cave," she said softly. "Does it have something to do with your parents?"

I said nothing for a long moment, long enough that she hurried to fill it.

"Never mind," she said. "You don't have to tell me if you don't wish to."

Yet I did wish to. It was baffling that I should want to tell anyone, but I could not deny the truth of it.

I came slowly to a stop, right there in the middle of the golden meadow. Marigold stopped as well, bringing her bow against her chest as she watched me. I pulled the shilling from my pocket, the silver dull and worn.

"I became ill first," I said. "A fever, chills. Nothing we hadn't seen before. I recovered, but my parents fell ill soon after. My mother had it the worst." I swallowed. "She died after only two days."

Marigold listened, head bent as she looked at the shilling in my hand.

"Father held on longer. I was certain he would recover." I shook my head. "One day, he called me to his bed. He pressed a shilling into my hand, told me to go to the bakery on the corner and buy a sweet for myself." I paused. "He told me that he loved me. That seemed strange in the moment, but I understood after."

"Oh, Tristan," she whispered.

I could not stop or I would never finish. And it was suddenly very important that I finished this story. "The bakery was closed. My father died before I returned. It was only years later that I realized he'd sent me away so I did not have to see it."

Marigold touched my arm. The slightest touch, nothing more, but it was all I wanted or needed.

"So you keep the shilling," she said.

"Yes," I said.

"It reminds you of them."

"Yes."

Marigold's face softened. "I wish you had a better memory for it, but I am glad you have such a way to remember them."

But it was a good memory. Not the pain or sadness, but the look upon my father's face when he'd given me the coin. It was something I'd clung to in the days following, when Uncle had come to fetch me and I'd had to endure a new home, a new town, and new acquaintances.

She reached for my hand and held it tight. She paused, looking up at me and capturing my eyes in hers.

"Never say you love less than I do," she said quietly. "I think you loved very deeply, once."

My throat had been overcome by an enormous lump, and I could no longer swallow. I managed a nod and slipped the shilling back inside my pocket.

But now that I'd told her, now that the words had vanished into the summer air, I did not want to dwell on the past anymore. Not when the present was so inviting. I pulled her with me as I started again towards the spruce tree, to where our arrows still waited. "Come. It is my turn to choose a target."

We shot for another hour, soberness soon giving away to our now normal teasing and laughing. I never would have thought it could be like this between us. If we hadn't been trapped in that mine, would I ever have realized who Marigold truly was? I did not think so. I was so convinced of my own opinions, I literally needed a crack to the head to change them.

Bless that rock.

We eventually made our way to the top of the cliffs, a mile or so from the manor house. Sandcliffe's steep white cliffs were not as tall or dramatic as Dover's, but they were stunning in their own way. Small, yellow wildflowers dotted the windblown grass, and the rugged cliffs fell away to white-capped waves. The gray clouds roiled above us, the wind throwing our hair across our faces.

"There." Marigold pushed back her curls as she pointed to the blackened stump of a tree at the edge of the cliffs. "The perfect mark, don't you think?"

"With this wind?" I cast her a dubious look. "We shall lose arrows."

"Always the optimist," she said with a laugh. "Come, it is your turn to shoot first."

I sighed but could not resist the challenge in her smile. I shot my seven arrows, fighting the wind with every release, and I couldn't tell if any of them would count for points.

She shot after me and was exponentially better. After her sixth shot, I realized why.

"I call foul," I said, crossing my arms. "It wasn't my turn to shoot first. You simply wanted to watch the wind."

She pretended offense. "What, precisely, are you accusing me of, Gates?"

"Cheating," I said grumpily. "I thought that was perfectly clear."

She winked and turned to take her final shot. Miracle of miracles, it struck the middle of the blackened stump.

"Aha!" she cried in victory. "What do you say to that?" She whirled back to me, grinning widely.

"I say that it should have been my shot." I wasn't really upset, but I enjoyed teasing her.

"As if you haven't been taking a step closer to the targets this whole time," she replied loftily as we both slung our bows over our shoulders and started off to claim our arrows.

"I have not," I said, indignant.

We bickered all the way to the edge of the cliff until we were able to tally our points. Even with my terrible shooting and Marigold's direct hit, my previous score kept me even with her.

"I do believe we are tied now," I said, stooping to collect my arrows.

"For now," she said, slipping her own arrows into her pouch and then moving to claim her last from the tree. When she pulled on it, the arrow did not budge, planted firmly between the overlapping edges of the bark. She pulled harder, setting her foot against the trunk, but the arrow held fast.

She glanced at me, watching her with a knowing grin. "I suppose you think this is amusing," she grumbled.

"Cheaters never prosper," I said. "Perhaps *that* is the adage you ought to keep in mind."

"I did not cheat." She pulled again on the arrow, though it refused to give.

"Of course not," I said, keeping my voice unaffected. "But what an excellent opportunity you have here, to show me that men and women are equally matched."

She placed her hands on her hips and shot me a calculating look. "How much will you tease me if I ask for your help?"

"Only every day for the rest of our lives." It was an alarmingly valid threat.

She blew out a breath. "Very well, then." She yanked again on the arrow. She would keep trying until she had blisters and raw skin. I knew her well enough to realize that.

I moved to her, the soft grass and fierce wind masking my steps. Her back was to me, and as I reached around her for the arrow, she froze. I did too, my hand hovering over the arrow's shaft. Only an inch separated us, an inch of frail air and heat. Her hair pins had loosened during our roving, and wisps of her fair hair curled about her neck. I resisted the urge to brush them back with my fingertips.

"May I?" I murmured. My hand closed gently over hers, still clutched to the arrow.

She did not move for a long moment, then nodded. I twisted and pulled, and the arrow came free with a small jolt. I released my grip and she brought the arrow to her chest, spinning to face me, her eyes wide.

"I loosened it for you," she said, her voice breathy.

"Undoubtedly."

There was room enough for her to step away, to draw back from me. But she did not. She stood close, looking at me with those dazzling eyes. The wind whipped her golden hair across her face, across those fine cheekbones and parted lips. She tilted her chin up, as if daring me.

And I was not one to back away from a dare.

Heaven help me. I was going to kiss Marigold Cartwell.

Chapter Thirty

MARIGOLD

I WAS GOING to kiss Tristan Gates.

How did I know? Because the heat in his eyes matched the flame in my chest. If he didn't kiss me, then I would kiss *him*.

He moved closer, the smallest step. His eyes raked over my face, pausing on my lips. He swallowed hard, and my stomach flipped madly.

"Marigold," he said, his voice hoarse.

His hands trailed down my arms and settled at my waist, warm through the fabric of my dress, and I did nothing to stop him as he pulled me against him. I was at his mercy, in his arms and unwilling —*unable*—to leave them.

My eyes fluttered closed, and the intoxicating nearness of him swept over me. Our noses brushed. He was close, so close. I could feel his warmth even as the wind whipped at my skirts. My breaths came faster, my pulse a loud hum in my ears.

His lips found mine, soft and slow. A burst of light illuminated the recesses of my mind. Every thought within me shouted that I was kissing Tristan, but every inch of my body already *knew* it. I blazed with awareness as his fingertips pressed into my ribs, as his lips wandered across mine with such care.

Perhaps too much care. I knew him well. He was *thinking*, and kissing did not require thinking.

I wanted more. I wanted the part of him I saw during prize shoots, that fierce competitor who held nothing back.

I circled my arms around his neck, pulling myself up to him, demanding more from him. A moment passed, and the world sparked to a stop. Then he responded, his hands sliding up my back, tangling into my hair, his racing heart matching the frantic beat of my own. He kissed me like he'd thought of nothing else for years, like he desperately feared he'd never have the chance again. Fire raced through me, scorching and blistering. But this was no destroying fire—it filled me with a desire and a wanting I'd never seen in myself before.

And I knew that I would never be the same for having kissed Tristan Gates.

Then it began to rain.

Not small, gentle sprinkles, either. The drops fell hard and fast, the wind suddenly whipping into a frenzy. I gasped and pulled away, the rain soaking my shoulders, slipping down my face.

Tristan cursed under his breath, hands dropping to my waist. He turned to scour our surroundings, but he knew as well as I did that there was no shelter nearby.

"We need to run for Crossdale." He almost had to shout to be heard above the rain.

"Do we?" I tugged his cravat. I wanted to stay right where I was, with him in the rain.

A slow smile spread over his lips, and I had to stop myself from throwing myself against them again. I'd never been drunk, but I imagined this was how it felt. "Your mother will be worried," he said.

I swiped the rain from my cheeks, my hair dripping into my eyes. He tracked my movements. Working quickly, he shrugged out of his jacket and draped it over me, bow and all. I held his jacket up with one hand so I could peer at him.

"There," he said. "Now come on."

He grabbed my free hand and we darted through the tempest. The rain pounded against his jacket, but it kept the worst of it off me. My hem was a different matter, soaked through in seconds. I did not care. The thrill, the pure *exuberance* of the moment made me laugh out loud as we ran. I must have seemed quite mad, but Tristan only looked back at me and grinned.

We ran hand in hand, Tristan guiding me around mud and puddles. I did not allow myself to slow, to think. I wanted to enjoy this. What a picture we must be, dashing through the rain. *Kissing* in the rain . . . .

We hadn't gone terribly far from home, winding our way through the countryside with our roving, and the familiar facade of Crossdale soon peeked through the trees. But I wasn't ready. I did not want to leave him.

Tristan seemed to feel the same. When we reached the enormous willow tree beside the pond, he tugged me toward it. He parted the dripping branches for me, then followed me inside. The thick, green leaves arched around us, a natural gazebo protecting us from the worst of the elements. It hushed the howl of the wind and pelting of the rain.

We stood facing each other, both breathing hard from our run. I peeked at Tristan as I recovered, lowering his jacket to drape around me, my bow jutting awkwardly from where I'd thrown it over my shoulder. His hair dripped, darkened from the rain, and droplets of water raced down his face, tracing the edges of his nose and jaw. His shirt and waistcoat were soaked through. They clung to him in a way I hadn't imagined before today but certainly would have no difficulty picturing after.

I stared for too long before snapping my eyes back up to meet his, prickling heat filling my face. But he did not tease me. In fact, his eyes intensified as he looked at me, head to foot. I don't know what he saw—I could only imagine my hair plastered to my face and my drenched skirts tangled in my legs—but it did not seem to frighten him away.

The moment stretched, taut as a bow string before releasing its arrow. Then it snapped.

He took me by the waist and pulled me to him, kissing me hard. I kissed him back, one hand clutching his waistcoat, the other curled around his neck. I should have been cold, my clothing wet through and my hair dripping. But my blood coursed fast, my heartbeat pattering more quickly than even the rain outside our little haven under the willow.

He pulled away a moment later, pressing his forehead to mine as he inhaled deeply. "I am sorry. I could not help myself."

"You are forgiven," I said, breathless. "I am hardly a paragon of self-control."

"An excellent point."

I dared not open my eyes. One of us would surely do something to ruin this moment. We'd only just become friends. Were we fools for pushing too fast?

"I am not entirely clear on the rules," I said. "Do allies kiss one another?"

Tristan did not speak, and I finally gathered the courage to look up at him. His eyes blazed, tracing my face with delicious intent.

"I think we can make our own rules," he said, low and rough. A shiver flashed down my spine. He splayed his hands against my back, the two of us a sphere of stolen heat amid the storm.

"I quite agree," I managed. "Rule number one: allies may kiss each other whenever convenient."

"Convenient?" His serious lips twitched as he bent his head forward again. "Not whenever they desire?" Those lips claimed the soft skin behind my ear and I closed my eyes, my stomach swooping like a swallow. Who would have thought that Tristan Gates kissed as well as he shot?

"I am open to suggestions, of course." I let my hands drift down his shoulders, his arms, tracing those taut lines of muscle. Was this allowed? He seemed not to mind, pulling me even closer as his lips explored my jaw.

"An addendum, then," he said, pausing at the corner of my

mouth. "Allies may kiss whenever and wherever they choose." He hesitated. "So long as both parties are in agreement."

My hands stilled on his forearms. Did he know what he asked? "I shall sign the contract now," I said, my voice a delicate thread. I was laying my heart out to him. I was taking a leap of faith and hoping he would follow.

I could feel him swallow, his uncertainty manifest. It was utterly terrifying to admit such feelings, more so for a man like him who kept his emotions locked away. I turned my face and found his lips, kissing him with all the sweetness I could summon. He responded, deepening our kiss to dizzying effect.

"Marigold!"

The shout came as if from a great distance, breaking through the cloudy haze of our embrace. I broke away, startled. My realization came slowly.

"It's Papa," I said, disappointment dropping like lead into my stomach. I wanted to stay here in Tristan's arms. I wanted to hear more of what he might say to me.

"Ah." Tristan drew his mouth to one side. "Seeing as I am still trying to win his approval, perhaps this is not the best way for him to find us."

I sighed. I knew he was right, even though every inch of my body protested at having to leave him. I pulled away reluctantly and slipped off his sodden jacket. "Thank you for this. I daresay it will need a washing."

"And I daresay it will have been entirely worth it," he said, taking it. "I will see you tomorrow. Do travel safe."

"You as well." Then I winked. "I hope you do not encounter any washed out bridges that prevent you from arriving on time."

Tristan narrowed his eyes. "No, I plan to arrive hours early and practice on the range. I play to win, after all."

I slowly leaned forward, my hand on his chest. I could feel his heartbeat quicken beneath my hand. "So do I," I whispered, my lips hovering a breath from his.

Tristan's eyes grew hazy and he did not entirely seem in control as his hands found my waist again. My lips slid into a wicked grin. I pulled back, and his arms fell away from me. "Until tomorrow, Gates."

He blinked, then exhaled a laugh. He knew precisely what game I was playing. "Temptress."

I took a few jaunty backward steps, still grinning. "If you think I won't use every weapon in my arsenal, you don't know me very well."

He crossed his arms but chuckled, low and deep.

"Marigold!" Papa called again, closer this time.

I allowed myself one last look at Tristan—dash it all, he looked utterly enticing with his rumpled clothing and dripping hair—then forced myself to spin and hurry away. When I emerged from the woods, Papa spotted me instantly, relief filling his face.

"There you are," he said. The rain had slowed, but the shoulders of his jacket were wet through. "I was about to send the staff after you."

"I am well," I said. I was far better than *well*, but that was not something I would ever admit to my father.

"Good," he said, taking my bow from my shoulder. "Let us get you inside before you catch a cold and cannot shoot against your betrothed tomorrow."

I laughed. "You are unexpectedly eager for this prize shoot. Would you rather watch me defeat Tristan or Lord Beauford?"

He winked. "It is fortunate I do not have to choose."

I held Papa's arm as he took me inside, but I glanced over my shoulder, looking for those telltale dark eyes. I saw nothing but the rain and clouds. I smiled all the same.

❧

My maid insisted on a warm bath, and I was happy to oblige. Once I was out of my wet things, I sank into the copper tub filled with hot water. I leaned back my head, closed my eyes, and let my mind drift back over the last few hours.

I conjured my memories of Tristan—shooting so skillfully, his back and shoulders strong, the fierceness in his face as he pulled me to him for a kiss. It seemed fully impossible that only a month ago I would have recoiled at the thought of kissing Tristan, and now I quite literally could not stop thinking of him.

How had it happened? Well, that was a silly question. I knew it was because of the engagement. It had forced us together in a way we'd never experienced before. But I tried to identify the moment when I'd realized that Tristan and I had become *more*. When we'd grown beyond feeling forced into this marriage. I couldn't say when it was. It was everything. It was his saving me in the cave, his honorable proposal, the vulnerability he'd shared that night at the ball, the kindness he'd shown by helping my society, his heartbreaking story about the shilling. It was the way he'd begun to look at me in the last fortnight, like I was someone worthy of admiration—and love.

I looked at him differently as well. It was as if the Tristan of my past was a completely different person, and this Tristan, the one I'd come to know, was the real one. He was kind and loyal and compassionate, and, if his kisses today were anything to judge by, more romantic than I'd ever thought to credit him for.

Romantic. I grinned as I lifted one toe from the hot water of my bath. Tristan would make such a face if I dared describe him so. But it was true. Even now, my heart raced at the memory of our kiss, the rain enveloping us, his lips warm on mine. If that was not romantic, then I knew of nothing more deserving of the word.

My grin faded. I'd enjoyed kissing Tristan. That much was undeniable. But did it mean . . . more? It was impossible to sort out what I felt for him. There was too much between us, our arguments and history, that it muddied the waters as I tried to peer into my future. Was what we had enough to endure a lifetime of marriage? What if these past weeks were an anomaly, and once we married, we reverted to the relationship we were used to? What if living together exacerbated our flaws and personal vexations, and we grew to hate each other once more?

My mind was too muddled. After washing, I dressed quickly

with my maid's help then went in search of the one person who could help make sense of everything I was feeling.

I knew Mama would be in her garden. The rain had stopped and there were still a few hours until dark. She especially loved to work when the ground was soft and pliable, claiming she was never happier than when she had dirt under her nails. It was perhaps an eccentricity for a lady of her status, but no one doubted her sincerity.

Today, Mama wore an apron to protect her dress as she weeded among the tulips. The gardener always reminded her that such a task was far beneath her, but Mama never paid him any mind.

She heard me coming. "There's a spare apron over there," she said, nodding to the stone bench. That was Mama's way. She never needled or pressed me to talk, simply presented opportunities.

I donned the apron, tying it in a knot behind my back, then knelt beside her in the dirt. I was well-versed in weeding—Mama had taught all of us when we were young how to care for her garden. We worked in silence for a minute, Mama saying nothing, and I tried to organize my thoughts. When that proved useless, I simply sat back on my heels.

"Tristan kissed me today," I blurted out.

Her hands paused, but then continued in their work.

"I do not think he planned to," I hurried on. "It just happened. It was during the rain, which I suppose did not help anything."

Mama listened, her brow furrowed. She still did not speak.

"I cannot stop thinking of it. It seems absurd, doesn't it?" I laughed. "That I should be so at odds because of *Tristan*."

She tipped her head. "What are you at odds about?"

I rubbed a bit of dirt between my fingers. "Everything. How I feel. How he feels. What this might mean for the future."

"And what might it mean?"

I pressed my lips together, staring at the tulips near my knees. "I don't know."

She smiled. "Forgive me if I don't believe that for a moment."

"It means . . ." I did not speak for a long second, then looked up. "It means I *may* be falling in love with him."

She stopped, her hands in the midst of pulling a weed. Blinking, she sat back and stared at me. "Truly?"

I exhaled a long breath. "It is difficult to know for certain. What I feel for him is so different from what I've felt for anyone else, even Mr. Eastbrook. Is that love? Or is this simply the natural consequence of being engaged?"

Mama shook her head. "No, darling. An engagement itself has no ability to produce love, or every arranged marriage would have a happy ending."

"I suppose," I said, "but surely it allows more opportunities for fondness to grow."

She peered at me closely. "Is it fondness you feel for Tristan?"

I swallowed hard. "No," I admitted. "It is far stronger than that."

Her eyes suddenly filled with glossy tears, and she broke our gaze, swiping at her cheeks and leaving a dirty streak on her cheek

"Oh, Mama," I said, taking her hand. "What did I say?"

"Nothing," she said, her voice hoarse. "Only you cannot know how I've worried over you these past weeks. I wanted so badly for you to find happiness, and to think you might have, with Tristan—" She blinked rapidly, looking at me again. "He cares for you, I know he does."

"What if it isn't enough?" I asked, my fears returning. "What if in a few months we realize that we truly were wrong for each other? And that this was all a horrible mistake?"

Mama laughed softly. "Forgive me, but that is not a problem I foresee. You both have changed so much, and for the better. Trust in him, and in yourself. All will be well."

I swallowed hard. Was she right? The hope in my chest blossomed, nourished by Mama's words. Of course, we would still have challenges. We would disagree, and no doubt marriage would bring a new set of issues to resolve.

But it was a future that no longer frightened me, not like it had a fortnight ago. It was a future that gleamed with promise. It was a future I wanted.

She clasped my hand tighter. "It is all I could want for you," she whispered. "To have the life you've dreamed of."

"It is certainly not the life I dreamed of," I said, laughing softly. "But I am beginning to think it is the one I should have wanted all along."

I left her a few minutes later, brushing my hands on my apron as I stepped back into the house. I wished I'd spoken to Mama ages ago, but then, I hadn't known precisely how I'd felt until today. Now it seemed so obvious, it was almost amusing. I *had* fallen in love with Tristan.

A lump formed in my throat, and I paused to lean against the wall of the corridor, closing my eyes. Could it be possible? Could our marriage—what I had presumed was the end of my life—be instead a blessing of happiness and love?

I was beginning to hope for that with all my heart.

Chapter Thirty-One

TRISTAN

"You seem cheery this morning," Uncle observed at breakfast the next morning, eyeing me over his plate of sausage and eggs.

"Do I?" I forced my lips into an even line. Uncle had been away when I'd returned home yesterday, which meant there was no one to wonder why I could not form full sentences. I had counted myself lucky. I did not want him to know how fully undone I was, all from a kiss.

"Indeed," he said, stabbing a sausage. "But then, you always liked the prospect of a competition."

I coughed to hide a laugh. "Indeed I do."

He thought I was simply excited for the prize shoot today, when, in truth, I'd barely spared it a thought all morning. Perhaps that was Marigold's true strategy—beguile me until I was a worthless, smitten milksop, then destroy me on the archery field. If that *was* her plan, then it was working better than she could have imagined.

I could never have planned for this, for Marigold. She consumed me with her vivacity and wit, her strength and stubbornness. And yes, with her clear blue eyes and tempting smile. I was not above admitting that a fair amount of my attraction was physical. But it was all of her combined, a potent potion, that drew me in. She was the honey, and I was the stupid, besotted fly.

I paused, lowering my tea cup. Perhaps not stupid. Just . . . careless? Had I not decided only the previous afternoon that being friends was good enough? Yet the next thing I knew, I was kissing her like I never planned to stop. I hadn't wanted to stop. Neither had she. If the rain hadn't come, I imagined we would still be up on that cliff, lost in each other.

"We are still planning to leave in an hour?" Uncle asked, setting down his fork and wiping his mouth with his napkin.

I jerked my head up. I'd been entirely lost in my memories of Marigold. "Yes. Yes, I will be ready. And Coultry as well. We'll collect him in town on our way to Mrs. Penrose."

Now I wished Marigold and I had not decided to travel separately with our respective families. But then, I did not think I could stand sitting beside her in a carriage for two hours without kissing her, so it was probably for the best if I did not wish to shock our fellow travelers.

"Very good." He made his way to the open door. "I do hope you have been practicing. Marigold has been in fine form lately."

I grinned and rubbed the back of my neck as he left. He had no idea.

After breakfast, I packed a small trunk with clothes and necessary items for a night away, then I carefully prepared my bow, extra strings, and every accoutrement I could possibly need. I would be prepared. I wanted to win. Didn't I? Lord Beauford's threat against Coultry notwithstanding, I thrived on competition. I shot my best under pressure. But my heart stopped a beat when I pictured Marigold's face if I won, broken and crumpled. She'd worked so hard for this.

But so had I, I told myself. Besides, it was not something I could choose. The best archer would win.

Once our carriage stopped for Coultry—who grumbled as he settled beside me on the bench—and Mrs. Penrose—who beamed and greeted us excitedly—we set off for Highstead Castle, a journey of nearly two hours. I tugged at my jacket, fidgeting with my cravat. I'd taken more time than usual tidying myself before the mirror that morning, though I'd felt a fool. I knew that beside the diamond that was Marigold, I was nothing but a rough rock.

Our kiss played again in my head. Marigold's lips, impossibly soft and sweet. That daring in her eyes. The way her damp skirts had shaped themselves to her figure—

I tried to stop that particular thought. It would not help anything.

But if Marigold's actions yesterday were representative of her true feelings, then she found me far from repulsive. It was an encouraging thought, and one that bolstered me as our carriage bumped along the road near the sea cliffs. I needed to speak with her —I'd decided the moment I'd woken up. I was not one to beat around the bush, and I had to know what she was thinking. If it meant confessing my own feelings, then I would take that chance.

My own feelings. I gulped, staring out the window without seeing any of the passing landscape.

Love, came the soft voice of my long-gone mother. How many times had she said it? "I love you," she'd whispered every night as she tucked me into bed. I'd fallen asleep for ten years with her voice in my ear, speaking of love. Since her death, I'd tried so hard to hide from it. I hadn't wanted love, or the pain it brought. Uncle hadn't given me a choice, though. He'd loved me unconditionally, and I could not help but love him back.

But Marigold was different. Before our engagement, before everything had changed, I'd assumed I would have a marriage of convenience for Uncle's sake, so he might have honorary grandchildren. I'd never intended to love my wife. But this . . . this was entirely and utterly unexpected.

Love. I exhaled a laugh. What a notion. No doubt Marigold would tease me mercilessly for being a romantic after all. I did not care. Let her tease me, so long as I could spend every second with her. That was the most baffling thing of all, that I should crave her company as much as her lips.

After two hours of Mrs. Penrose's chattering and Coultry's silence, I was more than ready to arrive at the small town near Highstead Castle. We had secured rooms at the local inn, and after settling in my room, I quickly prepared for the shoot, dressing in my shooting costume for the Sandcliffe Bowmen: a single-breasted green jacket with an arrow engraved on the button, a buff Kerseymere waistcoat, black Hessians, and a black hat turned up on the right side with a feather. Over it all I strapped on my belt and my equipment, checking and double-checking that everything was in working order. Then I took a deep breath and grabbed my bow, going downstairs to rejoin the others in the carriage as we finished the journey to Highstead Castle.

I leaned against the window as we approached. Though I'd previously attended the Lady Patroness's Meeting, the great stone castle perched atop the cliffs was never a sight I could resist, presiding over a wide, sandy beach and gently lowering hills to its rear. It certainly looked as if it might have withstood a fierce French invasion, with towering turrets and thick, high walls topped with battlements.

As we came to a stop before the front steps, Lord and Lady Englefield waited to greet us. The earl and countess were a handsome couple, he with flashing eyes and a commanding bearing, she with softer, brown curls and an easy smile. They greeted us warmly, and we all exchanged bows and curtsies.

The countess had invited Marigold and her family to stay the night after the tournament. Upon hearing about our engagement, Lady Englefield had extended the invitation to me as well, but I had kindly deferred, insisting I was content to stay at the inn with my companions. I had hoped I hadn't offended her, but her graciousness now made it clear my worry had been unwarranted.

While Lord Englefield asked Mrs. Penrose and Uncle about the journey, Lady Englefield turned to me, her eyes holding a lovely sparkle.

"I am especially pleased to meet *you*, Mr. Gates," she said, hands clasped before her. "The Cartwells arrived only a few minutes ago, and Miss Cartwell's first words were to inquire if you had arrived yet."

An unfamiliar pleasure slipped through my body even as my face heated. I cleared my throat. "I am not surprised, since I very nearly missed our last competition."

"I see." Her eyes danced. "Marigold is a lovely girl."

Lovely did not do her justice. Dazzling was more like it. But I was not one to correct a countess.

"She is, indeed," I said. "I consider myself the most fortunate of men."

"As you should." Lady Englefield smiled approvingly.

A maid led Mrs. Penrose, Uncle, and me across the grand entry hall—all polished marble and sparkling chandeliers. We followed her to the back of the castle, where the wide, double doors had been thrown open to the summer air. It was just as I remembered from last year: the enormous marquee, the crowds of archers and onlookers, the music and targets.

I looked for Marigold as surreptitiously as I could. Uncle would notice if I was too eager, and I could not bear his teasing today. But I could not see her anywhere. She must still be dressing.

I spotted a handful of archers already before the targets, warming their muscles with practice shots.

"I'm going to shoot," I told Uncle, nodding at the targets. "Just a few arrows."

He waved me off. "Take as long as you like. We'll be enjoying the food and company, so you needn't rush on our account."

"Perhaps mine," Coultry said, apprehensively eyeing the almost overwhelming crowd of attendees.

I tried to hide a grin. "Try to enjoy yourself. But if you happened to gather a few new commissions as well, I would not be too bothered by the idea."

"I knew I would regret partnering with you," he grumbled.

Uncle surprised me by wrapping one arm around my shoulders in an almost embrace. "Good luck today, Tristan. I expect to see you holding another prize at the end of this."

"Not Marigold?" I asked wryly.

He grinned. "You know I am fond of her, but I will always cheer for you first."

His words were unexpected. I knew Uncle cared for me, but everyone who knew both Marigold and me seemed to prefer her. I could hardly blame them. She was . . . she was *Marigold*. But knowing I came first to Uncle, that he would always stand behind me—

I tried to clear the sudden ache from my throat. "Thank you," I said gruffly.

Uncle squeezed my shoulder and stepped back. He knew me well enough to know what I was really saying. "We'll let you be."

"Best of luck, Tristan!" Mrs. Penrose said with a merry wave.

Coultry echoed her sentiments, albeit less excitedly, and trailed after the couple as they moved toward the marquee.

I strode to the targets, claiming an available one from the long line. I glanced around again, but Marigold was still nowhere to be seen. I strung my bow and checked all my equipment again, then nocked an arrow and raised my bow. My first shot was good, hitting the red ring just outside the center.

"Ah, Mr. Gates."

A voice came from behind me, certainly *not* the one I was hoping for. I grimaced and turned to face Lord Beauford, watching me with piercing eyes, his bow over one shoulder—the bow Coultry had made him, no doubt.

"Lord Beauford," I greeted him, not bothering to attempt any warmth.

"I hope your journey was uneventful," the baron said, straightening his shooting glove.

"It was."

He took a step closer. "And I hope you are resolved to shoot your best today."

My eyes narrowed. As if I needed another reminder of his threat. "Why would I not, my lord?"

He smiled tightly. "Excellent. Enjoy the shoot."

I set my jaw as he left, his stride slow and lazy. I certainly did not relish the thought of defeating Marigold, but I *would* delight in trouncing Lord Beauford.

I shot several more arrows, all hitting the inner rings—and two hitting the center. My chest was split in two. Half of me was pleased I was shooting so well. The other half hated it. The better I shot, the less of a chance Marigold had of winning.

It was just a contest, I reminded myself. If I *did* win, she would recover as she had before. But Coultry's livelihood was depending on me, and I would put forth my best effort.

Besides, I had a little pride. I still wanted to win.

I slung my bow over my shoulder and went to gather my arrows from the target, then turned to the crowd again. Where was Marigold? I tried to calm my impatience, but it was impossible. I wanted to see her again. I was *desperate* to see her again.

Needing a distraction and a respite from the unrelenting heat, I made my way to the shade of the grand marquee. I was greeted by several ladies as I went, all members of the Lady Archers looking lovely in their matching costumes. It still surprised me when they looked at me with such fondness, when they seemed *truly* pleased to see me. Would I ever grow accustomed to that?

After bidding Miss Weston good luck, I went to the table bearing an enormous bowl of lemonade. A servant handed me a full glass and I took a grateful gulp, my throat dry. I moved aside, to where one side of the marquee had been let down to provide further shade for those inside, and stopped just beside the temporary wall.

"Gates—"

I looked up, expecting to see someone approaching. But no one was looking my way. Who had said my name?

Then I heard the voice again. "—are fools, the both of them."

It was Lord Beauford, from the other side of the marquee wall, his words muffled by the thick canvas but still audible. I moved a step closer, holding my breath.

"They are indeed, my lord."

My jaw tightened. That was the nasally tone of Mr. Hutton, Lord Beauford's lackey.

"Miss Cartwell thinks to outmaneuver me," Lord Beauford said. "But she never considered that I would leave such a thing to chance."

"What do you mean?"

"I mean that even though Gates may have been taken in by a pair of pretty eyes, he knows better than to lose today."

My hand squeezed my bow, and I tried to keep my breathing even.

"They both will have to defeat you first, my lord," Mr. Hutton said loyally. "A near-impossible task."

"True, true," the baron agreed.

Was he deluded? He knew we were both far better than he. Or did he simply enjoy the praise so much that he actually believed it?

"Still," Lord Beauford went on, "even if it is Mr. Gates who earns the highest score, I will claim the victory—seeing that blasted society disbanded."

My eyebrows darted clear to the roof. What on earth was he talking about?

Mr. Hutton gave a short cackle. "Quite right, my lord. Miss Cartwell should have known better than to wager with you."

"She is young and naïve," Lord Beauford said. "It was not difficult to manage her. But once she loses and the ladies' society is no more, I can finally be at peace. I do hate contention, of course."

I stood stock still. Marigold had made a wager with Lord Beauford. She had wagered away her *society*.

The men kept speaking, but I moved away, dazed. It could not possibly be true. Marigold was not a fool—she would never do such a thing. She'd worked so hard for her society. We both had. Why should she risk something that important?

Except . . . except she was *so* competitive. When she set her aim at a target, there was nothing to stop her from getting her way. Was it possible that she had agreed to such a preposterous wager?

I left the cool shade of the marquee and blinked as I stepped into the blinding sunlight. I distantly registered the mingling guests, but I could not seem to settle my thoughts as they whirled about like a dust storm.

Then I saw her.

In her green shooting dress and her hair braided into a golden crown around her face, she looked like a wood nymph—impossibly beautiful and lively. She stood among a group of women from her society, all of them laughing. I stared at her. I wanted to forget everything the baron had said. I wanted to return to my blissful ignorance of two minutes ago. Perhaps the baron had lied. Except he had no reason to—he hadn't known I was standing on the other side of the canvas.

Which meant it had to be true.

Frustration knotted in my chest. Marigold had wagered away her society. How could she have been that reckless? Did she care so little for the other ladies and their hard work? What could Lord Beauford have tempted her with to make such a deal?

My temper flared like an ember inside me. Marigold knew the baron. She knew how calculating and manipulative he was. That she should go against common sense and make such a gamble showed a desperation I'd never seen in her. Was she really so obsessed with proving herself the best that she would sacrifice anything—*do* anything—to win?

I stopped short, the unanswered questions freezing like ice in my head. No. *No.* I knew this familiar path my thoughts were taking. I could not let myself fall into this trap once again, always thinking the worst. I was assuming I knew her reasons, assuming I knew why she had made the choices she had. But that wasn't fair. I knew her better than that. There must be more to the story. Although, in the end, it did not truly matter *why* she had made the wager—it would not change the reality I now faced.

If I won today, Marigold would lose her society. But if I lost, Coultry's livelihood would be at risk. And I hadn't any idea how I was supposed to choose between the two. Because, I realized with sudden, astounding clarity, if it was just about saving Marigold's society, I knew I would lose for her. Yes, I was crossed between wanting to shout at her for her recklessness and kiss her for her daring, but I would lose for her. I would do that and more because of how blasted much I loved the woman.

But with Lord Beauford's threat hanging in the balance, how could I sacrifice Coultry's trade, his means of supporting his family? How could I put Marigold's society ahead of a man's entire future? Even if losing her society would devastate her. Even if my victory made her view me with a trace of bitterness, a bitterness that could ruin our fragile relationship.

I stared at Marigold, at the excited glow of her eyes and the beautiful flush of her cheeks. It was impossible. No matter how many points I scored today, I would lose.

Marigold looked up and met my eyes, a brilliant smile lighting her face.

My heart sank.

Chapter Thirty-Two

MARIGOLD

THE LADY PATRONESS'S Meeting was better than I could have imagined.

As I stepped out into the shimmering sunlight, I could not help my wide eyes. A great red marquee had been erected on the back lawn, pennants flying merrily from their points in the strong ocean breeze, with several smaller canopies scattered around. Musicians played pleasant folk songs that drifted over the guests, and to my right, two rows of targets stood a hundred yards apart, their rings glossy with fresh paint. Everywhere I looked, I saw archers in their shooting costumes, many with their bows over one shoulder, all with excitement glowing in their eyes.

I'd been to grand meetings before, but I had not prepared myself for what it would feel like to enter as a competitor. This was what I had dreamed of. I belonged here, with these people. And I would make sure everyone knew it by the end of the day.

I quickly spotted the members of my society, and they all clamored to greet me as I joined them. Mama, Mrs. Vale, and Miss Weston chatted eagerly, while Cora generously endured the loud exclamations of Mrs. Mifflin, who—in spite of not planning to shoot today—had come all the way to support the society.

I smoothed the skirts of my shooting dress as I tried to calm my leaping pulse. Forest green was not generally my best color, but today it gave me confidence. I looked fearsome. Like Robin Hood, if he'd been a woman with golden braids and an insatiable itch to win.

I wanted Tristan to see me, and I wanted to see the look in his eyes when he did. Was that my vanity once again? Today I did not care. One was allowed a bit of vanity every now and then.

But where *was* Tristan? He had to have arrived by now, and I would be lying if I said I hadn't been searching for his intense dark eyes and teasing mouth. A mouth that I'd been dreaming of since I'd left him under the willow.

Then my eyes jolted to a stop. Tristan stood just outside the shade of the marquee. His eyes were also fixed on me, and I felt a surge of pleasure, my body remembering how it felt to be surrounded by his arms, my lips captured by his. I let myself take him in—his green jacket, fitted perfectly to suit his broad shoulders; his dark hair, so carefully arranged; the sharp line of his newly-shaven jaw. His mouth was more serious than I would have liked, but I could not complain overmuch when the rest of him was so deliciously attractive. I took a step toward him.

It was then, of course, that the bugle sounded, signaling the start of the tournament.

I quickly lost sight of Tristan as the mass of archers and onlookers began moving towards the great red marquee, where a low platform had been erected. I rose onto my toes, but I still could not see Tristan. Would he come find me? Of course he would.

"Searching for someone?" Cora came to my elbow, a mischievous glint in her eyes.

I dropped back down to the flats of my feet. "No," I said quickly.

"You needn't deny it," Cora said, propping one fist on her hip, her bow over her shoulder. "I know you are looking for Tristan."

My lips twitched. "Perhaps. Perhaps not."

She gave me a little pinch and I danced away from her, laughing

"Fine! I was looking for him. I saw him a moment ago, but there are far too many people here."

"Just more opponents for you to defeat."

"And you," I pointed out. "I daresay you are better than most of the Sandcliffe Bowmen at this point."

She waved me off. "I have no great aspirations today. I only want to support you."

I had to swallow hard, and I took her arm. "Thank you, Cora. You are a true friend, and I am lucky to have you."

She squeezed my arm. Neither of us mentioned the other friend who should have been there beside us.

"Come," I said, clearing my throat and pulling her toward the marquee. "Let us find a spot near the front."

We followed the surge of people under the shade of the great marquee, thankfully blocking the relentless sun. I searched for Tristan but could not spot him. Where had he gone off to? I'd assumed he would be looking for me as well.

No matter. I would find him eventually. Cora and I claimed a spot near the platform, so we had an excellent view of the earl and countess ascending the low steps. Lord Englefield wore the shooting costume of his society, the Bowmen of Kent.

"Welcome," Lord Englefield called, his voice carrying easily. "What a pleasure it is to welcome you all to Highstead Castle today. It is a singular thrill to see such a talented group, and I am certain we will witness a spectacular showing today."

A small round of appreciative applause.

"We are especially glad to see so many ladies participating today," the earl went on. "What a sight you are! I hope the fairer sex will bring a new element of sophistication to our tournament."

The applause was noticeably louder this time, and I joined in, excitement sweeping through me. Cora turned to grin at me and I beamed back.

"Now, let us have a word from our Lady Patroness." Lord Englefield stepped back, gesturing his wife forward. She smiled, hands clasped before her.

"I am so pleased to reveal the prizes for today's shoot," she said. A servant holding a cushion stepped to her side and the countess lifted a gleaming cup aloft. "For the highest score, a golden cup."

The guests murmured around us, craning to see the cup better. It was a significant prize, no doubt immensely valuable. But I did not care for that—I did not shoot for prizes. I shot to prove myself.

Well, and I shot to win wagers against narrow-minded barons. Although it was becoming increasingly clear that I no longer cared about gaining membership in the Sandcliffe Bowmen. What had seemed so unbearably important a few weeks ago now only left me with a bitter taste in my mouth. No, that was not why I wanted to win—*needed* to win. I needed to win for my society, for the women who had devoted their time and hearts to my cause.

"And for the best shot, a silver medal." Lady Englefield showed the medal to more excited whispers. It was a prize anyone might claim, if one was lucky enough to get closest to the center of the target.

Lady Englefield raised her hand to quiet the crowd, and then smiled once more. "May your arrows fly true."

A Mr. Kilorn was introduced, the vice-president of the Bowmen of Kent who would act as the archery marshal today, and he explained how the tournament would proceed. We would be divided into groups of eight and shoot in turn. The first round would be a double end, ten arrows each way for a total of twenty shots. The four highest scores would advance to the final round.

I squared my shoulders, setting my jaw. I *would* be one of those final four.

Mr. Kilorn held up a paper. "The first group will include: Miss Cora Atherton, Mr. Frederick Wilson, Mr.—"

I did not hear the rest, only snapped my eyes to Cora, who stood unblinking.

"I have to shoot first?" She paled so quickly I thought she might faint then and there.

I put one hand on her arm. "You have practiced for this. You are *ready*. Do not let anyone intimidate you."

"I imagined you would go first," she said faintly. "Everyone will be watching me, wanting me to fail."

"Not everyone," I corrected her. "Your whole society will be cheering you on."

Mr. Kilorn finished reading his list. "—and Mr. Tristan Gates."

His name sent a fluttering through my stomach. I tried to ignore it.

"There, you see," I said, hurrying to reassure her. "Tristan will be with you. Just follow him."

Cora nodded, her eyes a bit wild. "Yes. All right."

I felt a wave of guilt. This was not Cora's idea of a fine time. *I* was the one who enjoyed the attention and excitement of a prize shoot. She was only here because of me.

I took her shoulders and looked her in the eye. "You *can* do this, Cora. You're as good a shot as anyone here."

She gave a short laugh. "You needn't lie."

"You are," I said fiercely.

"Miss Atherton?"

Tristan appeared at my side, his gaze focused solely on Cora though his hand lightly brushed the small of my back. His touch sent a rippling heat across me.

"Are you ready?" he asked her. "I thought we might walk to the targets together."

This man. That he'd seen Cora's panic and come to help only made me love him more.

Cora twisted her hands over her bow's handle, glancing behind her as if she was considering making a run for it. Then she took a deep breath. "Yes," she said finally. "I am ready."

I squeezed her shoulders once more, trying to instill the confidence I knew she should feel. She was an excellent shot, and if she could find a way to relax, she would do splendidly.

Cora set her shoulders and started across the field toward the targets. Tristan moved to follow her, but I grabbed his arm.

"Thank you," I whispered. "She's terribly nervous."

He still would not meet my eyes. "I'll try to set her at ease."

I frowned. Why was he acting so strangely? "Is everything all right, Tristan?"

"Yes, of course." He stepped away, slipping free of my grasp. "Good luck to you."

I could only blink as he strode away. What had *that* been? He hadn't met my gaze for even a moment. Was he holding back because of our surroundings, because of the watching eyes and listening ears? But why, then, would he not at least look at me?

A twisting current took hold inside me. I tried to ignore it. He would not have touched my back so gently if something was wrong, would he? I was being overly perceptive, that was all.

I set aside those thoughts and instead focused on Cora, walking beside Tristan to the targets. It was time for my society to prove itself, and I could only hope I had done enough.

Chapter Thirty-Three

TRISTAN

I DROPPED my head as I walked away from Marigold, staring down at the grass. I hadn't meant to be so brusque, so cool. I simply hadn't known *how* to speak with her. I was trapped between two terrible choices and I could not look her in the eyes when I hadn't yet decided what to do.

But then, why was it *my* choice? Could I not simply perform my best and leave it up to chance? Let Fate decide? Although, the last time I had attempted that, I'd broken Marigold's bow. Perhaps that was not the best option.

I dragged a hand through my hair, withheld a groan, then hurried to catch up with Cora. No matter what I decided, I had to shoot well in the first round to advance.

Cora glanced at me as I came up beside her. "I'd wager you are glad to be shooting against me."

It took me a moment to understand her meaning, but then I frowned at her. She was so determined to see herself as inferior to all these other archers. "I *am*," I said, "though not for the reason you think. I am simply looking forward to watching the men's faces when you outshoot them."

She did not respond, but her back straightened infinitesimally.

"I shall try not to disappoint you," she said, the smallest grin tugging at her mouth.

We arrived at the targets along with the other archers in the first group. Cora was the only woman, and the men milling about sent her curious glances. No one was rude, but neither did they speak to her. I stayed by her side as a servant handed us cards with pins attached, so that we might poke a hole in the appropriate spot to mark our points.

When they grouped us two to a target, I volunteered to shoot with Cora. She shot me a look of gratitude, but it was hardly a favor; I simply did not want to make awkward conversation with strangers. I shook out my arms, as if that would loosen the tension in my limbs. It did nothing. I could only hope that once the shooting began, I would fall back into the normal rhythm of things.

The round started with a blow of the bugle. Cora shot first, and when her arrow hit the black ring, I could hear Marigold's cheer above all the rest. I could not help myself and darted a glance to the audience. Marigold clapped enthusiastically, bouncing on her toes, her eyes alive. She was far from alone—every member of the Lady Archers I could see was cheering and applauding. Cora grinned and gave a little wave as she stepped back to let me shoot.

I moved forward and nocked my arrow. My limbs felt unfamiliar, detached—as if they were controlled by marionette strings. My first shot was a disappointment—only one point—and as Cora and I took turns shooting, I grew more and more frustrated. I prided myself on my precision, but it was eluding me today.

Without thinking, my eyes flicked to Marigold. She watched me with arms crossed, her expression pensive. When she met my eyes, she straightened and gave a small, forced smile.

I looked away. Was her smile false because of how I'd acted when we'd spoken, or because she knew very well how much depended on her winning today?

I scrutinized the other archers in my group as we shot. Out of the eight, there were perhaps two or three who had notable talent. Cora was included in that number, with her steady hand and reliable aim. She did not have Marigold's natural skill, but I could see her influence in the way Cora drew her bow in one smooth motion.

In the end, only one of my arrows hit the gold center, and barely so. I grimaced as I lowered my bow after my tenth shot. The white flag waved and we walked to the targets to tally the score. I led our group, but only just. Cora was five points behind me.

"Well done," I said quietly to Cora as she regarded her score-card, looking surprised. Though not nearly as surprised as the men at the targets beside us, muttering to each other as they eyed the placement of her arrows.

She offered me a smile. "The same to you, Mr. Gates. Though, if I may be so bold, I know you can do better."

She was right. I *could* do better, and I would need to if I intended to advance to the final round.

We pulled our arrows from the targets and prepared to complete the double end, shooting back at the targets we'd just left. As I waited for my turn, Lord Beauford caught my eye, standing at the front of the crowd. He crossed his arms, expression dark, then jerked his head to the right.

I furrowed my brow but followed the direction of his nod. Coultry stood beside Uncle and Mrs. Penrose, watching the shooting with real interest. I swallowed hard, looking back at Lord Beauford. His eyes narrowed meaningfully.

I understood. Clearly Beauford was disappointed in my performance so far. I set my jaw, turning my back to the baron. That he should go to such ridiculous lengths to ensure my complicity made me want to rip the bow from his hands and smash it over my knee.

But I forced myself to focus, to take my time and make every shot count. I did better, scoring another center hit, and won my round. I still was not pleased with my performance, but my score should be enough to advance me to the final round.

"My congratulations, Mr. Gates," Cora said with a curtsy.

"To you as well," I said, bowing. "A commendable performance."

"I am only glad it is over." She pulled her arrows from the target. "I am not so fond of competing as you and Marigold."

"Perhaps," I said, "but now everyone knows that the Lady Archers of Sandcliffe are to be feared."

"I daresay Marigold will be the one to truly prove that." She gave a crooked smile. "And I wish you luck against her. I do think you shall need it."

"I have no doubt," I said dryly.

The next group of archers was preparing to shoot, so we parted. She headed for where her society had gathered, waiting to congratulate her on her success, and I could feel Marigold's eyes on me. I pretended not to see and hurried to join Uncle, Mrs. Penrose, and Coultry.

I knew I was being a coward. I knew it. But I could not stand beside her and feign that all was well. Not when she could very well hate me at the end of this tournament. I exhaled. That was an exaggeration. I did not think she would hate me. But if I won, I would take away the very thing that had given her life meaning when her future had been so cruelly snatched from her. I could not pretend it wouldn't affect how she viewed me.

"Tristan?"

My head jolted up. Uncle was watching me, concern creasing his brow.

"Yes?" I said quickly.

His brow only furrowed deeper and he glanced at Mrs. Penrose and Coultry, still watching the next round, then nodded to his left. I reluctantly followed him away from the crowd.

"What's happened?" he asked, crossing his arms as he faced me.

"Nothing's happened."

He gave a disbelieving laugh. "I haven't seen you shoot that poorly in years. No, something is the matter and I would wager it has to do with Marigold."

I blew out a breath. How did he do that? I put my hands to my waist and paced away, then suddenly spun on him again. "You're right."

"Am I?" He blinked in exaggerated surprise. "What a notion."

"Quiet now," I growled, "or I won't allow you to offer me advice."

"Very well," he said, holding up a hand in surrender. "Tell me what this is all about."

I explained everything: Lord Beauford's threat against Coultry, my overhearing the baron speaking of his wager with Marigold and all she had risked.

"And now," I said tiredly, "I do not know what to do. No matter what I choose—trying to win or losing on purpose—someone will be hurt by my actions."

"Not *your* actions," he corrected, his voice hard. "No, this is not something you can blame yourself for. The guilt lies solely with Lord Beauford."

"Be that as it may," I said, "it does not solve my problem." I'd been staring down at the grass at our feet as I'd spoken, but now I looked up at him. "What do I do?"

He gave a small huff. "I haven't the faintest idea."

"*Now* you decide to have no interest in guiding my life?" My words were meant to be joking but instead held a thread of desperation.

"It is not that I have no interest," he said, "but rather that I simply do not know what to tell you. Your situation seems impossible, truly." He paused. "Have you spoken to Marigold about this? Or Coultry?"

"How could I?" I asked. "They both would feel terrible if they knew what the other would suffer."

"Still," he said, "they might provide insight that could be useful."

"No," I said firmly. "I cannot push this onto either of them. I will solve this somehow."

Uncle examined my face, his eyes thoughtful. "I am sorry," he said sincerely. "You should not be in this position. But I cannot help but feel proud."

"Proud?" I gave a mirthless laugh. "That I am allowing myself to be blackmailed?"

"No," he said. "That you are putting both your future wife and your friend ahead of your own desires." He paused. "You've become an exceptional man, Tristan. One your mother and father would be proud of as well."

I blinked, my eyes blurring, and then looked away, unable to bear the blend of pain and love in his eyes. He gripped my shoulder for one long moment, then left to rejoin Mrs. Penrose.

I slowly went to stand beside Coultry, who nodded in greeting, having no idea what had just transpired. The competition went on, four other groups shooting over the course of an hour. I examined my situation from every possible angle but could see no recourse. No matter what I did, someone I cared for would be hurt.

Even amid my turmoil, I watched each of the Lady Archers compete. They shot as well as any of the other societies, and even better than some. Many of these men had been shooting for years, but considering archery was often regarded as a social club rather than a serious sport, I was not surprised that the ladies held their own. They had a fire of determination that most of these archers had never seen before, and it fueled their shooting.

When it was Marigold's turn, I could not stop myself from watching her. Considering what I knew about her wager with the baron, I thought to see some sign of nerves. But she showed none. In fact, as she shot, I could only shake my head in amazement. Three center hits and the rest within the inner rings—all while keeping her expression cool, her movements fluid, and her aim impeccable.

She won her round handily and did not look at me once.

Marigold left the field to a round of applause and was received excitedly by her family and friends. I stayed where I was. At the moment, I was neither.

Chapter Thirty-Four

MARIGOLD

TRISTAN WAS AVOIDING ME.

It was perfectly obvious. First, our strange interaction before he'd left to shoot, and then when he'd finished, he had very pointedly *not* come to stand by me. I knew he'd seen me, but he'd gone to join his uncle and Mrs. Penrose instead.

I very nearly dashed after him right then and confronted him. But I couldn't, not when I needed to throw my arms around Cora and praise her for shooting so well. Not when every round included at least one member of my society and I was determined to watch and support each one. Whatever was bothering Tristan would have to wait.

Then it was my turn to shoot, and even with my feelings in a muddle, I shot better than I ever had. As was customary, the bugle blew every time the gold center was hit, and it sounded thrice for me, each time sending a thrill across my skin.

I wanted to look for Tristan, to see if he was watching me, but I resisted. I did not need such a distraction, not when I was so close to achieving my dreams. But my chest ached. Why was he acting like this?

I finished my first round to great applause, though I noticed Lord Beauford away from the crowd, his back to the competition as if he did not care who won. He did, clearly, based on his reaction to losing his round not half an hour earlier. He had marched from the field with a scowl, not even bothering to congratulate the winner. At least I would not have to shoot against *him* in the final round. Of course, that did not mean my competition was any less steep. I'd always known it would come down to Tristan and me, and that was proving true. He hadn't shot particularly well in his first round, but that meant nothing. Likely it was just a strategy. He would not hold back in the final round, and I would have to shoot my absolute best to win.

I mustered a smile as I rejoined my society in the audience, each lady embracing me or patting my arm or exclaiming excitedly over my score. Oh, but it would hurt them to lose the Lady Archers, especially after they'd experienced this prize shoot.

How could I have been so abominably selfish to gamble it all away? How would I tell them if the worst happened?

My thoughts took a different turn. What would Tristan say if he knew about my wager with Lord Beauford? I pictured his face, his eyes dark with disappointment, his mouth flat and shoulders tight.

I had to push the image away. Doubt and insecurity would not serve me at the moment. I focused again on the range. Mama was shooting in the last group, and I clapped for her every shot. And when her last arrow pierced the golden center, the bugle blowing, I cheered, hugging Oliver.

By the time the last group finished, the success of our ladies' society was clear. Of the top twenty scores, six were members of the Lady Archers of Sandcliffe, including Cora, Mama, and myself. Only two other societies had done as well: the earl's own, the Archers of Kent, and the Sandcliffe Bowmen. I wanted to catch Lord Beauford's eye in the crowd and send him a satisfied smile, but he was nowhere to be seen.

We'd done it. We'd proven that we could shoot at the highest level, that we were equal to any archer on this field.

But that thought did not dissuade the twisting and churning in my stomach as the servants replaced the targets with fresh ones for the final round. The final four archers consisted of myself, Tristan, and two men from the Archers of Kent. It would not be easy, but I *had* to win. I had to win, or all of our efforts would be in vain.

"If I may offer a bit of advice," Oliver said, nudging me with his shoulder, "try to aim for the center. I've five guineas wagered on you winning."

I cast my eyes to the cloudless sky. "Do you? Then of course *now* I shall try."

He winked and sauntered off. I watched him go with a small smile. He may tease and poke and prod me, but I knew the sort of brother he was at the very core. I knew what he would do for me—dig me free from a cave and defend me to my so-called friends.

I turned to see Cora's eyes following Oliver, again with a strange intensity. Why was she looking at him like that? Like she . . .

And then I realized, and I nearly gasped aloud. Cora had *feelings* for Oliver. It all made a great deal of sense. Why she was always interested in news of him, why she'd been so affected by his quarrel with Sylvia. And why she'd never told anyone, considering what we had all assumed would happen between Oliver and Sylvia.

My heart ached. I loved my brother, I did, but there were some things he was very much blind to—such as how wonderful Cora was. Sylvia had always been there to steal his attention. But now . . .

Cora caught me watching her and straightened, a smile hurrying to her lips. "You'll do wonderfully, I have no doubt."

I wanted to take her aside and tell her that *I knew*. But now was not the time, and if she did not want to tell me, perhaps she had a very good reason. "Thank you."

We exchanged a small hug and she retreated to stand with her mother, who had watched the prize shoot with unimpressed eyes from the back of the marquee.

After Papa also wished me luck and went to join Oliver, I faced Mama. She pressed her lips together as she regarded me, her eyes shimmering.

"Oh, Mama," I said, pretending exasperation even as tears pricked at my own eyes. "You cannot be crying already."

Her arms came around me and held me tight. She spoke in my ear. "Show them who you are," she whispered fiercely. "You deserve to be here."

I closed my eyes, throat sore. "Thank you, Mama. For standing by me. For supporting me. For everything."

Mama gave a watery smile as she pulled back. "What else is a mother for?"

With one last squeeze of my hand, she left me standing alone at the side of the field. I waited for the bugle to signal the final round, shifting my weight as I checked my equipment yet again. Then I heard Mr. Raines's booming voice from somewhere in the crowd, and my eyes moved without thought.

Tristan stood beside his uncle and Mrs. Penrose. She spoke excitedly, gesturing at the targets as Mr. Raines listened. Tristan, however, stared blankly at the green field before him. What was he thinking about? What had caused that deep line to appear in his forehead, the flat press of his lips?

Then Tristan looked up and his gaze collided with mine. A rush of heat swept through my chest, a blazing wildfire. His mouth parted slightly, and—

The bugle blew, signaling the start of the final round.

I tore my eyes from Tristan's, breathing hard. His expression. It had almost seemed pained. Regretful.

I thought I might be sick. Something was clearly wrong. Had I done something to offend him? My memories of roving yesterday flew through my head, and I could not think of what I might have done. I'd thought he'd enjoyed our time together as much as I had. He'd certainly kissed me as if he had. Unless . . . was it our kiss? What if that kiss had revived something inside him, the part of him that fought against love and refused to entertain such flighty ideas? Perhaps he regretted kissing me and changing our relationship.

And yet . . .

I did not know every part of Tristan, but I knew he cared for me. This was *Tristan*. The man who had shielded my body with his in the cave-in. The man who had spent countless hours in the last weeks helping my society. The man who had kissed me so desperately, held me like I was everything to him.

Why, then, was he avoiding me?

Tristan and the other two archers competing in the final round had already started across the lawn toward the targets. All I wanted was to drag Tristan away and find a quiet place to talk. But that was impossible. Everyone was waiting and watching.

I took a deep breath, adjusted the bow on my shoulder, and started forward into the blinding sunlight. I was the last to arrive at the targets, a fact noted by Mr. Kilorn's hard eyes.

"Here is Miss Cartwell, at last," the marshal said, his voice holding an edge of disapproval. It seemed that Lord Beauford was not the only one who disliked including women in the shoot.

I opened my mouth to apologize, then shut it again, raising my chin. I'd done nothing wrong. "Yes, here I am."

Mr. Kilorn narrowed his eyes but seemed to think better of addressing me. He turned to the men. "The same rules as before apply. A double end, ten arrows for each target, twenty total. The highest score wins the tournament. Mr. Barnes and Mr. Gillingham, you will shoot on the far targets. Mr. Gates and Miss Cartwell, you will shoot on the near targets."

My lungs tightened. Tristan and I would be shooting together. I'd have to watch every draw of his bow and strike of his arrow.

The men were nodding, including Tristan, so I did as well. I did not want to protest our assignment and cause a stir.

"Very well," Mr. Kilorn said. "You may begin shooting when you are ready."

I stole a quick glance at Tristan and found his eyes already on me. The distance between us was a tangible thing, cold and rigid.

I tore my gaze from his. "Shall we?" I managed briskly.

He nodded and we walked to our target together, not another word passing between us. I set my quiver on the grass and filled my waist pouch with ten arrows, painted with my blue initials. Tristan stood nearby, checking that his string hadn't twisted, his movements so familiar to me after all our practices together. My hands shook. How was I to shoot with my heart trying its level best to leap out of my chest?

"First or second?" he asked, tightening his shooting brace.

"Second," I said without hesitation. I wanted to have the last shot.

He did not protest, only moved forward woodenly. He raised his bow, aimed, and released. His arrow hit the inner red ring of the target, a good shot. The crowd applauded. I watched as if from a distance, my insides swirling like the sea on the edge of a storm.

Tristan moved to the side, allowing me space to shoot, but as he passed me, my hand shot out of its own accord and stopped him. I looked up at him, at his dark, unreadable eyes. I suddenly could not go another moment without speaking to him.

"What is wrong, Tristan?" I asked, my words somehow even. Steady.

"Marigold—"

"I thought we'd moved beyond this," I said. "Are we not allies, Tristan? Are we not friends? Are we not—"

My voice cracked. His lips parted, but I pressed on. "Are you angry with me? Have I done something?"

He began shaking his head. I kept speaking. "Or do you—do you regret our kiss yesterday? If you do not feel the same way as I do—"

"Blast it, Marigold." He ran a hand through his hair. "Of course I do not regret kissing you."

My heart lifted slightly, but I still did not have an answer from him. "Then why—"

"Will you please allow me to speak?" His voice was crossed between exasperation and amusement. "And *you* need to shoot."

"Of course I need to shoot," I said shortly. "I simply cannot concentrate when you are glowering."

"I am not glow—"

Mr. Kilorn's voice interrupted him. "Miss Cartwell? Might we move this along?"

Now *I* was the one glowering, but at the marshal who watched us with impatience.

"Go on," Tristan said with a sigh. "We are skilled enough to shoot and speak at the same time."

"Very well," I muttered. I forced myself to raise my bow and aim, trying to calm the patter of my heart. I released my arrow and it hit the outer white ring. Not my best, but then I wasn't used to competing while also trying to hold my heart together.

"Your turn," I said, moving aside. "To shoot *and* to speak."

He took my place, and I thought he took more time than usual to find his shooting stance, adjusting his feet and setting his shoulders. He raised his bow and drew back his string. He paused.

"Why did you not tell me about your wager with Lord Beauford?" he asked quietly.

I stared dumbly at his back, my pulse taking off like a bird in flight. He *knew* about the wager?

He released his arrow. It hit the target with a distant thump, and Tristan turned to face me, eyes apprehensive.

"How do you know about that?" My voice did not sound like my own, strangled and cracked.

"I overheard him speaking to Mr. Hutton."

"Oh." I swallowed hard. Now I was the one who could not meet his eyes. "You must . . . you must think terribly of me. I thought so many times of telling you, but I could not bear your anger, your disappointment."

I was rambling, and I needed to shoot again—I could hear the other archers shooting, the cheers from the crowd. I stepped forward, though my vision was so hazy I could not imagine how I would even hit the target, let alone score any points. I managed to steady my arms long enough to loose my arrow, somehow striking the red ring.

"Marigold." He shook his head as we traded places yet again. "I am not angry."

That did not seem possible. "You needn't lie," I managed. "I know what a fool I was."

"I'm not lying." He paused, his back to me as he raised his bow. "That is, I *was* frustrated. I couldn't understand why." He released his arrow. The crowd cheered, and the bugle blew. A center hit.

I barely noticed, too ashamed at having been caught in a net of my own making. I took a deep breath. I had to try and explain, though my reasons were weak.

"The baron promised he would let me join the Sandcliffe Bowmen if I won," I said quietly. "It seems so trivial now. It was before the cave-in, before we were engaged. I still thought I would marry Mr. Eastbrook and leave Sandcliffe. I thought I took no risk in making such a wager."

"Mari . . ." His eyes were soft.

I hurried to finish speaking. "I could never have imagined what would happen, or how important the society would become to me." I shook my head. "How important *you* would become to me. I know now that I was supremely selfish to make such a wager. And since I cannot forgive myself, I cannot expect it of you."

He blew out a short puff of air. "Why on earth should you need my forgiveness?"

"Because of how much you've invested in the society," I insisted. "It is just as much yours as it is mine, and I risked it for nothing."

"I daresay you are blaming yourself enough for the both of us. But you could not have known what would happen." He lifted one shoulder. "Besides, I am far too aware of the mistakes I've made in my own life."

His words filled me with hope. Did he truly not hate me for what I'd done?

I glanced at Mr. Kilorn, who watched us with a scowl. I hurried to step forward and shoot, hitting the inner white ring.

"Still," I said as he moved to take my place. "It is no small thing, what I've done."

"No, it is not," he agreed, and there was something in his voice that made me pause. If he wasn't disappointed in me, then why did he sound so tortured? He raised his bow and aimed.

My mind made the connection in the next instant. When he

turned back after hitting the black ring, he faced my narrowed eyes and crossed arms.

"You *cannot*," I said shortly.

"What?"

"You cannot lose to me on purpose." My voice was firm. "I won't stand for it. I made the wager, and I alone will bear the consequences of my actions."

Something in my words sparked a reaction in him. He stepped toward me and the sudden heat in his eyes made me catch my breath.

"Marigold," he said fiercely, "I am to be your husband. I will stand by your side, no matter the battles you face. You will never be alone. Not now. Not ever."

I stared at him. My heart seemed to fill up my whole chest, warm and light. I wanted to bury my face in his shoulder, wrap my arms around his waist.

"You mustn't say such things when I am trying to be obstinate," I rasped, my voice weak.

Tristan's expression softened. "That is hardly fair. You are *always* obstinate."

I bit back the smile that tried to find my lips. I could not let him distract me. "But Tristan, *no*. I will not allow you to throw the tournament for my sake."

He looked away, scrubbing one hand over his face. "If only it were so simple."

I frowned. "What are you talking about?"

He sighed. "I shall only say that Lord Beauford is determined to do everything in his power to keep you from winning."

"Tristan—"

He nodded toward the targets. "Keep shooting, Mari, or Mr. Kilorn will faint."

I ignored his words, fixing my gaze on him. I would not let this be. "What do you mean? What has Lord Beauford done?"

Chapter Thirty-Five

TRISTAN

BLAST IT. I'd said too much. When I'd admitted I knew about the wager, I hadn't imagined how quickly our conversation would spiral out of control. Now she knew there was something else at play besides her wager with the baron. And yet, I could not tell her about Coultry. It was not her fault that Lord Beauford had caught my friend in his sights, and I had an inkling that if she knew the whole truth, she might very well quit the tournament right then and there in protest of Lord Beauford's actions. And I could not allow that to happen.

Because I was still hoping. I was still desperately wishing that a solution would present itself: a way for Marigold to save her society, for Coultry to keep his business, and for Lord Beauford to be made a fool. Well, the last seemed especially unlikely, but if I was making outrageous wishes, then I might as well add it to the list.

"Marigold," I said. "Please. I will explain everything after."

"Why can't you explain it now?" Her eyes flashed.

"Because . . ." My voice trailed off. What could I say? I groaned, shaking my head. "Because I want *you* to win, even though I *cannot* lose."

Marigold watched me, irritation painted across her expression. "You do know that doesn't make the slightest bit of sense."

"Yes, I know." I blew out a long breath. "Just . . . just keep shooting. Please."

"Miss Cartwell," called Mr. Kilorn, clearly irritated. "It is your turn."

"Devil take that man," I muttered under my breath. "Can't two people speak in peace?"

Her lips twitched in spite of everything. "It appears that the middle of an archery tournament is not the best place for an intimate discussion."

But she stepped forward, raising her bow. Even in the midst of my turmoil, I could not help but admire her shooting. There was something in her movements, her natural grace, that I could never hope to emulate, nor did I wish to. It was hers entirely.

The round continued, and the two of us spoke no more, focusing on our own shooting. I still felt off-balance, uncentered, but so must have Marigold. We met each other shot for shot, neither of us pulling away in score until Marigold hit the center with her tenth shot.

"Well done," I managed.

She gave a half-hearted smile. "You told me to keep shooting."

That I had. And with every one of her arrows, I felt both pride and panic. I couldn't lose. I couldn't win. I was trapped.

The white flag dropped, signaling it was safe to retrieve our arrows and tally our score. Marigold and I started forward together, but I paused when I saw a hand waving from the crowd. It was Uncle, Coultry at his side, their eyes determined as they gestured me to come to them.

I stared, mystified. What on earth could they want? Coultry perceived my confusion and waved me on more fervently. Well, whatever the matter was, it must be something of significance.

I turned to Mr. Kilorn, who watched with clear annoyance. "Might we take a brief recess? I need to . . . I must see to something."

His jaw tightened, and I was fairly certain he was about to refuse. So I turned away before he had the chance. Marigold had stopped as well, watching me intently. I could only shrug as I strode off the field, meeting Uncle and Coultry at the edge of the marquee as the crowd murmured and shifted to watch us.

"Has someone died?" I asked them. "I cannot think of any other reason to have stopped the shoot."

Uncle cleared his throat. "No, no, I have a very good reason." He looked distinctly uncomfortable as he glanced at Coultry. "Tristan, I told him."

I stiffened. "What?"

He held up one hand. "I know you spoke to me in confidence, and you can be angry with me later. But I could not help thinking that *I* should like to be aware of any blackmail involving my name."

Coultry's eyes flashed as he crossed his arms. "Indeed. I could not believe it when your uncle told me what you were doing. Do you think I care one whit what the baron might say about me?"

"No," I said sharply. "No, I don't believe you do. But that is the problem. You do not know his influence. The man could ruin you in a day if he put his mind to it."

"Even if that were true," Coultry said, "I do not hold with blackmail."

"But you've a family to think of, Coultry," I said, frustrated. Why did he not see things as clearly as I did?

"I am well aware," he said, casting me an exasperated look. "So please let me assure you that I am fully capable of caring for them."

"No one doubts your ability—"

He waved me off. "I've had six new commissions today."

I stared. "Six?"

"Two from Lord Englefield himself," he said, a bit smugly. "The earl saw Lord Beauford's bow and admired my work. Upon learning who had crafted it, Lord Englefield sought me out. Several of his acquaintances from the Archers of Kent did as well."

I could only shake my head, my thoughts spinning.

"Trust me, Gates," he said. "I may lose a few customers if Lord Beauford does follow through, but there are plenty who want my services. My business will be fine." He gave a wry smile. "I will even

297

commit to attending a few more prize shoots if that will ease your mind."

I exhaled a ragged laugh. "You are certain?"

"Lord Beauford has had his way of things for long enough," he said, voice firm. "I'll not allow him to bully you for my sake."

I rubbed my jaw. I'd been a fool to not involve him sooner. "I am sorry I did not tell you myself. It was an oversight I'll not make again."

He chuckled. "Yes, next time this happens, be sure to let me know." He sobered and held out his hand to me. "You're a good man, Gates. A good friend."

I gripped his hand firmly. "The same to you."

Marigold and the other archers were reassembling near the far targets, Mr. Kilorn tapping his foot and glaring at me. But I turned to Uncle, raising one brow.

He grinned. "No need to thank me. I was quite selfish, truly. All I want is for Lord Beauford to lose in every possible way today."

"I am still not entirely clear on how I can make that happen," I said. "Marigold will be furious if I lose intentionally."

He slapped a hand on my back. "You'll think of something. Hopefully within the next few minutes."

"Thank you for that," I said dryly, then started back across the field to join Marigold. She had already pulled her arrows from the target, Mr. Kilorn beside her recording the score.

"What was that about?" she asked suspiciously as I retrieved my own arrows.

How was I supposed to answer that? "Nothing," I mustered. "It was just business."

Her eyes narrowed, but before she could press me, Mr. Kilorn called out to resume shooting. We still had the double end to complete, ten arrows left apiece.

Marigold led by three points. It might as well have been nothing. An archery match this close could change in the blink of an eye. But now I knew what my aim was. Coultry was right—we could not allow Lord Beauford to win this. His words had given me the confidence I needed to make Marigold my priority. There was no doubt in my mind that I wanted her to win.

But how could I pretend to lose this late in the meeting? I nocked my arrow, my thoughts racing. The margin for error was so small, especially at a distance of a hundred yards. If I intentionally aimed for the outer rings, I had no doubt it would be perfectly obvious to anyone who knew my methods and techniques, namely Marigold. No, I needed another solution. And I had to be quick about it.

I raised my bow, aimed, and released my arrow, all without truly thinking about it. I hit the inner white ring. Two points.

Marigold sent me a searching look as she moved to take my spot, her shoulders tight. Was it because of how close our scores were? Because she was worried about the wager?

I watched her intently as she found her stance and peered at the target. She drew her bow, paused a moment as the crowd quieted, then released her arrow. It hit the black ring, only one point. I knew our scores were close—too close. Just as close as the match at the summer fair.

The summer fair.

An idea sparked through my mind. I straightened, examining it from all angles. Could it work?

"Tristan?" Marigold was looking at me, eyes squinted.

I gazed back, and I could not help the grin that spread across my face. "I've had an idea."

"An idea," she repeated doubtfully.

I stepped close to her. "Trust me, Marigold."

She tipped her chin up, and dash it all if I didn't want to pull her to me and claim those tempting lips. "What are you going to do?"

I winked, an action so very unlike me and yet one that felt perfect in this moment. "Trust me," I said again.

Then I prepared to shoot for the last time.

Chapter Thirty-Six

MARIGOLD

My heart was a wild bird, thrashing in my chest, and my head raced to catch it. What was Tristan doing? Would he intentionally lose, even against all my protests?

I could not let him. It went against every bone in my body to allow such a thing. Even with all I stood to lose, I could never accept a victory that I had not fairly earned. Besides, Tristan couldn't very well start shooting terribly all of a sudden. Everyone would know. No doubt Lord Beauford would insist that the competition had been fixed and refuse to honor our wager.

I swallowed hard, watching Tristan aim his second arrow. *Trust me*, he'd said. And I *did* trust him. I trusted him with my heart, my life, my future. So I stood back and said nothing.

He released the arrow, and the bugle sounded a second later. A center hit. And, though I could not be sure from such a distance, it seemed to be dead center.

But Tristan did not seem to notice or care. Instead, as the crowd applauded, he shook out his right hand, cursing under his breath. Cursing?

"Blast," he said, loud enough for the despicable Mr. Kilorn to hear.

"Sir?" Mr. Kilorn approached. "Are you all right?"

"I've hurt my hand," Tristan said, holding out the limb in question.

Hurt his hand? I'd never seen Tristan injure himself while shooting, let alone during the most important prize shoot of his life.

Mr. Kilorn seemed just as apprehensive. "And?"

"I do not think I can continue," Tristan said. "I am most disappointed, of course." His lips twitched.

Mr. Kilorn crossed his arms. "Do you wish to withdraw?"

"Sadly, it seems that I must." Then Tristan brightened, as if just thinking of a solution. "Perhaps I might substitute another gentleman from my society to finish for me?"

It was not my best moment, perhaps, taking so long to realize what Tristan was about. But once the thoughts connected in my head, I stared at Tristan, my heart leaping and bounding. Was he truly . . .

Mr. Kilorn frowned. "I suppose so. Have you someone in mind?"

Tristan grinned. "I most certainly do." He turned to the murmuring crowd. "Lord Beauford? Would you be so kind as to finish for me?"

I was afraid to look. The baron was not a man to be crossed, and here was Tristan, throwing down the gauntlet before a peer of the realm. But my eyes could not resist finding Lord Beauford. He stood in frozen shock, his eyes fixed on Tristan—burning, sharp as broken glass. Then he looked at me, and the darkness I saw there gripped my heart in an icy fist.

"Lord Beauford?" Mr. Kilorn called, and my regard for the marshal grew infinitesimally. He was not intimidated by the baron, at least.

The onlookers near Lord Beauford—well-dressed ladies and men in jackets of superfine—pulled away as if to make a path for him. It was clear, at least to me, that the last thing Lord Beauford wanted to do was step back onto the field of competition. But it was equally clear that he must. If he refused, it was akin to admitting he was afraid to shoot against me, a woman. His equipment was nearby and ready. There was no legitimate reason to refuse.

"Very well," Lord Beauford said stiffly. He slammed his glass of lemonade into Mr. Hutton's chest, the drink sloshing over the side. The baron grabbed his bow from a nearby table, his movements sharp and jerky.

I hurried to Tristan's side. He was already unstringing his bow. "What are you thinking?" I demanded. "He will be furious."

"Good," he said. "I must be doing something right."

I shook my head, stomach tight. "This is no laughing matter, Tristan. He is powerful." Why was he not taking this more seriously? It was one thing to beat the man fairly but another entirely to deliberately embarrass him.

Tristan took my elbow, turning me to him. "Believe me, I know. I promise there is more at play here."

My eyes widened. "What—"

He shook his head. "I will tell you everything once this is finished. But first you have a tournament to win."

I looked up at him, at his steadfast eyes and confident jaw. How had I ever looked at this man with anything but the real and raw love that coursed through every inch of my body?

"Thank you," I said, voice as soft as newly budded leaves.

He dipped his head closer to mine. "Thank me by winning."

He wanted to kiss me—that was clear from the way his eyes traced over my lips. But that would not help anything, especially not his ruse that he was injured. He exhaled and sent me one last scorching look, then withdrew to join his uncle on the edge of the field.

Lord Beauford moved forward at the same time, and the two exchanged emotionless nods as they passed. They both knew a different game was being played now.

The baron walked towards me, his strides slow and meaningful. He kept a hard set to his face, no doubt meant to intimidate me. It worked a little. It was a frightening proposition, competing against such a formidable man in this setting, with so many looking on.

This was not like our village shoot. No matter who lost today, it would be unforgettable.

"Miss Cartwell," he said shortly, dropping his quiver to the grass.

"Lord Beauford," I managed, holding tight to my bow.

His eyes narrowed to slits. "I suppose you arranged this, laughing at me all the while."

I blinked. Was he serious? And then, danger of all dangers, I nearly laughed. Not because I thought his words were amusing but because of how ridiculously parallel this was to when I'd accused Tristan of the same thing at the fair. Oh, what irony.

I forced my lips to remain in a flat line. "I arranged nothing, my lord. Mr. Gates has regrettably injured his hand, and he thanks you for taking his place."

Lord Beauford made a sound, crossed between a growl and a curse, then turned his back on me as he prepared his arrows.

"Miss Cartwell, if you please," Mr. Kilorn said, gesturing to the targets.

I nodded, stepping forward. Every inch of me radiated energy. The importance of these next few minutes were incalculable. Either I would come away victorious, or I would lose the society that had given me hope and purpose when I thought I'd lost everything.

I did some quick calculations. I had nine shots remaining, Lord Beauford eight. With Tristan's last shot, he had taken the lead by seven points, and the baron was a capable enough archer that I knew I would have to work for every point.

I glanced to my left. Tristan stood with arms crossed, watching intently from beside Mr. Raines, Mrs. Penrose, and my family. Cora and the other Lady Archers all stood nearby, hope in their eyes. My heart lifted. Come what may, I could not be surrounded by better people. They believed in me and wanted me to succeed, and I would do everything in my power to do exactly that.

Nocking an arrow, I raised my bow with steady arms. I'd practiced countless hours imagining such a moment. I was ready.

I inhaled one long breath, peering through squinted eyes as I aimed. I released, and the call came.

"Three points!"

I could do better. I knew I could. And I would.

Lord Beauford shot, earning himself two points. We exchanged the shooting position again and again, not meeting one another's eyes as we passed. I slowly chipped away at his lead. When I scored a center hit, the bugle sounded and a great cheer erupted from the crowd.

Our remaining shots dwindled. Lord Beauford was shooting as well as I'd ever seen him, even landing his own center hit. It might have shaken me on a normal day, but this was not a normal day. I could not fail.

The two other archers, Mr. Barnes and Mr. Gillingham, finished their ten arrows. Neither of their scores were close to mine or Lord Beauford's, so they stepped back. It would be down to us.

I stepped forward to take my last shot but one. Lord Beauford led by three points, and now was my chance to pull ahead. I could feel the hundreds of eyes upon me. My hands shook. To give myself a moment, I touched my gloved fingers to the concoction in my grease box and rubbed it over the leather of my shooting fingers to allow a smoother release.

Lord Beauford made a noise of impatience. I ignored him and took my time to raise my bow. I aimed carefully, the stillness in the air disconcerting. My fingers twitched, ready.

Lord Beauford let out a great, hacking cough. My body jolted, an irrepressible reaction, and my arrow went wide, missing the target entirely.

A loud groan erupted from the watching crowd. But it was nothing compared to the chill in my heart. I'd needed that shot. I needed *every* shot.

I moved to the left, allowing Lord Beauford forward. I refused to look at him. He'd done it on purpose, jarring me when it mattered most. He did not care how he won, so long as he did.

I met Tristan's eyes, which blazed with murderous intent. He knew what the baron had done. Judging by the dark looks and whispers of those surrounding him, most of the audience did as well. I took a deep breath and faced forward again. I had to remain composed.

"The last shots," Mr. Kilorn announced. "Lord Beauford leads by three."

The baron's face was impassive as he raised his bow. He took what felt like a month to aim, then loosed his arrow.

"Three points," came the call.

"Ah," Lord Beauford crowed, turning and finally meeting my eyes. "Even you will have difficulty with a six-point deficit, Miss Cartwell."

I said nothing. He did not realize he had just given me a backhanded compliment, and I drew strength from it. Lord Beauford might hate me, but even he acknowledged my skill.

I stepped forward to take my last shot, feeling the soft grass give way beneath my boots, the mischievous wind as it toyed with my curls. I closed my eyes. I imagined myself preparing to shoot, aiming, and releasing. It all depended on this shot.

"Anytime you like," Lord Beauford called out, his voice grating.

"Hush," came someone's voice from the audience. "Let her shoot."

I could not tell who it was, but I was grateful to them. Lord Beauford should not get away with his atrocious manners simply because he was a baron.

I nocked my arrow and raised my bow. Every inch I pulled back felt like a weight of incomprehensible significance. I was beginning to tire, but I forced my arms to hold firm.

For the briefest of moments, I paused. If I won here, if I beat Lord Beauford, what would happen? He would not take it lightly. He would find a way to punish both Tristan and me. Was that worth the thrill of winning? Was it worth saving my society?

Yes, I decided. Lord Beauford may be nobility, but that did not give him the right to intimidate everyone into submission.

I breathed deeply. I aimed, adjusting for the breeze. Then I loosed my arrow.

It flew straight and true. I knew before it hit. The bugle bellowed.

"A center hit," came the call. "Nine points!"

Shouts and cheers filled the air, hats flung into the sky. I stared, jaw agape, not truly believing. I'd longed for this moment for *years*. Years of endless practice and self-doubt and disappointment. But the arrow still quivering in the target did not lie, and neither did the sound of the bugle. The sweetest euphoria swelled inside me, and my eyes blurred. It was real. I'd won. I'd *won*.

I spun, heart in my throat. Lord Beauford was already stalking from the field, bow thrown to the grass in a childish fit. I did not care. All I wanted was to throw my arms around Tristan.

But Mama met me first and held me tight, crying in my ear. Papa and Oliver gathered around us, patting me on the back and laughing in disbelief. If words were exchanged, I could not recall them. I was too far gone, too lost in shock and elation.

After Cora released me from her enthusiastic embrace, I regained some sort of control over myself and looked around. Where was Tristan?

I spotted him some distance away, watching me with quiet pleasure, arms crossed and hair ruffled by the wind. I wanted to run to him, but dozens of people stood between us, waiting to congratulate me. I smiled and nodded and slowly edged forward, but then Lady Englefield was before me, beaming.

"Oh, Miss Cartwell! I am more pleased than I can say!" she exclaimed, taking my arm. "Come, we must award the prizes."

The crowd parted for her as she guided me to the platform, where her husband also congratulated me with a kind smile. When the crowd gathered around us, Lady Englefield raised her hand to quiet them.

"The prize for the highest score," she said, holding aloft the gold cup, "is awarded to Miss Marigold Cartwell. Well done, my dear. Well done."

I accepted the cup with a curtsy, applause and cheers filling my ears once again. My prize was heavy in my hands, its exquisite engravings blurred as my vision was obscured by unexpected tears.

"And," Lady Englefield went on, "the prize for the arrow closest to the center is awarded to Mr. Tristan Gates."

I straightened with a jolt. I had forgotten the second prize. But of course. Of *course* it was Tristan who won it. His last shot had been magnificent.

The crowd clapped again, and Tristan materialized at the front, climbing the platform and accepting his prize, a silver medal hung from a thick ribbon.

"If anyone has not heard," Lady Englefield said with a broad smile, "these two are soon to be married. Heaven forbid anyone oppose them, on or off the archery field."

The crowd laughed. Tristan's eyes met mine and he smiled, perhaps the truest smile I had ever seen from him.

"I present your champions," Lady Englefield called, and the audience erupted. Oliver made an embarrassing amount of noise, especially for someone who insisted archery was nonsense for children.

Tristan took my hand and led me to the front of the platform. I gave a low curtsy, beaming at my family, my society. I could not have imagined it would feel like this, because I had not known joy like this before.

Tristan leaned toward me, and I just heard his words over the tumult. "Meet me at the cliffs," he said, his deep voice brushing against my ear. Heat sparked up my spine, and my breathing shallowed.

Before I could respond, he and I were once again surrounded by well-wishers. For a quarter of an hour, I was forced to politely accept congratulations, when all I wanted was to run away and find Tristan. At last, the crowd around me thinned, the guests going inside to prepare for the ball to be held that night.

I had other plans.

I hurried across the lawn, not looking back to see if anyone watched. The grass flowed around the north wall of the castle and straight to the edge of the white cliffs, which dropped to the glittering sea below. Tristan stood on the brink, hair tousled and jacket flapping in the brisk sea breeze.

I stopped for one long moment, simply taking him in. That this man—this good, intelligent, wonderful man—should be mine was a thought beyond my comprehension.

Tristan turned, as if sensing me. I moved toward him, the wind blowing my skirts back, and he toward me.

"A decisive victory, Miss Cartwell," he said as we met, the corner of his mouth curled upward.

"One only made possible by yourself, Mr. Gates." I crossed my arms, eyeing him. "Are you not planning to tell me what inspired your 'injury'?"

"Is it not obvious?" His eyes gleamed. "I will soon be needing a new society to shoot with, and I cannot join yours if it ceases to exist."

My lips fought a grin. "That is rather presumptuous of you. I recall some very strict rules that bar men from joining."

"Ah," he said, stepping closer. "How fortunate, then, that I have a most advantageous connection. The founder of the society, in fact."

"Do you now?" I arched one brow. "And what makes you think she will break the rules for you?"

"Because I happen to know her greatest weakness," he said, leaning forward as if to share a secret. "She cannot resist a challenge."

I laughed softly. "That is true enough. But she has another weakness greater than that."

"Does she now?" Tristan stood within arm's reach now, hands clasped behind his back.

"Oh, yes," I said. "Everyone knows she is quite wild for her husband-to-be."

We'd been teasing each other, light and sweet, but now Tristan sobered, his eyes fixed on mine.

"Is she?" His voice was hoarse.

Did he really not know? Could he really not see how much I loved him? I stepped to him, slipping my hands up to rest upon his chest. He swallowed hard, staring down at me. His heart pounded beneath my palms.

"Yes," I whispered.

He took a long breath, closing his eyes. "Because if you did have doubts, I would understand."

I touched his cheek with my fingertips, lightly tracing the hard lines of his jaw. "Tristan."

"I know we were thrown into this engagement." His words poured out, as if he was worried there was not time to say them all. He found my eyes again, his gaze filled with knee-weakening purpose. "I know I was not your first choice, or even your hundredth. But you are mine, Marigold. My first and only choice. And I'll choose you every day, without pause, for the rest of my life."

I could think of nothing to say. How could I, when he pulled me apart and put me back together within the space of a heartbeat? His words stretched between us like a desperate line thrown to a man overboard. His eyes searched my face, as if my answer would be written there, in the lines of my features.

I could not have stopped my smile for a thousand gold cups.

"Tristan Gates," I said slowly. "Are you saying that you love me?"

He straightened, opening his mouth and then closing it.

"Because you really ought to be clear about your intentions," I said, tapping him smartly on the chest. "You've only proposed twice, after all. A third time would surely—"

Tristan kissed me, whether to quiet me or to answer me, I couldn't say. He grasped my elbows, pulling me snug against him as his lips captured mine. My surprise did not last long. I kissed him back, fisting his waistcoat to hold myself closer. His hands moved to encircle my face, those clever, strong fingers caressing my cheeks, his lips molten against mine. He matched me kiss for kiss, each one slower and deeper than the last.

I finally had to pull away, my breaths coming too quickly. I looked up at him, let my eyes run over every inch of his face. The turn of his lips, the strong ridge of his brow, the warmth in his eyes. I wanted to remember this, the moment when we both *knew*.

"I love you, Tristan," I whispered.

He stared at me as if no one had ever said that to him. And perhaps no one had since his parents had died. My heart ached. I slid one hand around his neck, gently tugging his forehead to touch mine. He watched me with shiny eyes.

"You are my choice as well," I said softly. "Now and forever."

He kissed me again, as if words were not enough to tell me how he felt. But he showed me, with endless searing kisses and impossibly tender embraces.

Epilogue

TRISTAN

I watched Marigold sleep.

Dim light slipped through the drawn curtains, falling on the curve of her cheek. I could just see her golden hair, her braid temptingly tousled after a night's sleep. Her lips were parted slightly as she breathed, slow and steady.

She had no idea how often I did this, simply watched her in almost bewildered disbelief. This woman had somehow consented to be my wife. She had said the vows and taken my name, had moved with me to the dower house on Uncle's property, and now lay beside me every night and every morning.

I was not terribly religious, but it seemed something of an ongoing miracle.

Blast. That had almost been poetic. Was Marigold right? Had I turned into a silly romantic? Or perhaps I was only a romantic because of her. I doubted anyone else could make me wax poetic at sunrise.

Marigold stirred, her hand coming to rest beneath her cheek, then she settled again. I sighed. I wanted to let her sleep, but I also knew if I did not wake her, she would be put out with me. We had so much to do today before the guests began arriving, and oversleeping was not on Marigold's agenda.

I moved closer and kissed the soft skin of her shoulder, the sleeve of her night rail having fallen down her arm. "Mari."

She did not stir, though her eyelashes fluttered.

"Mari, it's time to wake," I said, a bit louder. She still did not move. My wife was a sound sleeper, I'd learned in our month of marriage, and she disliked waking as much as she disliked losing. It was time to use that to my advantage.

"Marigold, the prize shoot is starting," I said, louder and agitated. "Hurry!"

She jolted upright in bed, her eyes blinking frantically, her disheveled hair forming a golden halo around her head. "My bow!"

I was already laughing. It took her a long moment to focus her eyes—and her thoughts—but when she did, her mouth dropped. "You wretch," she declared, throwing her pillow at me.

"What have I done?" I said, catching the pillow. "You told me to ensure you woke at a decent hour."

She glared at me, though her lips twitched. "Yes, but there are a dozen other methods you might have used."

"Hmm," I said. "Quite right."

"Oh, hush," she said, her cheeks pink.

"Next time, I will be more considerate," I promised with a rakish grin.

"Good."

She tried to keep her face severe but failed when I sat up and pulled her against my side. She sighed, tucking her head against my shoulder, reminding me of our night in the cave. It seemed so long ago. How incredibly improbable that things should have worked out the way they had.

"What time will Lord and Lady Englefield arrive?" I asked.

"Midday, her letter said." Marigold's hands toyed with the blankets. "I do hope the roads are serviceable. After the rains last week—"

"The roads will be perfectly fine," I assured her. "Everything will be. You're prepared."

"I want it to go well," she said quietly. "This is important to me."

"I know."

Marigold, nearly from the moment she'd won the Lady Patroness's Meeting, had begun plotting and planning. She'd worried that Lord Beauford would retaliate against her society, in hopes of ruining it once and for all. So she'd devised a plan—hosting her own prize shoot and inviting several societies from nearby towns to attend. The only qualification? The societies must allow women to join.

The response she'd received was surprisingly enthusiastic. Not only that, but when I'd quit the Sandcliffe Bowmen and joined the newly renamed Archers of Sandcliffe (formerly the Lady Archers of Sandcliffe), several of my fellow members had followed, including Thomas Lawrence and his father. Coultry had also joined, though it was more symbolic than anything. He hardly had time to shoot, as his shop was busy as ever. A deluge of commissions had followed the Lady Patroness's Meeting once word got out that both mine and Marigold's bows were his work.

Now Marigold's prize shoot was upon us, after weeks of constant planning. She'd promised me our lives would calm once it was over. I did not believe her, and neither did I mind. I could never ask her to restrain the passion that drove her—it was that same passion that drew me to her. No, I was content knowing our life together would be busy, happy, and filled with the people we loved most.

Most of the people, that is. For just a moment, I imagined what it would be like to have my parents meet Marigold. I pictured their beaming smiles and bright eyes. I had no doubt in my mind they would have liked her. Adored her, really. She had that effect on most people. But as it was, we were quite doted upon by Uncle and his bride, the new Mrs. Raines, married a week after Marigold and me.

It seemed the only person in Sandcliffe who still did not like Marigold—or me—was Lord Beauford. Yet he'd done nothing more than nurse his wounds and shoot dark looks at us during social events. We both had grown adept at ignoring him.

Marigold sighed, nuzzling close against my neck, and my stomach flipped.

"We'd better get dressed," she said reluctantly. "Mama is expecting us soon to help."

Her hair smelled of rose water and I brushed back a lock from her cheek.

"I think your mama can wait a few minutes." I kissed her cheek, my lips trailing down her neck. She shivered, and heat ignited within my chest.

"Perhaps just one minute," she said with a lazy grin.

I kissed her, the feel of her lips against mine now familiar but no less intoxicating. Her hand found my jaw, pulling me closer. Every touch set my nerves aflame.

Eventually, she pulled away, though I protested and tried to tug her back. She laughed, sitting up and straightening her night rail.

"Stop that," she said, smacking my chest. "Or I might accuse you of treachery."

"Treachery?" I sat up, capturing her hands in mine. "Do explain."

Her eyes glinted with mischief. "Clearly you think to addle my brain with your kisses so that I will underperform today. But you shall not succeed, sir. I am single-minded. It shall be victory or death."

"Quite the dramatic turn of events," I said dryly. "I daresay being married to me isn't as bad as all that."

"No, but losing to you is," she said. "I would never hear the end of it."

I kissed her hand. "Then let us see once and for all who is the better archer between us. We've yet to finish a shoot against each other since last summer, and I am ever so curious."

"As am I." Then she pushed me back in bed with a laugh, turning to hop from the bed. "Come on, then. You'll never win if you stay in bed all day."

"I did not realize that was an option," I said. "I choose that, for a certainty."

She cast me such a look of loving exasperation that I grinned. This was not the future I'd imagined for myself even two months ago, and now I could not picture anything else. I did not *want* anything else.

I followed her to where she stood tying her dressing gown around her waist. I bent to press a kiss to her forehead. "I love you," I said softly.

The words still did not feel natural to me. I did not know if they ever would. But I meant them, each and every time I said them to her.

She knew that. Her eyes met mine, filled with the love I knew she felt for me. "More treachery," she whispered.

"You know me well," I said. "Anything to win."

She tipped her head up to me, those sparkling blue eyes catching the morning light. "I can't imagine why you bother. You've already won the greatest prize in the world."

"I suppose you mean you?"

She grinned. "Why, of course."

I linked my hands around her waist and tugged her closer. "This might be the only time I ever admit that you are right."

Then I kissed her again, because I could not help myself, just as I could not help loving her.

But also because I hoped it would slightly addle her brain.

Anything to win.

Also by Joanna Barker

The Havenfield Series

The Truth About Miss Ashbourne (Book 1)

Otherwise Engaged (Book 2)

Standalone Novels

Miss Adeline's Match

Secrets and Suitors

Novellas/Anthologies

Beauty and the Baron

Romancing Her Rival

All Hearts Come Home for Christmas

A Christmas Promise

I would love to keep in touch! You can connect with me on Facebook and Instagram (Author Joanna Barker). To join my newsletter, check out my website, www.authorjoannabarker.com. If you enjoyed this book, please leave a review! Thank you for reading!

Acknowledgments

My list of people to thank has never been longer, and I have never been more grateful.

First, I have to thank my incredible readers! I would never be able to do what I do without you. You've given me my dream job. Thank you especially to my wonderful ARC team. I appreciate each and every one of your efforts to help my books reach new readers.

My beta readers were the true heroes of this story! Thank you to Jillian Christensen, Cassy Watson, Deborah Hathaway, Tara Cummins, and Jan Lance (or Mom to a lucky few). Thank you for clarifying and polishing my words in a way I never could! A special thanks to Mandy Biesinger for quickly reading a later version!

Thank you to my sisters, Janae and Jessica, for being the first to read the full story and for encouraging me when I needed it the most! You don't know how much it meant to me!

To my critique partners, Heidi Kimball, Megan Walker, and Arlem Hawks. This book would be an absolute mess without you. A MESS, I tell you. Thank you for talking me through plot holes, for pushing me to new heights, and for reading multiple versions of the ending so I could get it right. (Megan, here is the extra thank you I promised you, along with a hug. Now I expect one in return in your next book.) I love you all!

Lastly, I am forever grateful to my husband for enduring my endless complaints about how I would never get this book right and for knowing when I simply needed a listening ear. Watching The Office while eating ice cream together is my happy place. I love you.

About the Author

Joanna Barker firmly believes that romance makes everything better, which is why she has fallen in love with writing Regency romances. When she's not typing away on her next book, you'll find her listening to podcasts, eating her secret stash of chocolate, or adding things to her Amazon cart. She thinks being an author is the second-best job in the world—right after being a mom. She is just a little crazy about her husband and three wild-but-lovable kids.

Printed in Great Britain
by Amazon

16757351R00189